WAYFARER'S RIFT

THE WAYFARER CHRONICLES

BOOK ONE

ROBERT TILLSLEY

Wayfarer's Rift

Book 1 of the Wayfarer Chronicles

Cover design by Robert Tillsley

Cover copyright © 2025 by Robert Tillsley

All stock images used with permission.

Published by Black Sky Books

Magill, Australia

www.blackskybooks.com

ISBN 978-1-7642775-0-1

 A catalogue record for this book is available from the National Library of Australia

BOOKS BY ROBERT TILLSLEY

NOVELS

Wayfarer's Rift (The Wayfarer Chronicles Book 1)

Project Eclipse

The Last Cruise Ship (as R Max Tillsley)

The Darkness Without (Novella)

SHORT STORIES

Replication *in* Contact This!, Crickey! *in* Storming Area 51, Contours of War *in* On Deadly Ground, Red Snow *in* Slay Bells Ring , Silent Griffin *in* Fire For Effect, Where the Dead Walk *in* The Monster Within, Bloodstone *in* Zombie! Patient Zero, Clay Breath *in* Clash of Steel

CHILDRENS BOOKS

All as R Max Tillsley

My First Zombie (Picture Book)

THE SUSIE STEELE ADVENTURES

The Steele Trap

The Steele Bite

TANGLED FATES

Brainz

The Winter King

STAND ALONE NOVELS

Rebyrth

CHAPTER 1

ENDINGS

Children at the end of a school year are less a ticking time bomb of excitement and more a pack of snarling wolves circling the final bell. My fifth-grade class sharpened pencils, pulled the remains of Blu Tack from walls where posters had already been removed, and cleaned paint palettes among other busywork.

I eyed Nick and Ishaan, who sat on their table talking, and let it slide. They'd already mentally checked out of school, and I couldn't blame them—I wasn't far off either.

The school administration still hadn't allocated our classrooms for next year. And while I didn't want to leave a mess for the next teacher, it would be harder to leave it worse than the state I'd seen when walking in for the first time.

The front of the room had a mounted smart board, the attached speakers playing an inoffensive track from a carefully curated list. My creaking wood-veneer desk was off to one side to reduce the distance between my kids and me. A precious area of clear space allowed me to fit the entire class on the floor. At ten years old, they were getting a little big for it, but it helped keep them focused. Five groups of three tables sat six kids each. Their surfaces gleamed thanks to the effort of kids too happy to complain. Cupboards on the left held stationery, charging laptops, and a myriad of educational aids.

On the far right by the window was the most precious spot of all. The reading nook. I'd scrounged two short, wide-based bookcases the school library had wanted to dump, and paid for three big-fluffy cushions out of my meagre wage. Jackie Miller sat on the red one, staring out the window and tugging on a strand of oily brown hair. She had pale skin, dark beneath her eyes, and her clothes were always crumpled.

I sat on the blue cushion, giving her plenty of space. "It's loud in here."

She nodded. It could be hard to get her to talk sometimes. I knew why. I understood why.

"Did you want to borrow a book over the holidays?"

"No, Mr. Drake."

Mr. Drake. It always made me feel like a kid rather than an adult. But this wasn't one of those schools where the kids could call me Martin. And I'm not sure I'd have been comfortable with that either.

"Is your grandfather coming to visit?"

"He's sick again."

"I'm sorry to hear that. He seems very nice."

I forced a worried scowl away. Jackie wasn't easy to cheer up, and she didn't like it when adults acted concerned. A defense mechanism. If you were sure no one cared, you couldn't be disappointed. Unlike her useless parents, her grandfather looked after her when he came. You could practically see her cheeks fill out in a few days, and her hair was washed as well as her clothes. More importantly, she became more involved in the class, both socially and academically. She became happy.

At least until he returned home to his little hobby farm. I had met him several times, and on the last intimated that she'd be happier on the farm. "I'm getting too old," he'd said. And Jackie remained where she was, neglected, but not so badly that the overstretched child services department cared. I'd made three reports, and I wasn't the only one.

I hated this. Once they're out of the school gates, there's nothing you can do. Not until it's too late.

The background chatter grew loud. I needed to make myself visible and restore order.

"You're not in my class next year, but I'd like it if you checked on me," I told Jackie while standing. "Just to make sure the new lot of ratbags haven't eaten me alive."

She didn't look at me, but the corners of her mouth twitched. I'd given her permission to come and chat if she needed. It was all I could do, and I hated it.

As I strode to the front of the class, the noise grew. Children spoke louder to be heard over the rest, who in turn ratcheted up the volume. A quiet classroom tended to remain so. A classroom with every kid talking became a riot. That was Newton's first law of audio momentum. Stopping in front of the whiteboard, I turned and raised my hands like a wizard about to cast a spell.

I clapped a short pattern. A few children noticed and stopped talking. I clapped the same pattern, and several children copied, more becoming quiet. Once more I clapped, and the entire class —well, most of them—repeated it back to me. Magic.

"All right, agents of chaos. Any more tidying will only make the room messier. Put your chairs on your tables, then come and sit on the floor."

Ear-tingling scrapes followed, accompanied by the dull clank of metal legs connecting with each other. As the children flowed toward the front of the class, I picked up my now-cold cup of tea. Theoretically, it could be consumed hot, but I never managed to experience the state on school grounds.

Outside, unseasonal, ugly gray clouds assembled across the sky, stifling the sun's efforts. Inside, fluorescent lighting bleached color from faces, but couldn't steal the joy. Jackie took a spot at the back, a little way from the rest, but close enough.

I cleared my throat and glanced meaningfully at the wall clock. "The room appears acceptable. And in good time. What luck. We have time for one last spelling test."

Deadpan the whole way. And they bought it, crying out with a stream of protests. I grinned, saying nothing, and one by one they realized the truth.

"There's a sucker born every minute," I told them, "and I think I was given an hour's worth. Who's up for hangman?"

Most of the responses were positive, and ignoring the few groans, I woke the board, picked up a digital marker, and made several horizontal strokes, each representing the letter of a mystery word. I went easy on them, choosing *holidays.*

"Who wants first guess?" I said, taking a sip of tea.

The children took turns shouting letters at me. When they guessed correctly, I wrote the letter over its corresponding position. When Anastasia called out T, I drew the first line of the gallows with a dramatic flourish. A macabre game, but a good one.

Turning back to the class, a sensation of distant warmth bathed my front as if I were standing before a heater. A golden haze spread across the children. It faded as quickly as it had come, and a bitter cold oozed across my skin.

I dropped my cup. The icy sensation faded as it hit the carpet, and a fountain of tea sprayed upward, a few drops reaching the nearest students. The class erupted in laughter. It took me a moment to banish the experience, and reset my teacher mode.

After quieting them down with a gesture, I said, "Don't worry, Anastasia. Your suggestion was quite reasonable. However, it's clear that I need a holiday as much as the rest of you. Can someone grab the roll of paper towels?"

As my more helpful minions went to work, I asked if anyone wanted to take a guess. They'd already correctly picked L, D, A, and S. It took five more guesses, at which point the gallows was ready for the little stick figure, before Jackie called out, "Holidays."

"And we have a winner!"

The bell rang, and the children shifted.

"Wait," I said. "We need to make up time for late minutes."

I kept a tally when the class wouldn't settle, and we'd eat into breaks to catch up. It was collective punishment of a mild sort, but they kept each other in check. The children groaned as one, mouths open with horror.

"Got you again. Have a great holiday. Stay safe and try not to forget every single thing you've learned this year. Class dismissed."

Shouts of joy accompanied my statement, and the children were up. Some ran to the door, others said thank you, and a few handed me wrapped presents with cards. I took them with manly refrain, thanking the children, even as my insides squirmed. I hadn't received many presents in my life, and I knew budgets were tight for every family.

It was a relief when the last child left. Shouts and laughs filtered in, but there was a peaceful solitude, nevertheless. I packed up my few personal items and bagged the presents. I'd taken home my teaching resources the day before—schools were notorious for theft, and that wasn't from the children. All that was left was to check the windows.

"Martin. How did it go?"

Securing the first window lock, I half turned to the door. Ms. Brennan, or Victoria as I called her, stood in the doorway, a plastic basket hanging off one arm, and a potted plant in the other. Her long blond hair was tied back in a ponytail, from which many strands had escaped. Like me, she was twenty-five. I kept fit through hand weights, routines, and endless walking. Unlike me, Victoria was a runner, and she had an athletic look. A very nice athletic look.

"Alive, I think." I laughed. "I'm pretty sure I'll need to toss out everything I've done and start from scratch. I made so many mistakes."

Victoria raised a hand, the basket wobbling. "Stop. You'll make me stress about it all. If even one kid has learned anything from you, you're doing okay, right? Put your brain in neutral and chill. Oh, that reminds me, are you coming for drinks?"

There'd been a notice on the staff board for an end-of-year gathering at a local bar.

"I don't know. I hadn't really thought about it."

"You have to. I won't take no for an answer."

A shock went through my chest. I put a hand on my tie to straighten it, but stopped myself in time. I hoped desperately to not blush. I'd been torn between going and collapsing on my couch in a stupor. Stuff the couch.

"I guess I better go."

"Good. Now get out of here."

I watched her leave, then returned to checking windows.

There was a knock on the door. Francine Hart, the principal of Brythonic Park Elementary School, poked her head around.

"Are you busy, Martin?"

"No, Ms. Hart. Just packing up."

"Good, good. Before you leave, come by my office." She moved off before I could reply.

Whenever possible, I avoided her and the accompanying sense of judgment, but she must have finally locked down the class allocations. I really didn't want to get anything less than grade four. The younger kids were always sticky, as if a radioactive slug had bitten them and imparted a useless superpower.

It took me only a few minutes to grab everything, turn off the lights, and head to her office.

Books of the non-fiction variety filled the room. A whiteboard on wheels pressed against one edge, and a long set of windows near the main entrance gave the principal ample opportunity to see which students were tardy. To her credit, she seemed to know them all by name. Though, I thought as I entered, she might learn them purely to slap a name on the frequent punishments she doled out.

"Take a seat, Martin," Ms. Hart said while slipping off her reading glasses. Her sleek glass-topped desk gleamed. A slim monitor on one corner provided me with no cover.

I sat as instructed, waiting expectantly.

"I believe you've had a really solid year at Brythonic Park. I've certainly had positive feedback from parents and other teachers."

My eyes widened. Praise made me uncomfortable at the best of times. I adjusted my tie. What did it mean? Was I getting another grade five class as I had asked for?

"Ah, thank you."

Hurry up and stop leaving me hanging.

"It's been a good year for the school as a whole," she said, patting the table as if it were a pet. "Next year will be different. There are a lot of challenges coming."

Oh. She's buttering me up to stick me with a class of troubled kids despite it being only my second year of teaching.

"The economy has been struggling, and public schools aren't immune. Budget cuts are on the cards, and difficult decisions have to be made."

She'd gone into passive tense. My brow felt hot and damp, and I had to squash the urge to run.

"Very difficult. Classroom sizes will have to increase. That means staff savings. Employees are the most expensive part of a school."

She meant teachers. We both knew it. My stomach squelched.

"Unfortunately, as a contract teacher, you are one of those at the top of the list. And, let's face it, you haven't been as involved in the extracurricular activities as you could have."

Because I've been trying to keep my head above water, I screamed silently.

"Ask yourself, Martin, did you fit in? Were you *really* happy here?" She sighed dramatically. "In the end, that was the deciding factor. I need teachers who will put in everything they have. I'm sorry, Martin, but I won't be able to give you a class next year."

She may as well have punched me. I rocked back. "It's too late for me to get another contract."

"Don't worry, I'll write you a glowing recommendation. You'll find somewhere."

"But I just renewed my lease."

She put on her glasses, and one of her hands rested on a folder to one side of the desk. "I'm sure that can be negotiated. If you stay, we might be able to offer casual placements. You can let the office staff know on your way out."

I was dismissed, both from her presence and the school. I don't remember leaving. Other teachers would have offered their farewells not knowing it was final. They would have taken my shock for exhaustion, I'm sure.

To save money, I walked to the school most days. Today, I wished I hadn't. I wanted to be home and climb under my sheets. Instead, I walked out the school gates past knots of a few remaining parents, juggling my bags. I hadn't crossed the first street before the heavens opened up. Great fat drops of rain slapped me, one finding the back of my collar, an eel sliding down my spine. I had no umbrella. Why would I have needed one at this time of year?

By the time single-story houses gave way to shops and offices, the streets had grown busy with cars, and my clothes were soaked through. It was over half an hour door to door. I arrived at my low-rise apartment, dripping and shivering. It took three goes to get the damn key in the lock and two more to turn the rusty tumblers.

After dumping the bags to one side, I kicked the door shut and slapped the light switch. The blinds were still down from the morning. The apartment had a single bedroom, a combined kitchen and living room, and a dank little bathroom. Every single piece of furniture began at Ikea, and I'd bought it all second-hand. Or perhaps third. A repurposed Lack table—the square one sold with tiny chairs—held an aging monitor with an annoying crack in the bottom right corner. I'd usually plug in my battered laptop and stream.

I sniffed and raided the humming fridge supplied with the apartment and claimed a beer supplied by my second to last paycheck. This would get ugly, fast.

"Martin," I asked myself while walking into the bathroom, "what the hell are you doing?"

No answers came. I finished the beer, set the shower as hot as I could stand, and tried to scrub away the mess of my life. It didn't work. Towel wrapped around my waist, I prowled the confines of my existence. Everything of importance would fill a couple of suitcases, and that was mostly clothes.

I peeked around the living room blind. The rain was letting up, and lights from the streets and homes reflected off the dark surfaces, beautiful in their own way. People hurried from buses and cars, seeking cover, meeting loved ones.

Not me. I grabbed a second beer and dropped onto my couch. I'd move. It was the sensible thing to do. It was what I'd always done. Staying in one place too long meant getting to know people. Worse, it meant them getting to know me. And I never fit in. It was as if they could smell the damage if they stayed too close.

My gaze fixed on the one piece of furniture that stood out, the symbol of my otherness. The sword stand was off to one side of the monitor. It was a cheap design of sloppily varnished wood, ideal for fake katanas. What it held was a light cavalry saber, a British sword with a pronounced curve, a vicious tip, and a slender knuckle guard. The weapon's quality of finish and the handle's silver grip suggested it had belonged to an officer. It had come from my father. Not by his choice. The asshole would have sold it if he'd known it had any value.

My chest knotted, and I squeezed my beer bottle. No, my nana had given it to me when I'd left her *care*. Crazy old bat. She'd worked me hard and tried to fill my head with nonsense. I turned to get the sword out of my view. How many times had I been close to throwing it away? Maybe I'd known it was a bad idea. Nana, who'd had a collection of swords as big as any Texan's gun stash, had said it was an antique. That meant it was worth money, and I'd need plenty of that soon.

Damn it. I was screwed.

My phone buzzed. I grunted in annoyance and picked it up. Victoria had messaged me, asking where I was. I tossed my phone to the other end of the couch. I didn't need that. How could I go there and tell them Hart had fired me, that I wasn't good enough? The embarrassment. The shame. What would

Victoria think? My temple throbbed. I closed my eyes and rubbed at the pain. It didn't help. I was useless.

The voices came back. A slap to my head. Falling onto the ground. Begging. The memories merged, growing stronger. I needed another beer. I dropped the empty bottle and stood.

No, I didn't need another beer. I'd never wanted to be like that. Maybe it wasn't a good night to be alone. I rocked on my feet, pulled by choices, none of which I liked.

Reason elbowed its way into my dejection. If I could survive spilling tea in front of a class, if I could survive Hart, who was missing her namesake, then I could pull myself together and meet my ex-colleagues. They were decent for the most part. They'd shared a few laughs and helped me when I was drowning under lesson plans and paperwork. Perhaps they knew someone who knew a principal who was looking for a teacher.

Or perhaps I was just looking to rub salt into my wounds to see how much it would sting. Either way, I threw on some jeans, my last clean shirt—yellow, but don't judge me—and a burgundy sweater I'd bought for interviews. I still looked like a teacher. Brushing back my lengthening black hair didn't help. At least I hadn't yet succumbed to a tweed jacket with elbow patches.

With that image looming over me, I headed out into the storm.

CHAPTER 2

WHEN REALITY TEARS

Garry's was one of those bars that had been around forever, but it hadn't deteriorated into a dive, nor had its infrequent refurbishments turned it into a haunt for overpriced suits and gelled hair. A long rectangular bar cut through the middle of the space, its eternally sticky surface a red hardwood. On one side, wall-mounted televisions displayed sports highlights to an indifferent crowd of low-level office workers. The other side held tables suitable for those wanting a meal or to catch up with friends, have a few drinks, and work through endless bowls of fries.

That's where they sat. Eighteen, I counted. Not a bad showing. Drinks filled three tables pressed together, and laughter broke out here and there like firecrackers. If I were on the other side of the glass, I'd be able to hear the jokes, rather than watch a silent movie.

I'd parked down the street and used an umbrella to keep my top half dry until the bar's awning took over. The umbrella dangled in my hand, and I imagined raising it to smash my way inside.

The bar door opened, and a waft of warm air swirled out as an older man with a heavy jacket and a newsboy hat stepped outside. He passed me, singing what sounded like a folk song in a language I didn't recognize. I should have caught the door and walked in. It closed slowly on soft hinges, an impregnable barrier that may as well have been guarded by Cerberus.

"Come on, Martin. You can do this."

Why was it so much easier to stand in front of children than adults? Because the kids had no choice. The teachers were having fun without me. I'd smother the good mood. Victoria knew I'd been fired and had only been friendly out of pity.

No. I wasn't going to let that voice win. It was already waiting at the back of my mind, ready to judge, ready to assume the worst. Screw it. I took a step toward the door.

A loud thud stopped me. A keening followed. A dog hit by a car? I abandoned my resolve to enter the bar and peered into the darkness beyond the building. Bright headlamps of passing cars flowed past, strobing my vision as I headed down the street. If someone had hit a dog and kept going, I was going to be pissed. I'd never had a pet and didn't care to, but any animal deserved better than that.

I'd reached the end of the building, where an alley separated it from the next, and heard a scream. A woman's, hoarse and with an odd timbre. I couldn't be sure given the traffic noise and the rain, but I was guessing an old woman. And it'd come from down the alley. Was she an old drunk who'd had too much? Perhaps she'd been kicked out of the bar. The keening could have been her frustration. The thud could have been her smashing things in anger.

Not my problem. Turning back offered a sliver of a chance for a decent evening. All I had to do was go through that damn door. I glared at the rain, the transition on the sidewalk between staying partially dry and getting soaked. Where the awning lights caught a trace of red. I poked it with my shoe and smeared watery red. Blood. Damn. The old fool had probably cut herself on a broken bottle or stumbled against the building.

Checking on her promised nothing but trouble. The bar door beckoned, far more welcoming by contrast. By rights, the old drunk had done this to herself. I'd worked hard this year. I deserved to be inside. I deserved a drink. Maybe a little pity from my peers wasn't so bad.

The drunk could be seriously hurt. What if she died down an alley, alone, when a call for an ambulance could have been all she needed? I had to check.

My umbrella opened with a click. I turned on my phone's light and stepped around the corner into the alley. The gap between walls was barely wide enough for a car to fit down, but the boxes and assorted trash would have made it a rough ride. The same walls gave shelter from the rain. Near the end, a single, weak yellow light flickered, more off than on, revealing a dumpster and a chain-link fence.

"Do you need help?"

There was no response. The traffic and rain could have drowned me out, so I walked deeper into the gloom. A rotten stench pervaded the air, as protected from the cleansing rain as I was. My phone's light created shifting shadows among the alley's debris, hinting at movement while revealing nothing. I killed it, preferring not to see the rats that my imagination was already populating. It wasn't doing much, anyway.

A clang came from the dumpster. It rolled a short distance, jerking from spot to spot in the yellow strobe.

"Hi there. Do you need any help? If you're fine, I'll leave you alone."

Lightning cracked the sky, thunder rumbling in the same instant, right overhead, overwhelming any response. I blinked repeatedly as my eyesight filled with white afterimages and raced to collapse my umbrella. The thin metal and thinner polyester made a terrible weapon, but the hairs on the back of my neck were standing up. The palpable charge in the air had me on edge, caught between feeling stupid and worried. Ozone now overlaid the rot and my ears popped like I was descending fast from thirty thousand feet.

That was when I saw the dog. I shook my head. I'd been right the first time. The poor thing had been hit and limped down here to lick its wounds.

"Hey, don't worry about me. I'm just coming to check on you. That's right. Don't worry."

I reached the edge of the light. The dog was shaggy and white. Technically, the light made it yellow, but that was obvious. So was the fact that it was big. Hell, it was enormous. Several flickers of yellow passed before I could compare it to the dumpster. It was giant, with longer legs than I'd seen on any breed. And wolfish. Its large erect ears twitched, amber eyes practically glowing as they met my own, and its long muzzle opened, revealing far too many sharp teeth.

When it growled, loud, deep, and harsh, I almost wet myself. Instinct told me I should be inside a little cave, huddled around a fire, holding a spear, and hoping the gods were feeling charitable. I'd made a mistake. It was time to back away.

The wolf circled toward the chain-link fence, favoring one of its forepaws. Now was the time to step back. I moved closer to the left wall to see what had its attention, a stupid idea. From my new position, I spied an old lady. Okay, so I'd been right on both accounts. The dumpster had hidden her desperate attempts to hold the wolf at bay with… what I guessed to be a broom.

I froze. The scene before me made no sense. What was a wolf doing here? Had it bitten the old lady? I'd only gotten a glimpse of her before the wolf blocked my view, but she'd been swinging her broom with vigor. That couldn't last. She was in serious trouble. If that blood was hers, it wouldn't be long at all. I raised my phone. The police couldn't arrive in time. And if I walked away, this would get ugly, I was sure of it. Whether she'd annoyed it or happened to be in the wrong alley at the wrong time didn't matter. I couldn't leave her.

The umbrella wasn't going to help. I rummaged through the nearby debris and found a broken chair. Lion taming, anyone? Inching closer, I held the chair high. The padded cushion dropped free, bouncing off my head, musty and damp. The wooden frame gave it some mass, and it didn't have to be strong —I wasn't going to hold it out front like a matador.

The wolf's haunches lowered, ready to leap. Grunting, I threw the chair with every ounce of strength I could muster. While it recovered, I might be able to get around the dumpster and lead the old lady away.

Wooden splinters bounced in every direction, clattering like a tub of spilled pencils. I ran. The wolf stopped its leap. That was as good it got. The beast didn't even rock under the force of the blow. However, it did twist its neck and stare at me. And when it opened its mouth and roared—not growled, roared—three rows of teeth flashed, each dripping thick saliva. It was a mutant. Or perhaps a genetic experiment carried out by a mad scientist in a volcanic lair.

My run faltered as the icy knife of fear cut across my spine, severing control. I was dead. This thing was going to rip my throat out, chew me up, and crap me out.

It got crazier. Thunder boomed, and I was dragged toward the wolf by an invisible force, dancing madly to keep my balance. Several terrible, wet, harsh crunches followed, a series of firecrackers. The wolf's body crumpled in on itself, then collapsed.

The force stopped. I lost my balance and landed on a mass of rank fur. Thick yellow goo oozed from gashes in its hide, soaking my sweater. I rolled off and stood with my legs apart, ready to run, but the tension subsided.

There was something wrong with the wolf. Not just the fact that it wasn't moving. The wounds were obviously deadly. Yet, the thing that got me was how broken it was, how the ribcage had utterly collapsed. And how much mass was missing. That boom of thunder hadn't been an explosion—the lack of wolf intestines on the walls testified to that. The creature had imploded. Which made no sense at all.

Lightning crawled across the sky once more, casting the scene in stark white and shaking me out of my stupor. Answers could come later. I shucked off my goo-covered sweater and walked around the carcass toward the old lady, who was leaning against the fence, her head bowed.

"Are you hurt? Do you need help?"

"Need your help? Hardly, child."

Her clothes struck me as odd. She wore a gray-brown under-dress and a green overdress of a fine fabric that almost closed at the front, both held in place by a thin brown leather belt with irregular embossed lines. A blue cloak went over the top, closed at the neck by a chunky bronze brooch, though much of the fabric rested on her shoulders, leaving her arms free and revealing a black leather backpack with a diamond lattice pattern and brass buckles. Practical and classy. But definitely odd.

The broom drew my attention next, and I reassessed it. Carved and polished wood formed the long pole, with imperfections suggesting it had been handmade. The end held no bristles. Instead, the wood expanded and stretched like fingers around a sphere of clear glass. The clever maker had made it appear as if the wood had grown into this position. All in all, despite a rugged quality, the outfit resembled that of a wealthy cosplayer or LARPer well past her prime.

The voice replayed in my head. Hardly, child. I'd heard it

before. Where? I stopped a few paces from her and looked, properly looked, at her. Long gray hair flowed back into a loose ponytail held by a leather strap. Her weathered face possessed a stern nose, and dark, well-defined brows guarded piercing green eyes. Abundant wrinkles spoke of experience rather that frailty, and she wore no makeup.

"Jesus Christ," I said. "Nana, is that you?"

What was she doing out here? She was meant to be in a retirement village, being served generic meals and playing bingo all the while grumbling at anyone who dared to cross her wishes.

She raised her head, and I knew I was right. "It is, isn't it? What the hell are you doing here? Where's your walking frame?"

My question received a raised eyebrow and a withering glare.

"Leave now, for more of these tainted wolves will attend, even once I have passed through."

Whatever I'd been expecting, this was not it. I closed on her and put a hand on her arm, hoping to guide her away. Up close, I could see her nose was slightly out of alignment. Broken, I assumed. That was new. "You'll catch a cold. Let's at least go into the bar. I'll buy you a hot drink."

She slapped my hand away, and when she raised her stick, her staff, I took a step back. Had she developed dementia? Squiggles on the staff glowed, followed by the glass sphere lighting up like a lantern. Shielding my eyes, I searched for clues in her expression. It had been a while, but there was something a little off in her features.

"Touch me again, and I'll break your fingers. Go on, lower your hand."

She shoved the light toward me, and I obeyed, responding to familiar tone with frustratingly little choice. I thought I was over that.

"Huh," she said. "I'll be buggered. It's one of you."

"What? Nana—"

My eyes had adjusted, and I could see it now. She looked near-identical to my nana, but she wasn't the same. A sister maybe? An older one. If the timing worked, she could even be my nana's mother.

She continued. "I see it now. I'm not your nana. More like your great, great, great grandmother, but more so. Huh. I should have been more careful, but I always had a weakness for the big and pretty ones." She held my face and moved it from side to side with strong, blotched fingers. "Dark hair, strong cheekbones. Could have been Sampson or Andreas or maybe Benedict. It matters not. What are you doing here?"

"I was going to have a drink with—with friends."

"A likely story." She scowled and let go. While I rubbed my chin, she grumbled to herself, "Doesn't Kelwyn trust me? Cagey old codger. He should know me well enough. Is the council having second thoughts?" she snorted. "Worse, it could be the working of her if she ascended before time. No good could come from that. Or, what if it's *her?* We did not part on the best of terms, and *she* has a long memory. Fae love their tricks."

I schooled my face into a caring expression, brow gently furrowed, head tilted a little. The sort I'd use with a child that was on the verge of breaking something. Whatever she was up to, it was none of my business. At least until I got around the corner and called for an ambulance. She'd either swallowed a few too many pills, or she'd taken a knock to her head. Either explained the nonsense she babbled.

"It's really nice to meet you—"

"I don't have time for this. Cruel happenstance. Yes, it must be."

She rolled her shoulders, raised her staff in both hands and carefully stretched the sphere forward. Marks on the wood again brightened, turning a luminous blue, and the sphere's light shifted from white to the same blue.

With a sudden stroke downward, she set off fireworks. A thick line of sparks hovered in the air, growing wider until it formed an oval broader than my shoulders. Inside the sparks, the air shimmered. The alley was gone, replaced by shifting funhouse glass, distorting a reflection of the alley behind us. The distortion stretched beyond the fireworks, as if she'd warped the very fabric of reality.

At the furthest edges, it was already smoothing. Whatever she'd done, I was pretty sure it wouldn't last.

"Boy, you better run. Forget everything you've seen. It's just a nightmare."

Growling came from the other side of the chain-link fence. A wolf had approached, and it was sniffing at the wire. A second growl followed, not from this wolf. Another one was coming from down the alley.

Damn it, I thought. *I really can't catch a break today, can I?*

The old lady grabbed my shirt. "The plan's changed. You're coming through the *way*, or you're getting eaten up and shat out. Your choice."

I marveled at the insanity of her claim, giving her the chance to pull me closer to the fireworks.

No, thank you, I thought and set my feet firmly. "What is that?"

"Must have been Andreas. Pretty, but he could barely count to ten. Suit yourself, boy," she said and walked between the sparks.

And disappeared. Vanished. Gone.

Two things happened next. One, the first wolf leaped over the fence, despite its height. Two, the second wolf charged. Both of them growled. My nerves were getting pretty frayed by this point. I glanced at the sparks. The distortion was shrinking by the second.

Wolf one completed its leap. I could smell its musk. My legs wobbled. My skin was clammy. I really wanted that cave with a fire. I'd have taken a few dozen of my Cro-Magnon ancestors at my side as well. I'm pretty sure I could feel the beat of the second wolf's paws as they hit the ground. The beast was close. There was nowhere to hide, nowhere to run.

I did what anyone would do.

I threw myself backward into the sparks, screaming, "Shit!"

CHAPTER 3

DÉJÀ VU

The universe lurched. I stumbled and slammed into the alley wall, losing the air in my lungs and whacking the back of my skull on unyielding brick. Swearing, I rubbed my abused head. The sparks were still there, now only as wide as my arm and shrinking fast. There was no sign of the wolves. Where did they go?

Where did the dumpster go? More trash filled the alley than I'd remembered, everything from clothes through to packets of cereal, the various colors faded but not monotone. Which meant the light wasn't coming from that one flickering source, which made sense because it had a blueish tint. I raised a hand; it looked frostbitten. Above, the clouds had vanished, and the night sky along with it. Blue, intensely so. The ground—what little I could see of it—was bone dry, while my clothes remained damp.

I can be slow on the uptake, and I had hit my head, but it was clear some weird shit had just gone down. Time travel. It made the most sense—a bad sign. My not-nana had a time machine, and we'd gone forward or back. I ran a hand along the nearby wall. Solid and one-hundred percent dry. Wow. This had actually happened. Despite the earlier terror, my feet felt lighter. I was excited.

The sparks had gone. I listened carefully. No growling, yet the wolves continued to prowl in my memory, vivid and vicious.

"Time travel, right?" I said to distract myself.

There was no answer. The old lady had reached the end of the alley, and she turned onto the street.

"Wait up!"

I jogged after her, my balance off at first, passing more graffiti than I'd ever noticed before. But then, how often do you examine an alley on your way to a bar? How often do you go to a bar in the middle of the day? The stuff was weird, too. All strange patterns, bulbous symbols, but not a single word. The youth of today, I thought, ignoring the fact that I'd made a few bad choices myself along the way. The paint was old, peeling, as if it had been brushed onto wood rather than sprayed onto brick.

At least the stink had faded. In fact, the air was pleasant to breathe, similar to when I walked through the trees of Ascott Park. There were even small plants growing between the cracks in the asphalt and up through the trash. It would have been pleasant if not for said trash.

At the end of the alley, I stopped to find the time traveler, but my attention shifted away from ground level.

The entire cityscape had changed. Live in a city for a while, even just a year, and you get to know the shape of the buildings. They become navigation touchstones even when you're using GPS.

It was different. And that was only the beginning. Window after window was cracked, missing, or boarded up. Splintered doors gaped like hungry maws. Most had quarter-dome fabric awnings, the remains tattered and green with mold. A building to my right had collapsed entirely, and plants had already claimed dominion over its remains.

And the cars, they had a different design language: sharp edges and fins, and a good portion of them were burned out wrecks. The rest were filthy, their tires flat, bodywork dented, and glass shattered. Long shadows stretched from each, and pools of sullen gloom concealed their insides.

Time travel. Just how far forward had we gone? If an ape had come down the road on a Harley, I wouldn't have been surprised. Okay, I would have, but this was really freaking me out. I strode to the pub, hoping for something to ground me.

The Garry's sign had become unreadable scribbles in purple and white on blistered plastic. I peered through a broken window. Toppled tables, broken chairs, smashed plates, glass shards glittering like diamonds. The register, a shattered wreck on the ground, electronics sprayed like blood. It had all the hallmarks of a movie-scale bar brawl. Except there were no bodies of the unconscious or dead variety. It must have happened some time ago as copious leaves and loose rubbish had blown in.

What the hell had happened?

A nuke? Radiation could be ripping into my DNA, warping it, mutating me. I thought of the wolves. It was plausible. How long before I'd know? Would my hair fall out first, or would the first sign be projectile vomiting? The buildings were mostly intact. A neutron bomb could do that. My body shook. I spun round and round. There must be proof that I was wrong. My mouth was bone dry—an early symptom? My breathing was shallow and fast.

I must have scrambled my brains one way or another. Maybe I'd never made it to the bar. I might be on Hart's office floor having a complete breakdown. I'd wake up groggy, strapped to a bed, with some big guy sticking a needle in my arm. My hair would be long. Years gone by. That's what my mind was trying to tell me. I was sleeping through life.

Listen to yourself, asshole.

My internal monologue halted as my subconscious metaphorically slapped me about. I didn't know shit about what was going on. Panic had taken the wheel. That was dangerous. That led to mistakes. And mistakes led to…

I breathed in deeply and focused on the sound of wind on leaves, grounding myself. Better. It was time to think smart. I glanced down the road. The old lady was near the intersection with Haylon Street. She was turning. She was leaving me here. That was bad. If I was wandering through the dark corners of my mind, I sure as hell didn't want to do it alone.

True, I'm not a runner, but I gave it my all, and I caught up with her quickly. The street sign had been another series of unreadable squiggles, and the buildings were again unfamiliar and abandoned. The new angle revealed a fiery sunset of intense red at the horizon in a thin strip that shifted to yellow before giving way to the blue sky. There was an artificial feel to it, like a poorly made game.

"What happened here?" I asked, taking a few quick steps to catch up again.

The old lady sniffed. "So, you decided to follow. Eventually."

I bristled. "Like I had a choice. And where exactly have I followed you to? Or should I say when?"

"Nowhere of consequence, not for some time." Her staff tapped the ground in a steady rhythm.

She wasn't my nana, but she had the same annoying habits. Answering questions she didn't care for with nothing of substance. Hoarding information until she wanted to feel magnanimous.

"Don't screw me around. I want details. This isn't my town, not as I know it. I couldn't even read the name of the bar."

"It was called the Southern Oracle," she said with offhand boredom.

The muscles in my jaw tightened. I might only be twenty-five, but I was an adult. I deserved more than that.

"Hey," I said fiercely. "I could have gone into the pub, the proper one. Instead, I went down that damn alley to help you. You haven't even said thanks."

On she walked. Thud, thud, thud went her staff.

"Don't you care?"

"I didn't ask you to, boy. I didn't need your help then, and I do not need it now, so mind your manners."

I stopped in front of her and gestured to the buildings. "I deserve an explanation. Take a minute, just one minute, and tell me what the hell is going on."

"Foolish child," she hissed, her eyes narrowed. "To stay here is to court death for the both of us."

She cracked me in the shin with the base of her staff, the tip hard and heavy. I stepped back and rubbed my leg, and she was around me and walking before I could respond. Damn her.

I hobbled quickly. "At least tell me something. When is this, fifty years in the future, a hundred?"

"The answer would be meaningless to you. Suffice it to say, this world was lost long ago." She swerved to her left, avoiding squiggles painted onto the sidewalk, and crossed to the opposite side. "You ask the wrong questions. Its name is Astaria to those that still record such things."

"World?" I didn't like that. It made too much sense. Strange writing, different cars, a complete lack of humans. "This isn't Earth? We've traveled to a different planet?"

"Obviously." She picked up her pace. "Do try to keep up."

She'd made some sort of portal. Her staff must be a gadget. And she'd teleported us across the galaxy to an alien world that had a breathable atmosphere, cars, bars, and delinquent youths. I didn't buy it. An idea hit me. It didn't matter if I did.

"Take me back. Use your staff, press the buttons, and teleport me home. I'll step through the warp gate or whatever, and I'm gone, right out of your hair."

"I can't do that."

"We're far enough away from the wolves. I'd be fine."

"Boy, I'd do it if I could. It doesn't work that way."

I'd had enough. I reached for her shoulder. I wasn't going to rough her up, but I wasn't some child to scold. And I wasn't afraid of her, just like I wasn't afraid of Nana anymore.

She moved fast, stepping away with the grace of a dancer, then slipping her second hand around the staff, swinging the end, and catching the back of my knee. I went down hard, my ass taking the brunt of it. Before I could stand, she brought the base of the staff against my chest.

"Don't touch me, boy. I warned you before."

I froze, feeling tiny, fragile. Her shadow left me in darkness. I wanted to curl up, hands on my head to protect it, but I kept still, and she lowered her staff.

"I'm Martin," I said. I'd heard in a movie that hostage negotiators used their names to humanize themselves. "I'm Martin. And if you're my great-grandmother or whatever, doesn't that mean something to you? Surely you can burn ten minutes to get me home. I can hardly walk around here, hoping to pick up a job. It looks like the employment market's a little slow."

"Get up." She started walking again.

I joined her, but left more distance than before.

She glanced at me, her brow furrowed. "There is no going back. Not for me. Not now. There is no time. And you're still alive because you're one of my descendants. If you'd been anyone else, I'd have fed you to the wolves. I travel alone. Refuse to understand that, and I'll break your kneecaps to be rid of you. Or keep walking. Either way, I'm not waiting around for you to grasp the simple truth of your situation."

There was a matter-of-fact nature to her proclamation. There was no hint of threat, only the laying bare of natural conse-quences. I'd used that tone on recalcitrant children, sans the kneecapping. She meant it. I believed her completely. I was also confident she could follow through.

"Can you at least tell me who the hell you are?"

That brought a tight grin to her face. "Call me Blackbird. Now, hurry up." Her gaze switched to the sunset. "We won't reach the *way* before nightfall. If the wolves hadn't slowed me down—curse their corrupted flesh. I tell you, boy, if we're caught out here, you'd have been better off with the wolves."

She led me through a small playground. The equipment looked perfectly suited to human children, though it was made of varnished wood and rope rather than steel and plastic. An empti-ness hung over it all, far more than with the abandoned vehicles and buildings. The swings should have gone back and forth, laughter and shouts and the occasional cry filling the air. Parents should have been glued to their phones or sharing stories and bad advice. I'd always liked seeing how a real family was meant to work.

"There's no time to play."

I'd stopped without realizing. I jogged to the gate and went through, closing the safety catch automatically. "What do we have to fear? The place is empty. You said that whatever happened was long ago. Everyone's dead, right?

Blackbird sniffed. "That's exactly what we have to fear."

"You can't mean that."

She was already off again. I followed, staring at the inky shadows of open doors and broken windows. I hoped she wasn't pulling my chain. Actually, on second thoughts, I hoped she was. She had to be.

The darker it grew, the sadder this city appeared. Windows remained dark as did the streetlamps. Cars remained still. There was none of the hurry of rush hour. Yeah, it could be frustrating, but that busyness was life, the flow of humanity like blood cells down veins.

The similarities were too eerie to avoid comparing to Earth. This wasn't the future. And yet, it could be a mirror of what was to come. War, disease, climate change, the inevitable zombie apocalypse. I laughed at the latter, drawing a disapproving glance from Blackbird. We'd teleported to another world—science—not fantasy. Any way you cut it—virus, radiation, or toxic sludge—zombies made no logical sense. They violated the laws of thermodynamics for a start. She really was working me.

"We should start up a real estate agency," I said, feeling an urge to push back against her self-assured judgment. "Blackbird and Martin. No, Blackbird and Drake. That's got a better ring to it. You can zap the buyers over, and I'll show them around." I switched to a smarmy tone. "It's so safe, nobody bothers to lock the doors. Traffic's not an issue, and you'll never get a parking ticket. Sure, the houses are all fixer-uppers, but with a bit of elbow grease, you'll soon have your dream home."

She ignored me.

I wanted to ask where we were going, but I didn't like my chances on that front, either. Pushing her had risks. Hell, I was completely dependent on her. She would let me wander off whenever I wanted, that was clear. However, she was my ticket home. I couldn't lose her. I might have to get her to like me. I really hated that.

She was a hell of a tough nut, too. Yes, she'd saved me. Was I banking on her doing it again? There was no other choice. There was a small chance she'd come around to being reasonable at some point. Probably when she picked up her arthritis medication or a bottle of gin. Or Both.

Okay, I wasn't being fair. Which was perfectly reasonable. I'd been attacked by mutant wolves and teleported to a ghost town on another world. That kind of thing can color your opinion.

And Blackbird. Why did she have to be an amped-up clone of my nana? When I'd moved in with Nana, it had been better than before. I couldn't deny that. It hadn't been good either. Never knowing where I stood. The constant practice. The punishments for anything less than perfection. The strange diversions in her attention. Her twisted philosophy that grew more confused as she aged. I didn't hate her anymore. I'd just been glad to move out, and then to move away.

My life had all come full circle. I was the child again, desperate, damaged, and at her mercy. Here comes the new old lady, just like the old one. The old old one. Play along, I told myself. You're stronger now. Put on a mask and do what needs to be done. I knew I could manage that.

I was a survivor. I'd had to be.

CHAPTER 4
GHOSTLY ECHO

I hadn't traveled much. That's not in the picture when you're struggling with rent and bills and student debt, and day-to-day existence in general. I'd always wondered if McDonald's and Subway looked the same in Cairo or South Korea or Latvia—was there a fundamental building block of fast-foodness? The grease-on particle. We had come to a main road with a fast-food restaurant surrounded by parking. There was my answer. A tall pole held a wooden sign with dull neon shapes. I couldn't read the writing, but the shape of a burger was universal. The windows of the restaurant were all gone, and through the openings I could see a long counter and tattered posters.

As we passed a nearby trashcan, I peered inside. There was a wrapped burger atop a pile of plastic bags and other trash. I guess the recycling bug hadn't bitten this place. Curiosity woke and opened one eye, cat-like. There had been this time-lapse video going around of a burger decaying over months—or not if the video was to be believed. How long had this alien burger been here? Would it still hold its shape? Hesitating over whether I really wanted to stick my hand inside and fish it out, I checked on

Blackbird. She hadn't slowed. The burger would have to remain a mystery.

Blackbird was damn spry for her age, whatever that was. My nana had been the same in the beginning, and I guess I had a bit of it, too. A need to move, to get things done, or at least procrastinate with intensity. She barely slowed when we reached a pedestrian overpass that stretched across a six-lane road choked with vehicles. An ironwork railing kept us safe, but I could have jumped off if I were so inclined. The whole structure swayed as we crossed, metal grinding on metal. Or rust grinding on rust.

To keep my attention elsewhere, I used the new height to inspect more of the city. Towers still blocked much of the view, but through the gaps I could see that it was substantial. Millions must live here—had lived here. And I saw where some of them ended up.

Off to the right, next to a gas station, a fenced-off area resembled an oversized basketball court. There were vertical hoops, two a side, as if an unholy force had blended the sport with that crazy wizards-on-broomsticks one. I swore. Not because of that. There was a mass of dirty white and scorched black filling the court, almost luminous in the failing dusk, and as tall as me. The fence bulged under pressure. Bones. They were bones. Skulls, ribcages, femurs, all human, all sizes.

What kind of murderous nutjob would slaughter people, pile them high and, what, burn them? No, it would require more than one. You'd want machinery. I saw them. A bright pink bulldozer and two small cranes, abandoned after the grisly game was over. A virus. That was the only thing that made sense. They must have burned the bodies to contain it. And failed.

The sun disappeared beneath the horizon, and the first stars twinkled, oblivious to the markers of past suffering. It wasn't a cold night, but mist was forming in several spots, the court being the nearest. It flowed out of the bones, at first wispy, then in thick ropes that merged and spread quickly.

I licked my lips and pointed. "Ah, what is that?"

"It's a thrice-cursed alarm clock. I should have taken the safer route and accepted the additional ways. And yet, there is no safety to be found. Boy, keep walking."

Once off the overpass, she forged a path between office towers. I'd never seen the architectural style before. Thin windows rested between tall, protruding columns formed from smaller pieces, like Lego but with a sense of faded grandeur. The mist had spread, coming from multiple directions, and now caressed my shins. A faint silver light emanated, and if I fell over, I was going to hold my breath.

Darker patches writhed in the mist, and down one street, I made out silhouettes. At first, I thought them mannequins, but they moved from time to time, restless.

"I think I can see people. They don't look dangerous."

She glared harder than diamond. "People? Did you drink ditchwater as a babe? They are wraiths."

I looked at her blankly. There was no context to make sense of her claim or her insult.

"Ghosts, foolish boy. Spirits of the dead. A particularly vile sort. They will suck every last ounce of life from your bones if they get the chance, leaving you just as they are. Heed me well— do not let them touch you for any reason."

I almost laughed, but her glare still skewered me. Wraiths? They couldn't be real. Belief in the paranormal was essentially belief in magic, in rules separate from those of reality. Once you went down that path, anything could be true.

The distant figures whispered, the mist playing with their voices, sending them first as a torrent, then leaving nothing but a distant hum. Over and over. The figures inched closer, and the mist light confused their features as much as it illuminated them.

I saw people in old-fashioned suits with tails like a tuxedo, made from garish fabrics. Women in full skirted dresses with complex pleats, but all in shades of gray. The occasional child in baggy pants and sleeveless tops with floppy hats that would have been comical if they hadn't also been translucent.

As I stared, more details coalesced. Ripped fabric, filth, cuts, scrapes, hollow cheeks, unmoving and expressionless eyes. Slack jaws revealed filthy red teeth, a deeply unnerving contrast to the pervasive gray. One by one, they started walking toward us.

This couldn't be happening. This wasn't real. Ghosts weren't a thing.

My body believed otherwise. My skin grew chill, and my nerves prickled. A thought spun, over and over: we should run.

Blackbird kept to her purposeful, steady pace, only stopping when we turned a corner. A building had collapsed across the road.

"This is new," she said.

While she stood there, rubbing a cheek thoughtfully, I paced back and forth through the knee-high mist. A whistle came from beneath a bench not far away. A little bird, a finch, hopped to a lumpy weed that had grown between cracks in the pavement. Its red head transitioned to a purple breast. One of its yellow wings was bent out from its body. An injury. It chirped, what I had mistaken for a whistle at first, and pecked at a seed pod. The first animal I'd seen on this blighted world. I considered trying to get closer. No, it deserved the peace to eat its find.

A wraith approached. Its footsteps out of sync with its move-ment, a poorly inserted green screen special effect. I noted a missing ear and thin goatee.

Ghosts weren't real.

That sounded good, and yet… I took half a step toward the finch. It hadn't noticed the wraith stretching out its hands. It leaped for the finch. I clapped my hands. The finch twitched and hopped, darting away from the wraith. Flapping its wings, it took to the air, only to tumble to the ground a moment later, where a second wraith, one I hadn't seen, snatched it up.

The bird twisted and kicked slowly, as if drowning in molasses. I could see it all through the translucent fingers of the wraith. Colorful feathers faded along with the movements. Seconds later it fell from the wraith, stiff, dead.

"Holy shit," I said.

It was real. The wraiths could kill.

How didn't matter. I stumbled back, paralyzed by the choice between hiding or running. More wraiths appeared out of the mist. Staying was bad.

"Blackbird, we have to move."

"Indeed. This way." She headed for a narrow lane, and I hurried after, picking a path between two wraiths, clenching my teeth as I did.

She stopped just inside the entrance, shrugged off her backpack, and started opening the buckles. "Get behind me."

"They're close. Whatever you're doing, it needs to wait."

"Found it." She withdrew a velvet pouch. "Do not cross the line."

Look who's crossed the sanity line.

Loosening the opening, she poured a line of white powder from one wall of the alley to the other. A dozen wraiths approached, their whispers setting my teeth on edge.

"What is it?" I asked.

Blackbird closed the bag and slipped it into her backpack, seemingly unconcerned by the life-stealing wraiths. "Salt."

I retreated several steps down the alley. What did she think they were, slugs? Blackbird passed me, and I glanced back. The wraiths pressed at the alley's mouth as if blocked by glass.

"Why don't they walk through the buildings? They're not solid."

"There are rules, boy. Everything follows rules, even if we don't know them."

We exited the far end and discovered a barricade, a last stand. Crosses of wood held up barbed wire coils. Skeletons lay everywhere, some covered by decayed clothing or desiccated skin. Seeing them so close hit harder than the court full of bones. I imagined them screaming as they were taken by an enemy that couldn't die a second time. A folding table held several rust-encrusted rifles and a small lockbox, the key inserted. Blackbird slipped through the near side untouched, but my shirt caught on a barb, tearing a long line. Thankfully, the rusty point missed my skin.

I ran a hand along the box and tried the key. Rusted in place. However, the lid shifted. Unlocked. The hinge resisted before opening and revealing a pistol. A long, thin barrel, no visible safety, and a heavily rounded grip. It was rust-free, and I wanted some comfort, so I inserted the single magazine of steel-jacketed rounds that rested next to it. Cave man have weapon. Cave man feel better. Okay, so cave men—and women—only had rocks and sticks. But the feeling was the same.

Blackbird used this time to find a path between the barbed wire. I joined her, my body blocking the gun from sight. I had no reason to trust her.

What followed was a maze of turns that fried my sense of direction. No matter the direction we took, wraiths converged, and I was beginning to understand why everyone had died. Sooner or later, a human would tire or make a mistake, and there would be the wraiths, ready and merciless. The mist reached my thighs, a perfect height to hide a child wraith. A toddler could be crawling. I shivered, more vulnerable than if I were naked.

Taking a narrow circular staircase, we climbed above the mist and onto the covered platform of a train station. A curved brute of an engine rested on tracks at one end, its carriages stretched behind, never to reach their destination. Like the clothing, there was a historic feel to the design, not a steam engine of old, but a retro futurism.

And there were wraiths. They were walking along the raised tracks as if the train had broken down and they were late for work. Several were already climbing onto the platform.

Blackbird snarled. "So many. Well, we're close, boy. It's time to run."

She rested her staff over one shoulder and jumped off the edge of the platform onto the tracks. The acoustics of the station echoed the wraith's whispers back to me. I could practically feel their hunger. That put some energy into my tired legs, and I leaped from the platform, landing with a crunch on the gray rocks of the track ballast and sending several skittering away. I ran across two pairs of rails, a wraith close behind. I swear it picked up speed as it closed.

At the far side, I threw myself onto the platform. A wraith leaped at me. I swung the pistol around and pulled the trigger. Nothing. I cocked the gun and fired repeatedly. The bullets slammed into the wraith, slowing it, giving me time to scramble out of the way. By the time I was on my feet, the first bullet had plinked to the ground. The wraith kept coming, fighting the resistance.

Blackbird stopped by a wrought iron gate, blocking stairs downward. "Foolish, boy. You only attract more. Get rid of that."

Damn. She was right.

Every wraith in sight now float-walked directly toward me. I'd bought a few seconds and made myself a target. I tossed the gun. Blackbird opened the gate and went through. I slipped past, and she closed it so fast behind me that I wondered if she'd meant to keep me on the other side.

"Make yourself useful." She pointed to a wooden plank and

then to a window from a nearby building, its glass intact. "Get one end on the sill there."

Oh, God, I thought. We were two stories up, and she didn't want to take the stairs down. She meant to cross open air.

Judging by its gray color and battered condition, the plank had been exposed to the weather for decades. I lifted it, one end up high like a Scottish caber. It was heavy, an inch thick and about twelve feet long. I braced the lower end against my stomach and let the far end drop like a drawbridge, catching the edge of a sill on what I guessed was an apartment block. After shimmying it closer to the window, I lowered the near end.

"Do you think—" I began, wondering if we should test it.

Blackbird pushed past me and walked across, every step confident. The plank groaned under her weight, flexing alarmingly. Showing no concern, she reached the far side, and pulled up the window.

She was lighter than me and must have crossed before. I'd climbed trees, and could say with confidence, this wasn't going to be the same at all. Caution was sensible. Except the whispers were insistent. There was sadness mixed with anger—an accusation of selfishness, perhaps. I checked the gate. Wraiths crowded, and two pushed slowly through the metal, their faces contorted in pain.

"Really," I said to them. "You can't find someone else? Haven't you heard of buying local?"

They didn't answer. I put a foot on the plank. It wobbled a little, and my stomach lurched. If I fell, I might live. I'd break my legs and the wraiths would get me, but I'd live for a bit, screaming in agony with no one to mourn my end.

Yeah, I was being melodramatic. My impending demise justified a good dose of existential angst. I glanced at the stars. There were a lot of them now, not a single one familiar. Behind me, a wraith hand reached, fingers out straight, the tips seeking my flesh. I couldn't delay any longer.

I took a shuffling step. The wood bowed. I took another step. It bowed further, then wobbled. Throwing my arms out wide, I swore under my breath, my hips shifting. Vertigo pummeled my balance, and I felt myself falling a hundred ways, only to recover at the last moment. I didn't have butterflies in my stomach—I had dragons clawing.

You're better than this. As a kid, you used to climb trees no one else dared.

Because I needed somewhere to hide, not because I wanted to. This was the same situation, and it should be easy. It wasn't. I'd stopped running and hiding. I'd grown up, earned a degree, and shut the door on my past. Except, once again, I had no damn control of my life.

No, that was a lie. I had a choice. It wasn't good, but it was there. The secret to surviving was spotting it and picking the least-worst option. This time, it wasn't even close.

I wrapped the thought around me like a blanket, and shuffled across, a wraith on my heels. This close, its hunger tugged at my flesh, sucking the heat from my back, causing my muscles to spasm. The scent of mildew and sulfur tickled my nose, the need to sneeze forcing my eyes to close. Willing them open, I grabbed my nose, and my chest bucked while my sinuses burned with the explosive force. A misplaced foot sent me flailing.

The world spun. I threw my weight forward, feeling nothing but air before catching the sill, and slithering through the window. I held a hand against my pounding chest. Blackbird slammed the window shut, and I jumped at the loud thud. She had a bowl filled with salt on the floor, and once the window was closed, she poured the contents along the inside of the sill, a waterfall of fine grains spilling over the edge as she pulled across a heavy blind. Whispers and moans filtered through, but the wraiths couldn't pass. We were safe. I hoped.

CHAPTER 5

BRANDED VAGABOND

Geometric rose patterns in reds and greens with gold highlights covered the walls, reminding me of the art deco architecture my real nana had obsessed over—among other things. The scratchy indigo carpet had complicated squiggles of white, some in a circular design, others straight, and none of them repeating. A pair of chesterfields were positioned around a low coffee table. Depressions and worn leather spoke of heavy use and yet a mustiness pervaded the room.

A wide arch led to a kitchen dominated by a large oven and a fridge shaped with blocky protrusions of lacquered wood. Next to these were built-in cupboards with stained glass windows of black and white diamonds. A thin marble-topped island in the center of the kitchen held a clay bowl with more abstract lines. Though large, it only held three apples. They must be artificial, I thought, because they looked fresh. I counted three more doors. One with multiple locks that must have been the normal point of entry. The others could have been a bedroom and a bathroom. Was this Blackbird's home?

"Are we safe?" I asked, leaning against a wall and setting off a puff of dust.

Blackbird leaned her staff in a corner and headed into the kitchen, setting her backpack down on the island. "There is no safe. This shelter isn't in the official wayfarer archives, but that means little."

It certainly did. I moved to the kitchen entrance, wondering how long it had been since I'd eaten. How could you track time when the very meaning of day had changed? Which raised more questions.

"We can stay here, right? If those wraiths only come out at night, we should hole up until morning, and then you can take me back."

She took several small bottles from her backpack and clinked the last on the marble. "Do I paint the image of someone ready to wallow with my feet on the table, eyes closed, snoring like a wild boar?"

She retrieved more objects from her backpack, pouches and small boxes, while I searched for an argument more convincing than not dying horribly, a hard ask. Having apparently dismissed me, she rifled through the cupboards, taking out several jars and tins and using the contents to fill her little collection.

I folded my arms, refusing to offer help, and said to myself, "How did it come to this?"

"Greed, arrogance, love, or all three," Blackbird said, misunderstanding. "It doesn't matter. They did it to themselves and now serve the sentence for their folly."

"How can you say that? There were children out there. How did they deserve to become wraiths?"

Blackbird put away the containers. "The choices of the few affect the many. It is the nature of existence, and only gnat-brained sots pretend otherwise. Deserve has nothing to do with it.

The past is set. Affecting change requires charting the ways ahead."

The lecture rankled. It sounded like an excuse for giving up on people. That same attitude left troubled kids behind—as she'd been on the verge of doing with me several times. I remembered laying on the platform, blasting away at a wraith. She hadn't come to help. If I hadn't shot, I'd be dead. A question scratched at my thoughts.

"If those wraiths are ghosts, how did my bullets hit one? How can they even touch us?"

Pausing the repacking of her backpack, Blackbird gave me an assessing stare. "You are a babe waving your arms, wondering how the sun rises and snow falls. It's enough for you to know that they can. Act accordingly."

My cheeks heated. Not again. Not again. Nana had played with my mind before she lost hers.

Enough.

I planted my feet. "How the hell am I meant to survive if I don't know what's going on? You might not give a shit about me, but I'd rather keep my life—whatever is left of it. And think about this: you might need my help. What use can I be if I don't have a clue?"

She laughed. Worst of all, it sounded spontaneous rather than an act of cruelty. She thought that little of me, and it burned my pride. It shouldn't have. Her opinion didn't matter.

Still, I seethed as she walked up to me, no doubt ready to dig the knife deeper. When she grabbed my chin, I was too shocked to push her away. She moved my head from side to side, inspecting me like a horse.

"I have all my teeth," I said awkwardly as her iron-strong fingertips pressed into my jaw. Which wasn't strictly true. I'd badly chipped two when I was thirteen, and had lived with the pain until a student dentist fixed them for practice.

She let go and went for my hands, twisting them around in her firm grip. The backs were scarred: thin lines, jagged lumps, circular patches. I knew the story of each. She flipped them over and checked my palms. They'd lost their calluses, but they weren't soft. She squeezed my fingers and glared at me, her closed mouth moving from side to side. Was she going to pronounce the unfortunate shortness of my life line and ask for payment in silver?

"What did you do on your world, boy, pick berries and bake pies?"

I tilted my head. "No. I'm a teacher."

"A teacher?" Amusement brightened her eyes. "What did you teach—the great secrets of all that is, the energy flows that bind existences, the philosophy of the human condition?"

"I taught *useful* things. How to read and write, mathematics, science, and how to be decent. Call that philosophy if you like."

She sniffed, and I tried to pull my hands free, but she held them with ease.

"Let go already. What the hell are you doing?"

"Checking to see if you have the aptitude. Consider yourself lucky." Finally, she released me. "Remove your shirt and sit here." She patted the island.

I cocked my head. That was unexpected.

"Don't flatter yourself. Now, get up before I change my mind."

I started unbuttoning my shirt before choosing to do so. She might not be Nana, but I'd learned to obey that voice without question. And once I'd started, there was little point stopping. I'd look like an even bigger idiot. There might also have been a touch of the most dangerous substance known to humankind—curiosity.

She retrieved her staff and stalked around me. When she disappeared behind me, my back itched and I hunched forward, waiting for a beating that never came. Instead, she paused by my left arm and pressed on the side just below where I'd been vaccinated.

"This will do." She raised her staff. "Brace yourself."

Her eyes lost their focus. Was this some deliberate humiliation? If so, her heart didn't appear to be in it.

"Move to the left."

I shuffled along the island. She pressed down on my left hand, locking my arm in place, and brought the sphere of her staff near my skin. A fleck of light in the center burst into a blinding brightness. I forced my gaze back, ready to pull away.

A line of fire erupted from the sphere, hitting my skin. Pain. Fire. I swore and yanked my arm free. She backhanded my stomach, the slap stinging as much as the burn.

"Hold still. If I fuck this up, I'll cut your arm clean off."

Shocked as much by her swearing as her threat, I let her force my arm down, and she conjured more fire. I locked up, memories rising like the wraiths, fears clawing at my strength. My father had pulled his belt out, demanding I raise a hand. I'd dropped a glass and received a cigarette burn, tears streaming down my cheeks, too afraid to run, too ashamed to tell anyone. The anger. My mother had her own ways to enforce control, to inflict shame. And Nana, she'd loved the cane.

My eyes grew moist, and it was all that I could do to control my trembling. The acrid stink of burned hair mingled with that of cooking. Coward that I was, I couldn't watch, leaving me to wonder exactly how she was mutilating my flesh. How did it feel? If you've ever touched a frying pan by mistake, you'd know, except you'd have to keep running your hand along the edge over and over.

"Done," she announced thoughtfully, as if judging the quality of finished art. "You wanted to know things? Well, you've just entered the classroom, and you'd better use your eyes and ears.

Put your shirt on—you look like a gormless peasant farmer—and listen at the window."

A quick check revealed the damage. She'd branded me with a series of fine circles and lines as if a circuit board had disintegrated. It strained my eyes, as if it were simultaneously near and far. And damn, it hurt. It was going to scar. Simple first aid said that I should run it under water for a good twenty minutes. That would be admitting the pain to her. After the humiliation, I didn't want to give her that—offering up the evidence of my suffering for her delight. So, I pulled on my shirt, my teeth gritted, and let the fire of my skin wash across me.

"The window, boy."

"I'm *not* a boy." And yet, I found myself striding to the window, not to seek her approval, but to get it over and done with.

I startled. I could hear the wraiths. I *understood* their whispers. The terror of an endless cold. The fear of numbness, abandonment in a crowd. The despair of regret, of heated words that couldn't be taken back. The furious need to fill a hunger that couldn't be sated, a naked addiction that twisted shame into hate.

One voice was different, tortured yes, but ecstatic. "Praise him. Almighty Tenekal. He who craves will not be denied. Yes, we serve, we serve, we serve."

It was horrible. I stepped back, almost thankful for the throbbing that told me I still lived. Tenekal must be the name of whoever was responsible for the apocalypse this world had faced. No matter how much of a dickhead someone was, there was always another ready to kiss his ass.

"All they have left is want," I said, trying to shake off their misery. It had an infectious quality.

"The more they consume, the more they want—an affliction that extends beyond the domain of the dead."

I'd understood them. I glanced at my covered arm, the obvious and yet impossible cause. "What did you do to me?"

"I gave you a gift, ungrateful boy. And here's another. You resemble a vagabond." She pointed to an internal door. "Go. Pick clothes suitable for the journey ahead, and do it fast."

"What journey?"

"There lies a question with an unpredictable answer. Prepare yourself for any and all."

With that command, she wandered back into the kitchen. I pulled at my torn shirt, then my filthy pants and cheap leather-look shoes. They'd taken a beating. Well, if I was going to try her ex-boyfriend's clothes on, I'd better get to it.

The door led to another apartment. The internal wall had been ripped out and the windows and exterior door boarded up. Inside, several hanging lanterns shed weak light between rows of wooden shelving with steel uprights. These were packed with clothes of many styles, some so bizarre that they belonged on a catwalk. I wandered past formal clothes matching the wraiths and what looked like a corduroy baseball jacket with the words Dhuli Flamers embroidered on the right breast.

It didn't take long to assemble a set of sturdy boots, navy pants with the feel of heavy denim, and a white collarless shirt with a narrow waist and slightly puffy sleeves. I swear it was the best of a bad lot, though it had the weight and quality stitching of fancy clothes. At least the gray woolen jacket should fit well. And it looked good, reaching down to my thigh when I lifted it against me. All up, the outfit would have cost as much as a month of my wages. Which made my reluctance to dump my own clothes surprising. They were all that connected me to where I'd come from. And I felt like I was shoplifting. Who owned all this?

Who's going to arrest you?

I laughed at the thought, scraped my burn, and clenched my fists to handle the pain. I was being an idiot. If an opportunity came along, I needed to take it. The universe owed you nothing and would dish it out in spades.

In the end, I kept my underwear, socks, and belt. Changing hurt. The less said about it, the better. After, I slipped my phone and wallet into the jacket. I'd use them again. It was a statement, a promise to myself. It combined with the new clothes to renew my confidence. All I needed was a nap and a ticket home.

My mouth was open wide mid-yawn as the door opened. Blackbird strode in. "You're ready? Good. Time to go. We need to move before the nasty ones wake."

Nasty ones? There was something worse than the wraiths? I won't lie—my balls shrank and tried to climb inside my torso. Blackbird was already out of the storeroom, and I heard her working the locks of the apartment door.

Choices. I was either going to stay here and starve to death if the wraiths didn't find a way to break in, or I was going to follow this madwoman out and most likely die in the next few minutes. Most likely wasn't certainly. It was a fine distinction, but I grasped it tightly.

Time for a walk.

CHAPTER 6

SACRIFICE

W e stopped atop a hill, an oversized yellow moon staring down at us malevolently. My arm hurt like hell, my feet had grown a blister from the new boots, my lungs ached from running, and my nerves were fried. We'd reached an overgrown formal garden chocked with spiny weeds. Mist clogged the surrounding streets, a sea of potential death. We'd made it out of the apartment with only a few wraiths in tow, but they were everywhere. If Blackbird hadn't known the locations of so many wrought iron fences and gates, we'd never have made it this far. Wherever this was.

A plaque next to a nearby tree had a message for a loved one lost in the Grace War, whatever that was. Reading it was disconcerting. I knew it wasn't in English. Nothing here was. And yet, since Blackbird had branded me, I could make sense of everything from store names to street signs. My mind perceived the words as if an app was translating in real time. All except for the design on my arm. That remained a mystery and could stay one. My priorities lay elsewhere.

For example, with the wraiths pushing their way through the

51

fencing. Now I could understand their whispers, they were all the more terrifying.

"My poor Marchi, you tasted so good."

"No light. No sun. Why will nobody talk to me? Why will nobody touch me?"

"We are as nothing before his might and glory."

"Please, please, please, a little. Just a little."

Blackbird cut a path around a neat timber hut. We'd made our way through three- and four-story buildings to reach this point. There'd been one particularly beautiful example of carved stone, The Rival Theater. Depictions of what I guessed were heroes and villains filled its walls, some with proud gazes and others sly. The way ahead was different. The buildings were sparser, plainer. An industrial area. And in this direction, I spied a distant light.

"Hey, do you see that?"

She nodded. "It's an outpost of humanity, one of the few that haven't yet succumbed. We're not going there, but the way lies on the other side."

"Are they friendly?"

"It matters not. But they provide a convenient beacon."

A wretched scream pummeled my eardrums, wordless, fearless, deranged. The vibration rocked my skull and roared through my body. I twisted, searching for the source.

It stood upon the theater, a wraith, and yet different. More. It was as tall as the theater, with leathery wings glistening like an oil slick. On a heavily muscled torso, a neck stretched inhumanly long, and a spiked tail gave this balance. A heavy brow sat over eyes of swirling lightning. The jaw pushed forward, lending the wraith the look of a gorilla more than a dragon. Wraith? More like *überwraith*. My eyes widened; my fingers stiffened as if I still held a gun. Like one would do anything against that beast. Hell, I'd have taken my old sword for even a shred of comfort.

"A nasty one?"

"Indeed. They are the remains of creatures spliced with human traits."

A rumble shook the ground, followed by a deep roar. Then more, screeches, cries, growls. It was not alone. The überwraiths were shouting their challenges to each other. Or coordinating. I didn't like that idea.

"It is all too soon," Blackbird growled and jogged down the hill. "The wave is too strong."

I kept pace and worried. Her meaning was indecipherable, but her concern was palpable. I'd say fear, but I wasn't yet sure she was aware of the emotion. We reached a gate, thankfully wraith-free, and left the garden.

Descending into the mist shrank our world. Our footsteps echoed, coming from all directions. I strained to hear above my own labored breathing. And the wraiths, they flowed down streets and out of buildings, intent on eating our lives, our souls, whatever that meant.

A car yard caught my attention. Several vehicles were parked under a canopy, their condition remarkably good, at least as far as I could see.

"Hey, we should drive."

"Do you know how to hot-wire one?"

I looked away.

"Trust your body over machines," she said.

Easy to say when you were some kind of octogenarian athlete. But she was right on the first point. There was no reason to assume these were wired like the cars I knew. And, if I was going to be honest, the odds of one starting with its key were low after so long. So, I kept running—and hating it.

Turning left, we entered an open-air market filled with wheeled carts and wraiths. I had to leap over a cart with a broken wheel to dodge a brute of a man, his translucent hands swinging at me like hammers. In doing so, I lost Blackbird, and called her name over and over as wraiths closed in. Her response may have come a second later, but to me, it was eons.

We regrouped, dodging between carts, and were almost out when she shoved me beneath the narrow awning of a small permanent shop at the side of the market. *Rhuti and Co. Best Meat,* read peeling text on a flapping sign.

"What was that for?" I demanded while rubbing my side.

"Quiet." She squeezed under the cover, her elbow digging into my stomach.

The sign rocked further, and a bass beat pressed against my chest. I leaned over Blackbird and peered out.

"Holy shit."

"Nothing holy about it. Get back."

Another überwraith wraith flew overhead. Its wingspan resembled that of a small plane, but there were four, each gossamer like a fairy's. Six floppy tentacles writhed beneath it. What the hell animals had these people been splicing? And why had Blackbird chosen to come here?

The ordinary, merely terrifying, wraiths kept advancing. Blackbird checked the überwraith's progress, and then dragged me out. We left the market and slowed to a fast walk.

"I need to buy time," she said.

My gaze went to her staff. If she could teleport between worlds, why not turn back time? But she didn't stop. Way better than that, I thought, she took us toward the human outpost. It wasn't far off. And the artificial glow drew me on.

"The wraiths go at dawn, right? We say hello and goodbye to the locals, and off we go."

This time, she did stop. She rounded on me, and, curse me, I flinched.

"Boy, you still live in an illusion. You have so little compre-hension, I may as well be wiping your ass and giving you my tit to sup on. I can't stop. I am followed, and we'll all be damned if I'm caught." She gestured with her staff, but I wasn't sure she meant the pair of us, this city, the planet, or something greater. "All of us. Every. Last. One."

Her gaze was wild, wind picked up her hair, and her very presence grew more solid. I believed she believed what she said, and that frightened me.

There are moments in our lives when the familiar is ripped away. For the average Joe or Jolene, that might be when their parents divorce, when they are sent to boarding school, when they're fired without notice, cheated upon, or lose a loved one to an accident. I'd had enough to know them well, and this was different. I'd been walking on another world, but it was Blackbird that felt alien.

She was playing a different game. She was playing by different rules.

An überwraith howled from far too close, and she harrumphed. With no more said, we headed near what might have once been a school or a hospital. Made from squares of pale brick, the building reached two stories, had many shuttered windows, and a large moat of once-open land. Barrels cut in half had been laid like troughs, end to end, stretching around the building. This was replicated twice more, all containing salt. The equivalent of castle walls. Clever. As well, there were ditches dug at regular intervals with dull metal cylinders with screw tops. Enough light came through the shutters to decipher the symbols painted on their sides. Flames. Several wrecked vehicles dotted the space, their alignment suitable for cover or channeling the wraiths.

Painted squiggles caught my attention, clumps of circles and triangles and straight lines—nothing I'd seen before and yet reminiscent of the burn on my arm.

Behind us, wraiths had amassed, an army of ghosts. There

must be hundreds, thousands. We'd brought them with us like a dragnet, and they were spread wide enough to cut off our escape. Could it get any worse?

The answer walked between them, a cross between an albino giraffe and a ten-legged spider. Dagger-tipped legs rose and fell, scattering the lesser wraiths and sinking into my instinctual fear. Its crane-like neck dripped ectoplasm, and I wondered if it would feel wet—mostly to avoid thinking about its maw. Four fangs twitched around an ovular mouth with a tongue resembling the tentacles of an anemone. The wide head was eyeless. Neverthe-less, it marched toward us with steady confidence.

"Holy shit," I said, my eyes wide, the skin of my face taut.

"Keep moving."

Blackbird walked a zigzag route between the firepits, muttering as she went, coming closer to, but not directly toward, the outpost proper. The cries and moans of the wraiths steadily increased. I could no longer make out any individual phrases—hardly a comfort. The air was tight—that charged intensity before a summer storm broke with all its fury. And I swear my own energy bled into it, numbing my limbs, quieting the inner voice that said I'd make it, that I was a survivor.

A voice boomed from an unseen speaker, distorted like an early radio transmission. "Strangers, go no closer. This is New Hope territory. We will defend every inch with deadly force. Turn away immediately."

"I can't do that," Blackbird hissed. "Bigger problems."

A loud crack made me jump. My gaze went to the sky seeking a bolt of lightning before I processed the ricochet off the ground. The bastards were firing at us. It might have been a warning shot, but I dived behind a nearby vehicle already riddled with bullet holes on both sides.

"Assholes," I shouted as Blackbird walked calmy behind the same all too thin metal. There were bullets that could go right through engine blocks, or so I'd read. "How can they do that when people on this world are almost extinct?"

"Everyone does what they need to do to survive," Blackbird stated before dashing to the protection of a car with one side bent in.

I knew what she meant on a personal level, but she was also wrong. Cruelty for pleasure formed a thick scum floating atop humanity, but it wasn't all of us. I ran to her. A volley of shots echoed as puffs of dirt exploded around me. These were not warning shots.

"So be it. I should have from the start." Blackbird leaned close to me. "I need you to do as I say. There won't be time for your endless questions. Understood?"

Being shot at is nothing like watching it in a movie. To really get the feel without the guns, you'd need to lie down on some concrete, and then have some burly guy swing a sledgehammer an inch or so from your head over and over. The noise is incredible—your ears ring. And one slight shift of position will result in your brain splattering.

It sharpened my thinking. Blackbird hadn't panicked. She hadn't rolled up into a ball. She wasn't cursing our assailants or our situation. She had a plan, and it was no doubt better than mine: wait to see who gets me first, the outpost or the wraiths.

"Just tell me what to do."

"Follow."

She broke out of cover and sprinted toward the nearest line of barrels. I reached them soon after, my head low, flinching with every shot.

"Push this one over, now. Get your back into it."

I dropped to my knees and heaved. It was heavier than I had thought, and the edge flexed with my effort. The adrenaline coursing through me left my hands shaking. The barrel rocked— that was it. I pushed down on the near side, rocked it twice, and used the momentum to shove it up and over. Salt spilled with a hiss, and Blackbird ran her staff across, creating a gap as she went inward.

"Good, now run."

We dashed along the between the barrel lines, a hail, a torrent of gunfire chasing us, then cutting off. I guess we were out of the line of sight. The wraiths hadn't cared. They were closer than ever—right up to the salt barrels that we could have jumped over.

She came to a sudden stop and held her staff aloft. "This will do."

Do for what? The answer came fast. The sphere in her staff went incandescent, flashing across my vision as lines down the wood radiated scarlet. A line of flame hit a ditch. Night became day as a yellow fireball mushroomed up, spewing jerry cans that exploded like secondary fireworks. The air rumbled, and a heat slammed into me, blasting my hair back and drying everything from my lips to my eyeballs. Blackbird wasn't done yet. She took aim at three more ditches, always going for the outer edges.

When barrels from the second explosion smashed a hole in another line of salt, I finally got it. She wasn't blasting a way in for us. She was ripping up their defenses. Salt for wraiths, fire and lead for humans. Taking out the salt gave a path directly to the outpost. Wraiths were already streaming through the first break I'd made. They'd reach the second soon, and Blackbird's final effort had already breached the third line.

"You're using them as a distraction," I said, my voice harsh with disbelief. I gestured to the building. "How many people are in there? How many children?"

She visibly sagged, but I didn't think it was from my questioning. She looked tired. "How many live on this world? Are they the last or a drop among millions? It doesn't matter."

I bristled at her dismissal of their suffering.

She turned away and spoke before I could. "I don't have to justify myself to you."

I followed. What else could I do? Behind me, fire still roared, and the wraiths pushed through. The giant spider-legged über-wraith worked at this gap. A barrel shifted. The überwraith could move physical objects—at least once the salt line had been broken. I shivered, wondering if it would focus on the outpost or follow us, and hating myself for the outcome I wanted.

An air-raid siren whooped, and floodlights sent bright beams onto the chaos we had wrought.

We reached the far side of the outpost. A few wraiths were on our trail, but most float-walked toward the building. Shouting erupted, and I wondered if we had become easier targets in the bright light. But we were no longer the outpost's biggest problem. They'd been right to warn us off and to shoot at us. If their aim had been better, they'd still be safe.

Blackbird used her staff to vault the salt line. "We don't have far to go."

We've gone pretty damn far already.

I kept my frustration to myself and jumped a barrel. The first scream followed soon after. I didn't look back. I couldn't make myself. I should have. The slaughter should have seared my retinas.

Instead, I took in a long sandstone building. The words Public Book Hoard were engraved above a wide entrance, along with several stylized books. Book Hoard—it was a library. A broad set of stairs led up to a pair of heavy wooden doors, the kind that proclaimed the value of what was inside. Thankfully, they were ajar. Relief sizzled through me. We were almost there. Whatever Blackbird needed was inside. And then she could get me home. And this would be over, and I could reduce it all to a bad dream best forgotten. It was a lot of expectations to place on a library, but they'd been there for me in the past.

A pale shape loomed to the right, its translucent bulk pressing against the corner of the building. As tall as an elephant and with many short, stubby legs, it resembled a mutant triceratops. Four long horns pointed forward, and its beak curved down like a raptor. It opened that beak and screamed.

Kee-aah! Kee-aah!

A high-pitched hunting call that grated on my eardrums. Worse, it lumbered forward, clearly intent on catching us before we slipped inside. Putting on a burst of speed, I leaped up the stairs, my boots thudding an urgent drumbeat. I reached the doors first and pushed to no effect. The hinges must have rusted solid. Blackbird joined me as I shoved hard on the right door.

The überwraith picked up speed. I shoved again. Steel groaned. The door quivered.

"Come on!" Blackbird shouted.

We pushed. A great crack sounded and the top of the door bent inward. Another crack and it fell, smashing against polished wooden floorboards. We tumbled onto it. I rolled off—dodging the sharp, rusted edges of the hinges—and gave a hand to Blackbird. To my surprise, she accepted it with no fuss. Once up, she reached into her robes for a pouch and tossed salt across the doorway. Even I could tell there wasn't enough.

"Up the stairs."

The überwraith slammed into the remaining door. The hinges shattered, and the second door joined its brethren on the floor with an almighty bang. I looked at the size of the doorway and the überwraith. It was tight, but the damn thing was going to fit. Of course, it was.

We were in a large hall with busts of dead people, wood paneling to waist height, and several closed doors. The stairs started in the middle, built from a dark mahogany and carpeted down the center with black and white stripes. Partway up, it split to the left and right.

Leaves and other detritus crunched beneath our feet until we reached the first step. Blackbird activated her sphere, shedding light. Behind, the überwraith screeched in triumph as it cleared the doorway. I had an urge to tell it to keep its voice down, but any humor in our plight dissipated when it charged forward.

"Left," Blackbird called.

My legs burned as I reached the upper level. Several desks with simple chairs lined one side, back-to-back. Ahead and to the right, rows of bookshelves stretched into darkness. My English lecturer would have cried to be able to read just one of the alien texts.

The stairs groaned. The überwraith was on them, and any thought of taking a book fled my mind.

Blackbird strode to a pair of desks. "Help me move these."

"I don't think a barricade is going to cut it," I shouted while watching the überwraith push at the railings of the split stairwell. The upper sections were narrower. A creak led to a snap, and a section of railing fell away. Worse, two very ordinary wraiths had floated out of the bookcases.

"Tell me. Tell me. Tell me," one whispered.

"He knows," the second added as if replying.

I helped drag a desk clear and kicked the top of the second desk, knocking it over. We were getting surrounded again. The überwraith had shoved its way to the top and was struggling with the final thick post.

"What now?"

"Now, I open the way."

Blackbird raised her staff, the sphere growing in brilliance, and the marks on the wood—the runes—became a radiant blue. The sphere shifted from white to the same blue, and she sliced down. For the second time, I saw her create a portal, the sides sparking, stretching, creating a shimmering surface that reflected ourselves and a warped überwraith pushing up onto the level. Blackbird walked through the portal without glancing back.

I hesitated. What was through there? Could it get any worse? Would I be moving further away from Earth?

The last was a pointless concern. Anywhere was impossibly far unless Blackbird returned me. Another thought held me back. Earlier, Blackbird had said she was being followed. That was the reason for her haste. What could be so bad that she'd risked the path we'd taken this night? That she'd commit mass murder?

I didn't want to find out. I didn't want to be left behind. And I didn't want to get metaphysically chomped by wraiths.

The hairs on my arms tingled as I stepped through.

ONCOMING HEAT

A pungent, burning odor drilled into my sinuses as a bitter, ashen taste coated my mouth.

"Move. I have to close the way."

I let Blackbird push me aside as I took in our new surroundings. We were on a lush green hill, one of many, the grass dotted with a rainbow of wildflowers. The pale pink sky housed fluffy clouds. It was beautiful and so different from what we'd passed through that I sat on the grass, feeling the blades to make sure they were real.

My body ached, every part of it. I pulled off my socks and boots to rub my feet. Two ugly blisters greeted me. Just what I needed. Cries of the screaming survivors echoed through my skull, audible illusions. How could we be somewhere so peaceful, when we'd condemned others to a terrible death?

In the distance, there were people. I can't say how happy it made me to see them. They dotted the hills in small camps, packing up canvas tents and stowing them on brightly painted wagons of many designs. Others shouldered backpacks and walked off in ones and twos. I thought I spotted several swords and perhaps a rifle.

Their route became clear. A river of humanity snaked down a road, collecting more souls like a river with tributaries. The riot of colors put me in mind of a celebration. Perhaps there was a new king, a spring fair, or some religious event of significance.

The people flowed to a walled city far enough away to hide its details while creating an impression of scale. It must hold tens of thousands if not more. There might have been tall buildings, but distance made them waver, and I guessed there must be some kind of atmospheric distortion, or they had blimps, or perhaps overfed tethered dragons. It wasn't like I had any way to separate fact from wild imagining.

Overcome by a wave of exhaustion, I rested my head on my knees.

Blackbird leaned over me. "Are you seriously hurt?"

"Hurt?" I looked at her in disbelief. "I'm on my third planet, I can't remember the last time I slept, and I've killed who knows how many people."

"Don't be stupid. You'll know it when you kill. And what's wrong with your feet? I can see your caution."

"A couple of blisters. I've had worse."

"Always take care of your feet. If you can't walk, you're dead."

She kneeled next to me and pulled a narrow tube from her backpack. It had a cork stopper. She took out a rag, poured an oily green liquid onto it, and demanded my left foot. It's hard to argue indirect murder when you're being treated like a three-year-old. I gave her the foot.

And cried out when she rubbed the goop on. It felt so cold it burned.

"Hold still," she demanded. "This will toughen up the flesh."

I reluctantly handed over the second foot. "Got anything for not sleeping in forever?"

She pressed the rag hard against skin. I flinched, but she held it tight.

"Masking tiredness is risky, and anything that can wholly remove your need to rest is dangerous in the extreme."

I prodded a foot. The goop had dried, and while the blisters still hurt, pressure didn't increase the pain. That I could live with. Blackbird was already standing, so I hurried to get my shoes on, even as my thoughts churned. How could I reconcile this woman who had bothered to help with my blisters, yet had no problem with her earlier actions?

I tested my weight on my feet and her choices, "Surely, we didn't have to do that? I mean, condemning people to a terrible death. You knew that place. There must have been another way."

"Way? Huh. No, boy, there wasn't. Not one of use."

"Come on, that can't be true. There are always choices. What made you pick that?"

She pointed the staff at me—a gesture of emphasis, I hoped. "A god, a goddess. Depends on how you look at it."

God? Goddess? Damn. I knew the religious sort all too well. People like my father telling me I better pray to God that I didn't piss him off any further. People like Father Alvery, lecturing on deliverance, love, and power. I remembered his serene gaze as I asked for help, his assurance that God was with me. But when you were in the dark, hearing heavy footsteps coming up the stairs, you were all alone. When you were begging, crying, they weren't there. And after, they looked away from the bruises or said that you needed to behave better, that it was your fault. That damned serene face. As a kid, Father Alvery had made me feel small, bad. As an adult, I wanted to choke him until that same face turned purple.

I stared at the endless flow of people, not trusting myself to be civil. "Gods are just an excuse for anyone to do whatever they want without any comeback."

She walked to my side and watched as I did. "Believe me, if there were another way, I'd take it. I'm no priestess. I don't beg. I don't leave offerings. I don't pray. And I sure as a morning shit, never worship. But they exist, and they have power. Only a fool would be blind to them."

I cocked my head. "You can't be that backwards. You have advanced tech. You must have seen a lot. I mean, look at Earth. What a damn mess. There's nothing divine. It's all people being awful to each other."

"Oh, gods are all too real. Do what you've been avoiding since you passed through the way—look behind."

Avoiding? That wasn't true. I attempted to turn, but my body resisted the order. I was being ridiculous. Blackbird was playing with my mind. I was stronger than that. I'd prove her wrong.

I turned.

Thick gray and black clouds fill the sky in this direction, and silent lightning struck like vipers. It was everything the beauty I'd seen wasn't. The cause was natural, I told myself. Bright orange lava flowed through valleys, the edges and rear covered in a black crust with red cracks. Spurts of lava showered the plants ahead of the main flow, starting small fires. This flood of destruction undulated as if alive, shattering the crust, which quickly reformed. The source of the eruption was out of sight, the sheer width of its advance giving the impression of a slow-moving tsunami.

Sweat formed on my brow despite the distance. This was perfectly natural. No doubt my ancestors would have ascribed it to an angry god. And there were plenty of televangelists, priests, rabbis, and imams who would do so now. The forces at work were incredible, but no mind was needed to explain it.

We had, unfortunately, arrived right at the time of the eruption and would soon burn to a crisp. Damn, Blackbird was a bad-luck magnet. If I'd believed in luck, I'd have believed that.

"Look," I said as a stand of trees lit up like a birthday candle. "Whatever you believe, you go for it. Your god doesn't need me. You obviously have a map in your head with an X marked on it. Why not make one of those portals to Earth? I'll step through. You don't have to come with me. The wolves must be long gone. It's been nice to meet you and all, but I need to go home."

She held my gaze with her own, those familiar yet strange eyes fierce and determined. "Your home won't be the same. Not as bad as some others, I expect, but not the same."

"I already said Earth isn't perfect. But I'll do my bit to make it better. That's why I became a teacher. If I can help just one kid out there, it'll be worth it."

She laughed, a short bark, and my cheeks burned. What she thought didn't matter. I had my reasons. Clenching my hands, I glared at the oncoming flow of lava. Had it advanced appreciably? Was it getting hotter?

Sighing, Blackbird took several steps down the hill, then paused. "Perhaps we are not so different—only a matter of scale. Come on, don't sulk. We have some distance to the next way, and I suspect, limited opportunity to reach it."

Sulk? I was about to tell her where she could shove her words, when three men strode up from the far side of the hill, dressed in a motley assortment of clothes. Each possessed shaggy red hair, wispy beards, thick brows, pointed noses, and small round eyes. Brothers, I surmised. One wore glossy green boots with thread-bare pants. The second, leather pants, a tight-fitting shirt with torn, puffy sleeves, and a dirty blue vest with embroidered sun motifs. The last, likely the eldest, was all in dusty black. He held an ancient pistol, a flintlock judging by the weird prongs of metal sticking up above the trigger. They all had swords, but his remained sheathed.

The swords were short, slightly curved, and with false edges near the tips. The hilts sported plain steel baskets to protect the hands. Essentially cutlasses, I guessed, and probably made in bulk. Ugly but effective. My nana had drilled me in the use of sabers—real ones, not the Olympic sort or movie toys. These weapons would be weighted differently. They wouldn't have the same reach and flow. Then again, you don't need reach if your opponent is unarmed.

Thanks for that, me. You really know how to keep yourself positive.

I wished I hadn't left the pistol in the last world. But wishes were not weapons.

The eldest scratched a scarred cheek and waved his pistol in the general direction of his brothers. "I told you there would be easy pickings. We'll be able to buy tickets thrice over."

A softness in the words reminded me of French, but I understood him clearly.

Another brother, the youngest judging by his unmarked face and narrower shoulders, pointed his cutlass toward the lava. "We should make this the last."

Boy, were they barking up the wrong tree, I thought. Somehow, I didn't think the pathetic balance on my credit card was going to be of use to them. Time to set some expectations. I took a step forward with raised hands.

"Hey, we're just passing through. We don't have any money, and we don't mean you harm. So, you might as well let us walk away."

Blackbird narrowed her eyes and hissed, "Shut up, boy. Never show weakness to brigands." She planted her staff and glared at the three. "Begone. As the boy said, we have nothing of value to the likes of you, and crossing my path will not go well for you."

The three broke into laughter. To be fair, I would have done the same in their position. Not that I'd ever be in their position. I was no thief.

Just a murderer by proxy.

The eldest patted his flintlock pistol. "No one flees without their valuables. Hand them over."

A ball of lead would kill us just as easily as a bullet. Blackbird had the wrong idea this time. She needed to do some of her fire lasers or give them something shiny. We weren't going to intimidate them. I put my hand in my jacket pocket. Could I buy them off with my phone?

Blackbird hobbled over to the eldest, her shoulders drooping. "This is your last warning. Find others to bother."

What was wrong with her? Had she pushed herself too much in the last world?

"Final warning?" The eldest brigand slapped her across her face. "Silence, old hag." He stepped to the side and aimed his pistol at me. "Keep your grandmother on a tighter leash or she won't live long enough to burn."

The asshole thought I was the real threat. He had no idea, but that didn't comfort me, not with the gun and all. Damn Blackbird.

She swung the butt of her staff upward. None of us were ready for it. The end hit the barrel of the pistol. Gray smoke blossomed along with a blast, and a rush of air went over my left shoulder. I ducked, a futile instinct. Heart pounding, I kept low, my arms in front and a little wide, my legs apart, balanced, as my mind raced to solve the vital question: fight or flight.

The eldest, his face twisted in rage, shouted, "Kill the mukta shits!"

He dropped the pistol and drew his cutlass. Blackbird, having retreated a couple of steps, whirled her staff. She was ready for a fight, all signs of her feigned frailty gone. The second brigand ran toward me, apparently deciding it wouldn't take three of them to sort out an old lady.

The first rule of any fight is to run away. Usually, that's how you live. But Blackbird was my only way home. And, odds were, these guys could chase me down and chop me up from behind. Which meant rule two slammed into my mind. Don't be unarmed. Weapons were made for a reason. However, I didn't have one, and throwing my phone wasn't going to cut it. There went rule two.

My nana's voice spoke in my head, the tone different to Blackbirds, more frustrated and somehow lesser, weaker. "Pick a stance, and for God's sake, stay light on your feet. Control the measure. Make them work."

I'd had a rope tied around my waist, the other end connected to a pole. And she'd fired that pitching machine mercilessly, forcing me to dodge baseballs over and over. She'd loved it.

This time, I was facing more than bruises. I'd never been great at unarmed fighting, and I found myself dropping into a longsword stance, my legs a little apart, the right one further back, my torso facing the brigand, and my weight on the balls of my feet. I'd be ready to move in any direction. My muscles complained immediately. It'd been way too long since I'd last held the stance. That, or fear was turning my muscles to mush.

At least I didn't have long to wait. The brigand swung wildly, and I slipped back out of range, the blade whistling by. *Not bad*, I thought, burning precious time. His momentum carried him too close to swing full, but he punched with the basket, catching me on the cheek with a glancing blow, that split the skin and bruised my flesh. I tried to keep my balance, but I tripped and tumbled down the hill, swearing as I went.

I grabbed hold of grass tufts and stopped my descent. Blood trickled down my cheek as I raised my rattled head. The brigand was already there, anger visible in his bared teeth and bulging eyes. He stabbed down, and I rolled out of the way, hoping to get to my feet before—nope.

The brigand loomed. I kicked out, missing completely, but

the bastard merely slapped my leg with the flat of his blade. He definitely wasn't trained. No doubt he was a brawler, and they'd stolen these cutlasses recently. And that wasn't going to help me much.

All I had left was fighting dirty. I grabbed a handful of flowers and yanked them out of the ground. They came up with a clod of pale soil hanging around the roots. I threw it, scoring a hit in the brigand's face.

It was beautiful. The asshole stepped back and rubbed his eyes.

I couldn't afford to use the moment to regain my breath. Instead, I scrambled to my feet and jumped on him. On the person I'd just decided was a brawler. He staggered, and I went for a couple of cheap punches until he tried to skewer me. I leaned in close and grabbed his wrist to stop his thrust, putting both of us at the edge of our balance. His breath was foul: old beer, and even older scraps of food that were fermenting all by themselves.

"Holy shit," I said. "You smell like you've been kissing your brother's ass."

His eyes widened in surprise and fury. A vein throbbed in his forehead. I tried to pull away, but he grabbed my shoulder with his free hand. I kicked at the back of his knee, and he dragged me with him. This time, we both tumbled down the hill. A rock dug into my back, the brigand's elbow smacked my temple, and the whole time, I held his wrist tight, keeping the cutlass away. He kneed me in the balls. In the explosion of pain and nausea, I kept my mouth open, and got a mouthful of dirt on the next spin. But I didn't let go.

With a thud, we stopped. His grip on the cutlass loosened. I was on top. He'd hit his head on a large stone. My fists seemed to swing of their own accord, pounding his face over and over, matching the rhythm of the pain he'd inflicted on me. My knuckles stung, but it was the blood that stopped me. The stone he'd hit had acted like an anvil, and whether he'd cracked his skull first, or I'd beaten it in, he was down. He was dead.

Now, I had murdered.

My body shook. I stared at my bloodied knuckles. What had I done? I pushed off of him and stood, unable to believe the evidence before my eyes. How could it have come to this? I'd had enough of violence, of thuggish power. Was I becoming my parents? Screw them, and screw Nana.

A shout slapped me out of my thoughts. Blackbird was up the hill, holding the remaining two brigands at bay. They were circling her like wolves, testing, hoping to catch her from behind. One limped, and the other had a lump on his head. She'd taught them to be cautious, but she was slowing down.

I glared at the cutlass lying next to the dead brigand. This was stupid. It wasn't Hollywood. One mistake and I'd be dead. And if I didn't make a mistake… I couldn't stab someone. I'd cut meat; I knew that texture. I didn't want to feel a whole sword slicing through another living person. An alternative remained. With one dead and the others injured, we could persuade these guys that we weren't worth the trouble.

The cutlass was heavy in my hand. I gave it a few cursory swings, feeling how it moved, where it wanted to rotate. The blade was balanced toward the tip. It was no weapon of finesse.

Though they hadn't given it a second thought, my parents had taught me how to hide, and how to be hurt. My nana? She'd been something else. Just as vicious, but with a calling. How the hell had she known to train me? Had she known? Was this just blind luck? I trudged up the hill, finding no answers on the way.

"About fucking time, boy."

"I was busy." I pointed the cutlass down the hill. "Look. One of you is already dead. Back off, and we can all walk away."

Being an only child, I hadn't really considered the impact of telling them I'd killed their brother. This was a mistake.

The youngest screamed and charged. I gulped and dropped into my saber stance, right foot forward, the blade angled across my body. He chopped, and I brought my cutlass up. Metal slammed into metal, the force shocking my arm. I'd swung like I was trying to cut his sword, not parry. In my defense, I was scared shitless. The tip of his cutlass missed my scalp by an inch.

I stepped wide and lowered my tip to threaten his head. He pulled away, then hacked left and right in quick succession. And just like that, I was in a real sword fight.

There was no room for accepting a hit, for learning from a mistake. Giving him an inch was offering my life. Where I would have risked a clever cut around with blunt practice blades, here I disengaged, slip stepping, going wide, feinting—anything to keep myself clear and my guts on the inside. My arm ached with every effort. It had been too long since I'd trained seriously. And in my head, my nana nagged constantly. *Anticipate, don't just react. Maintain your measure and keep your options open. Use physics to gain a mechanical advantage.* But these were short blades, requiring close engagement and instant responses.

Excuses flowed faster than my defense. The brigand didn't have to be good because I wasn't striking at him. And whether through anger or fitness, he wasn't tiring nearly as fast as me. He stepped in, swinging for my neck. I caught the blow with the end of my blade, where I had no strength, while arching my spine back. The tip went past my throat, but the force of his attack wrenched the cutlass from my hand, sending it into the grass.

"This is for my brother!"

He raised his cutlass, ready for a killing blow.

"If you had trained with that, you'd know that pulling back so far is entirely unnecessary."

A snarl greeted my feedback. I would attempt to dodge, but it would be hopeless. Physics doesn't lie.

CHAPTER 8
CHARGE

A blur hit the back of the bandit's head, surprising both of us. He grunted and collapsed.

Blackbird adjusted her staff and bashed its butt down three times on his head.

Whack! Whack! Whack!

I wanted to look away as the impacts pulverized his nose and caved in his cheek, but I couldn't.

Blackbird wiped her staff clean on the grass. "Right. That's taken care of."

"Wait," I said. We'd just killed three more people. They'd attacked us, but we did it. I looked at her face. I don't think she'd enjoyed it. But she hadn't cared, either.

"Well?" she said while settling her backpack evenly on her shoulders.

It was no use. But I had a question. "Why didn't you use the flamethrower in your staff? You could have scared them off or given them a char grill. Then I wouldn't have—"

"Oh, so you know how the worlds conjoin? You're the wise one? How many centuries have you walked the ways? I should spend my rapidly depleting reserves so you don't have to see how ugly life is? How weak the stock of Earth has become."

"Hey," I shouted to her back as she started down the hill. "It's better than the shitholes you keep dragging me through. We've cured hundreds of diseases. Most of us can read and write, which I'm betting your friends here couldn't. Everyone having to fight for their life day in, day out, is not a virtue."

It led to broken people, to people accepting the damage as normal, to perpetuating the cycle of misery. I left that unsaid. What was the point? Blackbird had already moved on. I was about to follow when I spotted a horse off to one side. It was laden with a hodgepodge of bags. Odds were, it had belonged to the brigands.

Stifling a yawn, I hurried down to it. A stake had been driven into the ground, and rope held the animal. It needed to be set free.

"I'm Martin," I told it as I approached. "I'm not going to hurt you. Be patient, don't kick me, and I'll get you free."

Its head was bulkier than I expected, rounder, and its ears were long and fuzzy. Two large eyes watched as I kneeled by the stake, and it stepped back, putting light tension on the rope.

"I've had a hard day, too. I can't remember the last time I slept. My eyes are itching, and I've seen things that can't be real. We're living in strange times, right?"

The knot proved easy to undo. I considered the other end. "Shall I undo that, too?"

I walked up to it, one hand out. The horse sniffed my palm, then licked it with a thick blue tongue that tickled.

"Gross," I said, pulling my hand back with a chuckle. "No offense intended."

The horse stayed still, making it easy to remove the rope from its bridle. There were reins as well, and a saddle poked out from beneath the junk tied to its back.

"Can you ride?" Blackbird said, startling me as I gave the horse a rub down the side of its head.

Oh, hell, no.

Hissing came from above. I looked up at a dark speck that quickly grew larger. It was a rock. A smoking, black rock. There were others. The first slammed into the hill, tossing divots of grass at us. The stink of sulfur followed, and the surrounding grass smoldered. Lava bombs. That couldn't be right. The eruption must be miles away. More of them landed.

Blackbird, who was cutting the bags off the horse's back, asked again, "Can you ride?"

I looked at the horse. "How hard can it be?"

The dark eyes looked back at me, unconvinced.

"Take it easy on me, hey?"

Blackbird passed me a brigand's scabbard and mounted the horse with ease. After I belted on the scabbard and sheathed the sword, it was my turn. I don't need to describe how I managed. Needless to say, it wasn't pretty. The horse, as kind as any person I'd met, kept still. Although it did turn its big head to watch. Blackbird shook her head at my efforts, then squeezed the horse with her knees, and off we went down the hill, far too fast.

Thump! Thump! Thump!

Then again, as more lava bombs smashed around us, it was hard to argue with speed. This place had gone full Yellowstone. Wasn't that an extinction-level event? The last world had been the same in a way. Was there a connection?

We left the bodies of the brigands behind in one butt-aching trot after another. They'd died at our hands, but seemed destined to die no matter what. Had their deaths been the only way that Blackbird and I could live? And if they were going to die, then did our actions matter?

I didn't like it. I'd heard enough excuses and seen enough blaming of others to know there was always an argument to avoid blame. We should have done better. I didn't know how, but we should have.

And yet, as we headed toward the city, keeping our distance from the growing chaos along the road, I was happy to be alive. Guilt weighed me down, but between strangers and my flesh, it had been easy to choose me every time. No matter how we saw ourselves, were we only creatures of selfishness?

Selfishness and pain. My ass hurt more than my head. A horse, I decided, could be used by chefs as a meat tenderizer. My thighs ached from squeezing the horse—holding on to Blackbird wasn't enough to keep me from flying off. A thin piece of blanket sticking out behind Blackbird's saddle was my only padding. Airplane seats were more comfortable. Throwing oneself onto gravel at high speed was more comfortable.

To the horse's credit, it remained sure-footed and responsive the entire way down the hill, despite the deadly rain of hot rocks, and with the weight of two people. I didn't know much about horses, but I figured the animal was due a bucket of apples and some clean water after this.

We left the lava bombs behind. On flat ground, the steady pace had a hypnotic effect, and I must have dozed for a short while, only waking when I leaned enough to my right that I had to grab Blackbird tight to stop from falling. I looked away to avoid her death-ray stare.

The roar of humanity finally broke into my awareness as we circled a small outcropping. Tens of thousands of desperate, angry people, yelling, screaming, pushing, shoving, begging. They milled around wagons or climbed atop them to spy the situation. The line had spread like a river mouth, but the end had crashed into solid stone. We had reached the city.

Crenelated stone walls reached into the air, as solid as any dam, and stretched to either side in an enormous display of strength and wealth. Every hundred yards, rounded towers bulged outward, and thousands of bright pennants decorated the tops in a riot of color at odds with the impending disaster. Between the crenelations, soldiers in gleaming breastplates over puffy yellow shirts carried a mix of halberds—polearms with axe heads and spikes on the top—and rifles, probably of the same flintlock technology as that brigand's pistol.

A pair of huge gates remained open, guarded by a square of perhaps a hundred soldiers, halberds sticking point out toward the crush of refugees. How long before they were overwhelmed? I could only assume that they were waiting for someone *important* to arrive, and the rest would be left to outrun the lava. I didn't think any of them would be better off. Once the lava bombs hit, the city would burn.

"Is our way out in the city?"

Blackbird shook her head. "The way is far beyond."

I didn't like the sound of that. And yet there was one advantage. "At least we can go around."

"No." She gestured above the walls with her staff. "We'll need to take an airship. On foot or hoof, we'd never cross the distance ahead of the lava."

Peering beyond the pennants, I finally registered the balloons. Pointed like footballs, they were just as vibrant as the pennants. Each had four fins at the rear. The walls hid the lower half of most, but beneath the highest, I spotted a wooden platform hanging from ropes, shaped like a flat-bottomed ship. I remembered seeing photos of the Hindenburg, and the balloons on these airships didn't seem anywhere near large enough for lighter than air travel.

That was a moot point. How on earth were we going to get into the city to board one? Even if the walls were climbable, the soldiers at the top were hardly going to let us down the other side. And the crowd at the gates was one loud sneeze away from a violent riot. There were already waves of motion, bubbles in boiling water.

We had fed people to wraiths. I thought of her staff. How much fire could it produce? Could she burn a way through, our own lava flow? I didn't think I could let her do that. I wasn't sure I could stop her.

"You're not going to fry them all so we can walk inside, are you?"

She stopped the horse on a small rise two hundred yards from the edge of the crowd.

"They'll be dead soon enough," she shouted over the roar of the crowd. "But not by my efforts. It's too risky. Controlling a rip with enough heat is difficult, and projecting the opening is harder. No, we'll need a different approach."

I could only guess at her meaning, but I took comfort in her conclusion. I shouldn't have. The crowd grew and grew. People along the road left their most precious possessions to join the press. Something had to give. If the people poured through the gates, could we enter in their wake? And how could we secure a berth on an airship when every man, woman, and child would be after the same?

There was no answer. We were screwed. I watched the distant lava. How long did we have? An hour or less. Less. Maybe much less.

I ran a hand through my gritty hair. It was interesting that we weren't covered in ash or dying from poisonous gases. Yay, we'd get the most painful way to die.

"How are we getting in?"

"I'm thinking," Blackbird said.

Leaning back, I rested my hands on the horse. I'd never wanted a pet, but the short, stiff coat was reassuring. I closed my eyes. "What we really need is a monsoon or blizzard to slow down the lava. Then we could ride the whole way. Though, I think I'd take an SUV as first choice."

"Hmm, interesting idea." Blackbird raised both her staff and her free hand and swayed slightly. "There's a chance."

I straightened. "You can get an SUV? I can suggest a good model."

"Shut up, boy. I meant water. It's nearby."

A quick check to either side had me eyeing her with incredulity. I could see a stream, and I guessed there must be wells to keep the city watered, but that wasn't going to help.

"Do you know anything about volcanology? There's a lot of heat."

"Stop saying stupid things, and let me concentrate."

I swallowed a pointless retort, and she guided the horse along the rise, stopping right before it descended.

"This is as close as we can get, and it's not close enough." She held her staff in the crook of one arm and spat on her hands, rubbing them together. "It's been a long time since I tried such a difficult working. It's going to take a lot out of me."

"Do you need room?"

"I need to forget you're here. Don't move. Don't talk. This will drain me."

Maybe there was a fundamental law of the universe—every year lived accumulated crankiness until turning into a crotchety old cow or grumpy old fart was inevitable.

"Can I breathe?"

"If you must. But pay attention. You'll need to get us inside when the opportunity presents."

Opportunity?

The sphere on her staff woke, almost blinding me. White ebbed to blue, and then to purple. The air crackled, and the runes along the wood shimmered as if in a haze. My eyes watered as the sphere enlarged, or the light turned solid. It was like standing by a star as it went nova. There was a magnetic quality to it as well, pulling at my skin. My hair floated, and my tongue tasted like iron.

Blackbird grunted. A boom announced the release of energy, and the light vanished. Was that it? I looked nearby for sparks and found nothing. Had she failed?

A furious line ripped a sideways gash in the sky, spewing sparks and dripping power. Without a reference, I couldn't be sure of its size and position, but it had to be huge, and I guessed it was over some portion of the crowd. What good was that? We didn't have an airship yet.

Water cascaded down. Not a stream, nor a spray, but a full torrent, a dam bursting from nowhere. Rumbling accompanied a deafening white-noise hiss, and the air stank of ozone. The sheer power of this imitation of nature awed me, made me feel insignificant.

Down, down the water fell, smashing into the ground at an angle and lifting people off their feet. By the time the first screams reached my ears, the water had eaten into the crowd.

My mouth gaped open. What had she done?

Blackbird brought her hands together, then pulled them apart, and the gash tore wider. The furthest refugees ran for their lives. Those nearer were caught up and washed away. I'd never seen a flash flood before. I tended to think of water as something that would go flat almost instantly. But it didn't. When there's so much, it can't spread fast enough, and it becomes a broom, sweeping away all before its path. There was nowhere to run. If we hadn't been on a rise, it would have taken us, too.

As it was, the horse danced back when a salty brine sprayed us.

I leaned close to Blackbird. "Why the hell did you do that? You could have used the water like I said. You could have saved this place."

She didn't respond. I looked at the sky. The gash was thinning like a healing cut, the water slowing.

"Can you do it again?" I demanded. If she aimed better and kept that portal open, there was a chance to save everyone.

Blackbird said nothing.

I leaned around. "Hey, this isn't a game. These people matter."

Her eyes were closed, her expression empty. My weight on her back sent her slumping forward. I grabbed her before she fell off the horse.

"Blackbird, are you okay?"

She held her staff tightly, but otherwise, she could have been unconscious. I checked her pulse. I wasn't a doctor, but it seemed weak and the rhythm uneven. What had this earned her?

I forced myself to take in the destruction. There were bodies and overturned wagons. They'd been dragged across the front of the walls and off to the side of the gate. There were also people crawling, standing, a lot of them. And more still running.

The water was shin deep, then ankle, then a series of connected pools in a sea of mud. Sodden, filthy people stumbled to their feet. The toll was awful—unforgiveable—and far less than I had feared.

The gate.

The path to the gate was clear for now, the soldiers having been uprooted as much as the crowd. I wouldn't be the only one to notice. The city was as good as open. Damn her. She'd done it.

"Blackbird, we have to go."

No response. I clenched my fists and screamed wordlessly. It didn't help.

"Okay, when we wake, you and I are going to have a talk," I told her. To the horse, I said, "It's time to get your hooves wet. We need to get inside."

I fumbled for the reins. How did you make a horse go? I wasn't in a position to use my knees like Blackbird had.

I patted its rump. "Come on, let's go. There'll be food inside."

The horse stepped forward. Go blind luck! I tried my best to let it pick its path and only tugged gently to work around knots of people or wreckage, apologizing each time. We were halfway to the gates, and making steady progress when something flicked the tip of my ear.

"Ouch!" I rubbed the spot only to get a whack right in the small of my back. "Damn it."

I tried to turn to see who had hit me. We were dressed differently. Perhaps this crowd didn't like strangers. Impending doom could do that. Pools of water sprayed as rocks hit them. They were lava bombs. Well, small rocks. Pebbles really. I'd take that. Perhaps they were flying further because of their light weight. Still, they damn well hurt.

A large one hit the horse's rump. The horse let out a strange bark, reared for a terrifying second, and then galloped forward. I squeezed Blackbird between my arms and held onto the reins with pale knuckles. My aching thighs latched onto the horse's belly as best as I my terror-boosted strength could manage.

Water sprayed as hooves pounded the wet ground. The wind whipped at my face, stealing all warmth. When the horse leaped over a shattered cart, I closed my eyes. We careened left around a knot of people, then right around a wagon, spraying mud. If I'd needed to steer, we'd have been done for. Thankfully, the horse was set on getting behind the walls, too.

Several fresh soldiers emerged to check on their comrades. Our approach soon caught their attention, and they hurried toward halberds and rifles they'd propped against the gate.

"Stop!" one shouted. "Stop in the name of the Governor!"

As we bore down on him, I shouted back, "It's okay. We're just passing through."

I couldn't have stopped if I'd wanted to. They gave up on collecting their weapons, and I figured we were going to ride through easily, the threat of being run down too much for them. Wrong. All eight of them—yeah, I counted—pulled pistols from their belts. Each could only fire a single ball before having to reload. But they'd only need one hit, and we were sitting ducks.

Blasts shattered the air. Smoke billowed.

"Fuuuuuuuuuuuuuuuuuuuuuck!"

And then we were through, the horse's hooves clattering on slick stone. More soldiers dived out of the way as we barreled through a short gatehouse, and then we were back on mud.

White-painted buildings surrounded us on both sides, all made of overlapping timber slats. There were many narrow windows, each shuttered. Rope hung between those above ground level. The doors were bright reds, blues, greens, and pinks. A few even had stylized art, though we were moving so fast, I couldn't see the details. Debris littered the street, washed in by Blackbird's waterjet. Wooden crates, sacks, pots, pans, bodies. Arms and legs twisted and still, soldiers and ordinary people alike. The wind of our passage dried my eyes. If only it could as easily remove my horror.

Behind, soldiers streamed down staircases along the walls. Others hurried back through the gate, rifles in hand. That couldn't be good. The soldiers stopped and raised their weapons. Bad, very bad. Ahead, a pair of soldiers grabbed the rifles hanging off their shoulders.

Spying a narrow side street, I pulled the reins to the right. "We better turn, or you'll get more than a rock on your ass!"

The horse agreed, and we skittered as it bled speed and threw its momentum toward the opening.

A volley of blasts accompanied explosions of splinters as lead balls tore holes in the nearby wooden walls. Like the balls, we slammed into one side on, smashing my leg, before bouncing back into the center of a dim street that bent at odd angles around decrepit housing. There were less windows, the paint was faded and peeling.

"This is insane," I shouted as a final shot went wide. "This is completely insane. I'm a teacher. Just a teacher. I don't belong here. I can't do this. Whatever the hell this is. I mean, what the hell is going on? Is it too much to ask to sit in a bar back on Earth with a beer in hand, hoping I wasn't reading too much into an invitation?"

The horse snorted.

"Yeah," I told it, "me too, buddy, me too."

There was no way home, not yet. So onward we rushed, right into whatever new disaster lay in wait.

CHAPTER 9

HANGING

When narrow streets gave way to a long garden filled with established trees, I pulled on the reins. It didn't take much to convince the horse to slow, hardly a surprise given its chest heaving between my legs.

Dirt abruptly transitioned to pale cream stone paving. Chips and cracks suggested it had been laid long ago. The street split, framing either side of the garden. Houses were set back from the street, fronted by little gardens planted with flowering shrubs, many of them trampled. Unmatched shoes, broken pottery, a sharpened stick, smeared purple fruit. It reminded me of a class-room when kids were kept inside due to the weather.

Now that the horse's hooves weren't drumming, I could hear a crowd. No, that doesn't do it justice. The roar had several undercurrents, all of them ugly, as if I were surrounded by stadiums hosting finals with crooked umpires. I encouraged the horse up the street, wondering where everyone was: a high point, the airships? I could see floating vessels ahead, up high and off to the right, beautiful and a little unreal. By all rights, they should plummet to the ground.

The crowds grew louder and more distinct as we continued, filling me with a sense of impending trouble. Which was ridiculous as I hadn't stopped being in trouble for some time. We reached a junction with another, wider street. And that's when I saw them.

The far end of the new street opened onto an expanse—the airship terminal. Docks felt more appropriate, I decided as I noted many wooden structures. The details didn't matter, though. Between the docks and us were thousands of people crushed together, shouting, shoving, desperation and anger on their faces, sticks and paving stones in their hands.

Blocking the way to the docks was a hastily constructed barricade of crates and barrels. A row of soldiers stood in front, halberds lowered, blocking the crowd. Their breastplates and puffy sleeves were filthy, perhaps from thrown fruit. A few stood on top of wooden crates, rifles in hand.

Beyond them, an airship shot up into the air. Who was aboard? The wealthy, the powerful? I counted eight, maybe nine, left. There were nowhere near enough. And if there were other crowds behind other barriers, the odds of escaping the oncoming lava were near zero and shrinking by the second.

The crowd had the same thought. They swelled forward, roaring. A soldier lifted his rifle and shot someone at the front. A head tumbled out of view, and I wondered if the crowd was going to shatter into individuals, that group courage would turn into a personal imperative to flee.

I couldn't have been more wrong. A paver launched from among the crowd knocked the soldier off the barricade as he reloaded. I swear the crowd took a deep breath together, then surged.

Several fell to the halberds, their agonized cries mingling with the unleashed fury. More dropped to the rifles, but the momentum of the crowd couldn't be denied. They slipped around the blades and overwhelmed the soldiers, knocking them down and trampling their bodies. People climbed the barricade, the first clubbed by soldiers. More grabbed the soldiers' legs and pulled them down, a beast consuming its prey. This sparked a cheer, and the crowd poured over the barricade.

The way was clear, but our chances of reaching the airships were no better. It takes time for a mass of people to move. All crushed together, the bulk of them couldn't run—even walking was difficult. I thought of charging through the crowd using the horse's bulk, but I couldn't do it. Instead, precious minutes drained away until the path was clear. By that, I mean that there were dozens of broken bodies. People cried out for help, and I blinked back tears, my body folding in on itself as I fought against a profound futility.

I couldn't save them all. I doubted I could save myself. And I already had Blackbird's life in my hands. Excuses. Weak excuses. And yet, I rode between the helpless and did nothing.

The top layer of the barricade had been torn apart, but the crates were filled with soil and hadn't budged. This was the end of the journey for the horse. It would have to be a steeple jumper to manage the height and depth—and it'd need a tiny little jockey, not two adults.

I dismounted, my legs stiff and awkward. With no time to let life flow back into them, I pulled Blackbird off and lay her across the top of a crate, the staff knocking my head as I leaned over. It was still glued to her hand.

The horse nudged my shoulder. I ran a hand down its neck.

"Thanks for the ride. I'd take you if I could. You probably can't understand this, but if you do, you have to get out of the city. We can't outrun the lava, but you might."

What a crock of shit. The horse whickered, and I gave it one last pat, then climbed over the crates and settled Blackbird over my shoulder. How do movie stars lug people around while running? She was heavy, and the staff scraped along the ground as I walked into pure chaos.

The citizenry and soldiers battled in a space many football fields in size. A score of soldiers charged a running group, slaughtering first with the spiked ends, then chasing the rest down and hacking them apart with axes. Rifles and pistols spewed smoke that turned the air into a shifting haze with a sulfurous stink that scratched at my throat and eyes.

Ramps reached into the air, each in a square pattern that looped two times, finishing a good ten or fifteen yards up. Thick beams provided skeletal frames, and health and safety officers were nowhere in sight. At the top, gangplanks extended to the flat-bottomed boats held aloft by the long balloons. Ropes stretched from the boats all the way to the ground, where they were secured firmly.

People filled the ramps to overflowing. Several times, I saw some poor bastard drop off the sides to land on hard ground, unnoticed by any except their companions. Soldiers guarded the tops of these platforms, securing the loading of last-minute supplies and approved passengers.

I headed for the nearest ramp. It was riddled with soldiers. How was I going to get past them? A knot of soldiers at the bottom surged up the ramp. They'd abandoned their halberds and were tossing people off with their bare hands or using pistols like clubs. I think they'd worked out the truth. They were going to be abandoned just like the people they'd been holding at bay.

A howling, hot gust swept across the docks, rocking the airships and straining the ropes. If people had been teetering at the edge of humanity before, this tipped them into pure animal ferocity. Fights broke out among soldiers, between the city folk, and some kind of elephant-sized furry cow rampaged.

Keeping as far from the violence as possible, I made my way along the side of the docks. A green and white striped flag waved from the rear of an airship with a teal balloon. I traced its ropes down to massive steel bars fixed in stone. Soldiers at each of these waved red and yellow checkered flags back in a complicated pattern. They rolled up the flags, placed them down, then released the ropes.

The airship whooshed upward, the ropes whipping crazily, too high to hurt anyone. The soldiers walked from their different posts to a central spot, and opened a flask, handing it between them. They knew their fate and were resigned to it. Yet they'd still done their duty. I didn't know whether to be impressed or sickened. Perhaps it was their partners and their children aboard. If it was their masters, they'd just thrown their lives away.

Was I any better, lugging my ancient ancestor across a dying city with no hope of escape? I kept walking as the truth settled in my heart. We were dead. It was only a matter of time. Either a lava bomb would crush our skulls or molten rock would ooze out of the streets, burning my feet. I'd fall, and then it would flow over me. My skin would burn, then go numb like a shorted circuit as my nerves fried. Next, it would fill my mouth and boil my brain.

I didn't fear the pain so much. I didn't want it, but to finish like this… what was the point of pulling myself out of the burning shithole of my childhood to end here? I hadn't helped a single kid, not really. Any new graduate teacher could have replaced me and done better. They wouldn't have my baggage. When I'd encountered bullying parents, had I been able to stop them? No. My teeth clenched hard. I had no pretensions of being a vigilante, but sometimes, I just wanted to tear some thug limb from limb. And turn me into them?

I kicked an ornate silver belt buckle lying on the ground. Blackbird was no angel, but against all reason, she had chosen to rely on me. If she didn't wake, she'd deep fry without ever knowing my failure.

Why am I still carrying you? You were my ticket out, and now I'm meant to be yours. What a joke.

My spine ached. It would be easy to sit down and wait. All those years I'd survived—I hadn't given up. I'd cried, I'd shivered, I'd bled. And I had kept going no matter how much it hurt.

I paused in front of another giant metal staple where a soldier waited, flag in hand. The airship above sported a blue and yellow striped balloon. The wooden vessel gleamed, bucking as wind tested the strength of its tethers. The soldiers on its boarding ramp were smart—they'd hacked a section away, leaving them the comparatively easy job of kicking off those who climbed the framework.

The gangplank shifted. The airship was ready to leave. I couldn't accept that. One of the airship crew waved a flag. It may as well have been red. The soldier near me unfurled his own. That wasn't right. That would mean it was truly over.

Stepping forward, I had the mad idea that stopping the soldier from waving his flag would hold the airship. It was idiotic. No doubt whoever was up there would cut the rope, and they'd be off.

I swallowed. An idea twice as mad as the first sprung up fully formed, a rose with a thorny stem. The time to act was now. The soldier kneeled to release the rope. I stepped behind him, drew my cutlass, and gently pressed the point against the back of his neck.

He froze.

I looked at his waist. He had a small axe and a pistol hanging from a wide, woven belt.

"Take your weapons, one at a time, and throw them away. Do it slowly."

"Look, stranger—"

"Don't talk, just do it."

He hesitated, then did as I ordered.

"Now get out of here," I said.

"Can't do that," the soldier said, looking back at me. He was older than I'd realized. His bushy eyebrows were gray, and his lined face spoke of sorrow and endurance. "I've got to release the Valence. I've already given my life to the task, and I won't stop now."

Great, a damn hero. I checked the other ropes. Two were already free. We still had a chance. And, as stupid as it was to have a snap judgment, I kind of liked this guy.

"All right. Release the rope as fast as you can and run. Got it?"

"Right you are."

He worked swiftly, releasing a hook, then unwinding the rope. The last length swished out of the staple, the end dangling nearby.

"Run!" I demanded.

The soldier walked away without looking back. Mere seconds remained. I put Blackbird down by the rope and tied it around her waist. It was a good inch thick and hard to work. So much could go wrong. I'd left enough to tie myself in the same way. Whatever fate awaited, we'd share it.

"Oy!" A fresh soldier ran toward us. His puffy sleeves were striped yellow and purple, perhaps a sign of rank. He waved a sword in the air.

I grabbed the end of the rope, but he was on me, thrusting his blade. I swung my cutlass down, barring his attack, then tried to punch with the basket, as the brigand had done to me. The soldier, unsurprisingly, was better trained. He dodged out of the way and flicked his blade toward my chest. I hurriedly rammed my cutlass across my body to parry his attack.

The rope pulled, and I stumbled several feet. Blackbird slid like a ragdoll, the staff still in her hand. The soldier advanced, and I tried a combination attack to keep him busy. A cut from the right, a high horizontal thrust, then hanging my blade tip low and transitioning into a cut from the left. I was executing the final strike when the rope yanked hard.

It dragged me onto my ass, and I reflexively let go. The airship was rising.

The soldier shouted, "The gods say you're staying here. I'm going to wipe my feet with your guts, devil-lander."

I tossed my cutlass at him and ran for the rope. The thick hemp flicked up, and I caught it, my palms stinging. And then I was off the ground, dangling. I wanted to shout an insult, the sort of clever one you come up with weeks later, but I saw him run to the pistol the other soldier had thrown away. Clever bastard.

The fancy soldier raised the pistol and spent a precious moment aiming. There was a flash, smoke, and a boom.

Nothing. He'd missed. And now I was out of range. Because I was hanging from a rope in the air, vertigo nipping at my grip, desperate for me to fall. I curled my leg around the rough length of rope and settled my arms like I was in gym class. Better. Not good, but better. And who knew that the technique actually had real-world applications?

Higher and higher we went until I could take in the tableau in its entirety. The lava crested the rise where Blackbird had set the water on those outside the gates. It stretched away to either side, consuming all in its path. Fields that I hadn't seen on my way in were subsumed. Crops burned, then vanished. Smoke puffed at the edge of red, bright fires flaring. Orange lines stretched like wrinkles, and further back, the dull, inevitable black of a cooling surface. And this too didn't last. Sprays of lava shot up like coronal mass ejections, spectacular and plain wrong, at least to my limited understanding. It was all so wrong. Volcanic soil was meant to be fertile, but I couldn't imagine a single seed escaping this devastation.

A lava bomb smashed into a building just past the gatehouse, passing right through, and disappeared inside another. A breath later, and smoke billowed out. Soon after, flames licked at the wood. This was the first fire of many. And it spread with such ferocity that I wondered if it were alive.

The rope jolted, and I squeezed my body as tightly against it as possible. Out of all the things that could go wrong, the most likely was us being spotted and the rope being cut. The length of the fall would depend on how long we remained hidden. Our deaths would be quick, either way. We were jolted again. I dared to look up.

The rope was disappearing into the ship. My mind raced. That could be bad. Blackbird would be cut in half and I'd run out of rope and fall. Or it could be good. If I could climb up unseen, I might be able to grab Blackbird and pull her out of the knot. My understanding of ship etiquette, courtesy of cartoons and old movies, suggested that stowaways were tossed overboard. I'd have to be careful.

A face leaned over the edge of the ship. A finger pointed. So much for sneaking aboard.

Damn.

We were going to walk the plank.

CHAPTER 10

WHERE THERE'S SMOKE

Holding onto a thick rope as it jerked around rubbed a layer of skin off my fingers, testing my grip, each digit feeling like they were being crushed in a vice while dipped in acid. My palms burned, no doubt red and raw. Wind turned my hair sentient, a Walmart Medusa determined to choke me. And if I gave up, or relaxed for the merest instant, I'd fall, just another lump breaking up the city below. Above, Blackbird dangled, her staff swinging wildly—a danger all of its own.

The rope kept lifting us. We reached the body of the airship, and I focused on its construction to distract from the pain. Planks of a rich walnut-toned wood, glossy and slippery, reminiscent of a freshly waxed gymnasium floor. There were broad rudders at the rear, one beneath and two horizontal on the sides. Up, up we went, until Blackbird disappeared over the gunwale. When hands grabbed me, my limbs were so weak that I had no chance to resist.

It took two sailors to hold me upright. The airship had a raised front and back—castles, I recalled from teaching a history lesson. I had an impression of ropes strung like spiderwebs, of crates and barrels, of metal pipes, and a crush of humanity: refugees, sailors in baggy pants and tight, knitted tops, and soldiers. Damn.

I leaned forward to check Blackbird as a sailor worked the rope free. How long was she going to be out? Was she even breathing? As the sailor shifted her, blood smeared across the deck.

"Blackbird," I shouted, trying to shake off my guards. "She's hurt. Let me go."

One of my captors cuffed me hard, rocking my head. I tried to bite him in turn, surprising the both of us. I was just done, done with it all. Sawdust filled my head, hot coals my eyes, and my heart had burned in the lava below. I shook as hard as I could, a futile gesture.

"Ay up," said the sailor by Blackbird. "This one's not dead."

"Not yet, right?" said another, and they erupted in laughter.

A deep groan ran through the airship, and it rocked to starboard. The passengers squealed, but the sailors shifted their balance, and the grip on my arms never loosened.

"She's got the dead rigor though," the first sailor said, while pulling at her staff. "Hand's as fast as nails. Won't leave this stick here."

The sailors stiffened. A woman approached, her demeanor one of absolute certainty. She wore baggy pants, but they were of a finer fabric, a rich blue. Her shirt also had baggy sleeves, these in red with slashes of white. Over the shirt she wore a vest made of sheepskin, the fuzzy side inward. Assuming this world had sheep. Little triangles of yellow covered the vest, only one side sewn in, so that they fluttered with every breeze. A narrow belt of tooled leather and polished brass rested on her hips. From this, hung a cutlass in an ornate scabbard, longer than the one I'd thrown away, but not quite a saber. Intertwined ropes of metal formed the cup, some a glossy steel, the others dull, almost black.

The clever design hinted at a bushy-tailed critter with longs ears and a pointed nose.

"What are you playing with, boys?"

"Found 'em hanging off a mooring rope, Captain."

Okay, so the one in charge. "I'm Martin and this—"

One of my captors crushed my arm in his grip. I winced but tried to keep my expression between friendly and earnest. Apparently, it was a speak when spoken to situation. The power play sucked, but I had little choice.

The first sailor stood. "Rope's sturdy. No harm. Want us tossing the trash overboard, high and hard?"

Which meant us. We weren't even going to get a plank. My stomach dropped. I stared at the captain. She examined me with all the affection of a kid reading an assignment.

"We're right overloaded," said one of my captors. So, the not talking was only for me. "And there be many mouths."

I silently wished he'd shut the hell up.

The captain dismissed me and poked Blackbird with her boot. "They held on until now? There is something in that. Too many lives have already been lost. So many. No, we shall keep both for now. Perhaps they will bring us luck. Secure them in the brig as befits stowaways. I'll decide their fate on another day's wind."

She walked off, absolutely sure that her order would be carried out. I envied that certainty.

"Hey, look, guys. Blackbird's an old lady, and she's hurt—"

A fist slammed into my stomach, stealing my breath, radiating pain, and birthing nausea. I stumbled back, then bent over, vomiting acid and little else. The sailors jeered and dragged me along the deck, others taking Blackbird. They shoved me through a low door at the rear castle, and down a flight of suicidally steep stairs, and then another, and finally through a door into the brig.

There were two cells formed from woven staves of red

bamboo. A sailor opened a sturdy, if rattling, door and pushed me inside. I tumbled to the ground, my muscles flaccid.

"Check for a knife."

I was roughly searched.

"'E ain't got nothing but rubbish."

One of the sailors shook Blackbird's staff, her arm dangling from it. "'Ere, what we do with this?"

"Get rid of it," said another.

"I'll snap her fingers hard off, first. Captain didn't say she wanted that."

"By the Winged Aegis, Renniken, you test me. Just put her in, good. It won't help her none."

They placed her inside more gently than they had me, perhaps in respect for her age, but they also grabbed her backpack before locking us inside. I crawled over to her and leaned against the side of the ship. The sailors had taken several bottles, jars, and parcels out of the bag. I thought of my feet as a sailor pulled the stopper out of one such jar.

"Be careful," I said. I couldn't shake the feeling that nothing good would come from this. "I think they're poisonous."

Damn. That was stupid. What if they thought it was poison and that I was some kind of assassin? Or if they decided that Blackbird was a witch, and weren't worried about lighting a pyre on deck?

The sailor sniffed, his nose wrinkling. "What's it?"

I looked at Blackbird. Yes, I had an answer, and I wished she was awake to hear it.

"My nana has dementia. She's a bit old in the head, if you get my drift. I think it was all meant to be perfume at one point, but she's kept them for years, and she keeps adding to them— random things she finds on the ground, leaves, flowers, soap, oils. It's all in there, rotting. I'd have tossed the lot, but she wouldn't leave home without them."

It was time to really sell the story. "I mean, drink them if you want, but keep it to yourselves. When you die, I don't want the captain blaming us."

The sailors looked at each other, and one plugged the bottle.

"Nasty devil-lander habits."

"That be my luck. Every soul carrying all their silver, and we get a muddled-headed old goat."

When they slammed the door behind them, I had much to do. But I closed my eyes, and exhaustion mugged me.

I woke at some point, my throat dry, my eyes scratchy, and stomach both sore and ravenous. Groaning, I stretched and tried to rub life back into my arms. The air was stale and stank of pine resin. Small windows on either side of the hull let in beams of light, while being far too small for an escape. At one end, our cell had a folded blanket on a thin, filthy mattress. There wasn't even a bedframe. A large bowl sat at the other end of the mattress, its purpose both obvious and gross. Luckily, thanks to my ongoing dehydration, I didn't need to go.

"Blackbird?"

I rolled to my knees and carefully checked her. She was breathing, little shallow efforts. Blood had spread across her green overdress, but I found the hole. I tore this, revealing the taupe underdress and another hole. The soldier had missed me but shot Blackbird. The bastard. Why had he done that? It wasn't going to help him. He knew he couldn't leave the ground. And now he was nothing but contamination in liquid rock, his last action being to hurt someone out of spite.

The asshole no longer mattered. Blackbird needed a hospital. I rested a hand on her, unsure what to do. Was the ball still in her? Her risk of bleeding out, of infection grew by the second—I had to act.

"Help!" I shouted. "We need a doctor in here!"

A shadow moved in the other cell. A woman's voice spoke,

not old, but rich and intense, "Not a soul will come no matter how loud you cry. You may as well save your throat an injury."

She stood in the far corner of her cell, away from the light.

"I've got to do something." I shifted Blackbird's cloak and found the exit wound. The ball had entered, then gone up through her flesh and out her upper arm. A different angle would have found an artery—and she'd already be dead.

"What is wrong with people?" I demanded. Blackbird needed surgery. I was no doctor, but I was amazed she still lived.

"Rip up the blanket, cover the wound as best you can and weight it down," the mysterious woman said. "It will give her a little longer, but she'll die unless the wound is cleaned and stitched."

"Thanks, I'll call an ambulance."

I glared at the blanket. She was right. I tore several strips and packed the wounds as best I could.

The woman approached the bars between the cells as I worked, revealing her features. I guessed she was younger than thirty. Red hair framed a heart-shaped face with a hungry look. Pretty, I thought, in a wild fashion, and intense. She wore chestnut pants tucked into tightly fitted calf-length boots, a short and badly ripped yellow skirt of raw silk, and a wine-red shirt with the local fashion of puffy sleeves, each decorated with white embroidered fronds. A dark green belt held her shirt in at the waist. Her long fingers wrapped around the bars.

"There are enough hurt on deck to keep the ship's surgeon busy, and if you're down here, you are not on the list. I, on the other hand, am here. I trained as a farrier. If I were free, I could make a respectable go of it. Not the neatest, mind you, but respectable." She spoke in a strange way, mockingly placing emphasis on certain words.

I narrowed my eyes. "Farriers make horse shoes. I wasn't born yesterday."

"Farriers work steel and flesh for horses and those who tend them. You have very strange gaps in your sense for someone who has seen more than one sunrise. And you speak oddly. So, let me educate you. Sewing up a woman is easier than a horse. Men, of course, are harder, being such babies. But alas, all this is moot as I am on this side, and we have no needle and thread."

I scowled and paced the cell. I had no reason to trust her. She was also unlikely to make things worse, given that was practically impossible. And she was right—it didn't matter. The bamboo bars were too close together to slip between, and we didn't have so much as a travel sewing kit.

"Rather than trying to wear through the floor, why don't you try using that pole to break the bars?"

Why hadn't I thought of that? I carefully moved Blackbird and slipped the end of her staff between two bars. I leaned on one end. The bamboo flexed. I tried again, straining, pushing the sphere against the bars. It was no good. The bamboo wouldn't snap. I released the pressure.

"Try harder," the woman demanded.

"The bars won't snap."

"That was a hopeless effort. Don't give in so easily."

"Let's see your escape attempt," I shot back.

Damn, she was cocky. Who the hell was she to be telling me what to do? Who the hell was she at all?

"Why are you in the brig?" I said, suspicion dripping from my voice.

She raised an eyebrow, then her expression tightened into solemnity. "It is a tale of sadness and hardship. I couldn't possibly list all my travails. Such a recount would break my heart twice over."

And yet she launched into a tale of romance with a Tristian general. When said general's wife discovered the affair, the farrier had to flee for her life. With no tools of her trade or money, she was reduced to begging for food. And when news of the Great Doom arrived, she attempted to steal a ticket. The noble who owned the ticket demanded that she be brought aboard so she could be publicly tortured to death in a distant city called Darnessia.

Jesus, I thought, if they planned that for her, my prospects weren't looking good. We couldn't stay here. Not for Blackbird's sake nor mine.

"I have told you of my journey. Tell me of yours."

I'd sound like a lunatic if I gave her the full details, so I told her about borrowing a horse, riding through the city, and dangling as the airship launched. It sounded really stupid when I said it out loud.

The farrier laughed and clapped when I got to tying Blackbird to the rope. And at the end, she pressed her face against the bars.

"You must come from very far away."

"Very."

I returned to pacing. If only I'd had the courage to go into the bar. Would that have been so bad? Maybe someone would have known of another contract at a nearby school. Maybe I wasn't cut out to be a teacher. I'd not have almost died over and over, and there would have been a chance to find a life. Though it was the little deaths that always found me.

I went to the window. My eyelids closed against the brightness. If the damn thing had been a little larger, the cells wouldn't have been gloomy at all. I followed the motes in the beam down to the floor. A circle of light wobbled this way and that as the airship cut through the sky, resembling a laser. Now, I could have done with one of those. Traveling between worlds should involve lasers. Not that it would have helped. A laser would start a fire, and that was bad on a ship. It'd get attention too.

Blackbird needed attention.

My brow furrowed as I teased out possibilities. I didn't have matches or a lighter. Could I spin the staff quickly enough to make heat? No, scratch that. The staff. A glass sphere. It'd seen it make light, but it could also focus it. That was in the realm of physics.

I tore open the mattress, revealing dried grass like hay but shorter and finer. It had to be flammable. A short while later, I had formed a pile in the light. I added strips of the blanket, hoping it wasn't wool.

"What are you up to?" The farrier asked.

"I'm getting some attention."

Feeling along the floorboards, I found gaps and worked the cracked edges of several until I had a small amount of tinder and several splinters.

"Blackbird, I'm going to move your arm again. I'll be as gentle as I can."

She made no sign of hearing, but groaned as I rotated her arm and brought the sphere above my little pile of combustibles. Honestly, I was happy to hear anything from her.

I raised and lowered the sphere, seeking the smallest point of focus. Was it even enough light to do this? The airship rocked, and the sphere moved. I had to start all over again, my fingers shaking with tension. Did I see a wisp of smoke? I peered closely and blocked the light. Damn. I moved and tried again.

Smoke.

"Is that magic?" the farrier asked. "Are you a wizard?"

"Hah. No, anyone could do this. The glass bends the light so that it's all in one spot. Think about a summer sun, how hot that can be. If the heat from a bigger area is concentrated—"

"You make it very hot."

"Yes. And that leads to fire."

A little flame crackled. I quickly fed it more grass and the little pieces of timber. It smoked prodigiously.

"Oh, very good… what is your name?"

"Martin."

"Martin. An unusual name. You may call me Gwen."

Gwen. A pretty name. I fed the fire, coughing as the smoke thickened.

"Well, Gwen, can you pass through anything that'll burn? If we can make enough smoke, they'll have to come."

"And then what?" she asked, though she was already shredding her own mattress.

"And then they'll have to get us all out. And I'll do what needs to be done to get the surgeon or a needle and thread."

She passed through grass and material. "That is not much of a plan."

"I'm working with what I've got."

"As do we all," she said.

The fire grew. It wouldn't last long at this rate, but the smoke had to be leaking out into the ship. It was time.

"Help," I shouted. "There's a fire. Help."

There was no response, so I kicked at the bars as I shouted, causing as much of a ruckus as I could. Finally, the brig door opened, and a sailor entered the haze.

"What in the Forsaken Child's name be happening?"

Ah, yeah. I didn't want to tell him I'd been setting his airship alight. Probably wouldn't appreciate that. "One of those hot stones came through the window and landed on the mattress and now it's burning. The entire ship will go up if we don't put it out." There were more holes in that story than I cared for him to spot. "Come on, open up, and help us put it out!"

"It be needing water." The sailor turned away.

"No, wait. We don't have time."

But the sailor hurried away. If he put it out while we were still inside, we'd be right back to where we started. The sailor returned carrying two buckets of water.

"Out me way."

I shifted to be further in the way. "That'll never work from out there. The water will splash on the bars. You can't even see where the fire is. There's too much smoke. Open up and pass me the buckets. Get my nana away from the smoke, and I'll risk the fire."

"Are ye mad? Get gone." The sailor moved, hefted one of the buckets and threw the water.

I dived in the way, getting a face full of water, and saving the fire.

"If my nana is going to die, we might as well all burn."

The sailor's eyes grew wider before he shot me a dirty look and drew his cutlass.

"I'm a gonna enter. Be trying that again, and I'll stick you good."

Who ever heard of smart jailors? I moved away as he undid the heavy padlock that secured the cell door, eying me suspiciously all the while. The cell was too small for me to dart past him, and he knew I was up to something. If only I knew what that was. We were playing a game of chess, and I sucked at it.

The sailor picked up the bucket and held it out to me. "Take it, right. Put out yon fire." The cutlass in his other hand pointed toward my stomach.

With no more excuses, I edged toward him. Could I use the bucket as a weapon? He turned so that his back was to the bars dividing the cells. Did he know exactly what I was thinking?

Two hands poked through the bars at the sailor's head height, dropping a strip of her skirt round his neck, then yanking back hard. The sailor dropped the bucket and his cutlass to grab for his throat, but he couldn't find any purchase. Instead, his legs danced as his face turned red.

I grabbed the cutlass and pointed it at the sailor. "You can let him go now."

Gwen leaned back, and though it was hard to see through the smoke, I swear there was disbelief in her strained expression.

"Don't be a charlatan's mark. If this bird chirps to the captain, we'll be testing our wings. And unless you can fly as well as you can make fire, our only hope is no one noticing our escape until we can sneak off the airship."

I raised a hand imploringly. "You can't just kill him. It's not his fault."

"Watch me."

Her logic was sound. There was no going back from this. I hadn't thought beyond the immediate, and the sailor was paying for my mistake.

"What if we tie him up?"

"Do you think they won't notice him missing? They will look. If he escapes, we die. If he talks, we die."

The soldier stopped resisting. Gwen held her garrote for a count of fifty and let go. The body collapsed at my feet. I stared, shaken.

"It is done, Martin. Now, open my cell so that I may sew up this nana with the staff that makes flame."

If only she knew… I took the keys from the sailor's belt, trying not to think of the smell of death and how it clung to me. Blackbird lay nearby, helpless. What if this wasn't Gwen's first murder? Was she even a farrier? Could I trust her not to kill us both? I wasn't the best judge of character. My normal principle was to assume the worst. Here, there were too many worsts to compare. I needed to choose if I was going to trust her, and I needed to do it now.

Every second of delay could be Blackbird's last.

CHAPTER 11

MERCENARY

Trusting a cold-blooded killer? The problem was all about blood, and Blackbird was losing it fast. I stalked over to the fire and kicked the smoldering remnants into a puddle of water spreading from the bucket. That done, I had no more excuses, so I scooped up the keys from the sailor's belt and walked out of the cell.

I'd been in rooms in a police station but never a cell. The feeling of freedom once out of the already open door was powerful, almost tangible. Before, I'd been a trapped animal in a cage. Now—a flash of a dark closet sent a chill through me. Claustrophobia squeezed.

Not now. Not now.

I pushed the thought away and focused on releasing Gwen.

The stiff padlock mechanism opened with a hard twist. The moment I'd lifted it clear, Gwen was at the door, pulling it open, and pushing past me.

She rolled her head and cracked her knuckles. "That's better."

My knuckles were tight around the cutlass, though I let the blade hang. "What now?"

Gwen put a hand to my cheek and gave it a gentle slap. "Now we find needle and thread."

No doubt on a ship there'd be plenty. However, we could hardly wander around asking for some. And this was some old-timey ship's brig; I could hardly expect a medical kit hanging on a wall. How did Blackbird deal with this, traveling between worlds? If I were her, I'd carry medical supplies.

Her backpack lay on the narrow table in front of the cells. She was crazy, but she was a wily old cow. I put the cutlass on the table, and grabbed the backpack, surprised by its weight, and shook out the contents. Even empty, the leather was heavy.

"Help me look. There's got to be something in here."

Gwen joined me, opening bottles and jars, while I unfolded several small leather pouches. I found pencils, chalk, and several keys, among other equally useless items. In desperation, I searched the backpack, wondering if there was anything caught at the bottom. While feeling around, a discrepancy in the depth of the backpack and the base caught my attention. A false bottom? I tried to hook my fingers around the edges of the base, but it was all sewn tight.

Caught up in the puzzle, I turned to the outside and ran hands along the outer edge. My pinky finger scraped on a hard point. A rectangular panel appeared almost identical to the other side, but the stitching didn't actually go across the join. I teased out a small fold of leather, found a circle of metal, and pulled this. A tray slid out.

"Your nana is an interesting lady," Gwen said. She had sorted the jars and bottles into three different groups.

"You don't know the half of it," I said while poking through the tray's contents. A small pouch contained disks of gold and silver. A second held little gems. A decorated flask with a wax seal. I unrolled a long piece of leather, revealing needles, thread, tweezers, a scalpel, tongs, a glass syringe, a little folding saw, and several other items that made me wonder how much of this was for medical use and how much for extracting answers from unfortunates. It was all of a modern make, the sort any surgeon would be happy to use.

Leaving this out, I slipped the rest back into the hiding spot. Gwen could be a thief as well as a killer.

"Will this do?" I asked. It was time to see if she had been bluffing.

"I couldn't have asked for better. Your nana must be a great healer." She gestured to a small assortment of jars and bottles. "I recognize the scent of these. Numbing cream, wound-cleaning elixir. This is good. If she still lives, she stands a chance. Guard the door while I work."

She collected the leather and her selected medicines, and hurried over to Blackbird, leaving me in an awkward position. I couldn't watch the door and what she was up to.

Sighing, I picked up the cutlass and went to the door, pushing it a little further closed. Distant voices blended and muddied before they reached my ears. A thrumming underlay them. It came right up through my boots. It had always been there, I realized, since I'd stood on the deck. In defense of my oversight, I had been a little busy. Did the airship have an engine?

I heard tearing fabric behind me. This was followed by meaty, wet sounds. I studied the slim gap of the open door. The smoke was slowly dissipating, and it hadn't attracted more attention. Keeping it open was sensible. Besides, if I closed it, I'd end up watching Gwen work. Hearing was enough.

"Tell me, Martin, how do you earn coin?"

Surprised, I glanced her way. Blackbird lay on her back, clothes pulled aside. I slipped my gaze to Gwen before I could focus on the details, then back to the doorway.

"Teaching."

She grunted, then asked, "Did you work for a rich merchant or a noble?"

"Neither," I said. "My pay would have been much better. Most of the kids I taught were from poor families."

"If you don't want to say, you don't need to lie." She sounded like she was talking through closed teeth. "We all have our secrets."

A twang announced the snapping of thread. I rested the cutlass on my shoulder. I knew there'd been a time when there were no schools and when learning had been exclusive. And, my union rep had said, there were always those trying to bring that back. How could I explain modern education?

"I'm not lying. I just come from somewhere very far away. We do things differently." I leaned against the wall. "I don't know if I'll ever get back."

"Get back?" This was followed by the sound of a stopper popping free from a bottle. "You are a strange man, Martin. It doesn't matter where we came from. It's all gone. By the Lady's luck, everything we are doing is for naught. We'll all die when we reach the end of the world. We'll either have to jump off the great waterfalls or be roasted on land. All we are doing is buying ourselves a few days to choose the manner of our end."

She laughed, a genuine sound of pleasure. "But is that not life at its most bare? Strive for another day, burning one to grasp the next?"

That sounded like a monkey swinging from branch to branch. It was far too apt. But I had a way out. *If* Blackbird lived. And if we traveled to another place, what of all these people remaining? What of Gwen?

"The lava will have to stop at some point. Volcanoes don't go on forever." Life on Earth had survived whole asteroids. Without a shared context, I decided it was best to keep that to myself.

"That was what people said at first. There were rumors in the early days of destruction of a far-off nation. An angered god, an unfaithful people. The details were as varied as the shape of trees. I cannot say what is true and what is embellishment or outright lie. But it started across the seas. They are said to have turned to steam. I don't believe that. I went to the coast once. There was too much water. They say every nation to the west has gone, and that any airships that scouted have never returned. And still the lava comes."

Blackbird had said something about a god. I wondered if this was what she was talking about. Perhaps there was some high-tech civilization that had broken through the planet's crust, releasing pent-up pressure, and creating this disaster. They'd be gods to people who knew no better. Nature didn't care for us, but it didn't hate us, either. It just *was*. In the end, people were always at fault. I wanted to prove my point.

"What do you know about the unfaithful people?"

Gwen didn't respond immediately. I heard her moving, curse quietly, then the clink of glass. "Know? Nothing. Devil-landers, everyone calls them. The most common tale jumping round like a flea is of lunatics preaching damnation. A king of that land put them to the sword when the priests complained. Everyone protects their business. And soon after, a river of pure heat flowed out of the ground. But there are others: a murdered lover, a debauched priest, an evil from beyond. It matters little."

A susurration of cloth. A dry moan followed. I left the door. Blackbird turned her head and glanced at Gwen, who had a threaded needle and a jar in hand, then at me. The lines on her face were deep. Her mouth worked, then she coughed, a dry bark.

"Well, girl, get on with it or fate will snatch victory. We don't have all day." Blackbird's voice was quiet but surprisingly strong.

Gwen chuckled, and I examined the door.

"How are you feeling?" I asked.

"Like you let me get stabbed."

"You were shot," I said, immediately wishing I could take it back.

"And that's better?"

"You're alive. How about a little gratitude?"

Blackbird snorted and looked away. "Girl, you were talking about what has been. I only caught the last. Tell it all."

Gwen seemed happy enough to recount the rumors once more. Blackbird asked a lot of questions, but Gwen was either unwilling to share more or had no more to share.

"Ripples, girl," Blackbird said at one point. "The servants of a dark god created like a stone thrown into water."

"All done," Gwen declared, as if to stop the questioning. "To heal, remain as still as you can."

Blackbird grumbled. I entered the cell, knowing what she was going to do. Sure enough, she managed to stand with the staff to aid her. Only then did her fingers flex off the wood, her knuckles cracking.

She poked her staff at the ash. "How long was I out?"

"I don't know, an hour."

Gwen, who was cleaning and packing the medical kit, said, "You fell asleep. You've been aboard for almost a quarter of the day, maybe longer."

Blackbird took a step and winced. "I need specifics. Where exactly are we?"

I shrugged. "Near the corner of 42nd and Park Avenue. How should I know? We're on an airship that was heading out of the city. We could be anywhere for all I know."

"Don't dismiss me. The answer matters more than you know." Blackbird eyed the cell. "There will be those with the knowledge. Find out."

"Sure. I'll pop out of the cell and ask the captain. That'll go down well." I strode to the window. "Perhaps I'll see a street sign out here."

Through the window, I saw blue sky, and as I stretched up, the angle revealed purple squares with a dark line curving through—fields of lavender and a river? The shadow of our airship slid along. We were flying much lower than a plane.

A second shadow crept into view, and I pressed my face to see it.

"What are you looking at, boy?"

I ignored her tone. "Another airship is close. They must have left around the same time."

"What else?"

"Purple fields and a river."

The airship lurched, and I stumbled back, almost knocking Blackbird over. Gwen gave me a helpful shove, and I regained my balance.

"What the hell was that?" I asked.

Gwen furrowed her brow. "A sharp turn, though I can't think why."

Blackbird gestured to the window with her staff. "Go check."

I did—because I was curious. The second airship came into view. It was smaller and sleeker, the straight edges of its design utilitarian. A yellow pennant hung over its side, flapping in the wind. I described it all. There were a number of people on board with the puffy yellow of soldiers, but the new airship rose swiftly as it neared, hiding further detail.

"That is an ill change." Gwen said. "The Lady will have her games, and we must have ours. We will need to move, and soon."

The wisps of shouted voices reached me as the new airship came alongside its brethren while maintaining a small gap. I couldn't make out the words, but the tone seemed welcoming enough. Perhaps this was a patrol seeking news. They wouldn't hear anything good.

Ropes were thrown, landing with a thud, and the ships eased together, meeting with a solid *thunk* that reverberated through the hull.

A bellow was followed by a volley of gunfire.

I pulled away from the now-blocked window.

"What the fuck is that?"

There were more booms.

Blackbird took the leather medical kit from Gwen. "Did you take anything else?"

"No. Only that which heals." Gwen pointed to the table. "The rest is there."

"And you?"

"*Everything* is there," I stated, annoyed by the suggestion that I'd steal from her little horde.

She shoved the kit into my free hand. "Good. Then pack it all up. As your new friend says, we need to move."

What was I to do? She'd just had surgery, and she'd lost blood, meaning she deserved a little slack. I collected all the containers and placed everything where it belonged as best as I recalled. There were no more gunshots, but a general hubbub filtered down to us, one of panic and anger.

After handing the backpack to Blackbird, who wouldn't let me carry it for her, I asked Gwen, "Are they pirates?"

"In the governor's colors? I doubt it. Whoever they may be, they have done us a favor."

I cocked my head. "Favor? It sounds like they started a war up there."

"War is chaos, and chaos gives us an opportunity to escape."

"Correct, girl." Blackbird said while struggling toward the brig's door. "Boy, I told you to get us aboard, not into battle—or a prison. Must I do everything?"

"Next time, carry yourself."

Gwen opened the brig door, then closed it. "The stairs are clear."

A blood-curdling cry of anguish echoed from above.

"Wait," I said, my hand slick on the cutlass's grip. "The way to where? We need to find a spot to hide."

Gwen smirked, first looking at me, then at Blackbird. "Where did you find him?"

"He followed me," Blackbird said.

"A lost puppy," Gwen said. "The best place to hide is among the chaos. Once the fight is over and we are discovered missing, they will search every hold, every crate. We must go."

I walked in front of the door, hating myself for the logical next step.

"Then I'll do a recon first. I'm armed, and I'm uninjured."

"Armed," Gwen said. "You'd use that to shave before you'd kill."

I heard a scuff and held up a hand. "Shh."

She straightened. "Don't shush me."

"No," I hissed. "I can hear someone."

The door slammed open, knocking me back against the bamboo bars. A soldier entered the tight space. His breastplate rose high on his shoulders, perhaps a little too big. He wore the yellow shirt beneath, but a red sash tied around his right arm pulled the puffy sleeve tight. A thin, bent nose centered a face marred by scars. He froze for a second, clearly as surprised as us.

The soldier started toward me at the same time, his cutlass rising to parry an attack I never made. Yay me, the obvious threat. Gwen grabbed the cutlass from my hand and hammered the stubby pommel down on his head. I ducked as the soldier struck out, his cutlass lodging in a bamboo bar. As he staggered from her blow, she drove the blade up into his underarm. Blood fountained, coating my face. The soldier put a hand on the wound, collapsing right after. His body twitched as he bled out, then stilled.

"This is yours." Gwen shoved the cutlass back in my hand and wiggled the soldier's free of the bamboo.

"You know how to use a sword, too?" I said, lamely.

"I know how to poke someone."

"Focus, the pair of you." Blackbird nudged the red sash. "See this. We have one of the attackers. This is for identifying themselves to each other. The attack is an ambush."

I tried wiping the blood from my cutlass onto the bamboo. "Is that good or bad?"

"It depends on what they're after."

Gwen stepped over the body. "He's a mercenary from Straia. Look at the thin nose, small mouth. He's short, too. It would take a lot of money to get them all the way from the Blue Mountains. And that could be trebled or more given the impending tide of fire."

She slipped out the door. I offered Blackbird a hand over the body. To my surprise, she accepted it. I went out last, and up the stairs last as well. Blackbird climbed jerkily, but short of getting her over my shoulder again, I couldn't see a way to help.

Three bodies lay at the top of the stairs, the floor slick with their blood. The poor bastards. They could easily have been us. The uproar from the deck soared to a crescendo as Gwen opened the door. She'd talked about chaos, and she was right.

Soldier fought mercenary, the arm sashes hard to spot in the midst of battle. There was no room for halberds, and I guessed the rifles and pistols had all been used and discarded. The steel of cutlasses flashed as blade struck blade, ringing unlike any bell. More bodies coated the deck. Civilians cowered or defended themselves with swords or makeshift weapons. A red-sashed mercenary beheaded an old man. Another chopped through a wooden bowl and the hand of the woman holding it. It was wholesale slaughter, and the scale of the savagery shocked me for its impersonal terror.

"They're killing everyone."

"Then good luck and farewell. Let us all see if we gain a few more grains of sand if it is not to be another day."

I scanned the deck, looking for a way out, a way off. The small airship remained tied to the larger, a parasite draining its host. It appeared empty. The crew must have come across for the fight. "Gwen, wait. The attackers' airship. It's our ticket out of here."

Blackbird sniffed. "A viable proposition. I think we are close to the way as it is. We must land."

"Close to what?" Gwen said, her eyes on the carnage.

I leaned close to Blackbird. "We have to take her with us. She knows how to handle herself, and she patched you up. She'd be useful, and she has nowhere else to go."

Blackbird screwed her face up. "Very well. This one time. But I am not a collector of wayward children."

A spark of something too small to be hope warmed me.

"Gwen, we have a way off this world—Blackbird does—I can't tell you where it leads, but it won't be here. No lava, no waterfall to infinity or whatever. It's another choice. Help us, and we'll take you."

She snorted. "Another world?"

"Different people, different place," I said, not knowing more than that.

Blackbird harrumphed, as if she didn't approve of my amateur explanation.

Gwen pointed her cutlass at me. "You sound mad, but who doesn't on this day? You have a deal. Get yourselves toward the cutter, and I'll foment a distraction." She flourished her blade, and then darted off to the left, behind two dueling soldiers.

That mattered to me. Not because it increased our chances

of survival. It meant we'd be saving a life. It was a drop in the ocean, but it was something. An uncharitable thought crossed my mind. We could be Gwen's distraction so she could take the airship for herself. Two lives for her own. She'd already made that bargain.

I firmed my grip on my cutlass and willed some energy into my exhausted body. Nefarious plan or not, our course was clear. We were going to walk into a raging battle and hijack an airship.

All I needed was a damn eyepatch.

CHAPTER 12

CAN YOU FLY?

Metal on metal, raw screams, bodies akimbo on a blood-slicked deck. A wooden doll looked up, painted face dotted red. The tang of blood merged with the stink of shit and piss and the lingering sharpness of gunpowder.

We'd headed upward since the attack began. The chill of the air stole my body heat, and each breath wasn't enough to fill my need for oxygen. Ahead, low clouds loomed, wisps already reaching like an airborne kraken. I assisted Blackbird across to the gunwales, looping around one fight and pausing as another passed.

A red-sashed mercenary kicked a passenger off the rear castle, then leaped down to finish him. On the far side, three passengers grabbed another red-sash, and tossed the bastard over the edge. A shot went off, and one of the three collapsed.

"We don't have far to go," I said, leading her alongside the gunwale.

"I'm not blind."

A group of six passengers blocked our way. I paused, considering how best to get past. Could I recruit them? One darted by me, and the rest ran as if on cue. A woman in gold brocade fell, and the others trampled her in their desperation. The last one leaped onto a soldier. The clouds enveloped us at that point, and I lost sight of the struggle, of the anarchy.

Sounds grew muffled, and my view shrank to a bubble of white. We appeared to be in our own little pocket universe. I wasn't fooled. Death lurked all around, and we were far from safe.

We shuffled forward. More passengers swept past. A mercenary materialized, cutlass swinging. I caught his swing and threatened his wrist with a flick. He stepped back, and a soldier advanced, engaging the mercenary, who blocked my way. When the mercenary slashed down at the soldier's head, my instincts kicked in and I brought up my cutlass to stop the blow.

The soldier lunged, and the mercenary had to spin out of the way, cursing as he went. The soldier kept pressure on the mercenary, and I added a few half-hearted stabs and cuts. I had a chance to run him through, but I couldn't do it. Not by choice.

However, my last swing at his leg gave the soldier an opening. He shoulder-slammed the mercenary, sending him over the edge. The mercenary grabbed the soldier's arm, dragging him halfway over the gunwale. I leaped for the soldier's legs and caught him. The weight almost sent me over, too. The soldier twisted, there was an angry cry, and the weight lessened enough for me to pull the soldier back onto the ship.

"My endless thanks," he said, then he looked at me closely. "You're one of the stowaways!"

"We are not enemies. Think of us as neighbors coming by to borrow a cup of sugar."

He gave me a look. Perhaps they didn't have sugar here. Before the guilt of the dead sailor in the cell showed on my face, I added, "We're not with those mercenaries. How about a short truce?"

"Until we crush the enemy," the soldier said.

We looked at each other with mutual recognition. We were just two people trying to survive.

I held out my hand. "Agreed."

He looked at it, bringing his own hand a little forward. I took it and shook. He didn't know what we'd done. He didn't know that we were going to leave him to die. It felt cruel. I was a liar by omission. But Blackbird was hurt, and she needed my help. Was she my responsibility? No, but she had the pull of my nana, and as self-serving as it was, she was my ticket out.

Two more mercenaries stepped out of the clouds.

"Which one?" The first said, a barrel-chested brute.

"All of them," the second boasted, a slim man on light feet, and then charged forward.

We became entangled in a series of strikes, our blades whirring, sweat and condensation flinging from our limbs. I ended up with the first. He swung hard, but I focused on catching his blade near my cup, where the mechanics of the contact gave me an advantage. His slow footwork allowed me to retreat, but I couldn't leave Blackbird.

The airship dipped, a pocket of low pressure, perhaps, and we all stumbled. The two mercenaries and the soldier ended up several paces away from the gunwale, turning the fight into a two on one. I took a step to help, but Blackbird grabbed my jacket.

"It is not our fight. Get me to the other airship or all is lost." I hesitated, and she pulled me close. "Do you really think you can fight them? And then what? If every last mercenary lies dead, the defenders will turn on us."

Her lack of faith in my fighting stung, no matter how accurate it was. But it was the finality of that path that I accepted. To live, we had to leave. I moved on past the soldier, thankful that he couldn't spare a glance to cut me down with pure contempt.

We reached the spot where the airships pressed against each other. Ropes bound the two tightly. They'd be a problem later. I helped Blackbird over, a task made more difficult by her insistence on holding the staff at all times.

She'd just gotten her feet on the other deck when a flash and a bang announced another shot. The wood near my hands splintered. A mercenary appeared from behind a small platform at the front. He must have been there to guard against exactly what we were doing. He leaped up onto the gunwale and ran toward me, a short straight sword in his hand. Perhaps this was the mercenaries' usual weapon when they weren't impersonating others.

When he closed, I swung at his legs. He easily jumped the attack, as I knew he would. I tried again, working him away from where the ships joined. His footing would be more at risk with only the surface of one to stand on, and that might get him down to the deck where I didn't have to worry so much for the safety of my scalp. It was a plan, but I felt he was playing with me, letting me easily drive him to the narrow prow to build my confidence. He jumped clear again, and this time brought his sword down in a two-handed swing. There it was. I'd been right. I caught the blow, buttressing my blade with my left hand against the blunt edge.

Seizing on my inexperience, he kicked out, and caught me solidly on my chin. My head rocked back, and he went for me again.

A massive explosion filled my vision with sparkling white. Everything went silent as a wall of force tossed me against the gunwale, and my cutlass went over the far side of the cutter, flipping end over end. My entire right side ached. I looked up, waiting for the killing blow.

Just in time to see a long piece of bent and blackened piping punch through the mercenary's chest. Sound returned. Screaming, wailing, hissing, and the whoomph of combustion. I staggered to my feet as he fell.

The ringing in my ears confused me, and I turned away from the small airship, seeking my bearings. The captain stumbled out of the thick mix of cloud and smoke, her gaudy clothes tattered and stained. She walked right toward me, dropping a flintlock pistol, but keeping her fancy cutlass in hand. Each boot stomp was the drum of an advancing army.

Oh, shit, I thought. She was going to kill me. She must have decided all this was my fault and she was going to make me pay for the ruin of her ship and the deaths of her crew. Blood dripped from her arms and her left side. Maybe her revenge was more personal.

A mercenary darted at her from behind. She spun, grabbed the man's arm, and ran her blade through his unprotected thigh in one fluid motion. He stood staring for a moment, the wound gushing, and she head-butted him. When he dropped, she flicked her blade, shedding his blood, and advanced on me.

I raised a hand, feeling the loss of my cutlass, while being sure it would have done me no good. "I'm not your enemy. I'm not one of them. I don't even know them. I'm just trying to get away."

The captain made a pained expression and put her free hand to the wound by her stomach. "You don't know them, but they sought your hag?" She coughed and blood flecked her lips.

"I swear it on anything you believe in. I never wanted this. I was just trying to save an old lady. Anyone would have done the same."

"You would protect those you owe nothing to?"

"I tried."

She grabbed my shoulder, her eyes unfocused. "This is my ship. All aboard her are my responsibility, even stowaways."

She wobbled, and I went to steady her, but she took a step back and raised her cutlass.

"My father gifted this to me on my birth flight. It has bled raiders, Venitarian soldiers, and helped bring down a roc. It has never known defeat, not in my darkest days. And yet, we are at the end of all there is."

I expected Blackbird to tell me to hurry, but perhaps she feared the captain was about to skewer me and chalk up one last kill. To me, the captain appeared after something different: comfort, hope, meaning, a yearning as strong as that of the wraiths.

"If we escape, they won't be able to catch us. If we live, you've defeated the mercenaries. And, I don't know if it's true, but that… hag would say you will have saved many more lives. I believe you can be the victor of your final battle."

The captain laughed, a wet, sickly action, and put a hand on my shoulder. "Make it taste the blood of your enemies. And always remember your duty. Without it, we are nothing."

She pressed the sword into my grip, then slid down to the deck, her blood on my hands in a very real sense. Her head slumped, and her eyes closed.

Blackbird jabbed my back with her staff. "If you've finished flirting, get over here and cut the ropes."

I clambered over to the cutter. So much death. I'd seen it on the news, but up close, it was different, personal.

The airships bucked, then rolled to the left, the larger dragging the cutter down. I grabbed one of the ropes holding them together and sawed.

It parted slowly, then snapped under tension. I moved to the next. "What about Gwen?"

Blackbird sniffed from behind me. "She makes it or she doesn't. If you don't cut us free—"

"I know," I said, surprised by the anger in my voice. "We die. Everyone seems to be dying."

We drifted beneath the clouds, and much of the larger airship came into view. There were pockets of fighting, but each side had culled the other harshly. The center of the deck had a great hole, and flames roared out of this. The surface of the balloon had darkened and bubbled. That couldn't be good. There were runes on the fabric, too, subtle like a woven pattern in a single color. Interesting, but I had more pressing concerns. I worked on a third rope, and then a fourth.

The last one mocked my sense of right and wrong, but I sliced with the captain's cutlass, certain that delay would kill us all. It was as taut as piano wire. I raised the blade high and brought it down to cut the last twists holding the airships together.

Out of the corner of my eye, I saw Gwen. She'd climbed out of the hole and was sprinting across the deck. Momentum carried the blade down. The edge dug into the hemp, severing fibers one by one, until the force on those remaining was too great, and the rope snapped, the ends cracking like a whip.

The airships pulled apart.

"Hurry!" I shouted.

She ran on, the larger airship sinking lower and lower. At the gunwale, she leaped into clear air, arms outstretched.

My stomach soured imagining the feeling of having no tether. She flew across the gap but was too low. I dropped the cutlass, grabbed hold of the ship, and leaned down.

Closer.

Closer.

I strained.

Gwen grabbed my arm, holding it vice-tight, almost wrenching it out of its socket. Grimacing, I pulled myself back over the gunwale, and she climbed in, grinning maniacally.

"You weren't leaving without me, were you?"

I sat on the deck, rubbing my shoulder, speechless.

She laughed and patted me on the head. "Oh, don't be so downhearted. We were all taking risks. And I lingered too long before setting off the distraction. Blowing a boiler is much harder than I expected."

"Airships have boilers?"

The look she gave me made me feel like I'd just failed a spelling test for the word cat.

I reached over and retrieved the captain's cutlass to hide my embarrassment. The weapon was mine now.

"That is a nice sliver of metal you have there. May I?"

Standing up, I passed it to her reluctantly and wandered to the side of the airship. The larger one hadn't strayed as far as I'd expected. As I watched, the fighting ceased, and a cheer rang out. I believed the captain's people had won at great cost. I hoped they had, for her sake.

The remaining soldiers converged on the side nearest to us. If they were hoping for a ride, they were going to end up disappointed. I squinted. They were doing something. What was it? Steel glinted.

Wait, I thought. I know. I know.

"They're going to shoot."

"Then get down, boy!"

I dropped as several shots went off. Balls slammed into the wood, and I flinched with every one.

"Girl, do you know how to fly the airship?" Blackbird said from her crouch.

If I hadn't seen her when healthy, I would have thought the old woman was fine, despite her shaking hands. The slumped shoulders were the giveaway.

"I can fly well enough," Gwen said, sliding my new cutlass to me along the deck, then dancing toward the rear of the airship.

"Land us as fast as you can."

"But the sea of fire—it will spread here, too."

"We won't be here to see it."

The farrier examined both of us. "And I'm to wager my life on the word of either of you?"

"What have you got to lose?" I shouted over more rifle shots.

Gwen worked a panel of levers near a large wooden wheel, pulling and pushing them until the airship drifted downward and away from its bigger cousin. Another volley of shots followed. I considered counting how long between reloads, but what did it matter? They were either going to fire off some lucky shots or we were going to land. It was out of my hands. And for now, that was a relief.

The wind shoved us this way and that as we descended, angry at our abandonment of the sky. Each time we dropped sharply, I expected it to continue, for us to be pulverized against the ground.

And who was to say we'd be okay if we did land in one piece? The captain had said the mercenaries were after Blackbird. Could more await us below? I dared a look over the side. I couldn't see the other airship. Below, endless purple fields stretched. Ahead, a storm brewed—heavy clouds flashing with lightning, the sky itself short-circuiting.

"Seriously?" I raised my hands and let them fall helplessly. Was the entirety of nature against us? I didn't need to guess. I knew. I damn well knew.

"Passengers," I shouted, "please fasten your seatbelts. In case of emergency, you're screwed."

CHAPTER 13

EMBERS

Blackbird refused to lie down and rest, so I rigged up a seat using crates and a rough blanket that stank of eucalyptus. She'd sat down grudgingly only once I'd shifted it to the front of the airship. I stood close by, holding onto the rigging that connected the balloon. The ride was rough. Hot winds battered us, then cold, then back to hot, leading to sudden rises and dips. Gwen, picking up on our inexperience, warned this could get worse near the ground as it was flat and treeless.

Blackbird really should have gone below deck. She was looking off to one side and wore an almost constipated expression. Did I dare say anything?

She craned her neck to stare at me as if she were a mind reader. I walked to the bow, holding rope and wood for support as needed. Of course, she couldn't read minds—no one could—but I felt better without eye contact.

We were perhaps a hundred yards above the fields. Pale white stalks bent with the wind, shaking large purple heads that resembled wheat, giving the impression of a night sea. It must be near harvesttime—a time that would never come.

A shadow passed over us. The original airship screamed by, on fire and trailing smoke. With no other way to escape the oncoming lava, they had tried to keep the vessel aloft. Now they were burning *and* were going to land hard.

On impact, the structure crumpled, pulled along by the balloon, which exploded in an angry red fireball that sent debris high into the air. Actually, it wasn't just fire. The balloon must have been filled with red gas. It spread further than the flames, like a gargantuan jellyfish, then hung there being nibbled at the edges by the wind.

The blast slapped our airship sideways. Wood strained and groaned. I made a very manly noise and held onto the bow tightly as we almost capsized. Our own downward trajectory gave a sense of impending doom. We rocked back, no more than fifty yards above ground.

The crashed airship still continued to burn, and there were pockets of fire from debris. If this purple wheat proved dry, we might have swapped one form of fire for another.

"Could anyone survive that?" I wondered.

"Hopefully not," Blackbird said quickly. "The way is close."

Several sharp *slaps* and *tinks* drew my attention. A burning piece of timber dropped an inch from my nose. All the bits thrown up from the explosion were raining back down. I swore. We needed to take cover.

"Hold on tight!" Gwen shouted from the rear of the airship.

The airship groaned again as heavy wood and metal pipes pounded the vessel, a giant shotgun blast. We were damn lucky the balloon acted as an umbrella, saving us from the worst.

An ugly pop sounded above. Red gas spewed from the side of the balloon. There were more leaks, at least four. I checked on Blackbird. She'd fallen to one side, but was still on the crates. Damn it. She was too injured for this. I ran on the heaving deck, stumbling left and right, on the verge of falling again and again, until I gripped the crate she lay on and wrapped a protective arm around her.

"I don't need your help," she complained.

"And yet, you've got it."

Just like my nana—rejecting help when anyone could see she needed it. I'd always been sure it was a way to avoid saying thank you.

A ragged sheet of metal spun toward us. I covered Blackbird, but its path was higher—right through the balloon. My stomach lurched, and I felt like I was floating.

"Hold on!" Gwen shouted. "Impact!"

My legs tried to break through my pelvis. A horrendous grinding, crunching, snapping cacophony announced our landing. The airship didn't stop, though. We shot forward, shedding wood as we went. The balloon lost its shape, but it still strained at its rigging, having become a sail. With the ground acting like a giant grater, we were going to be shredded.

Gwen leaped and ran, dodging both sliding and flying debris to join us. "We have to dump the balloon. Cut the main ropes."

I glanced at Blackbird.

She glared in return, one hand holding onto the crate beneath her, and the other holding her staff, which she'd wedged into a small hole in the deck. "I don't need a nursemaid."

The ship bucked, and I slid toward the airship's starboard side. Grabbing a rope, I drew the new cutlass carefully out of my belt, wary of wickedly sharp blade, and sawed. Fibers gave, and the rope strained. With a crack, it split in two. An end flicked up, punching my cut cheek.

I staggered, my eyes watering from the pain. The airship rolled onto its side, and I crashed into the gunwale, my face over the edge, slapped by endless stalks. I arched my back and twisted clear.

"Keep going!"

That could have been Blackbird or Gwen. Details were hard to make out thanks to the terrible cacophony. My body juddered endlessly, the wind dried my eyes, and up wasn't in the right place. But I saw another rope holding stubbornly to the balloon and knew what had to be done.

I climbed the tangled rigging, struggling to keep hold of both rope and cutlass in the same hand. My palms burned with the friction as I closed. I never wanted to see another piece of rope after this world. Stretching out as far as I could, I worked at the damn thing, cutting back and forth.

The final strands of rope snapped. The airship's bow dug into the ground, and I went flying. I saw Blackbird, staff tip still wedged in the deck, standing as if physics wouldn't dare lay a hand on her. A cloud of dirt and wheat sprayed from the bow, and I shut my eyes and mouth against the sharp flecks that left no part of my unprotected flesh untouched.

A hard surface hammered my shoulder. I spun, and more blows pounded my body. The sound of a thousand bones snapping. I was rolling over and over.

Silence.

A soft bed wrapped around me, comforting. A hospital?

I opened my eyes. Purple wheat surrounded me, held me. The wreckage of the airship lay nearby. Rising on unsteady legs, I noticed the absence of my cutlass and cursed. A lot. The airship had dug a channel through the field, but the wheat didn't have to be in a stack for me to have permanently lost my needle. Perhaps I wasn't meant to have a sword. *Meant.* That was childish. There was no such thing. But it had been a pretty weapon, and I was feeling naked without it. Getting attacked over and over will do that.

A small farmhouse in the distance looked promising. With Blackbird's coins, we could trade for food or at least water. First things first. Get everyone together. Blackbird would be okay.

Being shot hadn't stopped her. Nothing would. That better be true. My fluttering heart refused the certainty, and I hiked to the airship at a fast pace despite the weariness weighing me down.

It had snapped in half, and a variety of sharp smells cautioned me—the burning of chlorine, the sweetness of WD-40, the brain-eating fumes of varnish.

Gwen leaped down, swinging from a rope that proved to be the perfect length, and landed in front of me.

"I believe you are missing this," she said, holding my cutlass out.

"Thanks," I said, reaching for it.

She pulled it back, and I glared, but she handed it over on my second attempt.

"That was the worst parking I've ever seen," I said. "Your license should be cut up and burned."

She gave me a quizzical look. "My proof of skill? I need none. You're alive." Then her mouth twisted, and she put a hand on my shoulder. "Did I scare you? Do you need a hug?"

I brushed her off. "Yeah and no. You scared the crap out of me."

Crashing, being dragged along, thrown through the air—all of it was truly terrifying. And yet, I realized with shock, it had been exhilarating. I couldn't contain a smile, though I didn't want to give Gwen any satisfaction. Fear and excitement, all mixed together, a first for me.

I looked over her shoulder. "Have you seen Blackbird?"

"I'm fine," came the old woman's crabby reply.

She sat on the side of the gunwale of the overturned airship, her legs dangling, her shoulders slumped. I pushed through the wheat and offered her help down. She offered the slightest nod of acknowledgement, remaining silent as I lowered her.

"Do you need me to carry you?" I offered. The muscles in my body tightened—angry with my betrayal.

"Certainly not."

I shook my head. "Seriously. You're old, and you've been shot. There's no reason to be stubborn."

Blackbird poked me with her staff. "You see only that which is on the surface. I have lived near two thousand of your years. My body well knows how to heal itself. I will manage."

And off she walked at a good pace, ignoring the farmhouse. Gwen and I followed. I would have protested, but my mind was busy. Two thousand years. Surely, Blackbird had been exaggerating? No one could live that long. Cancer, disease, wear on the body, or sheer bad luck—one had to win in the end. Some things had to be impossible.

What if she had told the truth? What would it mean to live that long? It would explain her mood. Who she was? What she was doing? Who was after her? How did her tech work? Why was she stopping me from getting home? How could I change her mind? Was it even possible to do so?

Her route took us toward the wreckage of the large airship. To give Gwen some credit, this one was in much worse condition. It burned, a pyre marking the end of the vicious mercenaries, and perhaps a tribute to their victims. Gusts of wind whipped the mammoth flames, and smaller fires merged into larger threats. The air filled with ash that caught on our sleeves and coated our hair like dirty snow.

Judging by the sun's position as it peered through ever-thicker, ugly red clouds, we were heading west, and night would fall in a couple of hours. Red clouds when it was too early to be dusk. My mouth dried. The lava. Was it a trick of the planet's curvature or was the flow accelerating? It couldn't have caught up to us otherwise. We'd been making good speed for hours.

The storm clouds marched ever closer. A bolt of lightning smashed into the distant ground. What would it be like up close?

All I knew was that you didn't want to be outside when lightning played. Around us, there was nothing *but* outside.

"I'd rather swing wide around the airship," Blackbird said, breaking into my gloomy thoughts. "But I can't risk the extra time."

As we closed, we came across torn sacks and crates spilling clothes and other possessions into the field. Two small paintings on framed wood captured the same family at different ages, the eyes staring up into the sky, unblinking.

The first charred body made me flinch. Blackbird walked right on past, and I only caught sight of it by chance. The metal breastplate resembled a colander thanks to countless punctures. The poor bastard might have died well before the crash.

More bodies followed, limbs twisted with bends that didn't belong. Caved-in skulls, crushed ribcages. Faces burned to ash on bone or eyes wide with eternal terror. It was different from the battle. There hadn't been time to take it all in back then. Now, the details seeped into my awareness and found niches in my memory to lie in wait.

They weren't all dead. Among the hiss and crackle of fire were the moans and pitiful cries of the injured.

"We could help some," I said, my gaze low. I didn't want to see more. The suffering sickened me. "There must be a few that might live."

Blackbird gestured toward the west with her staff, never looking back at me. "None of them will. You need to engrave that on your thick skull. This world is doomed. This is more than a ripple. There are machinations—yes, I am sure of it. Betrayal or opportunism, I know not which. But that matters little to you or to these. They will die."

I hurried to her, careful not to block her, even as frustration sizzled in my veins. "We can bring a few with us. I'm not saying everyone. But we could give them a chance."

"No." Blackbird cut the air with her hand. "I cannot afford more weakness."

Weakness? Was I a weakness? Was Gwen? I bit back the questions. I shouldn't care what she thought. She might look like my nana, but she wasn't. And I'd outgrown caring what my actual nana thought long ago. I'd wised up to bullies and hard-asses. Or so I had thought.

To my right, a passenger lay. Hints of colorful clothes resisted a crust of soot and dirt and blood. His eyes were open, his breath ragged. His neck was tight, and one arm trembled, the other bearing the sash of the mercenaries. Suffering. I clenched my teeth. Blackbird must have something for the pain among those jars of hers. If only she'd stop. Helpless and useless, I continued past. Did I have any more right to survive?

A meaty squelch came from behind. Gwen pulled her cutlass from the man's chest. His body quivered, then stilled. I stared, horrified. Had she finished him off for the fun of it, or, more charitably, had she put him out of his misery—something I'd not even considered? She pointed to the pistol in his hand with her cutlass. I had completely missed it. She couldn't be implying he was trying to shoot us, could she?

Damn. What was wrong with people?

Heat from the burning airship baked my left side. I slapped an ember that settled on my arm. Blackbird was slowing. She needed help. Screw her. She deserved the same consideration she gave to others.

As the smoke thickened, she abruptly veered away. In the distance, a pile of stones stood above the purple wheat. Each striated uncut chunk was more or less flat, and often several nestled alongside one another to complete a layer. The cairn narrowed as it rose, finishing a little above my head height. Finding the tiny monument in the sea of wheat was inconceivable. Unless, I decided, it was a beacon giving off a signal. Perhaps disguised from the locals.

The wind strengthened as we approached, and I leaned into it, my hair as wild as the flames. If the last world had been post-apocalyptic, this one was in full swing. A stone flipped off the top of the cairn, then another. A spear of lightning shook the earth, burning afterimages into my vision. The pounding thunder couldn't have been more than a second behind. My hair floated, crackling, and I tasted ozone.

Blackbird planted her staff in front of the cairn and closed her eyes, unmoved by the forces closing on us.

Gwen folded her arms, then, as long seconds passed, walked over to me. "Who does she pray to?"

"Pray to?" I stared at the self-proclaimed farrier. "She talks of gods, but I doubt she prays to anything. I suspect she's more of a hostage taker."

Gwen picked up one of the fallen stones and examined it. There were faint markings that could have been deliberate or the result of stone-on-stone scratches.

"Then what does she do? You promised me a way out."

How could I explain it to someone who had never seen a science fiction movie?

"Think of it as a magic doorway. She kind of slices an opening. I guess it creates a wormhole."

"A hole for worms?"

"A tunnel."

"You must have big worms where you come from."

"Forget about the worms. She can create a tunnel between worlds."

"Why isn't she?"

More stones tumbled off the cairn. My skin felt stiff, dried by the hot gale. If Blackbird took much longer, we'd get airborne for a second time.

"Give her time. She's hurt."

We waited, but Blackbird remained unmoving, and there wasn't a spark to be seen. If she'd broken her tech in the crash, we were all royally screwed.

"I'll check," I shouted at Gwen when my patience ran out and hurried to Blackbird.

"What's the problem?"

She spun and grabbed my shirt, pulling me close. "I don't have enough energy, boy. I've used too much."

"So we're screwed?" I said as she released me. "I don't see any power sockets around here."

"It doesn't work like that. It's my energy."

Gwen stalked closer and tossed the stone in her hand. It shot up and away. "Martin, you are a bedpan full of shit. I could have flown us far from here. You don't have a way off this world, do you? You were lying to get my help."

"Lying?" I growled. "I doubt you've spoken one word of truth since we met. And don't forget, you would still be in that cell if it wasn't for me."

"Then I'd still be on my way to safety. They were after your hag, not me."

"What happened to getting tortured to death at the destination?"

Blackbird whacked my chest with her staff, then hit Gwen in the stomach. "Shut up, the pair of you. I need to think."

We waited to a soundtrack of moans that came and went with the howling wind, the pops of burning wood, the hisses and crackles of grassfires.

I came to notice Blackbird staring at me.

"What?"

"There is no other option. I need your help."

"I'm so happy to be your last choice. What do you expect me to do? I don't know a thing about electronics."

"Stop talking and start listening. How do I put this in terms you might understand? See my staff."

"Yeah, I do."

"And the runes."

"I'm not blind."

"And yet you don't see. These channel energy. In the right order and in the right amounts, it creates a resonance with the stuff of reality. That is how you understand the language of this place."

"And the balloons?" I said.

She jutted out her chin. "Exactly. I need to cut a thin line in reality so that we may pass through."

I scowled. "That sounds more like magic. Is this some quantum thing?"

"If you say so. It would take decades of study and practice for you to comprehend even the basics. If you're capable of that. But you may have what it takes to lend me your energy."

That sounded dangerous. I half expected Blackbird to open her mouth, reveal two pointy fangs, and take a bite out of my neck. Had she been waiting for this moment—not for fangs, but to use me as a human battery? If I did what she wanted, would she use me up and leave me behind?

Even in my head, it all sounded ridiculous, like magic as I'd said before. Humans would be the least efficient battery since potatoes. Which meant we were out of options. I didn't believe her, but I wanted to. I wanted out of this world.

Gwen watched me like a cop watching a kid outside a liquor store. She hadn't blinked at Blackbird's explanation. Then again, she didn't appear fazed by much. This was ridiculous. And yet, what would refusing do? I had no choice.

"Do it," I told Blackbird.

"It is you who will have to. That is the point." Blackbird grabbed my right wrist as a burning ember floated past. "Stand still with your legs relaxed and close your eyes. Good. Energy flows from life. It is in the grass beneath your feet, in the soil, in your legs, your balls, your heart. Silence your mind and listen for it. Listen to the hum. Feel the tingle. Focus on it. Block out all else. Can you sense it?"

I squeezed my eyes shut, trying to feel what she was describing. It sounded like new age crystal bullshit. Questions appeared unbidden. What was happening to my apartment? Had I remembered to cancel that overpriced streaming subscription? How long before the milk in the fridge went feral?

Focus, asshole.

I'd always had this. My mind never stopped. I pushed the questions away. Perhaps my arms tingled. That might be from the tension, or the air pressure changing from various impending dooms.

"Can you, boy? Focus."

"I think so, maybe. This is stupid." I opened my eyes.

"Shut them. Try again. Now."

I closed my eyes, my body tense for the swing of a cane that never came.

"Focus. Feel the energy. You have the capacity. Put in the effort."

Might as well light some incense, dance, and chant. I kept the thought to myself. Eyes closed, I was vulnerable. I hated that. And there was light breaking through the thin skin of my lids. Just how close had the fire come?

"Good. Hold your hands out."

I did so, waiting for my knuckles to be struck. I was small. I was weak. I was a bad boy. It was all my fault.

Wood pressed against my palms. Blackbird has given me the staff. No, wait, she held it, too.

"That's it. Now, let the energy flow into the staff. I'll direct it. You're the dog turning the spit."

I didn't know what she was smoking. There was no energy. I was exhausted. If she wanted me to align my chakras or chi or dowse, she was going to be disappointed.

"Come on, boy. You've slowed me down and bled my energy. Can you do this, or should I have left you behind with the wolves? Try."

"I am trying," I shouted.

"Then try harder, or we'll all be dead, and it will be your fault."

My skin burned with anger and shame. I tried to sense the bullshit she'd been raving about. All I could feel was heat and light and the force of the wind mocking my waning strength. My pupils tightened. I wanted to close my eyes twice over. It was too intense, a flashlight shone directly into my eyes from an inch away. Afterimages flashed of things I'd never seen. A mishmash of creatures, of strange plants. Away!

The staff moved in my hands, up then down.

"It's not enough. You're hopeless. We're stuck."

Blackbird yanked the staff from my hands. I looked around, shocked.

"We won't be stuck for long," Gwen said, my neck tingling with the discomfort of someone behind me. "It won't be lava that burns us."

She was right. The fires weren't as bright as I expected, but they were all around. The air scoured the inside of my lungs, and each breath wasn't enough. If only I'd stayed home and fallen asleep. Damn it, I missed sleep, proper sleep. Or if I'd had the courage to enter the pub. Stupid coward. I was the worst.

Blackbird sat on the grass, legs crossed, the staff in her lap. She looked as exhausted as I felt. The captain had called her a hag. Harsh, but at this point, accurate. Her gray hair had tangled thanks to the storm. The deep lines on her face spoke of endless hard years. Maybe she wasn't two thousand years old, but she'd lived a long life. And it was going to end because of me. It no longer mattered that I didn't believe her. She did. And she had the right of it.

I might as well get it over and done with. I walked toward the approaching line of fire.

There was a brighter, taller patch where the blazing fingers transitioned from orange to gold. A soft voice brushed against my ears, whispering urgently. I need you. Help me. Please! It drove a dagger into my heart, taking me back to when I was young, crying in bed after another beating. My parents arguing in the living room as they sorted through booty from their latest burglary. I'd lay there whispering, pleading for help from some-one, anyone—too afraid to shout because I knew what would happen.

The bright patch faded. I called out, but there was no answer. The smoke must have been playing with my head, a harpy luring me in. I looked at the treacherous flames. No, I wasn't going to give up. That was my one strength. I kept going.

I'd been in hostile classes, fresh out of college, instructed to run poorly planned lessons I'd never seen before. How had I gotten through? I kept at it, using the old adage: fake it until you make it. I had nothing to lose. I'd fake it well.

"Blackbird, I want to try again."

"Why bother?"

"Because I'm going to do it this time." I held out a hand.

Her head tilted, and she examined me. "Very well."

She accepted my hand, and I pulled her up. The fire couldn't be more than thirty yards from us. No chance to back out. No chance to run.

I held the end of her staff and closed my eyes. If I failed, at least there wouldn't be much time to look stupid before we all cooked. I pushed the thought away. It was replaced by a strange voice of fear and desperation that was both familiar and unknown, as if it were an amalgam of all the unanswered cries of hurt children.

The sea of lava sloshed at the edges of my mind. The mercenaries capered, their faces distorted into demonic visages. One by one, the horrors of my journey presented themselves. Life and death, over and over. The fear had given me the energy to keep going. So to had the excitement that bubbled beneath. I imagined collecting this energy, scraping it off like cream on fresh milk, and pouring it into the staff. A sense of relief flowed, and I opened my eyes.

The runes on the staff were glowing. I couldn't believe it. And the sphere, it was brighter than the fires. Blackbird moved this end, and for an instant I imagined I could hear her thoughts as she directed the energy through the runes and out the sphere, cutting a line in nothing.

Sparks exploded, and the line widened into an oval vortex that reflected twisted flames.

Gwen peered closely. "Is this a door? What's on the other side?"

Blackbird grinned hungrily. "Find out if you dare."

"Oh, I dare." Gwen walked right through without hesitation.

Damn.

Blackbird snorted. "Come on, boy." And then she was gone.

The vortex was shrinking. I guessed I'd only juiced it enough for a little while. Juice it—was I really going to believe in magic? A cinder landed on the back of my neck, and I yelped, slapping it off. At least I was the only one here.

Which reminded me that I needed to go, the whole mortal peril thing still being on the cards. The next world better be a beach resort with free cocktails.

I walked through the vortex with barely a flinch.

CHAPTER 14

OLD FRIENDS AND FRESH WOUNDS

Astream gently burbled as it wended its way between rounded boulders, its banks softened by short reeds. On the far bank, the bushy crowns of enormously tall trees waved in a gentle breeze. Thick sinuous roots buttressed the main trunks, winding down into a mat covered by leaf litter. A flock of four-winged birds swooped to land on branches, their calls sounding more like babbling toddlers than chirps. A herd of long-legged animals headed away from the creek, feathered bodies gleaming above chocolate-colored grass. Unseen insects chirped and trilled. The air was warm but not unpleasant.

In the distance, jagged mountains of dirty gold projected great shadows thanks to a spectacular orange sunset. Above, a streak of brilliant stars shone amid a nebula of blues and pinks.

I did a double take and checked the sunset, my heart racing. Not lava, just a sunset. A completely alien scene, but a beautiful one that didn't promise death by fire. So far. I was alive.

Which gave me a moment to stare at my hands. Had that been magic? There was no scientific basis for what I had done. I knew I was no Einstein, but I felt confident about that. Berating myself for even considering magic would have been easy, except the world we'd crossed into was so tranquil that I couldn't do it. The impossible had happened.

Rather than frustration, my body tingled with a wisp of delight. I'd done—whatever it was—and it was kind of cool. And this setting felt like a reward. I crouched down and pushed my fingers into the loamy soil. A piña colada or mojito would have been better, but this was nice.

Gwen, who had crouched by the stream, scooped a handful of water and drank. "I will never doubt the Lady Organa again, no matter how fickle she may be. She bestows more blessings than I deserve. She told me I would be safe. That I would find paradise and know… it doesn't matter. But this—"

"Don't be foolish, girl. There is no safety. Not for long. And paradise is for fools and poets. The world you live in is the one you make."

Blackbird gazed at the stars as if they were a book to be read. She must be the life of the party.

I rubbed my eyes and yawned. "It seems safe enough for now. We can't go on forever without rest. You need to heal, and I can barely keep my eyes open."

My hands were filthy. My clothes were beyond filthy. I joined Gwen by the stream and cleaned my hands and face as best as I could, only drinking when I figured I had more chance of getting sick from the water than my grime. The coolness refreshed my parched throat, leaving a mineral tang like fancy restaurant water.

"A short break is called for. There is a spot downriver. We will rest there." Blackbird marched away.

I pulled off my jacket and shirt and scrubbed them with a rock, refusing to give her the satisfaction of making me run to her heels. Was I being stubborn or petty? I preferred to think of it as setting boundaries.

The jacket turned out to be a write-off. It had enough rips to be a fashion statement, but its career as clothing was over. I'd be leaving it behind, mildly guilty there was no trash can to throw it in.

A splash caught my attention. Gwen had the same idea. The washing, that is. And with no modesty. She wore an elaborate midriff bra underneath her now removed shirt, shaped with bone rather than plastic or steel, I guessed. And she filled it out well. I decided to look away too late—she met my gaze and chuckled.

I scrubbed my shirt very, very hard. When the material was at risk of eroding, I wrung it out and slipped it back on. My pants needed the same, but they were staying on. Doubtless, Gwen would have broken into a stand-up routine at my expense.

"I'm, ah, going after Blackbird."

"Wait for me."

I heard her dress, and then she joined me, the red fabric dripping. We looked like drowned rats. Well, I must have. She looked good.

"Where is this place?" She asked as we followed the stream.

"I have no idea." I swept a hand to indicate all that we could see. "I come from a very different place. Big cities, tall towers, roads, street lights, cars, planes, spaceships, satellites."

She examined me. Her face wasn't stern, but I definitely had the impression there was disbelief. Perhaps she thought we played a game of lies. Or the translation was coming up with interesting results.

"Martin, man from a world of wonders, why are we here in a place with nothing but trees?"

That was a great question. Did I have the slightest clue? No. What could I say? Because Blackbird is doing something for a god or in spite of a god? Or because I was in the wrong place at the wrong time, and disasters snowballed from there?

I put my hands on the back of my neck. "You're better off

asking Blackbird. Just don't expect a full answer. Hell, if you get anything, tell me."

We caught up to Blackbird. Her pace told the story of her condition. Holding my tongue, I slowed to match her gait, and we walked in silence for some time. Ahead, a blob on our side of the stream resolved into a single giant of a tree. Its isolation when so close to its kind resonated.

My stomach rumbled, loud enough to be a tiger in the woods. Screw metaphorical flora—a few millennia had passed since I'd last eaten.

"Anyone seen a vending machine? I could do with a packet of chips." My mouth watered. "Maybe some lasagna. Not from a vending machine. I'm starving."

Gwen glanced at the trees. "I am not tired. When we stop, I will see how clever those birds are. Or I might try a snare if there's any game on the ground."

"No," Blackbird stated flatly. "Not here. We must travel lightly."

There was meaning behind her choice of words, but I couldn't tell what. So, when we reached the trees, I had little hope of filling my empty belly.

Blackbird put a hand on a huge, curved root. "We stop here. Sleep as best you can, even if you don't feel the need. We can only spare a few hours."

She walked around to the far side of the tree.

"Shouldn't we take watches or something?" I called to her retreating back, getting no response. I swore she had to pay a dollar for every word she spoke.

After searching for the densest patch of grass, I lay down.

Gwen grabbed handfuls of grass and cut them free just above the base until she had enough to form a pillow. Did that count as traveling lightly? She looked very pleased with her efforts. I wish I'd thought of doing the same, but now I didn't want to copy her.

"I could get used to this," she said after a few minutes. "I've earned peace and quiet."

"How so?"

She peered at me through lush stalks of grass, her face barely more than a silhouette. "The same way every woman has to: with daring, cleverness, and stepping over the bodies of men."

Dead bodies, I was sure. Did I really need to close my eyes right now? Perhaps I could wait until our next imprisonment when she was safely behind bars.

Chirping insects wove a hypnotic tapestry of sound, and despite my unsettling neighbor, I drifted off.

When I woke, the nebula and its stars still dominated the sky. I couldn't have been out for that long, but I felt a little refreshed and even more ravenous. Gwen lay on her side, facing away, most likely asleep or scheming quietly. Assuming the former, I slowly stood and silently stretched before walking around the tree to check on Blackbird.

She was kneeling next to an ancient, weather-grayed piece of wood sticking up out of the ground. Carved deeply on its front: Lucan. A few bright blue flowers lay before it, their shiny petals catching the weak light. Blackbird's eyes were closed, and I wondered if she'd fallen asleep in front of what must be a grave. It was the first time I'd seen anything personal, and it felt like an intrusion.

I started backing away, but she spoke.

"He was the first I stayed with until the end. And the last. The path I walk is a lonely one—but not without its rewards. Help me stand."

As I gave her my hand, I considered this small revelation. Her voice contained fondness, and yet she wasn't sad. That wound must have healed long ago. Had my nana had a long-lost love? I didn't remember my grandfather at all, and she'd never spoken of him. I'd seen her as a cardboard cutout, pre-made to inflict misery, weird philosophy, and anachronistic skills. Had she kept some bit on the side, someone I'd not noticed as I hid in books to forget the real world a page at a time?

It didn't matter, nor did Blackbird's memories. If I wanted to get home, I needed to remember what she'd done. Blood may be thicker than water according to the long-misunderstood proverb, but that only made it a better trap. She wasn't some nice old lady who'd lost a husband years ago.

"Boy, keep your mind focused." She poked me with her staff. "We enter the forest of Celian. I hope for us to pass undetected, but those who reside within can be a prickly sort."

Compared to Blackbird?

Gwen joined us. "You should be at ease then, old one, for you will be in like company. This journey you take, do you head to a city?"

"There are cities of a sort in the same direction," Blackbird said cagily.

Gwen's eyes narrowed, but she didn't press further. "Then shall we walk together?"

I hadn't considered her leaving. I suppose there was no reason for her to stay beyond having traveling companions. She'd escaped the lava, and now there was a whole new world for her to explore. Wherever she ended up, she'd come out on top, I was sure of it.

Blackbird crossed the stream on two conveniently placed stones and aimed for a gap between the vine-covered giants at the forest's edge. Gwen and I followed, and soon the sky gave way to a thick canopy. Rather than the darkness I'd expected, there was a faint teal glow from thousands of dots on the trunks, a kind of lichen.

Blackbird must have recovered somewhat—she activated her staff, adding a bright glow that animated disturbing shadows as she passed. Our slow passage snapped twigs and crunched leaves in a steady monotonous song, and apart from the need to wend our way between trees, we were uninterrupted.

Long, shiny red fruit hung from a vine nearby. My mouth watered. "Is it edible?"

"Not by you," Blackbird said firmly.

"They're poisonous?"

"They could get you killed."

I stared at them longingly, wondering what they'd taste like, but Gwen gave me a gentle shove, and I moved on. A little while later, I jolted when a critter peeked out of a hollow. It had thick striped fur, and a long tail rivaling a snow leopard's. On seeing us, it trilled like a bird, then scampered away.

We pushed through shaggy undergrowth that wafted a honey scent as we bruised its leaves.

"Paradise," Gwen said, but she didn't sound particularly happy.

The forest smelled better than a city, but I couldn't shake a crowded sensation with the trees reminding me of tall office towers, anonymous and aloof from little me. Perhaps it was more like a mall food court when I had no money. Or maybe I was just hungry.

A chittering cry sounded in the distance, followed by the babbling above of unseen birds. I stopped, my hand on my cutlass.

"What do you see?" Gwen asked.

"Nothing."

"Precisely," Blackbird said, looking at them from over her shoulder. "Keep going. I want to spend as little time here as poss —" She cocked her head.

Rustling spread around us, and I drew my cutlass. A voice in the darkness, dry and angry, demanded, "Remain still, interlopers, and drop your weapons."

I had started lowering my weapon carefully, when Blackbird hissed, "Don't you dare."

So, I held it at an awkward forward-leaning angle, wondering if I was about to be riddled with bullets or robbed.

Figures slipped out of the shadows, surrounding us. They were tall and thin, their ears pointed and their faces pretty in a gaunt way. Elves. Their skin was mottled blue-green, and they possessed diminutive antlers. Close enough to elves for me. Each wore wooden plate armor, the surfaces intricately carved, waxed, and polished to a luster. It moved differently to metal, creating an almost toy-like impression, and yet the grooves and chips bore testament to its battle-tested effectiveness. The elves' firm expressions told me they meant business, that and the bone-tipped short spears and recurve bows with knocked arrows.

I counted twelve of them, three bearing poles strapped to their backs with small flags hanging above their heads. One of these stepped forward, stopping well out of range of staff or cutlass.

He pointed a spear at us. "You test the resolve of the Argante. Drop your weapons, lesser creatures, or be considered enemies."

Blackbird worked her jaw, then said quietly to us, "Imperial guard. They are far from home. This could be good or bad. It has been some time since I last walked this world."

It would be nice, I thought, to walk by someone and give a noncommittal nod and go on to our own thing. Was that too much to ask for?

Blackbird had other plans. She closed on the elf. "I am no enemy of the Protectorate. Indeed, I merely seek passage along the public road to the Heart, where I would have words with an old friend."

Gwen leaned closer to me. "What is all this babble?"

"Sounds to me like she's trying to negotiate with the local cops."

The elf gripped his spear tightly. "Who are you to make free with our lands? Name this soul you claim to know."

Blackbird straightened her shoulders and thumped her staff on the ground. The sphere grew bright.

"I am of the Wayfarers Council, born far away to a people you will never know, in service to the Greater Fabric. Call me Blackbird." Her voice took on a resonance that vibrated in my chest. "And I seek audience with she who is High Priestess of the Seven Blossoms, Warden of the Forests, Protector of the Heart, and Head of the Convocation of Isamir—Queen Nyashoth, who is dear to me."

The elves twitched and whispered to each other.

Blackbird continued. "She will not take kindly to my ill-treatment. Since when has a guest been greeted thus?"

She had to be bluffing. Guest? Everything about our journey so far told me that we were not expected by anyone. The elven leader talked to his two flagged friends. Their words were intense and animated but unclear.

Finally, the leader approached once more. "You will come with us."

Blackbird nodded and started walking, the elf then hurrying to take the lead. Gwen and I followed, with the other elves forming a moving cordon. I had expected them to hold us back, so I could live with this, though their seven-foot height was unsettling.

The route they took twisted back and forth enough that I wondered if they were trying to make us lost. It was a waste of time as I already had no idea where we were or where we were going. At one point we circled round a large pond, and further along we passed through a clearing dotted with saplings. The route was easygoing, but my legs were growing stiff, and I struggled to focus, making a bridge over a sinkhole a mildly terrifying experience, despite the aid of a brightening sky.

The transition to a village was instantaneous. We exited a wider gap between trees, and then there it was: single-story buildings built from wood, wide verandas, and shingled roofs. The designs were simple, but elegantly put together—the sort shown on a YouTube video as an easy home project where you don't see the hundred carpenters working behind the scenes. Every vertical post sported intricate carving and paint in clashing colors that hurt my eyes as they adjusted to the morning light of a clear sky.

Elves labored in small open workshops or on the verandas. I saw weaving, bowl carving, painting, the drying of fruit. God, how I wanted to eat the latter, poisonous or not. They worked with calm efficiency and frequent conversations. Our passage drew attention, but I didn't see fear. It took me a while to spot the children. The few I saw watched from the shadows of houses, through open windows, and even from rooftops.

Rather than having roads like a proper city, the houses were placed in such a way that we constantly tacked back and forth. I spotted a stable with several horses and wondered how they'd get wagons through the village maze. It didn't seem the kind of place for delivery trucks.

The elves marched us to a house on the far side. It was a little larger than the others, and the finish made the rest appear slovenly by comparison. Delicate patterns softened every hard edge, and a mural on the front door showing trees, buildings, the sun, elves and more must have had symbolic meaning. A hard-packed dirt path led to this, its sides marked by cubes of different woods, some a dark cherry, others a bright ash. The tops of each were carved with scenes of hunting and dancing.

The elves halted at the beginning of this, their bodies tense as they turned to face us. I guessed we were about to meet the mayor, and they didn't like that we were still armed, though we had sheathed our weapons along the way.

The elven leader walked down the path. Before he could reach the door, it opened, and another elf walked out, every movement one of grace. She was older, a little more filled out, with thick braids of hair tipped in gold. She wore a dress of muted gold with embroidered flowers around the neck and down the sleeves. A thin circlet of living flowers rested on her brow.

"I see you have brought me guests, Beralius." Her tone was rich like a blues singer. "I will oversee all the proper greetings. You may return to your patrol."

The leader of the patrol scowled. "The elder claims—"

"Yes, yes. I am sure she does. That is a matter for me. Return to your duties."

The leader's stern expression twitched, but he raised his left hand, pressed it to his heart and ordered his soldiers to follow.

"You had better come in," the woman said.

CHAPTER 15

QUEEN NO LONGER

The door opened onto a hall covered with woven mats. Thick candles rested in small niches, each surprisingly bright and burning with a plum scent. The internal walls were fashioned from trunks planed mostly flat. Designs of leaves, flowers, and the four-winged birds added color, using a style reliant on a few suggestive lines. Up close, I could see little embellishments on the critters: sharp teeth and four eyes. Gwen may have found hunting harder than she expected.

An arch on the left opened into a room. The seating was more in line with a presenter and an audience than a living room. The chairs were large and narrow, clearly not designed for us. A single couch was a more likely option.

Large hinges and handholds fixed to the ceiling suggested it could open up to see the night sky, unless I was way off base, and it had a more kinky function.

The elf rested her hands on the presenter's chair. "Blackbird, it has been too long."

Blackbird placed her staff in a corner and stood in front of the elf. They clasped each other's hands. "Queen Nyashoth, it has been too long indeed."

"Not queen, merely Nyashoth in these days." The elf made an inclusive gesture toward Gwen and myself. "I see you travel in company once more."

Blackbird twitched. "A short-term arrangement. This is Martin, who holds a little of my blood. And that is Gwen, whose world has been destroyed."

Nyashoth didn't look at either of us, but said to Blackbird, "Please rest. I will bring refreshments."

My eyes widened. Food! "Would you like help?" If it sped up the process, I'd have done an interpretive dance.

Blackbird shook her head at me as if I'd committed some kind of faux pas.

Nyashoth, who had stopped at my offer, examined me as if checking to see if I was making fun of her. "That will not be necessary."

When she left the room, I said to Blackbird, "What was that about? She's a queen, and old. I was just being polite."

"She *was* a queen," Gwen said. "What's that mean?"

Blackbird settled awkwardly into the lowest chair. "It means that all is not well here, either."

Gwen walked to a wall with a shelf holding several carvings of unusual animals and a variety of bottles formed from glass, clay, or a mineral resembling tiger's eye. Each had wrappings or coils of metal and leather, the patterns unique. "It is always a matter of how deep the shit in the middens reaches. This land appears well enough. Are there… people like us?"

Blackbird eased deeper into her chair. "Like you? Humans? There are those close enough to pass. Where possible, I travel through ways hospitable to myself, and in such worlds, there is a bias—at least in this cluster. Elsewhere, I have seen beings that defy easy description and others that I wish I could burn from my memory. But heed this: there are monsters hiding within flesh such as yours."

I walked over to a window opening to the village. An elf carried a long stick with several bloated fish hanging from one end. Would I be able to settle in a place like this, giving up on Earth? Would the elves shun me as different? It didn't matter. This wasn't the place for me. I wanted to go home. And damn, wasn't home becoming more nebulous every time I thought about it?

A short time later, Nyashoth returned and placed a tray on a table to one side of the chairs. On its flat tortoiseshell surface rested glazed earthenware plates with fruits, strips of something pale blue, and little cakes. The ex-queen used a pot at one end to pour herbal tea into handleless cups and passed them around.

Her tasks complete, she sat in her chair, all grace and confidence, and said, "Please eat."

I glanced at Blackbird. She'd claimed the fruit was poisonous earlier in the day.

"You will not sicken," Blackbird said.

That was confidence-boosting. But I was starving and didn't need encouragement. I sipped the tea, which had a meaty-mushroomy taste like a broth, and picked at the food. Gwen collected several pieces of fruit and sat on the couch, her legs crossed. When Blackbird didn't move to try any, I offered to bring her some.

"Later."

Nyashoth leaned toward Blackbird. "Tell me of your circumstances."

"I have a name for the dark god. Tenekal. He advances at a pace I had not reckoned with. Either his power is far greater than I hoped, or his need is greater. He will come by soon enough. For your sake, I hope you only feel the ripples of his passing. Every way I have crossed, every world I have walked, shows signs of his corruption."

I stopped chewing to listen carefully. Answers. I was finally hearing answers.

Nyashoth rested her hands on the arms of her chair. "When you visited last—near a hundred seasons ago—we spoke of the stirring. I promised you a hundred of my mystics to aid you."

Blackbird closed her eyes. "I remember."

"As the seasons change, so does power. Having heeded your warning, I channeled the resources of my people into the mystics to find answers. Yet I was not careful enough to salve the hurt pride of our warriors. They did not accept the nature of the threat. At first, questions bloomed within the Convocation. These same words spread fast, echoing in the halls and forests. Questions with imperfect answers. Few alive remembered the service you performed for us, and so your warning held little weight."

"What power could a distant god have in our world, they asked. What proof was there of growing malevolence? Did I have no faith in the seven guardians, they demanded. Within our chapels, the mystics argued with each other. They knew the guardians have been dormant for an eon. Were they no longer needed? Had we risen so far? Dear friend, the ancient scourge of our cousins is all but forgotten. We live long but then do not trust that beyond which we remember. None can threaten our dominance, they said."

The ex-queen paused, perhaps contemplating the folly of her race, which sounded about as human as it got. Was hubris a universal trait?

With a wave of her hand, she continued. "Signs and portents were twisted to suit individual needs. Factions riddled the Convocation like boring beetles. It had not been so ill since my mother's mother ruled."

"My loyalists worked tirelessly on my behalf and on our

cause, but we missed the truth—the fires of dissent were being fed."

"Tenekal?"

"Or Titania. Or nothing beyond a thirst for more. My nephew spied the weakness of my position and desired the throne more than to honor his kin. After that—you know well that it is easier to tear apart than it is to hold together."

Blackbird sighed. "Indeed. How do you still live?"

"By retreating. I renounced the throne and exiled myself. Not for my life—I have seen more than enough seasons. I did so for my few remaining loyalists. I live in shame so that they live at all. And now I wait and watch as my great nation pulls itself apart."

"Tenekal destroys in many ways, but I fear what you describe is the surface. Your guardians might—"

"Blackbird," Nyashoth said, heat in her voice. "I did not ask for aid before, and I have not now."

"I will say no more on it."

They both relaxed a little. This was clearly old ground. I, however, was pretty damn tense. They believed what they were saying, and their manner was more war council than reunion.

Nyashoth flexed her long fingers and opened her palms. "Despite what we have shared, you carry hope?"

Blackbird didn't respond immediately, and I found myself leaning closer. It wasn't my problem, and it was barely understandable let alone believable, but I'd become embroiled in her schemes. That, and the earnest worry, carried far more weight than a dramatic performance.

"A wisp of hope, fragile as a newborn babe and as small." Blackbird let out a breath and shifted slightly.

"But a newborn can grow." Nyashoth's brow furrowed. She stood suddenly. "I see what you hide. Will you ever look after yourself?"

Blackbird's expression soured. "As you do?"

"Do not try that on me. I am not some shortsighted human to be distracted with meaningless turnarounds."

I swallowed a laugh at the scolding.

Nyashoth bent over Blackbird and ran a hand above her wound. "Stubborn as ever. You should have rested. Though I may be a queen no longer, my arts have not faded. I will do as I can. Come."

"Once a queen, always a queen," Blackbird growled while accepting Nyashoth's assistance to stand.

Nyashoth gestured to Gwen and me with a subtle movement that intimated a meaning I couldn't grasp. "Be at peace here."

When they were through the door, Blackbird called back, "Don't get into trouble."

What did that mean? Exactly how long was she going to be away? She needed to rest for weeks, if not months. So we were to be here for a while. Yeah, that would delay my return as well, but she was old, exhausted, and the risk of infection must be high after all we'd been through. I'd live. I stared at the door, genuinely worried for her. Where had that come from?

Was I projecting? Was it because I'd wanted someone to care for me? To my parents, any sickness, any hurt had been an inconvenience at best and a deliberate provocation at worst. I'd grown so good at hiding weakness that the teachers never saw it. I was just a weird kid.

No one should go through that. No one should suffer alone. I wanted to wave a wand and make it all go away. What a fucking joke. I wasn't a kid anymore. Fairy tales belonged in books, not in minds.

Frustration heated my skin, making it itch. The scale of the room diminished me. I was Alice after a sip of potion labeled drink me. Sweat formed on my brow. I hated it. I wanted to be anywhere else. It reminded me of how helpless I was, how dependent on Blackbird.

Gwen had taken one of the small bottles from the shelf and was tossing it from hand to hand. "This isn't the city Blackbird was talking about, is it? I've seen larger households."

That was all she cared about? I turned on her. "You said that Blackbird would be fine if you sewed her up. I got you what you wanted, and she's not."

Her eyes hardened. "Don't talk like a fool. It makes you far less pleasant to look at. I'm a doctor, not a miracle worker. She walks, which you should be grateful for."

I bit back a retort as I remembered she didn't have the translation runes that Blackbird had burned into my skin. Gwen had only heard one side of the conversation at best. She had no reason to worry.

"I'm sorry," I said. "You're right. I'm feeling trapped, and I took it out on you."

"I'm going for a walk." Gwen stopped at the door to the hall. "Want to join me?"

A thought scratched at my mind. I needed a chance to follow where it led. "Maybe later."

"Your loss." Her footsteps traced her path out the front.

What was it? Gwen. She'd called herself a farrier when they'd met on the airship, and now she claimed to be a doctor. Was that the translation failing, or was she a compulsive liar? Did she even owe me the truth? It was easy to blame others. My scalp itched, and I scrunched my hair for relief and to contain my frustration.

I returned to the food tray on the basis that if I didn't have answers, I could at least have a full stomach. The tastes were pleasant, but I wanted something familiar. A strawberry, a hamburger, a slice of toast—I'd settle for a salad. We weren't being chased. We weren't being attacked. I should be relaxed, but I wasn't.

Discarding a large slice of fruit, I crossed to the couch and sat, feeling bloated and slow. We were in the calm before the storm. I was sure of it. And when heading into a storm, one should know why. A destination would be a start. Yes. I'd talk to Blackbird when she was better. We couldn't go on the same way. She'd have to understand that. And she'd be more reasonable after getting some rest. She couldn't be less so.

I closed my eyes, imagining her nodding at my sensible argument, and fell asleep.

THE GENTLE CREAKING of wood woke me. I pulled my hair back from my eyes, ran a hand across itchy stubble, and tried not to notice my stink.

Nyashoth stood before me, her hands clasped.

"How is she?" I asked, walking to the window to gain some personal space.

Night had fallen, and the glorious nebula was once more in the sky. Several lanterns hung outside houses, and elves sat at tables set up haphazardly, talking, eating, and drinking. Some held small crafts and used deft fingers to shape their creations.

"I have lent her all the spirit her body can accept." The ex-queen joined me at the window, her imposing serenity intimidating, her very presence disarming. "Tell me, Martin of Earth, what is your place in this task?"

She knew I was from Earth. She and Blackbird had been talking. Of course. It was a strange question to ask.

"Place? I don't know. You tell me. I'm just a teacher. I spend all day with kids, hoping not to damage them further while trying to instill hope—any hope. And I lost that chance before Blackbird showed up." The bitterness in my voice surprised me, as did how much I'd admitted. "I'm no one. I have nothing to do with Blackbird's whatever-it-is. All I want is to go home. If I still have one."

"That will not do. Blackbird needs your help though she will not admit so." Nyashoth rested a hand on my shoulder. The grip was strong, almost painful, and yet my body relaxed.

"You're wrong. She let me tag along only because she doesn't have the time to get me back. If we weren't related, she'd have ditched me at the start, and I'd be mutated-puppy food. Her religious pilgrimage matters more to her than anyone else does. In fact, I don't think she gives a shit about anyone."

I should have felt concerned about swearing in front of royalty, but it felt so good to get it off my chest. The journey had tied me in knots until I no longer recognized myself. I thought of Gwen, and the small bottle she'd casually stolen. I thought of the wraiths and the people I'd helped slaughter. "I don't think anyone does."

Nyashoth released my shoulder and pointed to an elf braiding strands of mustard and black cord into a thin rope. "Does Closara braid for herself? There is only so much rope she could need."

I knew where this was going. "She'll sell or trade it to others. Her work is only for her benefit, even if others find it useful."

"Closara once served as a court scribe and was known as an accomplished poet." Nyashoth lowered her shoulders to look into my eyes. "When watching only the surface, we see ripples but not their cause."

That was all anyone could see, and it wasn't a bad thing. It was armor that protected our true selves. I wanted to tell her as much, but her eyes held me, the amber glints in her irises as good as a net.

"Let me tell you a story, Martin of Earth. Not every word will be true, as no one soul commands knowledge of all that has been. Even the mystics of my court debate the details. A long time ago, when elves first began to know themselves, we sought, hand in hand with our cousins, to learn what lay beneath the ripples. That search brought about our seven guardians—that which you would call gods. Whether our desires created them or attracted them does not matter. They became part of us and we became part of them. Our worship provides them with sustenance. In return, they provide guidance, whether we accept it or not. The mystics believe this is the same throughout the many worlds. Blackbird and her wayfarers said as much when they first passed through our lands."

"Many seasons ago, a new god was born, one who was small and weak. Such are said to fade away, their monuments consumed by time. This god, unsatisfied with his lot, discovered a way to gain in power beyond that of his worshipers. He consumed the essence of an even weaker god, one tied to a single shrine. Now a little stronger, he searched for another. With each hunt, his might increased until none on his world remained to challenge his supremacy. He was worshiped in fear by lesser beings such as ourselves, yet his appetite could not be satisfied with such morsels."

She clasped my arms, and I felt like a fly trapped in a spider's web.

"One dawn, this god found a way to push beyond his own world and into another, opening up new ground to hunt his own kind. Even if he were not a force of hunger and spite, his passage would bring upheaval. He is not of these worlds, and his mere presence strains the fabric of our existence. He not only spawns cataclysms in every world he invades, but he taints those he merely passes by."

"You're talking about that Tenekal guy?" I blew air out like a mechanic setting the price of a repair. "Look, I've seen things I can't explain easily. But gods, cannibal gods? You can't expect me to take you seriously."

I braced in case she chose to lift me up and throw me outside.

Instead, she chuckled. "It could be allegory. Mystics love it. Such stories feed their egos."

Perhaps she was more chill than I had believed. At least I'd made it clear from the start that I wasn't along for a ride on the crazy train. I looked away. Gwen walked down the street, a large bottle in one hand, two elves keeping pace. It irked me for the silliest reason. She'd only been along for the ride.

"Who is she to you?" Nyashoth asked.

"Just someone we were trapped with on an airship. I helped her escape, and she treated Blackbird."

"A barter between two merchants."

"I guess so."

"Would you have helped her if she couldn't heal Blackbird?"

I scratched the back of my neck. "Possibly. It's hard to say. All I know of her for sure is that she's unpredictable and dangerous."

"Do you know yourself?"

It was a meaningless question. I chose not to answer. I thought I knew myself all too well.

"Some wisdom, I see. Let me ask again, would you have helped her?"

I sighed. "Yes, I would have."

Nyashoth left the window. "Come for a walk with me. Your weapon must remain."

That didn't sound good. Had I angered her? I didn't want to go, but I wanted answers, no matter how opaque they were. Besides, disobeying a queen, even an ex, had to be dangerous. I put the cutlass on the couch.

She led me down the hall and out the back of the house, each step graceful despite her height. Multicolored rope stretched between two nearby trees, and clothes hung on this, a jarringly domestic scene. It must be strange, I thought, to do chores after having spent a lifetime with servants. Did she resent it?

We walked down a path of wood chips, green with moss, our footsteps near silent. It continued into the forest, finally stopping at a glade no more than fifty yards across. Bushes thick with glowing orange blossoms hid the bases of the trunks, sealing off the space. A small spring at the far end disgorged water into a cracked wooden bowl. The crack leaked and fed a mini waterfall that flowed over small stones that appeared natural and yet so artful that they must have been set there by hand. As peaceful as it was, clicks, chirps, and other strange noises suggested the night was busy.

"This is where I venerate the guardians."

She paused in front of a small bed of thin-stalked green plants that resembled the tops of carrots.

"Here is where I consider Pachiya of the soil."

She was welcome to believe whatever she wanted, but I didn't have the energy to feign interest. "Is this Pachiya going to save you from Tenekal?"

"Does it matter to you? My guardians are not yours. I will leave you here. Perhaps, you can listen to yourself."

Her dress swept the ground as she left. Was she rebuking me, or did she expect me to pull out little bells and dance around calling for wisdom? I'd need a few mushrooms before that. I stalked around the glade's border, convinced that I needed to wait a little before taking the path and returning, lest I offend the queen. *Off with his head.* She'd need to get in line. I rubbed my temples, trying to ease my frustration. Once again, I was being jerked around with no good explanation.

I stopped by the spring, cupped my hands, and took my fill. A massive stump to the right looked comfortable enough, so I lay down and kicked off my boots. I'd joked about a second prison to Blackbird, and now I'd found it. Nyashoth had wanted me to listen to myself, but that was the last thing I needed. Better to get out of my own head.

When I was studying a teaching degree, another student had shown me mindfulness. I'd dismissed it at first, but after a hard week at a school placement, I'd given it a shot.

Closing my eyes, I leaned back and felt the wood—slightly spongy. A cycle of slow breaths quieted my thoughts. That drew attention to the messages my body was sending. Cuts, scratches, bruises, strains. I had them all. Fuzzy grass tickled my feet as they hung over the side of the stump. The air was still and earthy, the splash of water hypnotic.

A voice called out, muffled. A figure appeared before me, golden yet indistinct. I tried to work out if I had stood or if she was floating over me, but the notion collapsed as soon as I grasped for it. Had I fallen asleep again? Was it an effect of the flowers or the water? My head was too muzzy to make out her words. There was urgency tinged with despair, a longing to be saved. I knew it well. Tears wet my cheeks.

"Where are you?" I shouted. "What's wrong?"

A slap on my shin ended the vision. I sat up. This time it was Blackbird staring at me. She held her staff as if considering a second blow. Her clothes were clean and whole, and I couldn't see a trace of the repairs.

"Enough sleep. It's time to go." With that, she left the glade at a steady pace.

I stretched and wiped my face. The sun was up once more. The nights must be short. I thought of the voice. It couldn't be real. If it was, what else would I have to accept?

Nyashoth waited for me in front of the doorway. "Do you know your part?"

The sort of question I dreaded as a kid when I hadn't been listening. A yes might prove dangerous.

"Look, your highness or whatever I'm meant to call you, I don't know my part. I don't want one. I'm just trying to find my way."

She nodded. "Seeking is its own reward."

I got the feeling she wasn't going to accept an honest answer.

She pulled a small pouch of plain tan linen from her belt and held it out. "This will take you back to Earth if you can wield it."

From behind her, she retrieved a sword. It was my cutlass, but it was sheathed in a scabbard of tooled leather attached to a deep blue belt. "This will take you into mortal danger."

She pushed both at me.

"Ah, thanks."

"None is deserved. Now come inside and clean up. You will soon be on your way."

I stayed as she entered her house. She'd given me a way back to Earth. *If you can wield it.* My stomach fluttered. I had what I wanted. But the cutlass… back to Earth or mortal danger. Wow, such a difficult choice. Ha!

I snorted and strapped the sword around my waist. Once I was home, I wouldn't need it. Home. I opened the pouch and reached inside. A polished stone, yellow with green flecks. Runes had been etched into its surface. I could believe in magic, just for a bit. I thought back to helping Blackbird with her staff. There'd been a sensation of energy. I tried to will something into the stone, like a kid trying to use the *Force* to pick up their dirty clothes.

Nothing.

"Yeah, well," I said to myself. "What did you expect?"

"Martin, by the hairs of my ass, hurry up."

I shivered at the thought. Was it possible to dip my memory into sulfuric acid? Yet another question without a satisfactory answer. I'd learned a lot during our short stay, but I had no idea how much of it was real. I'd decided to confront Blackbird, and I still would—when I could tell if she spoke the truth.

I slipped the stone back into the pouch and tied it to my belt.

"Coming," I shouted.

What else could I do?

HOLDING BACK

The eight-legged, broad-faced horse undulated as it picked its way along the forest floor. Cloven hooves dug into the leaf litter with confidence and surprisingly little noise. The elves had shortened the stirrups to fit my stubby human legs, and the padding underneath the saddle was thick. It hadn't helped. My ass ached liked I'd been hit with a paddle over and over.

We rode in single file, two elves leading the way with lanterns on long sticks. They hadn't talked since we left the village, yet remained alert the entire time, putting me on edge from the start. When no ambush occurred, I settled into the ride as best I could.

Gwen had the tail position, and I'd spied her picking fruit, nibbling some and storing the bulk in a woven satchel. She greeted my surprise with a grin and tossed me a bright yellow berry. I ate it without checking Blackbird or the elves. Challenge met. What a rebel.

About half an hour later, we came upon a ruined stone structure covered in ferns and saplings that elsewhere would have been full-height trees.

Blackbird called a halt. "Get your things. We walk from here."

Groaning, I slid off the horse and rubbed my thighs. Gwen landed on the ground and stretched ostentatiously. I guessed she'd ridden a lot. Which would make sense for a farrier, not so much for a doctor unless she made house calls. I retrieved a ceramic water bottle covered with woven cord and a pack. I'd already gone through the latter and found wooden boxes of dried fruits and meat. A thick woolen blanket filled most of the remaining space. There had also been a scrap of cloth, a flat textured piece of stone, and a clay bottle with oil, no doubt for my weapon. I slipped the pack over my shoulders, wishing for the adjustments of a proper hiking backpack. Then, to recover the blood flow in my legs and not to protect my pride, I strode toward the ruins rather than collapse in a numb-legged heap.

At the front of the line, Blackbird spoke to the elves, thanking them for their help in a formal manner. One of them responded, referring to her as Wise One, and then the pair collected the horses and started back.

I ran a hand along the nearest slab of stone. A luminescent moss covered much of its surface, but the sides were as smooth as if cut by an industrial saw. There were patterns chiseled into a nearby piece, similar to Celtic knots and entirely different from the elven style. I reached for my phone to take a photo, a near-lifelong habit resurfacing. My phone was gone. When? On the airship, when we crashed, back by that stream? There was no hope of finding it. And, the obvious point shouted at me: it would have long ago run out of charge.

Everyone complains about phones distracting people from what was around them. Right then, I needed it to remind me of where I'd been. It had been a tether to my life, a reminder that I belonged somewhere. My wallet. Panic gripped me as I patted my pants. Gone, too. My proof of identity. My cards, my cash. I could be anyone. I could disappear, right now. If I returned to Earth, who would remember me? Leaning my head back, I laughed at myself. Damn. I was a wraith of another sort. Might as well float on.

Continuing around the ruins, I gained a sense of scale, if not one of perspective. They were about the size of a country town hall with a gap in the center that may have been open ground. Round, flat stones lay like sliced pickles. There were cuts in stone slabs, perhaps from timber supports that had long since rotted. I picked up a lump of dirt and broke it apart. In the center was a shard of glass. I wiped it on a flat leaf and spotted fine lines traced on its surface. My fingers tingled against its surface, as if there were a slight electric charge. My first guess had been a window, but I wondered if this was from a mug or tumbler filled with something poisonous to my anatomy.

Gwen walked up to me and pulled my arm so she could examine the piece. "That's not a gem."

"I worked that out."

"I used to do a little treasure hunting. Trust me, anything worth looting will be long gone."

"That's one way of looking at it." I dropped the glass and moved to a slab of dressed stone with chiseled markings. Letters. My fingers traced the design, and the word came to me: Wayfarers. Another started, but the roots of a tree covered most of its letters. That was fine. I had enough to go on. Wayfarers—Blackbird was one. This had been part of her club. Had it been the headquarters? Had she been inside when it still stood? What did its destruction mean?

"You can read it?" Gwen asked, kneeling on one leg.

"Yes. It says wayfarers."

"I've seen that, though in my language, at Vale Brocel."

"Where?" I asked.

"You've never been to Vale Brocel? It is the largest city in the world, my world. The outer walls straddle the River Bain and stretch as far as the eye can see. The great port holds many water-going boats, and airship towers grow like grass."

"You know it well?"

"Very. Not that it matters. It must be gone by now. But among the noble compounds, there was a place such as this. No one paid it heed. I was only ever curious because it appeared abandoned."

Why would that make a farrier curious? A doctor perhaps, might. Now, a thief, they'd be interested.

"Was it where you grew up?"

She stood. "No. Not in the end."

"You sound like you've traveled a lot," I said. "I'm surprised you're going with us and not heading for an elven city."

"According to Blackbird, we still follow the same path, at least for some time."

I was a little disappointed. "So, you are staying in this world?"

"We shall see."

Blackbird, who had been pacing back and forth, brought light to her sphere and called out, "You two, get moving. We have a long hike from here."

I wanted to press Gwen further, but I'd glanced at Blackbird when she spoke, and Gwen walked past, slapping me on my unguarded ass. "You heard the boss."

After gathering my dignity, I caught up. When we reached Blackbird, I said, "Why not keep those horse things? Don't get me wrong, I'd rather an SUV, but we'll be much slower."

Blackbird's face shriveled up. She worked her jaw, then said, "Because it's a bad idea to lead the uninitiated to the exact location of a way. We are vulnerable at the transition. Already I run risks not dampening the cut's bleed, but that takes time and energy, and I'm already wasting too much on things like explaining the basics to you."

That term again, *ways*, I thought as she pressed on. A way must be a portal. Or at least where she opened them.

Onward we marched, past a fallen giant of a tree. A net of yellow fungus covered its bulk, and the interior proved to be hollow. Five young trees vied for the opening it had left in the forest canopy. A nest of woven sticks as high as my waist rose among its rotten roots. The top, wide enough for a large goose, was covered with a mat of fine brown fibers and many small bones spread down the sides and onto the forest floor. Macabre.

A thunderous screech echoed through the forest. I drew my cutlass from the new scabbard and held it out, searching for danger. Gwen had done the same. We shared a look—neither of us knew where the sound had come from. Blackbird, for her part, hadn't even stopped walking, and the absence of her light left us in deep shadows.

Seconds passed.

I heard the shifting of a stick and pointed with my sword. Gwen nodded and took a slow step to orient herself. The screech repeated. This time nearer, and we were ready to trace its origin. We waited. A small head popped out from behind a tree, and then a round body that was distinctly mammalian and striped yellow and brown. I thought of it as a beaver crossed with a tiger, and it was no bigger than a rabbit.

"Careful, Martin. It's more than you can handle."

I glared at Gwen. "Why don't you go over and give it a pat?"

The creature opened its mouth, revealing two rows of wide, jagged teeth that would have been terrifying if it hadn't been pint-sized. It screeched a third time, and I winced. So damn loud.

"I knew a man who sang like that," Gwen said, walking on.

Probably some poor bastard who'd had to spend time with her. I lifted my cutlass to sheath it and paused. There were markings on its side. Flipping the blade showed the same on the other —runes etched in the steel, black on silver, a few vaguely familiar. I saw sharp lines, curves, distinct characters without any clear order, and yet there was a beauty to their placement.

Who had done this, the elf queen or Blackbird? Surely, Blackbird would have said something… except for all the times that she'd said nothing. If I asked her, she wouldn't give me a simple answer, and if it was Nyashoth, then she might have kept quiet for a reason such as Blackbird not approving.

I put away the blade and considered Blackbird. She stepped confidently over a large stone, a sign that her health had returned. Either Nyashoth had filled her up on painkillers or Blackbird had healed impossibly fast. Magic? A word that meant nothing and could be used to describe everything, ending all questions. Either way, I was grateful for the change. Why? Because I needed her, I told myself.

The ground became more uneven as we hiked, eventually leading us into a shallow valley that curved to the left. A landslide blocked our way, and we turned back, taking a new route over a low ridge until we hit a thicket of bushes with spines as long as my fingers. On the other side, we crossed to a narrow path more suitable for goats with cleats on their hooves, and eventually found a gentle upward slope.

The trees thinned as we went, and the dominant species shifted to a washed-out-teal colored spruce that exuded a musty odor whenever I brushed past. Blackbird stopped at a point no different from any other as far as I could tell. Were we lost? She harrumphed and angled to the right where a flat-topped hill dominated the skyline. I took a swig of water. My hardened feet were managing the never-ending walking with only mild agony. My legs had settled into an ache that went through muscle and bone alike. I cinched my belt one hole tighter, wondering if I'd be recognizable after another week of this. My hand went to my cheek where a thin scab had formed over the cut I'd received in my first real sword fight. What would I see when I next looked in the mirror?

"Oh, look," Gwen said as she kicked aside a seed pod the size of my fist. "A man primping over his scars. You're all the same."

"Primping? Hell, no. I'd rather not look like a Hollywood pirate."

That led into an explanation of movies, and our discussion continued as we took a slow spiral path that climbed up the hill. Gwen described shadow theater and the intricate tricks used to make the silhouettes come alive. I tried to explain CGI with little success, though she liked my attempts to act out explosions.

As we walked, the land brightened, and a sun rose—different to the one I'd seen before. This was smaller, dimmer, and an angry red. How could that work? A binary system? That might explain the short nights.

We reached a small plateau, and Blackbird stood at the edge, pointing into the distance. "Thrinidar, heart of the elvish folk on this world."

I'd been about to sit on a large rock, but I grumbled and walked over. The land smoothed and grassland spread, broken by dotted groves of trees, the result wholly unlike the sudden transition at the stream we'd first encountered. On the horizon, a dark patch of ground surrounded a green-gray smudge of rectangles. In the center, a hoop reached high into the sky, a monument of some kind. Thrinidar was big. Massive like New York, Tokyo, or London—not that I'd been to any of them.

Gwen toed the edge of the plateau, her gaze distant. Perhaps she was planning her route or wondering how many chumps walked the streets.

"It looks nice," I said lamely.

"Everything looks nice from a distance," Gwen responded.

Blackbird headed for the spot I'd planned on using to rest. From here, I could see it was worked stone, and there were more pieces. Another ruin? Remnants of a war?

I left Gwen to her thoughts.

"We'll rest here," Blackbird said to me.

That sounded good, but a restlessness kept me from joining her. As likely, I was evading the questions I needed to ask. I walked along the plateau, well away from the others, and drew my cutlass with the intention of cleaning the blade. The runes caught my eye, and I examined them. Were some similar to those on Blackbird's staff? Would that mean anything? Both crap and carp used the same letters.

With the cutlass in my hand, memories of the recent sword fights stirred, almost more in my body than in my mind. The terrifying rush as a sharp edge swung, as a tip plunged forward. If only I'd had a gun. A nice chunky pistol, a bullpup rifle for convenience, or a fucking cannon. I laughed at my stupidity. I'd probably shoot myself in the foot. At least I knew how to use a sword. Or I had once.

I closed my eyes and saw Nana demanding that I shift my feet, lower my hips, and keep my torso vertical. When I'd had to put down a longsword and start on rapier, the new stance had almost killed me. One hand out, back curled forward, back leg bent, holding much of my weight. She'd never stopped shouting, never stopped hitting me with her practice blades—over and over.

Tradition, Martin, tradition. Honor thy ancestors. Always be ready. Keep the faith. Learn the way. Darkness will always find you.

I squeezed the leather grip. Darkness had already found me by then, the old bitch. But she had taught me how to fight. Had she known what would happen? No, she couldn't have. She'd been mindlessly passing on the mangled family history, one that led back to Blackbird. I looked at the old woman and gritted my teeth. She'd been responsible for it.

No. I kicked a pebble off the plateau. At a certain point, people had to take responsibility for themselves. It had been all my Nana, substituting one form of abuse for another. But I would be an idiot to dismiss what she'd taught as tainted.

Moving the cutlass in a gentle sweep, I felt its balance and tested how it liked to rotate, how my hand fit on the grip. Saber was the closest blade I'd trained with. I worked through a few stretches, then controlled gathering steps before bringing the blade up and practicing the various cuts: the diagonals, two down, two up, and the opposing horizontal slashes. The strikes numbered one to six, forming a star at the base my imaginary opponent's neck. I worked them down toward the sternum, focusing on the flow of my swings, until my shoulder muscles fatigued. Wiping sweat from my brow, I transitioned into thrusts. The drill calmed me, gave me a sense of control that appealed no matter how illusory it was.

Gwen approached. "Look who's been holding back. Sword Master, are you willing to show me how to use these lumps of metal?"

She'd already killed with hers. How much more did she need to know? That reminded me of another Nana-ism. *It is easier to kill than not be killed.* Gwen was a survivor, no doubt about it, but she was in a new world and would have to make her way without anyone at her back. That should be reason enough to help. And the way she looked at me made it difficult to refuse. I doubted many could refuse her anything.

I started with the cuts, but her footwork and posture were terrible, so we went back to basics with footwork. She was a quick learner and fit, so I moved us on to a starting guard from outside of range. In the process of correcting her stance, we ended up close together. I tensed. She really was pretty. And smart. And the fact that she was dangerous didn't dampen my interest as it should have.

I stamped down on the thought and said, "Let's do a transition from a high parry to a cut. Rule two of sword club is don't die, so controlling your opponent's blade matters."

She raised an inquiring eyebrow. "What's rule one?"

"We don't talk about sword club."

"You are a very strange man, Martin."

"I get that a lot."

I demonstrated the combination, pommel high on the left, sharp edge up, the tip a little lower on the right, catching a high cut, letting the tip drop to circle around, then finishing with a cut. Essentially, using the opponent's momentum to fuel the return strike.

"Are you heading to the city?" I asked casually.

"Do you want to get rid of me?" she said, cutting close enough that I leaned back to be safe.

"No. I didn't mean that. You're valuable."

"Like a gem? Because I look pretty?"

"No—not that you aren't. I mean, you can handle yourself." I settled into the number two guard. "Start on the opposite side and try again."

"Handle myself? Where's the fun in that?" She went through the actions several times, then stopped. "I don't think Thrinidar is what I'm seeking."

"Oh," I said. "And what are you seeking?"

Sighing, she said, "I'll tell you when I'm sure. I thought—it doesn't matter. I haven't found it yet."

She walked a short distance away. I couldn't be sure what was eating at her. Perhaps it was the shock of losing her world. She hadn't spoken of friends. There must have been many, though. Perhaps family or lovers. And now her disconnection equaled or exceeded mine. If so, she was handling it better. I wanted to offer comfort, but she was no child to be soothed with vague words, and I had nothing to offer.

"If you two aren't going to rest," Blackbird complained loudly as she stood, "we may as well pass through the way."

Thankful for the interruption, I wiped my blade on my pants and said, "Do you need help?"

"Hardly."

Yeah, she was back to her old self. I watched as she gathered her energy. It wasn't obvious, but I could see it in the way she stood, legs a little apart, staff in two hands, and her distant expression. Her mind looked within. Then the runes on her staff lit, and the sphere flashed white before settling into a brilliant blue.

Another light tugged at my attention. I glanced at my unsheathed cutlass. The runes on the blade had the faintest green tinge, almost overwhelmed by the blue of Blackbird's staff. A forced twitched the blade, so weak that I could almost explain it away as my own action. Unsettled, I hurriedly slid the blade into the scabbard.

Blackbird cut open the way, creating the usual border of sparks—tinsel connected to a few thousand volts. Usual? I needed my head examined.

Gwen sauntered over, and Blackbird pointed her staff at the pair of us. "You've heard me speak of Tenekal, a god of vile thirst for power. We are ahead of him for now. That may change at any moment, so be alert, be ready for whatever must be done. Everything you have encountered so far is a child's game compared to what will pass. And watch your balance."

She entered the way.

Gwen gestured for me to go first. My back itched at the thought.

"You're coming?"

"I can hardly stay here when Blackbird makes it sound so exciting."

Good, I thought as I walked through the way, her decision was reassuring. But thinking that was reassuring, I decided, wasn't reassuring.

Sometimes my head can be the worst place of all to walk into.

CHAPTER 17

DEAD GODS

An icy wind scoured my cheeks, numbing the tip of my nose and drying my breath. All around, harrowing agate mountain peaks speared a golden sky, their crooked shapes built of swirling bands of red and dirty white. The tips were snow covered, and flat green growths like giant lichen colonized patches of rock here and there.

We'd come out on a small shelf beneath a tiny overhang. Snow draped the slopes beyond, dotted with broken black stumps. The howling of the wind covered any other noise, though I expected there wouldn't be much in an isolated location like this.

Oh, and I was absolutely freezing. Blackbird walked back and forth across the ledge, shoving her staff into the thin snow.

A sudden push from behind had me teetering on the brink of the ledge, my precarious position offering a long, cold drop followed by a brief career as a growing snowball—at least according to cartoons. Eyes bulging with fear, I waved my arms, trying to shift my center of balance. A hand grabbed my shirt and pulled me back. I spun around, furious.

Gwen stood there, smirking. She gave me a wink and said, "Remember what Blackbird said. We need to watch our balance. You should be aware of what's going on around you. I'll teach you how sometime."

The anger bled from me, released by disbelief. "Now I know why you were imprisoned."

"No, you don't," she said loud enough to beat the wind. "Not at all."

"Stop squealing like randy pigs and save your energy." Blackbird said as she cautiously stepped off the ledge and onto what must have been a path, though it all looked like a continuation of the mountain's slope. "We must pass through this world with haste."

Haste or not, I took a moment to fish the blanket out of my pack and wrap it around my shoulders. Gwen used a silver pin to close hers around her neck like a cloak. She scooped up a handful of snow, and I readied for her to throw it at me, but she merely let it slide off. I waited until she followed Blackbird before I, too, dared the hidden path. Gwen belonged in front of me, where I could keep an eye on her.

The route took us steadily down, reducing the wind's ferocity. I tried to use the others' footsteps to guide my own. It was a grueling, miserable task. Following each other meant we were essentially alone, and it was too hard to speak over the gusts that whistled past. I rubbed my fingers for warmth, occasionally daring to take one out and place it on an ear to defrost my flesh.

Blackbird paused at an obstruction. A small landslide had brought down rocks from uphill and left an enormous boulder in our way. Thick ice had collected on both it and what I assumed was surrounding rubble, making its dark surface slick and distorted.

We ascended the rubble cautiously. The slick surface cracked and popped underfoot, almost as if the stone beneath flexed. I gave up on holding the blanket and tied it around my waist so I could use both hands and feet to grip as needed. My fingertips tingled and burned. Near the top, Blackbird set off a mini avalanche of stones and ice that scraped like sandpaper, but were far more dangerous thanks to their mass.

Blackbird shoved her staff into the ground, anchoring herself. Gwen slid several feet as the material battered her legs. I offered a hand from the relative safety of my position, but she refused and leaned into the last of the debris.

"Easy," she said, "like climbing a sand dune."

I rubbed my hands. "I'd take some sand right now."

The avalanche hadn't just moved snow. We continued along the ice, finding large sections sheared off.

"What's that stink?" I asked next to one such spot.

I sniffed around, my cold nose discovering the source with ease. The ice had completely sheared away from a section of the boulder. I peered at the surface, wondering how it could smell so bad. The formation was strange—palm sized lumps that overlapped like scales—quite unlike anything I'd ever seen. Running a hand along it, I was surprised to find it warm. As well, the surface gave a little when I pressed with my weight.

"Blackbird, check this out."

"We don't have time for geology," she said, shaking off snow from a leg.

"I don't think this is geology."

Scowling, Blackbird made her way back to my position and kneeled down. She tutted and placed a hand as I had.

"A dragon, an elder one judging by the bulk of its body." She scanned our surrounds and pointed to a patch of yellow-gold uphill that I hadn't noticed. "That will be feathers from its wings."

If it was anything like the body of a western dragon, it would put a T-rex to shame. We were walking on a dragon. I wondered how large its teeth were. How sensitive was it? Would it notice us?

"This dragon," I asked, "is it hibernating?"

"No. The dragons of this world have the same wit as us and are long-lived. They would not stay in the winter by choice. The people who inhabit the lowlands worship them as gods." She stood and surveyed the mountains. "Dying here makes no sense, and the body remaining—impossible. They eat their own dead, and one of such age would never reside alone. I must ask myself whether this is the work of Tenekal. Is he here or does he close on us once more?"

"It couldn't be coincidence?" I asked.

"To die on the path I must take? I do not believe it. Evil is at play. It is only a matter of who and why. We have time to consider neither."

Gwen prodded the dragon scales. "I'm starting to think that elven city had promise."

"Do not look back. I cannot afford the time to reopen the way, and it matters not in the long term. Any nearby world will be torn asunder if I fail, and into the future, none would be safe."

I stared at the downed beast beneath my feet. It must have been immensely powerful. What could have killed it, the god Blackbird talked of? That was scary, but a fighter jet could easily do the same with a modern missile. The sea of lava bubbled in my thoughts. That, a fighter jet couldn't achieve.

This was the opening I needed. "What exactly are you trying to do? What can't fail? If there is actually some big, bad evil god wandering around, how are you going to stop it?"

Gwen stepped onto the exposed scales. "I have a proposal. Why don't we head as far away as—"

The scales sunk in a good inch. We all looked at them. Gwen kept her balance, unperturbed.

"As I was saying—"

A strange groan like an upset stomach emanated from the dead dragon. The scales shifted, then split around her boots. She dropped suddenly, accompanied by a slurp, and only stopped when waist deep. I put a hand to cover my nose, and my eyes watered. A trashcan out the back of a sausage factory in the middle of summer smelled better. Why hadn't the cold mercifully switched off my nose?

"Cursed offering, I'm stuck." Gwen's expression twisted in disgust, and she pushed against the sides of the hole, shimmying without progress. The dead flesh squished, squelched, and sloshed, holding her like a vacuum. "Give me a hand."

The grossness of it all sunk into me. I started laughing, perhaps in defense of my sanity.

"It is not funny."

I reached out a hand, careful to stay on the ice. "It kinda is."

Blackbird chuckled as well. "There's not many that can say they've been inside a dragon and come out alive."

Gwen took my hand, and I leaned back. She didn't budge, so I leaned further, working my exhausted thigh muscles. Inch by inch, she came free with the sound of a noodle being sucked up, accelerating at the last. We hit the ice with a loud *crack*. I moved away and wiped my hand, still laughing.

"You're right," she said. "It's funny. No hard feelings. Give me a hug."

Gwen lunged, and I leaped aside. She stepped on her blanket, and it came off, taking most of the dragon sludge with it. A mercy, as she caught me, and we rolled. The warmth of her body contrasted with the cold of the ground.

"All right," I said, as we risked tumbling down the entire mountain. "You win."

"That was never in doubt."

"If the two of you are done," Blackbird said. "We had best be careful where we step."

Shivering, Gwen and I worked our way along the dragon.

"Why isn't it frozen?" I asked Blackbird.

"Fire gland. I'd wager it hasn't been dead for more than a month. It'll take another to lose the last of its heat."

When we reached solid ground, I offered Gwen part of my blanket. The path was still narrow, so we huddled close, and I felt carefully before placing all my weight on my boots.

"Have you been skiing?" I asked.

Gwen tilted her head. "What's that?"

"You stick two planks of wood to your feet and slide down snow. You can go fast."

"That sounds insane. I've never even seen snow before."

"Do you have it on your world?"

"No. What's it made of?"

"Frozen water."

She laughed. "We have snow, you idiot. I know what it's made of. But I haven't seen it before."

I considered pushing her off the mountain, but said, "I was joking about skiing. It's not a thing."

Her eyes narrowed. "You're telling the truth?"

"Absolutely," I lied.

The path wended its way back and forth as we walked and talked, sometimes steep, sometimes barely present. I knew I should be afraid—of our precarious journey, of this evil god, of the very notion of traveling worlds—but I was too tired for it, too cold, too inured to the threat of ultimate doom. And with company, all that seemed further away.

Sporadic blackened tree trunks gave way to bright green pines with multiple trunks oozing a pink sap with a sweet scent. They reminded me of Venus flytraps. I passed them warily. As well, the air grew less bitter, and I gave up the blanket entirely. Blackbird powered on, keeping the lead. Nyashoth really knew what she was doing. Painkillers couldn't have kept Blackbird in motion for so long. Magic. Or advanced technology indistinguishable from it—made by elves who were running around a forest in wooden armor. Magic. Crazy.

There was light, but I never saw a sun, even as the sky darkened to a tarnished brass. We had nowhere to stop, forestalling any complaints, and on we hiked until we reached a point where several small ridges almost joined.

The remnants of more than one stone bridge lay all around, though I couldn't fathom why anyone would want to wander these mountains. Okay, it was beautiful and would make a great hiking spot in summer, but I stunk of dead dragon, and my extremities had hurt like hell since blood returned to them. My dislike was perfectly valid.

Blackbird surveyed the spot. "We'll stop here for the night. Make yourselves useful. Collect firewood."

Her tone grated on me, but even if she was fit, a wrinkled face like hers demanded first dibs on resting. I gave a mock salute, dumped my pack, and went searching for wood. It proved easy to find. Sticks lay beneath the trees, and I approached one slowly, instinct warning me that all was not well. When I found a particularly long stick, the kind a kid would pretend was a sword, I used it to poke an arm-thick branch of a tree right where it exuded pink sap. The branch curled in suddenly with a crash of foliage, the sap pulling on my stick which I let go with no regret. *I knew it.* If I'd been careful before, I was now doubly so.

Wood and hungry trees weren't the only things in the area. More stone had fallen farther from the bridges. Shapes took form, and I inspected several. Arms, legs, short and burly but human or humanoid. I ran a hand along one, noting the detail. Given the number, there must have been a whole museum's worth of statues. Unless they weren't statues: dead stone people, petrified corpses. After that thought, I gave them a wide berth.

Gwen started a fire with the first load I brought, and by the time I'd found enough larger pieces, she and Blackbird had set up a flat piece of metal to heat small parcels wrapped in leaves, and had water boiling in a small kettle. Who had brought all that? Was I meant to have put things into my pack? Gwen placed two sticks of what looked like curled cinnamon into the kettle, and a pleasant herbal scent mingled with the smoke.

I sat down, and Gwen handed me a small wooden cup with a carved pattern in the elvish style. I figured it was as likely stolen as given or traded, but I drank from it, nevertheless, and damn, the warm tea felt great as it cooked my esophagus. The heat spread to my limbs, softening my muscles.

"Here." Blackbird handed me one of the leaf parcels. She'd been holding a loose end, and I had to juggle the bulk, blowing repeatedly. While it cooled, I watched Blackbird eat one whole. I took a tentative bite. The leaves had little taste, but the inside was a mix of fruit, minced meat, and perhaps coconut sugar.

The mood in our little trio shifted. We ate and drank, and Gwen spoke of a time when two angry guards chased her down a dead-end street at night. When one slipped on the water from a barrel she'd pushed over, she'd snatched his pike, set it against a wall at an angle, and ran up it, leaping high enough to grip the top of the wall and climb over. Her impression of the guards' fury had me in stitches.

After we quietened, Blackbird poked the fire with a stick and said, "When I was much younger, I traveled many ways to a world with another kind of dragon. A mite larger than a horse, and nasty bastards they were, sharp of tooth and claw. I had found a tavern and was a dozen drinks into the evening when a particularly fine specimen of man walked in. Bronze skin, scarlet eyes."

"We got to talking, and he boasted of his brush with a swarm of dragons. I knew it was a lie, but I wanted to show off, to prove how much more impressive I was. Quick as lightning, I dragged him outside and into the forest, where I'd spotted a dragon's nest earlier by a stream—love the water, they did—and swore that I could ride one. I kept light on my feet, all hunched over, and used a patch of undergrowth to close on the beast."

"White of scale, blue of wing, and snoring like a saw. I tiptoed to its back, threw caution to the wind, and leaped upon it, laughing like a banshee. It growled and turned its spiteful eyes toward me. I had a smaller staff back then, perfect for whacking its nose. It reared, then kicked off, and we were up in the air."

"Oh, I thought I was so clever, right until I dropped the staff and had to cling on with all my might. The beast banked left and right, ducked and rose. It gave me one more look, and swept low and fast, back toward the tavern. It bucked and spun full upside down, dislodging me. I thought I was going to die as I plummeted."

"Down, down, I went, landing smack in the middle of a cesspit, wet to the brim from an earlier storm. I swear the bastard was making a point. Anyway, I climbed out, and the man had followed my flight, and we stood across from one another, me triumphant. He called me crazy, told me I stunk, called for his horse, and rode off. I learned a valuable lesson that day."

Gwen nodded. "Don't get on the back of a dragon."

I laughed.

"No, girl," Blackbird said. "It pays to be clean when you want to make an impression. I wouldn't have given up that ride for anything. Still, it was a shame I didn't get to ride the man."

This time, Gwen laughed. I joined in while blanking my thoughts against the mental image.

"If a little filth could halt him in his tracks," Gwen said. "He wasn't worth your time."

Blackbird put a hand where she had been shot. "Time. Worthless until you have little of it.

I didn't want to break the mood, but I sensed an opportunity.

"Since we have some time tonight, will you answer a question? What exactly is it you are trying to accomplish?"

Her eyes rested on me, glinting in the fire. I waited for her secrecy to burst into anger, but it didn't come.

"I am on my way to meet a goddess."

"You should have stayed on my world," Gwen said wistfully. "We have many, but the Blind Lady, goddess of luck—fickle, fearless, and the rudder of my heart. The things she would whisper to me."

"All the gods of your world are dead." Blackbird said, her voice stark.

The calm I'd enjoyed fled.

Gwen bristled. "You can't know that. If anyone would know, it would be me. A goddess of luck can't be captured, even by your Tenekal—I don't care how powerful and evil a god he is. It can't be done. None can fight her will."

"That's not how it works," Blackbird said, her shoulders sagging. "At least not for most of them. Put it aside. We gain nothing with this talk, and we are losing the rest we need."

No one spoke after that. With only one blanket between the two of us, Gwen and I kept close, but her mind was far away. Sleep came fast.

I walked a school hall full of gods sitting cross-legged on a wooden floor with the worn lines of a basketball court. Some wore togas, others armor, and one had a leather jacket. Some were fat, others painfully thin. There were animal parts and protrusions I couldn't name. Up I went, a camera zooming out. There was no ceiling, just a dark shadow that blotted out the stars. Great big hands reached down and scooped up the gods, one after another. The floor became a plate, and the remaining gods ran around, bumping into each other comically in their need to flee.

The menace switched to a fork, skewering the gods and lifting them out of sight. A delicate figure tumbled off the side of the plate into darkness, only visible thanks to a faint glow that pulled at me. The fork descended in that direction, accelerating as it went, the silver tines dripping a viscous golden fluid. I tried to call out a warning, but no sound came. She was in danger, though I could not say why or even articulate who she was. She needed me.

I woke with a start. The fire burned low, and Gwen was relaxed against me. We were fine. It didn't take long to slip back into sleep. But there was a tug on my heart, a pressure that bypassed the defenses I'd built up since early childhood.

"Don't worry," I mumbled. "I'm coming."

CHAPTER 18

HELLSCAPE

Our morning started with a climb over the crumbling remnants of a stone bridge. My back was stiff and sore from sleeping on the ground, but there was no room for pity or slowness when shards of stone cracked and fell with little notice. We all held hands and kept each other safe. Once we were across, I'd well and truly warmed up, and the pain had faded. We continued steadily downhill, and though the path remained narrow, there was no trace of snow, and the surface held firm.

Shortly after a switchback, I spied a cave not far ahead. As far as I could tell, it appeared natural, though it was suspiciously tall enough for a person to walk inside. Little tufts of grass sprouted from grooves in the stone at the opening, and I couldn't shake the feeling of a mouth.

Blackbird stopped us in front.

Gwen peered into the darkness and said without enthusiasm, "Inside there?"

I wholeheartedly agreed with her caution as I put a hand on the side and leaned in. My skin tingled unpleasantly. The morning light lapped at the rough stone within, hinting at color on the wall—perhaps faded paintings, but I wasn't keen to investigate.

"Martin, get back. That way is no longer… healthy." Blackbird said. Then, when she stamped her staff on the ground out front, she added, "Our way is here."

"How do you know where?" I asked, idly curious and very much relieved.

She narrowed her eyes. "Practice sharpens innate talent. Experience heeded develops skill. And as with any woman, man, or other who travels, my path is founded on the efforts of those who have gone before and survived to tell the tale. The tradition of wayfarers goes back to the beginning of time, or near enough."

Raising her staff, she fed power into its runes and cut open a way. As well as the usual sparks, there were colors at the edge of my vision, ones I couldn't name. Did the opening of ways leak radiation?

That thought had me hastily following Blackbird and Gwen, and we stepped through into a new world. If what we found could be described as such.

I felt a sense of dislocation, of shifting balance, and a heaviness that pushed at me from all sides. The ground beneath our boots was smooth white glass, the sort you'd see on a kitchen backsplash, except it was clean—completely unmarked—and it extended in all directions along a single plane. Not a hill, a slope, a valley, a tree, an animal, a leaf. A swirling gray filled the sky, amorphous and sunless. There were no shadows, either, and I could only guess that the light came from both the sky and the ground, or perhaps from every molecule of air.

A default universe. That was how it felt. I imagined a game designer loading a framework, but called away before adding valleys and mountains, grass, cities, armies. I breathed in and smelled nothing. The air was warm and stale.

Gwen, kneeling and running her hand along the glass, said, "It would be easy to get lost here. Should we drop a marker? Perhaps this could be chipped?"

"Quiet, girl," Blackbird said, her eyes closed. She held the staff extended in her right arm, and had the other out to the side, the fingers gently trembling. "Yes, this way."

The endless expanse swallowed the dull thuds of our footsteps. It says something about our recent experiences that the long view brought me some consolation—we were unlikely to be ambushed. Strangest of all was the sensation that we were moving, heading toward a destination. Our passage left no signs of progress, and no markers meant no proof of advancing. Yet, a static in the air grew denser. I was about to mention it, when Blackbird called a halt.

Once more, she cut a way, and we stepped into another world.

My eyes soaked in the rich detail. Our boots sank into coarse black sand littered with great curving shell fragments, iridescent under a lavender sky with a pale blue sun. Above the shore, tangled brambles with arm-long spines formed a barricade as unpassable as any wall. The broad, thick leaves rustled as wooly spherical bees landed or took off inland. The gently lapping water had a pink tinge and a salty odor. I'd have had to be much thirstier to try it.

Blackbird set off down the coastline, and we followed. The sand ground underneath, stealing energy from each step and ensuring we were announcing our presence to anyone wandering by.

Ahead, I noted an artificial hill on the shore, all a gloss green that I assumed was part of a modern beachside resort. At least until large flippers emerged to propel it forward, throwing sand far into the air and producing a racket like steel being scraped along concrete. Each time a flipper hammered the ground, small shockwaves went up my legs. It raised its head, revealing a long neck and a beaked head large enough to swallow a van.

"I bet it would make a tasty stew," Gwen said while releasing a steady stream of dry sand from her hand.

I raised an eyebrow. "You know, I wouldn't tell it that if I were you."

She laughed. "A fair warning. Besides, imagine finding a pot large enough to fit it."

"And you'd need a forest of spices," I added.

There was a majesty in the way the turtle swam when the sea deepened, each flipper propelling it with great speed. It must be the apex predator of this world, unafraid of anything it encountered. That would be nice. The sun glistened off its wet shell. Why would it need a shell? Defense from its own kind, or was some larger predator swimming in the pink sea, a creature that even an ancient Earth megalodon would fear?

Add no swimming to the no drinking.

I grew more unsettled as we continued. This place wasn't for us. It didn't welcome us, and I had no doubt there were no humans or human analogues. There was more, too—an unpleasantness that scraped along my mind, warning me that we should turn back. The air tasted wrong, and yet it had no taste. I breathed and wished for more oxygen.

"Boy, listen."

Shaking my head, I turned to Blackbird, who had stopped a short way back. She'd been talking, but I'd taken none of it in.

She tutted without humor. "I said you need to be careful. The next place is not one I would tread under any other circumstance. Once was more than enough for a dozen lifetimes, and to bring the pair of you—I doubt my judgment altogether. But what must be must be, and all we can do is stretch the boundaries of what may come to pass."

This darkly philosophical Blackbird disturbed me. Before I could ask what we'd be walking into, she continued.

"It will be absolute darkness without reprieve. We must hold on to each other at all times. To let go is to die, and you will pray that happens quickly."

Gwen grabbed Blackbird's cloak and held out her hand to me. "Let me know if I squeeze too tightly."

I took it, hoping she had no plans of letting go. Her skin was warm and dry, her grip firm. "Lead on, milady."

Blackbird sent up a shower of sparks, opening the way, and letting in an unseen aura of oily cruelty. She wasted no time, and Gwen followed, pulling me through.

There were no sparks on this side of the way. There was nothing at all, I thought at first, no hint of shadow, no stars, no lamp, no glow of Blackbird's staff, nothing. Cool, clammy air filled my lungs, and I wished I'd held my breath.

A crunch ahead announced Blackbird's position, more followed, and then Gwen pulled me along like a child in a first-grade class. And boy, was I grateful for it. Each step had an odd descent, as if gravity were a shade less, and the lumpy pile we traversed shifted unpredictably. Her hand was a lifeline, telling me that I wasn't utterly alone and helpless.

The grinding of our passage hid other sounds at first. I didn't know if they were growing louder or my ears were adjusting, but I noticed what at first sounded like whispers, and with little else to do, I dissected the mélange, identifying wails, shrieks, and gibbering that scraped along my nerves like fork tines across a plate. Damn it. Surely, Blackbird could spare a little energy to make some light?

I stepped on a long, thin object that rolled under my weight, sending my legs in different directions. Letting go of Gwen, I extended my arms, trying to find my balance, but only succeeding in having them as far away as possible when I hit the ground. Except it wasn't ground. Lumps, sharp spikes, odd holes. Bones, my fingers told me. The rough texture, the curves, the dry dusty scent similar to rock. Seeing might be believing, but a few million years evolving around constant danger did wonders for touch.

So many bones. I swallowed, panic seeping into my limbs, searching for my rapidly-beating heart.

I slid to my right, grabbing desperately but finding no solid purchase. I was moving too fast. Bones clattered and snapped as I sailed over them. Swearing over and over like it was a mantra, the remaining rational clump of brain cells left to me decided I had to change tactics. Fast.

Heaving myself up, I then threw my hands down under my weight, and dug them deep, like I'd seen Blackbird do with her staff. My legs continued sliding down and out into thin air, even as my arms anchored my upper body. I cried out, waiting for my momentum to pull me down and over. Bones rattled by, but I never heard them hit the bottom of wherever we were, and that scared the crap out of me.

"Martin?" Blackbird shouted. "Stupid boy. Gwen, find him quickly."

She didn't need to let go. I'd done it. Now, if she wanted to do me harm, she could push me right off, and Blackbird would be none the wiser. A perfect solution if she wanted to be Blackbird's only traveling companion. What if she wanted to steal Blackbird's abilities? These thoughts burrowed into me. They were my own, but fed by fear and helplessness.

I stretched my head above the surface. "I'm here!"

Another wave of bones spilled past, and I slipped further over the edge. The gibbering was louder now. Would I fall endlessly, tormented souls shouting in my ears? I'd been stupid. I'd grown complacent, trusting in Blackbird and relaxing around Gwen. As a kid, I'd learned to rely solely on myself. Neglect and betrayal were two sides of a coin.

Bones swept by, as strong as a river current. This was it. My heart thudded, and I couldn't tell if sweat or tears ran down my cheeks.

A hand gripped my arm, and I shouted, trying to pull away.

"Martin, it's me," Gwen said. "Stop fighting."

"Gwen?"

"No, it's the Spring Nymph. Now stop trying to get away."

"I'm not. Not anymore. My legs are over a ledge."

"Well, don't let go this time. Try to get a leg over when I pull."

I ignored the double entendre and twisted awkwardly, straining to get my left leg up over the lip and hold it there as the bones shifted. Another hand gripped me, and Gwen dragged me off the ledge. I stood shakily, holding her tight, feeling her breath. It was as if I were holding life itself. And it was more. I'd been unfair. Whatever she'd done, I'd been wrong to doubt her, and this proved it. I didn't want to tell her, but I wanted her to know that I respected her, that she impressed me, that she was clever, and brave, and… I leaned in close.

"Hurry," Blackbird said from nearby. "They're close."

Gwen found my hand and drew me uphill, breaking the moment.

"What's close?" I demanded as we regained level ground.

"Do you want to find out?" Blackbird said coolly.

I glared in her general direction. No, I didn't want to know. I imagined demons capering, tortured souls screaming as they were flayed alive, and then wailing as their flesh was ripped from their bones, their mewling only stopping when their lungs were devoured. Pure despair—the place oozed it.

Our hurried walk became a reckless jog, which turned into a deranged sprint as the cacophony erupted all around. And the darkness, it never gave up, transporting me back into a locked wardrobe, my father hitting the wood with a thick plastic tennis racket.

You've been a bad boy, Marty. You need to learn, kid. Do as you're fucking told, you sniveling little shit. You're worthless.

Blackbird clattered to a halt, and we bumped into her one after the other. This was the way out. I could feel it. A tightness in the air, but not as toxic as where we stood. It was better. It had to be. Now that we'd stopped, the sounds of tumbling bones couldn't be our own. They were close, an underlying rhythm to the song of hell. Infused in the despair, as with the wraiths of that first world, was a predatory hunger, and we were doe-eyed prey.

My free hand went to my cutlass. Drawing it would fill me with confidence, but left-handed, I'd as likely hit Gwen as whatever was coming. Instead, I huddled near, my hand slipping around her torso, a toddler holding a teddy bear before they learn there's nothing that can protect them.

She rubbed the back of my hand with her thumb and moved forward, the crunch of her footsteps drowned by the unseen horde. They were on us—I was sure of it—mere seconds away.

I stumbled, my innards freezing, and then my eyes burned as if they'd been burst by hot pokers. Unable to help myself, I let go of Gwen and covered them against the onslaught. I wanted to face our hidden tormenters, meet their gazes, but I couldn't force my eyelids open.

For the second time in minutes, I was on the precipice of death, and there was nothing I could do.

CHAPTER 19

HERE, KITTY

The shattering of skulls morphed into the crackle of a closing way, and this faded to nothing. Exhausted and strung out, I sat down, unable to comprehend what had occurred.

Gwen kneeled by my side—I could smell the faint whiff of expired dragon—and we found each other's hands.

"Let your eyes adjust," Blackbird said. "It won't take long."

"I should have brought some Ray-Bans," I said weakly.

Blackbird was right. It took a minute or two, but my pupils remembered how to shrink. I let go of Gwen so I could peek through gaps between my fingers. She looked as shaken as I felt.

"Thanks for saving me," I said. "I owe you one."

"One?" she said, her voice soft. "Martin, my dear, I'm keeping a tally."

I forced a laugh, and I think it did me good.

"Where were we?" I wondered. "Hell?"

Blackbird sniffed. "Nothing so civilized."

After letting out a settling breath, I stood and offered Gwen a hand. She didn't need it, I was sure, but she accepted the help.

Golden grass covered rolling hills that surrounded us in all directions. Scattered trees with bulbous trunks pocked their sides, foliage spreading out from their tops like mushrooms. The sky was a familiar, reassuring blue, and thin clouds dotted it artistically. Bucolic, I remembered from a spelling test I'd given an advanced class. All it needed was a farmstead and a few cows. Preferably ones of normal size, with four legs, no wings, and without a taste for meat.

"Ready?" Blackbird left a small rocky outcropping and started down a hill. We soon passed one of the trees. The broad trunk had light gray bark. Thick vertical lines had been cut through this, and green sap had oozed down its side before drying. They were too large and too deep to be from a bear and were parallel their entire length. I wondered if it were a tribal marking, or a field boundary or some such.

Once down the hill, we headed up a larger one with no more trouble than the occasional small burrow that could catch a toe or heel. We paused at the summit near a stone-sided well to eat spherical nuts that Gwen offered. They were salty and a little bitter. I used a winch and tested the water, finding it clean enough to refill our bottles.

A winding river headed to what I decided was north, and along its near bank, a stone-walled town stood, whitewashed buildings reaching at least a couple of stories high with shallow-sloped thatched roofs capping them. They were pretty and inviting. I considered the likely technological level of their builders. I'd seen thatching in photos of England, but I wasn't holding out hope for vibrating chairs and big-screen TVs.

"That is where we'll go," Blackbird said. "And we'll get there faster if we leave now."

Gwen quickly closed her pack. "I hope they have some soap. If I don't get the dragon guts off me soon, I'll stink forever."

"You have my full support," I said, then added, "No offense meant."

She smirked. "None taken, my sweaty companion. You are hardly all flowers and honey."

Yet more walking. People burned their work leave and paid good money to travel to isolated locations to hike. You could sell some people on anything, I decided when I paused to extricate a rock from my left boot.

I shared this wisdom with Gwen.

She chuckled. "You can sell *any* man on anything if you decorate it with the right bow."

"Just men?"

She sighed dramatically. "Sadly not."

We encountered a patch of crushed grass shortly after we left the hill for plains that continued to the river. We should have gone around, but Blackbird liked her direct routes, and so we stumbled onto several dead bodies.

Curiosity beat my caution, and I crossed the short distance to look closer. My mouth dried. Small bodies. Children? I forced myself to consider the details. No. Relief flooded me, though it was unfair to these poor bastards.

They were men and women, but no taller than my chest. I leaned down to inspect one. She wore armor, but it had the texture of fabric under resin, a medieval version of fiberglass. I suspected the armor was formed from multiple layers laminated together. The victims all wore skullcaps of the same substance but painted in stripes of blue and white rather than the beige of the body armor.

None of it had proved good enough. Huge rents in the armor were brown with dried blood, and several of the thirteen bodies were missing arms or legs. Their faces were frozen in masks of pain, displaying pronounced canines in the upper and lower jaws.

"Poor bastards," I said. "Were they locals?"

Blackbird examined one of the dead. "Most likely. There was a small settlement when I last came through."

I looked toward the town. "And no one's come to bury them or burn their bodies."

"Or loot them," Gwen pointed out.

"Or loot them," Blackbird agreed. "It changes nothing. We must go on."

It sure as hell changed my outlook. This place was less bucolic and more bubonic. Blackbird continued, unfazed. We passed through fields of different crops, none of which were familiar. They were also untended to the last.

The town wall dominated as we approached. Several sections of the top had crumbled, the fallen remains on the outside. Chariots littered a road leading to a pair of tall gates, but there were no horses or bodies.

Reeds covered the riverbank. Downstream, in a clearer patch, I spotted a cat slinking out of the water. It resembled a British shorthair—gray, of stocky build, and fuzzy once it shook its body dry. The cute little guy took a moment to wipe its head with a paw, crushing reeds beneath its chonky ass. I struggled to process the movement with the size of the reeds, and its distance from us.

My blood chilled.

"Big cat," I managed, pointing. "Like elephant big, bigger."

Cats were cute. Tigers were cute but dangerous. A giant cat? I thought of the shredded and dismembered locals.

"What's a cat?" asked Gwen, her voice wary.

I screwed up my face as I dredged up an explanation for someone with no reference. "Four legs, furry, bad attitude, sharp teeth, and sharper claws. They think they own the place, and we keep them as pets on my world."

She gave me a look. "Why?"

"I guess they're cuter when they can't disembowel you for fun and profit."

"Enough talk." Blackbird gestured to the gates. "Walk slowly and steadily. We'll use whatever cover we can and work our way inside. With any luck, it won't see us."

Not being seen was a specialty of mine. I knew how to avoid sudden actions, how to let my body slouch, and how to avoid litter on a street. We just had to get to the chariots, and we'd be fine. Damn, that sounded hollow.

We crossed over a small stream, ducked behind a thicket, then crawled along a roadside ditch. The nearest cover was a large cart thirty yards down the road.

"On a count of three?" I suggested.

They agreed, and on three, we hurried behind the cart. Dried blood spattered its side. Next, we darted toward a chariot and squeezed behind it.

A growl thundered. I check over top of the chariot. It really wasn't big enough to hide us all. The cat watched us with enormous bright amber eyes.

"It's seen us."

"That was inevitable."

Gwen stood. "We run?"

"Yes," Blackbird said. "We don't have far to go."

So we ran, covering ground much faster now we'd given up on hiding. I checked over my shoulder, bracing for the vision of it bounding toward us. That was not to be. It unfurled two enormous furry wings and kicked off the ground, rising into the air with heavy beats, then quickly shifting into a glide.

"It can fly," I shouted. "I repeat, the damn cat can fly."

I mustered my remaining energy and sprinted to the gates. Gwen was through first, and I followed Blackbird inside, expecting a thud as the cat smashed the thick wood. The fuzzy monster was too clever—a shadow flitted overhead as we hurried down a cobblestone street.

"We can't stay in the open," Gwen said.

"This way!" Blackbird dodged to the right and through a door.

I was the last inside, hunching to clear the low height. A loud scrabble accompanied a thud as the shock of the cat's landing passed through the ground. At least it couldn't fit through the door.

It was a cat.

I leaped away as an enormous paw reached inside, claws slashing like swords. Remembering I had one of my own, I drew my cutlass. It looked tiny against the red-marbled scythes sweeping toward us.

But it couldn't see. I tried a stab after its paw whooshed by, but the thick fur caught my blow. The paw swung back, knocking me against a wall and winding me. Anger flared in my aching skull. I'd taken a lot of shit from people over my life, but a damn cat?

Gwen dragged me through an internal doorway. I started to protest, but the paw retreated a little and started ripping stones from the front doorway.

We had entered a room filled with boxes of dyed yarn, and for a moment, I had a crazy idea to distract it with a toy. I thought of Blackbird's staff. That was like a laser pointer. And then sanity caught up with me.

"Blackbird, can't you do something about it? Fry it, soak it in a few million gallons of water? I'll settle for exploding it or whatever you did to those wolves."

"If I do now, then I won't be able to later."

She hurried out a door in the back, and we followed her into an alley. The front of the building collapsed, stone smashing against stone, throwing up dust and a rain of loose thatching.

"If you don't, there won't be a later."

"Quit whining. This way." She cut back toward the main road.

The cat landed on either side of the roofs above the alley and glared at us with its wild eyes, giving me immediate sympathy for every consumed mouse throughout history.

We reached the road, and the cat leaped down. With no time to discuss, we all ran in completely different directions. I reached a small street, puffing, and checked on the cat. It danced around Gwen, then swiped with sheathed claws, sending her rolling across the road like a skittle. Blackbird made it to a workshop with various tools hanging from a bar and disappeared inside.

The cat advanced on Gwen. Fuck that, I thought.

"Hey, pussy, wanna play?" I tossed a clay bottle that had been lying on the ground.

It didn't reach the cat, but it smashed loudly, drawing the furry beast's attention. The cat twisted sinuously, bringing its massive head around, and bared its copper teeth that dripped gobs of saliva. Those damn teeth were hideously long and more thickly packed than any Earth feline. It growled, loud enough to put any tiger to shame, the shock going right to my chest like the bass from a nightclub.

My plan worked. Gwen was forgotten. I, on the other hand, was now at the top of the menu. It leaped toward me. I jumped behind several barrels, and the cat knocked them away with a single swipe of its paw. That had been stupid. I ran, jumped up onto a cart, then over a fence. The cat roared and pursued.

I'd entered the forecourt of what I guessed was a warehouse. Several wagons lay in various states of destruction, most on their sides. Not wanting to share their fate, I ran into the warehouse. Huge tubs of water dominated the space, but dozens of sheets hung from lines that traced back and forth. A laundry. I picked up a small bucket with curls of white and smelled. Yep, soap. What a find. We could be clean. A shame there wasn't the time.

The wooden building shook, and dust dropped from the roof.

The cat smashed a wall with its paw, splintering the wood. It held for another two blows, then a section gave way.

I looked at the tubs, wondering if I could hide. Cats don't like water. Then I remembered seeing it leave the river. Nope, water wouldn't save me. I ran for the sheets.

The cat pushed against the hole, snapping timbers, ducking to keep its head free of the rafters as it struggled in. It was through before I'd reached the far side. My back itched as I imagined its claws dicing my ribcage. Eager to show me exactly how it felt, the cat advanced, pushing through the sheets, shaking its head with annoyance as it went.

I reached the far wall. Stacked barrels lined it, a few on the ground open and filled with soap. This was a dead end. Very dead. I had seconds before the giant cat cleared the sheets. I stared at a barrel. Could I hide in one? No time, and I was screwed if it didn't work. I glared at the wall. There were no windows to escape through. I spun, finding nothing new.

Why was everything constantly trying to kill me? I shoved a barrel over in frustration.

The barrels. That was all I had. I shoved another over, giving in to pointless anger, and it rolled. Damn. That gave me an idea.

I angled the barrel off to the left and kicked it into motion, doing so again to build its speed. Soap poured out one end, in a line heading back to me, but I didn't stay still, instead, tiptoeing to the right and passing between the sheets. If the cat realized what I was up to, I'd have no chance.

Sheets tore, rope stretched. The cat was after the barrel. Relief washed over me, but there was no time to admire my handiwork. I flailed at the edges of sheets, pushing past rows and rows, giddy with fear-laden excitement, until I glanced down one and saw the cat's head. I froze. The cat's ears twitched, and it looked my way, great eyes widening as its pupils locked on me. Farther away, the tip of a tail twitched above the sheets.

"Bad kitty!"

Sprinting, I charged through the last of the sheets. The cat tried to push through, tangling itself as I reached the entrance I'd started at. Not stopping, I curved through the yard and went right, followed by the sounds of ripping sheets and crashing wood.

"Blackbird! Gwen!"

Debris littered the street I ran along, and I wondered how similar this was to the lava. A force that couldn't be reckoned with, passing through and consuming all in its wake.

"Blackbird! Gwen!"

"I'm here," Gwen called.

It took a zigzag route and a few more shouts before I found her. She was still on the main street, sitting on the ground with her back against a wall. A slight grimace told me she wasn't there by choice.

"Are you okay?" I asked despite the obvious answer.

Her eyes were red-rimmed and glassy. "No, I'm not. The Blind Lady. She's gone. Blackbird was right. I don't know how it can be, but she's dead."

I scowled. "Blackbird doesn't know everything."

"I know it is true. I felt it. When I needed her, there was nothing. For the first time in my life, she was gone."

Crouching, I put a hand on her shoulder. I'd always known I was alone. That certainty made my life steadier. For Gwen to find herself with this ugly truth—it must be hard.

As hard as it was, we couldn't stay.

"Blackbird!"

Nothing. Well, at least Gwen and I were alone together. We needed to be somewhere else together, and fast.

"I hate to say this. You're going to have to stand."

She let me help her up, wincing and grunting, and I encouraged her into a limping walk. We didn't get far before the cat climbed over several buildings and managed a leaping glide that brought it right in front of us.

We squared off with the cat, cutlasses drawn, a surreal version of a western standoff.

"Run," Gwen said dully. "I'll buy you a few more breaths."

"And let you steal all the glory?" I said with much more enthusiasm than I felt.

The cat stalked toward us, unhurried, and perhaps a little cautious. It rose on its hind legs and raised a paw. I glanced up and wondered if I stuck my cutlass high, would it pull back in pain before it had driven me six feet into the ground.

A whip crack sounded, and the cat growled with fury, batting at the air.

"This way," Blackbird called from a doorway of what I guessed to be a café or tavern.

I helped Gwen inside as Blackbird raised her staff, and another sharp crack infuriated the cat. There were many wooden tables inside with benches or simple chairs. A large hearth held nothing but ashes. Wooden cups and clay bottles lay everywhere. Blackbird chivvied us behind a long bar and had me push over a stand holding more bottles. Booze and ceramic shards went everywhere in a great crash loud enough to hurt my ears.

A trapdoor lay where it had stood. I yanked it open, and accepted a lamp that Blackbird retrieved from behind the bar.

A ladder descended into a plain, cold room filled with barrels and several bodies with no clear injuries. Had they starved to death or drunk themselves into oblivion? I put the lamp aside and helped Gwen down the stairs with Blackbird following.

Crashes confirmed the cat hadn't given up. Wood groaned and shattered, and heavy paws pressed on the ceiling above us. A huge eye glared through the trapdoor. Why hadn't I thought to shut it?

"Blackbird. Time to do your thing."

"Boy, don't you hurry me."

"Simba the murder kitty is doing the hurrying."

Blackbird rolled her head from side to side, pressed her lips together, and opened the way. My cutlass again glowed with some kind of resonance. After she was done, she leaned on her staff, head bowed.

The way wasn't the same as the lightless hell, but I didn't like the way's feel. No good would be on the other side, I was sure, though I couldn't say why. The cat tried to shove its paw down the narrow trapdoor, but it wouldn't fit.

"Bad kitty," told it. "Go the hell away. You're not eating us."

I sheathed my weapon and helped Gwen to the way. Blackbird hadn't entered yet, so we stood there, all three of us, alone with our thoughts.

Alone together. Perhaps that was enough to survive Blackbird's quest. I put my hand to the pouch that held the stone I'd been given by an elven ex-queen. When we were done, I'd ask Gwen if she wanted to see Earth. She'd like it. So many opportunities for chaos. Yeah, that was something to look forward to. And I'd get us there, whether or not Blackbird was willing to help.

"Let's go," I said, and we all walked through.

CHAPTER 20

FOUR AND TWENTY

Stone monuments encircled us, each made from two enormous pieces driven into the ground with another giant resting across the top to form a lintel, the result bearing a striking resemblance to Stonehenge, or what it would have been like before a thousand or more years of erosion. On the near faces, runes blazed, each on a scale far larger than Blackbird's staff or my cutlass. Their blue-tinted light cut out beyond the border of the circle, giving way to a dark sky with only three visible stars. Power sloshed between the stones, raising the hair on my arms like static electricity. To what purpose? It didn't matter, as long as it wasn't directed at me.

The stones were set within a depression, beyond which came the roar of a crowd as if I were standing outside a concert gone wrong, angry fans rioting, or an entire city. Bass booms rocked the ground, and flashes of light strobed the darkness.

While Blackbird walked a circuit, examining the runes, I checked on Gwen.

"What's the damage?"

"Very little to mention. My head rattles, bruises bloom like spring, and my ankle complains like an aged man by a cooking fire."

She spoke without her usual inner fire, worrying me, but I sensed that she didn't want to be pressed, so I offered my shoulder and helped her walk to Blackbird who had crossed out of the henge and was making her way slowly up the rise. Blackbird stood statue-still as we caught up.

"Oh, shit," I said.

Ahead waited a scene that would make Weta Workshop cry. A terrible battle roiled before us, combatants massed without end. In the distance, I spotted trebuchets tossing balls of fire, and closer, ballistae on wagons loosing barbed darts of silver. Teeming around them were knights on horseback, archers, pikemen, unarmored warriors wielding spears and shields. They clashed with monstrous creatures: writhing masses of teethed worms, two-headed dogs that breathed fire, giant lizards with small mouths sprouting across their backs, chicken-legged giants, twice as tall as any human, with six arms, each wielding a stone sword. And worse. There were creatures of such hideous appearance that I couldn't even compare them to anything I knew. But I could feel their wrongness. It beat at me, angry waves crashing on a seawall.

In the middle of this great conflict, shone a golden star. I narrowed my eyes. Was this the figure of my dreams? No. My eyes adjusted, revealing a knight in golden armor astride a similarly protected horse. The fighter spun his mount and charged, lance forward into a tentacled mass, retreated, then brought the horse around again, drawing a long straight sword.

"The king of Arallion," said Blackbird. "He commanded well more than a million a few years ago. Before us is less than half that. A mighty force, but no longer an overwhelming one."

Half a million, all fighting in one spot and the same if not more on the other side. The scale filled me with horror.

"They're losing, right?" I asked, my voice choking up.

"Yes. He has no chance when the very nature of his world is being corrupted. Yet he stands and fights."

Gwen tensed at my side. "It is you. You are the harbinger of death. Even gods die as you march. I should have taken the airship by myself and flown to the edge. At lease I'd still have my luck."

Blackbird glared, her fingers pale and tight around her staff. "No, you wouldn't. I told you. Whatever boon your worship offered is ash. Your god has been consumed by Tenekal—and no action of yours could have stopped that. You don't matter."

Gwen pushed away from me, snarling. "But you do?"

"Right now," Blackbird said, a bitter anger in her voice. "I may be the only one who does."

What chilled me was the lack of arrogance in her tone. That, and before she turned away, I could have sworn I saw the glint of a tear. And, as bad, the tension between them. We'd been through a lot together. We had become a team, if not a willing one. These were the only two people I… I had a connection to. I couldn't let us pull apart, so I changed the topic.

"Do we have to cross the battlefield?" Trepidation filled my voice. It would be pure suicide.

"No," Blackbird said sharply, but her voice softened after. "We'll skirt behind the lines. These poor souls buy us time even though they don't know it. He was a good king, as they go."

Having dismissed the king and half a million others, she angled to the left of the battle. I offered Gwen my shoulder again, but she refused the help and limped after Blackbird. I kept pace, wanting to offer solutions, a starkly stupid desire when I didn't understand the problem.

We drew closer to the fighting and had to wind our way between the corpses of humans and *things*, our boots picking up coatings of mud and blood and worse. The stench curdled my stomach, and I wondered how long the battle had raged. How long could the strength of humanity stand up against this onslaught?

The ground rose sharply, and we turned onto a hard-packed dirt road, a much easier surface to walk, and, I feared while staring at the nearby chaos, a much easier position to be seen. At least we couldn't be heard. That would be bad, very bad. A mail-clad fighter swung a mace, bludgeoning the skull of a bipedal rat with scales. Seconds later, he was wrapped by pallid worms that bit into his neck, spraying blood. My hand went to my cutlass. It was a stupid gesture. What could I do? I walked on, the hollowness of my convictions on display for all.

A short while later, we encountered an open-topped wagon with spoked wheels, and a horse. The animal lifted its head from the grass at the edge of the road and shifted restlessly. Its eyes were blinkered, no doubt the only reason why it hadn't fled along with its owner.

"Here's some luck," I said. "Gwen, you need to rest your ankle, and we could all use a break."

"Don't tell me what I need," Gwen snapped.

Blackbird approached the horse. It was tall, with a broad body and high shoulders. When she touched its flank, the horse skittered to the side, but the tack held it to the wagon, and she whispered to it until the animal calmed.

"Get on," she said.

I positioned myself to help Gwen, but she pulled herself up. At the top, she looked at me as if about to say something but moved out of sight. As I climbed after her, Blackbird settled on the raised seat at the front, urging the horse forward without delay.

Wide clay bottles with narrow necks, each around half a gallon in capacity, sat on the bed of the wagon, toward the rear. As well, lumpy hessian bags filled the front. Gwen lay across several, staring up. I selected a spot on a thin bench along one side and searched one of the sacks. It held rich brown ovular loaves of bread, hard enough to produce an audible thump when I tested one against the wagon.

Wax covered the bottles' corks. I scraped enough clear of one to pull out a cork and take a sniff. The fumes immediately cleared my sinuses and claimed the lives of innocent brain cells. I sneezed and shook my head to dispel the burning sensation. If paint stripper and licorice had a love child, this would have been it.

Gwen wriggled into a sitting position and reached out. Surprised, I handed her the bottle without a warning. She briefly placed her hands on mine—the gesture catching me off guard— then took the bottle, and rather than smelling it, she put it to her lips and gulped a mouthful, followed by another. When she handed it back, her eyes were watering.

I forced myself to watch the battle and took a swig. My throat burned, and I wheezed as the syrupy liquid clawed its way down my throat and nested in my stomach. Blackbird glanced back, and I passed her the firewater. I think we were all mourning, though I wasn't sure what I'd lost that I hadn't lost before. To keep myself busy, I tore apart a loaf and handed pieces around. It had a nutty taste and needed much chewing. The bottle made its way around, a silent offering.

I rested my eyes and thought of Earth, of all those places where people far less fortunate than me faced starvation, disease, and the tyranny of thugs. How much of their fate had come from the invasion of other peoples. No one was innocent, but damn, we tried our hardest to make everything worse.

There was beauty, too. I remembered the Kallen Valley waterfall, nestled in a ravine near where I'd studied. The mist over mountains burned away by a familiar sun. The star-filled sky while driving down a lonely highway at night. The craziness of city sidewalks at rush hour.

My hand slipped down to the pouch on my belt, and I took the stone out. In the dim light, the polished yellow surface was a murky brown. I ran my fingers along the runes, wishing the translation ability Blackbird had given me would work on these stubbornly obtuse characters.

What if I could get it working? Gwen could receive medical attention, and Blackbird would be free of us. If only Nyashoth had explained how to use it. My brow creased. What if she didn't need to? Blackbird had used me to channel energy—magic—into her staff.

Magic. I shook my head. No point pretending. It was magic or a fundamental particle or a different force. Yes, there was a reason why I wasn't teaching high school physics.

That was a distraction. I stared at the stone. It hadn't worked the last time I'd tried, but that had been nothing more than a moment's test. With nothing else to do, I had time to really give it a shot. Nyashoth wouldn't have given it to me if she didn't believe I could use it.

I took my third mouthful of firewater and relaxed, trying to go deep within myself. I imagined a pipe and tried to push magic through it and into the stone. Nothing happened. Maybe it needed to be more specific to Earth. I formed impressions of coffee, of my first apartment, taking a left turn as I remembered the empty cupboards, getting evicted, living in a derelict car by a creek until a local scheme to clean the waterways hauled it away.

Things had gotten better, I promised myself. Yeah, I could already be locked out my current place, but I'd be able to get work if I looked hard enough. I'd lived off dried noodles before. I could do it again. The stale bread on the wagon had more appeal. I focused on a bakery I passed regularly, every detail I could recollect of the windows, the door, the signage, the smell.

Nothing happened beyond my head hurting from concentrating so hard.

Damn it.

I put the stone away, my actions rough. Nyashoth had made a mistake; the stone was as broken as I was. Yet I lived while the poor bastards we traveled alongside were cut down. What right did I have to complain? So much misery. They were brave beyond my understanding. I could never do that. I was a survivor, and that came with a dose of cowardice.

"Be ready. We have company."

Blackbird's warning shook me out of my self-pity party, and I clambered up to the front seat and looked over her shoulder as she slowed the wagon down. The road passed through a thicket of trees. A young boy, no more than eight years old, lay in the middle, one leg under a thick branch that had fallen from a shattered trunk at the side of the road. He waved at us, no doubt calling for help, but Blackbird was already turning the wagon off the road to avoid him.

"Wait," I said. "It couldn't take us more than a minute to help. We can drag the branch off if we can't lift it."

She stared at me as if I'd suggested up was down. "I won't risk stopping for anything, and this reeks worse than a barn full of cows with the runs."

Coward, I'd called myself. But this was something I could do. I leaped from the wagon and hurried toward the boy, Blackbird cursing my back. She gave in, though, bringing the wagon back onto the road.

I crouched by the boy. His hair was ragged, with leaves and twigs sticking out. He wore a knee length smock even filthier than his hair. Large, dark eyes stared at me.

"Don't worry," I told him. "I think the end of the branch is light enough that I can lift it off your leg. All you need to do is get out from under it when you can."

Grunting, I strained until the branch shifted. The boy scooted clear, his leg undamaged.

Blackbird pulled the horse up and said, "I don't like this. Ask yourself, what's a boy doing—"

People emerged from the trees, fifteen or twenty, surrounding the wagon. They all wore filthy clothes and were armed with a variety of weapons from spears to axes to crossbows. Their gaunt faces held desperation. They weren't soldiers. The boy ran to them, his leg completely fine.

Damn it. Damn it. Damn it all!

Blackbird had been right. I was such an idiot. Stepping back from the branch, I drew my cutlass. "We don't need trouble. We have food, but you can take it all. Just let us pass."

One of the ambushers approached. He wore long hair in a ponytail, and serviceable breeches beneath a smock cinched with a belt and half-covered with a short cloak. A large gold chain hung around his neck, dangling a star of black opal flecked with blues and reds. If he'd owned it for long, I had wings and could breathe fire.

"You won't need nothing," he said in a high-pitched whine. "Drop your weapons, all of ya."

Gwen stood on the seat near Blackbird, her cutlass drawn. Blackbird held her staff casually, as if it could not wreak carnage. The old woman met my eyes with a stony gaze. My screwup would be remembered.

She switched her ire to the motley group. "Piss off and go back to whatever cave you've crawled out of. You should be fighting the darkness to the last soul, not interfering with the work that must be done. Let us pass." The last words came quietly, but they carried on the air, a clear threat.

"Hear that? Fat like lambs and running. Says that to us." The man strutted back and forth. "I'll be having that shiny stick myself."

This had room to get messy. They outnumbered us, and a crossbow was as good as a gun for the first shot. I gave the asshole, who I assumed was the leader, my most unthreatening look and backed toward the wagon. "She's an old lady, and her legs don't work so well anymore. I'm sure times are tough, but we're all human, right?"

Blackbird poked me with the end of the staff. "What have I told you?"

"Look," I said to her, "you want to keep moving, and you want to conserve your energy. Why not give my way a go? There's a lot of them."

She ground her teeth and glowered at our ambushers' leader. "The boy wishes for me to be generous. Heed me well. I knew this land when there was peace and prosperity. I remember when there were rules of hospitality."

The leader gestured to the battle beyond the trees. "Hospitality? We live at the end of all. The old ways are dead. There is no trust. There is no welcome. Only survival remains."

"No honor," Blackbird demanded, fire in her voice.

"None."

That was a lie. The half a million fighting had honor. These brigands were contemptible, and yet that was about as hypocritical as I could get. Death and destruction waited wherever we had gone, and all I'd thought to do was escape and get home. I'd made it this far walking on the bodies of others.

"A bargain," Blackbird offered. "You take the wagon, food and all, and we walk on in peace. Survival for all. It's what you want."

"You cannot bargain. We have the numbers. Accept your fate." He waved his arms at his people. "They're hiding something. Strip them of all valuables. Kill them if they defy me."

And there it was—the second time I'd been wrong in the past few minutes. Blackbird must be boring holes in my back with her eyes.

I heard her staff hit wood. She couldn't be giving it up, surely? She'd held onto it even when unconscious.

Flame shot over my shoulder, and I ducked to the side, swearing in shock as heat curled stray hairs. Blackbird directed her staff, and the ray incinerated three of the ambushers. They screamed, flailing, then froze, falling to the soil as blackened husks. The air grew dry as I sucked it in, and my lungs strained, desperate for any remaining oxygen. Shouts of nearby horror overlayed the distant battle as she continued, immolating a man and a woman holding crossbows, then directing the flame toward another.

One of the crossbows bucked with a twang as the holder lit up like a torch. A short, stubby bolt hurtled forward, striking Blackbird's right shoulder where she'd been shot before. Time slowed. Every detail tattooed itself on my retinas. A fine dark spray. Cloak billowing out as she whirled around, and for the first time, the staff dropped from her hand involuntarily. Down she went, into the bed of the wagon and out of sight, so much meat.

My face buckled into a grimace.

Was she dead?

She couldn't be. She was a force of nature, immortal for all I knew.

But why wasn't she getting up? Why wasn't she exacting revenge?

"Blackbird!"

CHAPTER 21

RAMPANT

Shock crushed my chest with the careless glee of a demented giant, holding me as time returned to normal. Or sped up. Gwen leaped off the wagon and onto an ambusher, knocking him down. Another ran toward the pair, a rusty sword in hand.

The threat to Gwen freed me. There was no time to check on Blackbird, to help her, to mourn her. Sickened by the admission, I sprinted to Gwen's side, blocking a swing from the second ambusher as she ran her victim through. She yanked her blade free and released a spurt of blood. More ambushers pressed on us, and we shifted back-to-back, defending ourselves and each other.

I easily controlled the first, but struggled when a second joined the attack, my flat bladed-slaps goading them on rather than frightening them away. They knew my hesitation, what I couldn't bring myself to do.

Gwen danced this way and that at the edge of my vision, holding back three, her shoulders bumping mine when she slipped out of range. I laughed, a ragged, crazed sound. She knew how to use a sword as well if not better than I. She had played me again, harmlessly so. More fool me.

She cut at one ambusher but left her side open. I hacked at the haft of a spear-wielding asshole who tried to take advantage, knocking it down and carving a deep chunk of wood. The action left me vulnerable, but inexperience led the rusty sword ambusher to cut at my blade rather than my arm. It saved my life, but I lost my grip as the force jerked the blade, the cutlass bouncing on the road and out of reach. Another ambusher shoved me, sending me tumbling into Gwen.

We tangled and collapsed, and in seconds, yet another damn ambusher stood on her blade, immobilizing it.

"Make it hurt!" the leader shouted.

They milled around us, kicking, stabbing with spear butts, slapping with the backs of axes and sides of swords to prolong our pain. At first, I tried to cover Gwen, but as the beating continued, confusion transformed into dizziness, resolving into helplessness. My mouth tasted of blood, my stomach convulsed, and my arms refused all demands.

Existence shrunk. The ghosts of my parents stood over me, cheering on the attack. I was small, so small. Worthless. Wretched. Weak.

"That's enough. We need to move on. Kill them."

An axe rose high, glinting despite substantial rust.

I was entirely helpless, entirely useless.

A grating roar ripped the air. At first, I thought the sound was my own desperate cry, but another came when my mouth was closed.

"The devils are upon us," an ambusher cried. "Run."

"Do and die," the leader countermanded. "We're not leaving all that behind. Move the branch. Get the wagon. Hurry, or I will flay you myself."

Lying in a daze, I listened to them scramble. The wagon

rolled past, and the roars continued but never drew close. Time passed, marked only by waves of agony. When I attempted to speak, my split lips refused to do more than quiver. I closed my eyes.

Sometime later, I woke. The sound of battle continued. How long before every last human life was quenched, never to shine again? Why did my ember remain? With great effort, I rolled my head to one side then the other. Gwen lay there, unmoving. She'd died while I slept. Both of them were dead.

I wanted to fade to nothing, but Gwen's presence kept me there, a chain that wrapped around my throat, around my soul.

She couldn't be dead. Not after what we'd been through. A sob ripped free of me. I forced myself up onto my knees and shuffled over to her, sickness a raging dragon in my stomach.

Please. You can't die. Not you and Blackbird. Don't leave me alone.

I ran a hand along her dusty red hair. She didn't respond.

"Gwen, are you with me? You're the toughest woman I know, short of Blackbird, and you might even give her a run for her money."

I slipped a lock of hair behind her ear and examined her face. Cuts, bruises, swelling. She was still beautiful. My chest filled with an ache that wasn't physical. She *needed* to be okay. I'd never felt anything like it. Being shredded by the giant cat would have hurt less. This sun-hot need entwined with the chill river of misery and forced burning tears to run down my aching cheeks.

"I need you. I don't want to be alone anymore. I can't be."

Gathering her up into my lap, I closed my eyes and wept in front of another for the first time since I turned six, since I'd finally understood that it only made things worse.

"You can lie to me as much as you want, just don't leave me. I'm begging you."

The soundtrack of my despair was the rhythm of battle, the beat of weapons, heavy guitars conjured by dark imagination.

My loss mingled with the king's, with every poor bastard striving to live.

We were tiny specks in a cosmos bigger than I'd ever imagined. I'd thought I had a chance to matter. I had turned my life around, sealing off my youth with rigid determination. My goal had been to help children, so they didn't have to go through what I had. Not alone. But life loved kicking dirt in my face. That guiding vision was a mirage. I was beyond help and incapable of helping.

Here I was, cradling a beautiful woman I barely knew, one who lied with ease, one who I'd entrusted with my life and would willingly do so again. I had failed her. She wasn't the first I'd failed, not even the first in the same day.

Blackbird. Not a child for a millennium or more, a prickly soul who had placed the weight of everything upon her own shoulders. I had failed her, too. I couldn't save either of them. I couldn't save anyone. I sure as hell couldn't save myself.

Gwen slowly turned her head toward me, sending a jolt through my body.

"Go away."

"You're alive!" My nerves coursed with a million volts. Despair sizzled, darting around like water on a frying pan, shrinking, shrinking. It was too much. I was going to burst.

She licked her dry lips. "How else could my suffering continue?"

I took a deep breath. There was hope. I'd been wrong, and I loved that. I wanted to infuse this foreign joy directly into her blood, to wrap her in silk and carry her to a thick rug before a fire in a cozy cabin where everything was okay, where she was safe, to hold her and never let go.

We'd have to make do with reality, however.

"You'll heal. We're alive. That's more than many can say. That's a start."

"A start? It's all over. I have no luck. My lady is dead." She grabbed my shirt. "Haven't you seen? Don't you understand? I've lived every day of my life with her. The things I've done—the impossible, the glorious, the mad—it's all ashes. And her last promise is just as worthless. I will never have the paradise she foretold. The dead cannot make good. Everything I touch is now tainted by a cursed fate. I have nothing. I am nothing."

I gently raised her into a sitting position and looked into her eyes. I knew that pain. She was strong enough to bear it, but I hated the thought that she had to.

"It's not over yet. How do you know your Blind Lady didn't make arrangements? Perhaps her promise is waiting for you."

"Does this look like paradise? Does this resemble anywhere peace might be found?"

"No, but as I said, this isn't over. If your goddess was one of luck, then was it her luck that had you meet us? How else could you have escaped your world? Trust me, Gwen, the journey is not over."

She gripped my arm. "You saw Blackbird. She's dead. We're stuck."

I shook my head, pushing aside my own doubts. "I won't believe it until I see it. She's a tough old bitch."

"We're stuck. Give up and leave me alone."

Every statement of surrender only made me more determined. It didn't matter that I'd been where she was seconds ago. I burned for her.

"We're not stuck, not necessarily." I pulled out the stone. "Nyashoth gave me this. It's meant to open a way back to my world."

She glared. "But?"

"I haven't worked out how to use it—yet."

Her expression could have set water on fire, and I loved it. Fury smoldered within her, and that was energy. That same fury had kept me going so many times when despair had its hands around my throat, when adversity dragged me underwater.

That same fury ran within Blackbird, too. We were like a three-sided coin. The impossible metaphor slipped away. I saw the old woman in my mind, spinning with the force of the bolt. I thought of the people she'd willingly sacrificed. Was she as evil as the god she fled? I'd seen no joy in her decisions. But I bet fury was there. And arrogance. So much arrogance.

She'd demanded unquestioning obedience as if from a worshiper, but I'd always been free to leave. She wore the same face as the woman who'd shaped me with cruel deliberation into a young man. But she carried loss with her, held as tightly as her staff. Blackbird she might be called, but she was all shades of gray.

If she still lived, was she worthy of saving? Were any of us? We were all arrogant in one way or another. Sparks flared in my aching chest, crackling with the rhythm of my heart. I lived because of her choices. She had saved *me*. Again, and again.

We'd walked worlds together, fucking worlds. She was the closest thing I had to family, and I didn't want to lose her, just as I refused to lose Gwen. Yes, that was it—that was the fuel for the fire I needed.

How dare these fuckers hurt them? How dare they take Blackbird from me?

The thought echoed in my skull. I remembered the emotions that rushed through me when I'd helped Blackbird open a way, but this was a different mix. Anger, determination, and a sliver of something alien, something scary—caring. This new magic flowed into purpose.

I pulled Gwen to her feet, despite her protests.

"I'm sick of being chased around, of being bullied. I'm sick of losing. I'm not going to lose you, and I won't lose Blackbird. I'm going to save her. You're going to sew her up—again—and then she's going to lead us out of here. All three of us. If not to your paradise, then to somewhere better than this. When we get there, you can walk away and never look back, but please, please, give me this."

She scowled and shoved me away. "What rancid swine shit. You're cute, but you're weak. You're afraid. I've seen it when you fight. You play. You've never done what it takes to survive." Her voice cracked. "You won't, and I can't anymore. I just can't."

My cheeks heated, but I felt a sharp pain, a sense of dislocation, as a cage broke open inside my mind. I'd held myself back because I didn't want to be like my parents. I didn't want to be violent. I didn't want to be a monster.

That was over.

"Yes," I growled. "I will. I will gut every single one of them if that's what it takes."

I reached out and grasped Gwen's hands. "I need your help. Are you with me, or are you the coward you accuse me of being?"

Gwen stepped in and grabbed my shirt. "Don't put this on me. We have no weapons. You're selling me a dream, and I know what that's worth."

The ambushers had claimed our swords. She was right. It didn't matter.

"I'll take you over a sword, any day," I told her, leaning in close, eagerness and fury on my stinging lips. "Come on, Gwen. I don't believe in gods, but I believe in you. Let's rescue Blackbird."

Her breath was hot on my pulverized face, but I welcomed it over and over. Eventually, the corners of her mouth twitched into a feral grin, and she patted my cheek. "It's as good a way to die as any other."

Damn, she was scary, and it only made her more beautiful. I didn't believe in gods, but an avenging angel was fair game. We were so close, drawing closer. I was Icarus, and the sun had nothing on Gwen. I stared into her eyes, wanting to take her, wanting to be taken. Too much. How could people feel this and not shatter into a million pieces? I wanted her to break me.

A monster roared, its challenge met by the furious cry of the brave. Gwen shuddered in my arms and I in hers.

I retreated a single step—the hardest I'd ever taken.

We had things to do.

CHAPTER 22

TORCH OF HUMANITY

A ball of fire soared through the air high above, its light revealing winged monstrosities that flew beneath its arc. Each creature possessed broad wings, three long necks and three tails whipping like cut worms. They screeched and banked back toward the battle, one after the other. The fireball continued on, reaching its apex, then dropping far away, its energy spent to no avail.

Gwen and I took the road as far as we dared, unwilling to lose an ounce of speed. Our targets would keep moving, so we had to more than match them. They may have been drawn to the battle to pick from the carcasses, but with such a rich find, they'd be fleeing to somewhere safe to gorge.

Nowhere was safe for them.

When we heard the creak of the wagon, we gave up the road for the cover of a low drystone wall, its length broken twice by mutilated bodies that must have been dropped from high above to achieve such damage. Lines of trampled plants in rich, loamy soil behind the wall's protection hinted at a farm. The only harvest was death.

Most of the ambushers walked around the wagon at some distance, several with torches producing as much smoke as light. They scoured the ground as they went, talking excitedly, no doubt about their theft or joking about how they'd beaten us, boasting of a kick, a strike. My fists clenched.

"What's the plan?" Gwen hissed. "You take the ten on the left, and I take the ten on the right?"

I surveyed the group, a hand resting on a loose stone that shifted under my weight. "There's less than twenty. Or is it fewer? That doesn't matter. We're not going to take them out that way. What about grabbing one as a hostage? A life for a life?"

She tilted her head, a fist-sized stone in her hand—the perfect size for slamming into an unsuspecting skull. "Do you think they'd exchange a mouth to feed for anything of value?"

"True." I rapped the wall with frustration. That asshole of a leader might even see thinning his herd as a favor. An idea burrowed its way up from the depths of my imagination. *Damn*, I thought. *Martin, you're a cold son of a bitch.* "They're desperate and ruthless. So are we. Do you think you could give me a distraction?"

Her lips parted as if she were tasting my demeanor. "There's nothing to blow up."

I raised her stone-wielding hand. "I trust you to come up with something impactful."

She smirked. "You're getting to know me too well."

"Not nearly enough," I said.

Gwen slipped away from the wall and dug into the soft soil. She proceeded to rub dirt down her arms and legs, then across her face, dulling her skin. Returning to the wall briefly, she checked the ambushers. When no eyes looked back, she loped across the road and disappeared into foliage on the far side. I silently wished her good luck.

The rearmost ambusher trudged along twenty yards behind

the wagon, a torch in hand, muttering to himself. I couldn't have asked for a better target, which meant it was go time. My skin chilled while sweat trickled down my temple. Fear tightened my lungs. I was scared. So what? I'd been scared for such a long time. This was nothing new.

Leaving the wall's cover with a stone of my own, I paced along the road, watching the surface for sticks to snap or loose pebbles to kick. A single glance from any of the ambushers would reveal my approach. Thankfully, after their victory, they thought we were done, that they only need look ahead. They'd pay for that mistake.

As I closed, I matched the timing of my steps to the rear-guard, if he could be labeled as such. He wore a ragged cloak with holes revealing a long brown woolen tunic and pants at least a size too small. There was no sign of a weapon.

Martin, are you ready?

I thought of Blackbird. They hadn't thrown her corpse off the wagon, which meant she lived. A disturbing alternative was that they were keeping her for meat.

Acid burned my throat. I'd know soon enough. I rolled my shoulders to loosen tight muscles. It was time.

Two quick steps to catch up. I slipped an arm around the man's neck like I'd seen in endless action movies and brought my other arm around to strengthen the hold. His sour, cloying stink forced my nose to the side. He was light, almost light enough to lift off the ground. A sign of starvation? His feet scuffed the road, and I feared the noise would bring attention, but the wagon rolled on, creaking, and the rest of the band continued talking and walking with the stealth of an elephant. Their ignorance lent an air of unreality. Surely, I couldn't be doing this if there was no response?

I dragged him to the side of the road, out of the small the circle of light left by the torch he'd dropped to grab desperately at my arm. Applying all the force I could muster, I choked him. He switched from grabbing at me to writhing. Pity tested my resolve. I wanted to stop, to grant mercy, but I dared not. He had to die for Blackbird to stand a chance.

So, I held tight while his movements slowed, and kept holding for a count of a hundred before shoving him face down into the dirt and stomping twice with all my weight.

Kneeling, I looked at my hands, their shape barely visible in the darkness. I'd killed someone, a cold, calculated act, and my hands tingled with eagerness, with a power coiled, waiting to be freed once more. Who could hurt me now?

I squeezed my eyes shut. That was sick. That was not who I was. Except, it was who I needed to be, at least for now.

The dead man's cloak barely fit across my shoulders, but I forced the hood over my head and hurried to the guttering torch. A few breaths brought it back to life, and surrounded me with thick smoke and an odor of rancid fat. The smoke gave as much cover as the light took away.

My acting skills had never been tested beyond high school drama assignments with poor grades. However, I did my best to mimic the tired gait of my victim, deciding against mumbling. With each step, I closed on the wagon, hoping my gradual approach would remain unnoticed, unchallenged.

Two of the ambushers on the right were close enough to hear the specifics of their conversation.

"Ain't right not warming our chests with a dram of varik when we all put in. A drink for the dead, an' all."

"Tie that mouth shut, mudcock. Didn't listen to Rufus, did you? The sorceress could have wished a curse upon it all. When she wakes, he'll force her to try it—then we get our fill."

"I heard his words. It's all we hear night and day—his words, his words. Think on this. Who's to say tomorrow she wakes? He's looking after his share and taking from ours."

The second speaker thumped the first. "Keep those words buried, fool. You might be heard, and then it will be you in a ditch."

Blackbird lived. I tried to keep the hunger from my face, and my focus on the task at hand. This wasn't revenge. This was a rescue.

A shout from the distant left. "Learium's dead, and Tiyala doesn't answer!"

The ambushers erupted into shouted questions and useless answers, panic gilding each. Bowing my shoulders further, I raised the torch above the hood to deepen the shadows around my face. The ambushers congregated on the left, and the wagon stopped. Gwen had come through as I knew she would.

The leader, Rufus, I presumed, appeared atop the wagon. "Silence, weak-hearts, or I'll cut your throats and feed your bloodless meat to the beasts yonder."

His slurred command had the desired effect, and the sullen ambushers waited for more.

"Is there sign of beast or patrol?"

"Beast it was, Rufus. Learium's all hacked up, Sun guard his soul. Must have been big teeth. It wasn't sword or spear."

Rufus walked along the wagon but stayed off the ground.

"Beast, or more likely, Tiyala sickened of his stupidity and refused and word of it. Mavis, Isodan, Dwathor, search to fifty paces, no more. And don't forget Learium's axe, or you can stay with his body."

I shuffled to the right of the wagon and peered inside. A second clay pot was open. I guessed Rufus had been testing the merchandise. He could have drunk the lot for all I cared.

Blackbird had been dumped on the right of the wagon bed, close to the front. She looked so small and frail. Fresh anger stoked my determination to see her away from this second-rate thug. Her staff lay nearby, along with Gwen's cutlass. Rufus held mine in his murdering hand. It was the only thing keeping me from climbing up and punching him there and then.

A solution rested in my pocket. I retrieved the stone I'd picked up earlier and shifted it in my hand, testing its shape and weight. I'd never been one for sports, but I'd tossed plenty of stones into rivers and a few eggs at houses of the deserving.

I threw it. The stone cut the air, too close to lose much height but higher than I'd hoped for. It smacked into the crown of his head, glancing off. Rufus grabbed his head, his face filled with pain and surprise. As he cried out, I was already climbing onto the wagon, an awkward task with a flaming torch in one hand.

Our packs were stacked at my feet, sticky fluid leaking from Blackbird's. I picked it up, reassured that it was still heavy, and pulled it over my shoulders. If I'd left it behind, she'd never let me hear the end of it.

The action drew Rufus's attention.

"You!" He pointed at me with my own sword and stepped into the middle of the wagon. I should have gone for Gwen's cutlass first. My head wasn't quite right after the beating. I needed time to think.

"Clever, boy, Rufie. I can see why they picked you as leader."

Bravado was all well and good, but he had a sword and I had… a torch. Dark thoughts coalesced. A torch was all I needed. Mostly. I tossed it to him, a gentle action. He caught it easily, confusion on his features.

"Witless scum. I'm going to slice your balls off."

"Everyone needs a hobby," I said, then barked out a laugh. "But it's not playtime."

I grabbed the nearest clay pot and threw it at him, two-handed. "That's for Blackbird!"

Rufus sneered and slashed at it with my cutlass, shattering the clay with ease and spilling the sticky liquor all over himself. Splashes went through the torch flame, igniting with a whoosh, and the bastard went up in flames, stinking of fennel. He staggered back, screaming, and dropped both torch and my cutlass in a doomed attempt to wipe away the alcohol. The stuff was napalm. I ran at him and kicked, catching him firmly in his stomach, and sent him off the wagon.

Little flames clung to the wood where he had been, and to the road where the spirit had sprayed. The remaining ambushers moved closer, shouting scared questions. They would soon make sense of the situation, of Rufus's agonized screams, and I'd be in trouble. I grabbed clay bottles two at a time and tossed them off the wagon, grinning maniacally when each shattered and caught alight. In a minute at most, the wagon would become a pyre.

A figure climbed onto the wagon. I reached for the nearest cutlass, Gwen's.

"I believe that's mine," she said, the backdrop of flames adding to the burnished red of her hair. My heart leaped with relief as she continued. "I see you have been busy."

"I've been cooking." The savagery in my voice shocked me. "But we had better clear out before it's time for dessert."

I handed her cutlass over along with Blackbird's staff and retrieved my weapon. An ambusher appeared in front, holding a spear awkwardly while he climbed. Without hesitation, I dropped to one knee and thrust into his chest, missing his ribs. There was only the slightest hint of pressure as I punctured his clothing and skin. More resistance came as the point separated flesh, then deflected off his spine. When I yanked my cutlass free, a gush of blood sprayed from his chest, painting my face.

This was more personal than strangling, than immolating. We were eye to eye. Grim satisfaction to horror. Then I'd wanted to stop. Now I wanted to slice this bastard's throat to be sure. I was different now. I was someone who would kill. But not for what I wanted, only for what was needed. I held to that distinction as a talisman.

The corpse fell away, and I had no time to waste—the horse jerked from side to side, snorting and stamping its feet. With its blinkers, it couldn't see the state of the wagon, but it must have felt the heat.

I wiped my blade on my leg, sheathed it, and dragged Blackbird away from the nearest flames. Her shoulder was a bloody mess. I wanted to shake her and see her eyes open. But if she still lived, being unconscious was a mercy. As gently as I could, I picked her up, sat on the edge of the wagon, swung my legs over, and dropped to the ground, bending my knees to absorb the force.

Steel rang on steel, and I waited beyond the growing inferno, confident. Sure enough, Gwen dismounted, limping a little as she joined me, her blade dark with blood.

The ambushers streamed around the wagon, facing off from us at a safe distance. They held their shaking weapons out, and I remembered Blackbird's approach.

I lifted my sword, the rune-etched blade gleaming. "You caught us off guard before. Now we are ready. Get in our way, and we'll kill every last one of you. Follow us, and we'll do the same."

Gwen shook the staff at them. "With this, I can burn off your hands and feet, leaving you to be feasted on. I will boil your eyes so that you may only hear them scratching the road as they approach, sniffing your charred flesh."

I repeated her words, so the translation could work. The ambushers backed away.

"Good choice," I said.

We walked confidently down the road as the poor horse dragged the wagon to one side, spreading the fire. Its life was in their hands. I couldn't save it and live.

When we were far enough away, I gave in and trembled. My muscles were rubber, my mind was numb, and I wanted to vomit.

"Keep going," Gwen demanded when I slowed.

Soon after, a massive explosion gave us seconds of daylight—the remaining alcohol had gone up—a mushroom cloud in a fantasy setting. Directors would do anything to get the money shot of special effects, I joked to myself. Then I remembered the horse and hoped they had freed it.

"It would have been nice to have the ride," I said to cover my guilt.

"Says the man with two working ankles."

"Hey, I'm carrying Blackbird."

"Hmm," Gwen said, putting a hand on my shoulder. "Sucks to be you."

"Very philosophical," I shot back, amused the phrase translated so well.

"I can get philosophical if you like. I didn't think we'd survive that, not without the Blind Lady. And yet, we are both here and walking, our hearts still beating. We can make our own luck. At least a little."

I nodded, unsure I had the energy to speak further. We'd need more than a little luck. Blackbird was still limp in my arms. Was she okay? We couldn't stop and check, not yet.

I'd just have to hope that, as Gwen said, we were making our own luck—but at an industrial scale.

CHAPTER 23

AN IMPOSSIBLE CHOICE

We stopped at the remains of a small roadside building constructed from wood. The main room had been ripped apart, its pieces scattered, but a small extension stood. The words 'Gradock Tollbooth' painted above its entrance proclaimed its purpose. Something told me they weren't raking in the tax dollars. The inside stank of old smoke and mold. At least, it provided protection from the biting wind that had picked up. Or it would have if I had been inside.

Clouds blotted out the sky, subjecting me to a steady drizzle that flattened my hair. Reflected light from the battle gave us the little visibility we had. I used it to watch the road in case the ambushers gave chase. That and the roiling mass of battle in case it shifted our way.

The crazed rush of adrenaline had faded, leaving me shaking and nauseous. The waiting gave me too much time to think. Lady Macbeth had nothing on my hands. Three people dead in the space of a few minutes, unless there were more that burned. I'd let my rage loose and rode it, cheering all the way. When my mother said having me was a mistake, she might have been right.

Did she see it in my eyes? When my father had tried to beat the weirdness out of me, had he known what I was capable of?

My stomach convulsed. I was never meant to be a teacher. I'd never known how to fit in with people my own age. How on Earth had I thought I could be responsible for kids?

Today, kids, we're going to look at burning people alive.

An implacable truth stared down my horror—put me back in time and I'd do it again. So, did I really hate what I'd become?

"Martin."

I rubbed my hands and entered the tollbooth. In the far corner, a small brazier burned the remains of coal we'd scraped together. The tip of Gwen's cutlass rested in the hottest part, glowing a dull red. Blackbird lay on her cloak. Since I'd stepped out, Gwen had torn the old woman's dress, revealing the wounded shoulder and upper chest.

My eyes widened. Her skin was carved up, burned, tattooed, all to form runes, so many that she resembled an unreadable word cloud. Beyond that deliberate marking, puckered scars spoke of five or more injuries long-healed. The bolt still stuck out of the latest. That couldn't be good.

Gwen, on one knee in the cramped space, looked up at me. "Get down and give me a hand. The bolt is stuck in her bone, and I can't budge it. I'll hold her down; you pull it out."

I winced at the idea.

"Think of it as the reverse of stabbing. Hurry up. She's already spent much of her lifeblood."

The reverse of stabbing. That didn't make it sound any better.

"Will she be okay?"

"How in the den of a rooster-snake should I know? You can't put a leash on fate. That's what the Blind Lady wanted everyone to understand. We do what we can and pray for the best."

I nodded and kneeled by Blackbird, trying not to think of

what a rooster-snake would look like. Gwen placed her weight firmly on Blackbird, and I hovered my hands near the bolt. Blackbird looked so weak. I didn't want to kill her by trying to help.

She's a survivor. She's tough. She'd demand you do it if she could.

I breathed in to steady my hands.

Please don't die.

The bolt had wooden fletching with several nicks, suggesting it had been fired more than once. How many lives had it taken?

You're not getting this one.

I put a hand on the shaft.

Blackbird groaned and whispered something.

"Hurry," Gwen demanded.

"Give me a sec." I leaned close to Blackbird. "What is it?"

"Ambrosia."

I furrowed my brow. "What?"

"Do you have it?"

"I don't know what you mean."

Her eyelids fluttered. "Can't lose."

I put a hand on her forehead. "Don't worry. You're safe. We beat them."

"Where is it?"

I glanced at Gwen.

She scowled. "I don't know what a god drink is."

Gwen was hearing a translation. Ambrosia. God drink. Blackbird had been carrying a lot of liquids in a variety of containers, none of them labeled.

"Don't worry, we've got your backpack."

She relaxed. "Do it."

I gripped the shaft. "On the count of three."

"Just do it, damn you," Blackbird hissed.

I pulled on the bolt, lifting Blackbird before Gwen redoubled her effort. The bolt stayed lodged in bone. I pulled hard. Blackbird grunted. I strained, muscles tensing, harder and harder, until the bolt popped free with a slurp and spray of blood.

Blackbird screeched, then flopped, as unmoving as the dead. I threw the bolt out the doorway as if it were planning to attack again. Gwen grabbed her cutlass, pressed it into my hand, then resumed her hold on Blackbird. I hadn't thought about this bit. I swallowed hard, my hand shaking.

Gritting my teeth, I pressed the tip against the two-inch long gash. The flesh sizzled, filling the air with the scent of cooking meat. Blackbird screamed and writhed. I screamed internally, horrified that I could do it.

"Hold the tip steady," Gwen demanded.

My bile rose, and I tried to breathe through my mouth, a poor combination. The smell was sweetness overlaid with a metallic sharpness. Sweat added to the rain on my skin. My bones turned to ice. No more. I couldn't. I pulled the cutlass away, the tip sticking at first, and threw it aside. Without a word, I fled outside.

Rain couldn't wash away the sickness inside me. My chest ached. The world span. I dropped and vomited, acid burning my esophagus, finally rolling away when I had nothing more to expel. Hands on face and resting in a puddle, I shook, over-whelmed as I'd never been before, not in my darkest moments.

A hand squeezed my shoulder, and I reached for my cutlass.

"It's me," Gwen said. "We can't stay here."

"Blackbird?"

"I wrapped her as best I could. She's awake, mostly, but she can't walk."

Awake was something.

Gwen offered her hand, and I took it. When I was up, she pressed her forehead against mine, her hair framing our faces.

"You're going to take me somewhere nicer, right?"

"You don't like the rustic ambiance?"

She gave the tiniest of smiles. "I think the Lady would have liked you." Then she pecked my lips and pulled away.

I shivered as my existential dread drained into my subconscious, leaving me space to think.

"We need a stretcher. A couple of lengths of wood, and some rope or material to sling between them."

She rested a hand on the shelter. "The tollbooth for the wood and your cloak for the sling."

I nodded, hoping the fabric was up to the task. We kicked out several planks and hacked the ends with our cutlasses to make handles. After that, we tore strips of fabric from Blackbird's overdress, punctured the cloak, and tied it to the planks. Blackbird groaned when we placed her on the makeshift stretcher along with her staff and backpack. She watched me, her lips tight and her skin ashen.

"We're going to carry you."

"That much is obvious," she said shakily.

"But you have to guide us. Do we keep heading down the road?"

"For now."

We carried her outside, and I shuffled the handles so I could walk facing the right direction. The ground was slick under my feet, and exhaustion dulled my balance, forcing us to keep a slow pace. The hue and cry of battle appeared distant, but that might have been the weather. On and on we walked, my legs and arms aching.

Bodies littered the sides of the road in clumps. Armored soldiers, civilians, and yet more monstrosities, killed before they could feast on the dead. I kept checking to make sure Gwen hadn't disappeared, that I wasn't walking alone. She managed a smile the first time, but thereafter only stared. She was struggling. We both were.

Another road intersected ours, and I signaled to put the

stretcher down. With the weight gone, my arms were so much meat, burning and useless, and my fingers were hooked like talons.

I bent close to Blackbird. "We're at a crossroads."

She coughed and opened her eyes. "What a damn cliché."

"No, actual crossroads. I need to know which way to go."

Blackbird bent at her stomach, trying to get up. I put out my arm for her to hold, but she gave up. "You'll have to find it."

"Me?" I raised my barely functional hands. "I can't do that."

"How do you know?"

"I—I guess I don't."

"Good. Now, listen up." She grabbed my arm and held it with a weak grip. "We should be close enough. This way has been used many times, and that leaves a scar in the local reality. You won't be able to feel it directly, not yet. But it bleeds just a little of that which it presses against. The differences react like when you have two groups of strangers standing next to each other. Nothing is said, but you can sense the tension. Drown out all else and find it. Hurry."

I left her coughing and walked to the middle of the crossroads.

Gwen joined me. "What are you doing?"

"I'll tell you when I know."

Gusts stole my body heat and carried the sound of battle so well that I feared the forces would crash over us. Gwen squeezed my shoulder, giving me strength.

I closed my eyes and turned a slow three-sixty. I'd felt other ways, at least when we were very close. How hard could it be? I was only looking for a scar of some kind, tension. Except I wasn't looking. I had to *feel* it, and all I felt was my own discomfort. A second rotation gave the same result. And a third and a fourth.

Come on. Do something right, something you can be proud of. They're counting on you. It's easy to take a life, but now you've got to use your brain. They don't know you're damaged, that you're a failure. You can't let them.

I forced my body to relax even as I tore into my self-worth. I noted the wetness of my boots, how they'd sunk into grooves left by wagons. The air smelled of dirt, a richness like blood, a bitterness I could only ascribe to my feelings. Around I went. And again. Nothing. I was nothing.

Do you remember not knowing why they hit you? You've been bad, Marty. You're a bad boy. Don't understand—you're stupid. Why'd you do it? Don't you ask what—you lying little shit. We don't need you. I never wanted you.

The shame burned, and self-hatred spun like a dynamo. Fuck them. I'd do this. The only people in the world I gave a damn about were relying on me. I'd feed my damn soul into the furnace if needed. Around I went, arms extended, pouring out my recriminations and determination in equal parts.

There. I turned back, scrunching my eyes tight. A tension, a fizz interwoven in the hiss of rain. Three steps closer. Maybe. Another three. Yes. No. Another step. Hands grabbed my arms. I shook them off and opened my eyes.

I was at the precipice of a short drop on the far corner of the crossroads. The corpse of a spiked beast lay corkscrewed, its spine broken multiple times. Each spike was as long as my arm and wickedly sharp.

Pointing, I said, "I know where we need to go."

Gwen pulled me back. "And let's get there by stepping around the stabby dead thing."

Hard to argue that. We stretchered Blackbird off the road. I paused frequently as we walked to reconnect with the feeling I'd had. A short while later, we hit the spot, and I indicated to lower the stretcher again.

"We're here."

Blackbird raised an arm. "Help me up."

"Oh, come on," I said. "You're in no state to stand."

"Don't be stupid, boy. There is no alternative."

I searched for a reason to deny her. She was right. Giving in, I held her carefully and helped her to her feet.

Gwen had moved away, and now she hurried back. "They've caught up with us. Five, no I see a sixth."

"Are they following the road or actually heading our way?" I said, hoping we could hide until they passed.

"Guess."

I didn't want to.

Blackbird leaned against me, only standing with my continued support. "I need your energy."

I heard a shout and looked back at the crossroads. The ambushers were easy to see, torches in hand.

"There they are," one shouted.

Blackbird tugged on my sleeve, her staff awkwardly between the two of us. "Focus."

This may come as a surprise, but I found it hard to focus when people wielding medieval weapons raced toward me, revenge filling their minds.

Gwen unsheathed her cutlass. "I'll keep them busy. Get that magic door open, and don't you dare leave me behind."

I nodded. "Not a chance. You're stuck with me—us."

If they hurt her… I pushed aside my worry. The way to keep her safe was to get us out of there. Easy. I'd found the way, hadn't I? But I wasn't feeling it anymore. Time to delve deep again.

This time I dredged up a scene, one where my parents shouted at each other while I hid under the kitchen table, only able to see their legs.

"The fucking cops are on to us," my father said. "Little Jimmy talked or one of Gary's boys. We have to disappear."

My mother hit the table with her fist. "You said we wouldn't have to move again."

"You said we could trust Little Jimmy."

I cringed at the anger in my father's voice and imagined the flying spittle.

My mother wasn't cowed. "We killed a security guard. It's on us. We brought the heat down on ourselves."

My father kicked a chair. "It doesn't matter. We have to clear out."

The distant sound of sirens bled through the open front door.

"Fuck." She turned toward the narrow hall that led to our bedrooms. "Marty! Get your ass here."

But I was too afraid. If they knew I'd been there all that time, if they knew I'd listened, they'd beat me.

My father picked up a bottle and threw it at the wall. It hit with an almighty smash and sent glass and whisky flying. "Marty, you fuck. Show your face, or I'll shove it through a door."

The sirens screeched their hunter's cry.

My mother hurried to a low cupboard and swept aside plates on little wire racks so she could grab two bags hidden behind. I tried to shrink myself into nothing in case she turned around and saw me.

She stood and called my name.

"Fuck him. We're outta time," my father said, grabbing the bags.

"But—"

"Come on. It's not like you ever wanted him."

"I—we'll go faster, just the two of us."

They hurried out of the house. I heard their car start and the engine roar. And then they were gone. Forever.

Emotion, magic, whatever it was, it flowed from me into the staff. Panting, I opened my eyes, only vaguely aware of holding Blackbird around the waist while she cut the way with a shaking staff. The sparks were closer together than normal. It wouldn't stay open for long—I was sure of it. Where was Gwen?

She was goading the ambushers, darting near one, then dodging out of the way, despite her ankle. Five remained. The sparks of the way caught the attention of all, and Gwen used the chance to stab the wrist of one on her right, forcing him to drop his axe. I wanted to cheer her on, but she was on the wrong side of the bastards.

"Go through," I said to Blackbird. "We'll be right behind."

She grabbed my hand, which had fallen to my cutlass. "There's no time. I can't lose you."

I pulled myself free. "I'll find the time. Go. I swear it."

She gave me an inscrutable look and stumbled through the shrinking way.

An ambusher peeled off from the rest and charged toward me, sword brandished. "You brought them down on us! We're all that's left."

"Kiss my ass," I said and readied myself to meet him. I'd need to be quick.

He swung wildly and with incredible force, shaking my arm each time I parried. I dropped my blade and stepped back, flicking the tip at his forearm when momentum carried him past. He grunted and hacked at me again. Our blades caught, and we pressed at each other, my weight and strength giving me an advantage, even in my current state. He punched my face, bringing an explosion of pain. I'd been here before many times. I knew how to cope, how to silo the pain, the damage.

Spitting in his face, I slid my cutlass back, keeping his blade running along the guard at the start of my cup to gain mechanical advantage. Then I dropped my tip down to his face and thrust my blade along his, stabbing him in an eye.

He fell screaming, my cutlass slipping free. I kicked his sword away with a vicious cry and took stock of the situation. Gwen had downed another, a woman with a club. But she still had two blocking her path, and they'd pushed her farther from the way.

The way—it was so narrow. Soon, it would be gone.

Even if I could sneak behind each of her attackers and slaughter them, there'd be no time for us both to reach the way.

If a Gwen is approaching a way at full sprint, and a Martin is headed in the opposite direction, at what time will they meet? Answer: too damn late.

I tensed and screamed at the sky, at the universe. I couldn't leave her behind, and we'd both die if we remained. On the other hand, Blackbird was terribly injured. How long would she last alone? She was so sure her death would be the death of all.

Who to save? An impossible situation. Gwen met my gaze. She didn't ask for help. She didn't beg. She didn't demand. A tear slid down my cheek, lost in the rain. She'd reached the same conclusion. She knew she was dead.

I screamed again, unable to contain the roiling emotions.

An idea flared. I grabbed the stone from the pouch. Nyashoth has said the stone could take me home. A direct route. My energy had fed the staff—why not the stone? When I'd last tried, I hadn't scoured the depths of my soul enough.

I focused, pouring all my anguish into the stone, willing the runes to glow. It didn't work, and I had seconds left. No time for despair. Something new was needed.

Gwen was ruthless, playful, and clever. I fed these thoughts and the emotions they conjured. The electricity along my lips when she'd kissed me for the shortest moment. I imagined taking her to her first movie, popcorn and wine in our hands, our legs brushing, her eyes shining. A bed later that night. My body filled with desire, heat, need, and this I poured into the stone.

The runes flashed and spat sparks.

I'd done it. I'd charged it. It thrummed, practically begging to be used.

"Gwen! Catch!"

I hurled the stone over the ambushers.

She caught it and retreated. "What am I meant to do with this?"

"Cut your own way. It'll take you to my world. I'll find you there. I promise."

Blackbird's way had shrunk to a sliver. There was no time to see if Gwen used the stone—if she could even make it work. I abandoned her and leaped through the way moments before it closed.

CHAPTER 24

SEEN

Sunlight kissed the soft, spongy groundcover beneath me, a rejection of my suffering, a dismissal of my abandonment of Gwen. The blotchy yellow fern leaves were so intertwined that I couldn't tell where one plant started and another finished. A rosemary scent exuded from the leaves I'd bruised, woody with a hint of menthol.

Fluffy white clouds dotted a teal sky dominated by a large lemon-yellow sun directly above. Midday. Insects chirped all around, and a zebra-striped beetle crawled over my left hand. Blackbird lay by an outcropping of translucent, gold-flecked quartz. A distant herd of dark spots wandered across the horizon.

Ahead, the land sloped gently down to the shore of a glittering lake, the far side only visible due to the mountain peaks rising high. Water lapped at ochre sand, and nearby humans—or similar—moved among the buildings of a small fishing village. A single sloop rested on a wooden frame. Repairs?

Nothing indicated danger of any sort. She should have been here with us. It wasn't fair. I rolled onto my back, checking where the way had been. Gwen wasn't there. I knew she wouldn't be.

Maybe this wasn't the paradise she was chasing, but she'd have appreciated the change in weather if nothing else.

My clothes were already dry. Had I slept? I didn't deserve rest.

Was Gwen lying in muddy ground at the edge of an epic battle, slaughtered by cowards not willing to stand up even when their world was ending? I shifted my shoulders, uncomfortable with my own behavior. If Blackbird was right—and how else could any of this make sense?—then this journey was my battle as much as hers. Maybe Blackbird was the king in gold, and I had to choose to be by her side or a scavenger at the edge. I'd already decided, hadn't I?

Gwen—was she collateral damage, a dead soldier forgotten as one of countless? No. She was alive. She was no tag-along like me. She had to be okay. Why? She was smart, a survivor. She'd make it to Earth. I willed it with every ounce of conviction I could muster. She'd get there because I'd go back for her, and I couldn't do that if she wasn't there. Even on a planet of eight or so billion people, she couldn't be that hard to find.

It wasn't just guilt. Love? A dangerous word tossed around too easily. What then? There was something, a feeling I'd never encountered before. I wasn't naïve enough to think she was in love with me. We'd been caught up in the moment. What drove me then? I owed her a simpler, less confronting answer. I wouldn't abandon her, not like my parents abandoned me. Not again, anyway. The idea cut me as easily as any blade. The truth was, I admitted, I was still caught up in that moment.

Stewing in my own thoughts wouldn't make the rescue any faster. I walked to Blackbird, noting the grimace on her face despite her snoring. Still, each loud breath offered comfort. Her staff lay in the crook of her arm, and her backpack acted as a pillow. If she'd died, it would have all been for nothing. Putting a hand on the quartz, I stared down at the village. Could I get help?

"She died for a good cause," Blackbird said, surprising me. "She died for hope. That's a better end than many claim."

"She's not dead," I stated.

When Blackbird held out a hand, I helped her up, surprised yet again by her resilience. The weight of her steady gaze forced me to explain the stone, activating it, and that desperate throw to Gwen. It sounded hopeless, a waste of resources that would confirm my stupidity.

"Do you think she could work it?" I asked with a child's desperation while staring at the lake, waiting for judgment to fall.

"Likely so, if she had the chance. It was a *way bridge*. Such devices were crafted long ago for those without the requisite aptitude to cut between worlds, though they were found to have a more flexible use, one which you put into practice. They are very powerful and very rare, lasting but a single use. It was a valuable gift—to leave her with hope. Be proud of that."

I glanced at Blackbird, surprised. A compliment? She must have hit her head as well as being skewered. Or maybe it was the pain of her injury. Either way, it was nice.

Right on time, a terrible thought occurred to me, dulling the positive vibe. Could the way bridge have taken us directly to Blackbird's destination? Were our recent hardships all my fault?

"You look constipated."

Dreading her disapproval, I admitted my mistake.

She harrumphed. "Put aside that worry. Yes, you should have told me, but no, it could not have taken us where we need to go. I have tried a number of techniques to hasten the journey. Each time, I have been thwarted by a force that is… smothering all such attempts. A defense that bodes well, even as it causes us difficulty. At least, that is one possibility. One can never be sure.

Forget the way bridge. Only by cutting world to world can we advance."

"If a force is blocking way bridges, how did I make one work?"

"Do not think yourself some kind of savant. The bridge you connected took a route heading away from the force. Nyashoth knew where you had come from and must have surmised that it would benefit you, though I wish she had shared her plan."

"I suppose that makes sense." Her dismissal offered me little comfort. I'd been too slow to learn how to use it, and that delay had consequences. "Even if Gwen cut open a way and escaped, she's on Earth, all alone."

"Remember this," Blackbird poked me with her staff. "In the end we all walk our path alone."

I smoothed my shirt. "I don't believe that. Look at us. We're together."

She sighed and put a hand on my arm. "Time will tell."

Her touch surprised me. My immediate impulse was to pull away in case she meant to follow up with a hit, but she didn't move, and made no sign of aggression. I stilled, growing used to the experience, finding comfort, yet waiting for a sting.

"I didn't bring the stretcher," I said to change the direction of the conversation. "If you wait here, I might be able to trade with the village for parts, perhaps even for a wagon or a horse. Doesn't seem like the place for an ambulance or hover-car."

Blackbird let go. "Absolutely not. I shall walk, and you shall lend me your strength. The next way is close. You will feel it soon enough if you put your mind to it."

Stubborn and proud, her two defining characteristics. I wasn't going to change her mind. I held out my right arm, and she took it. As we descended toward the village, she stumbled and hissed multiple times, but I kept her up, and on we went.

"We're going to make it," I said, unsure if I'd done so for myself or Blackbird.

"Of course." After a pause, she added, "But it's time you learned a few things."

Blackbird was right, though I didn't admit it. A prickling sensation began soon after we started walking and transitioned to a thickness in the air within ten minutes. She ordered me to provide the juice needed to cut the way. I didn't want to delve into the memories that fed my darker emotions, but it flowed easier this time.

When I stepped into the sparks, I thought of Gwen and wondered how many worlds were between us.

A city stood on the other side. Tall towers of metal and glass stretched into an ordinary sky. Sleek, glossy cars rested alongside curbs dotted with immaculately pruned trees. Flowering plants cascaded artfully over raised garden beds. Not a single piece of litter dirtied street or sidewalk.

I followed Blackbird across the street we arrived on, then continued right. We passed a quadcopter drone cleaning a window with one articulated arm spraying foam while another used a squeegee, creating an awful wet, dragging sound. Which had me checking up and down the street. We were alone apart from the machine. Where was everyone? In the distance, a background hum thrummed with peaks of high-pitched whines. A second, smaller drone zoomed around a corner and whizzed closer, its purpose unclear.

Blackbird interrupted my thoughts. "Tell me where the next way is."

The little drone stopped nearby for a count of three, then headed off. Was it checking us out?

Blackbird rapped my shins with her staff. "Pay attention. Where is the way?"

I bit back a Star Wars reference, figuring she wasn't the kind to catch a movie, and slowly performed a three-sixty. A slight tension toward the glass foyer of a large office tower, and a weaker one further away. Yeah, I thought. I was getting the hang of this.

After pointing out my finds, I waited for her grudging respect.

"Don't be a fool," she said, gesturing down the street. "That's not a way—it's a void crack. Try to go through there, and there'll be nothing left of you."

"It's a vacuum?" I asked.

"It's nothing." She gave me another glare and shuffled toward the office tower.

I clenched my teeth with annoyance and followed her up a set of broad steps. Several small tables and chairs dotted the paved ground outside of the foyer, each of them spotless, and the chairs perfectly positioned as if for a photoshoot.

Through the closed glass doors of the building, I spotted a chrome reception desk with gloss black detailing. An emblem of a big-toothed fish rested above the words: Barramundi Automatons. On the side of the foyer closest to the tables were vending machines with pictures of food and drinks.

Blackbird pushed the glass doors, but they barely moved. Locked.

"How do we get in?" I thought aloud.

"I knock your head against the glass until it shatters." She raised an eyebrow when I looked at her, and I wondered if she'd been making a joke.

"Ha, ha. Can't you—" I considered her injury and her reliance on me to cut open a way. My question was better left unasked. It was amazing that she was mobile at all. Expecting her to toss magic around was selfish.

My cutlass wasn't a sledgehammer, so I picked up a chair, considered my impending act of vandalism with a hint of guilty delight, and swung it at the doors. The impact let off a sound like gunfire, but the chair rebounded with no damage. It was too light. Blackbird watched me silently as I threw it away and picked up a table, hefting it experimentally. Heavy. Good.

I carried it back to the doors and swung it like a baseball bat. The table whizzed through the air, then impacted with a loud crunch, sending jagged lines through the glass.

"Again," Blackbird demanded.

What did she think I'd do? Give up after one go? I gave myself a run-up this time, and the table shattered the entire panel, continuing through as shards rained onto the foyer's marble floor. I'd let go, and the table bounced along, hitting the reception desk and denting the front.

"At least there's no alarm." Or receptionist, I noted silently. Had we arrived during a weekend?

Blackbird walked inside, popping and crunching. I followed, scowling. A building should have an alarm. A fancy building like this could have round the clock security or a direct link to the police.

Neither mattered. The way was clear, hovering in front of several arches along a wall. Numerals followed the curve of these. Elevators, I guessed, licking my lips. There was something wrong with the way. A drumbeat sounded in my head, flat and unpleasant. Maybe Blackbird's injuries were clouding her judgment.

"Are you sure this is the right way?"

She straightened her shoulders and back, using her staff for support. The lines on her face seemed deeper than ever. "If the journey was all sunsets and wine, any fool could walk it. Now, listen carefully. You mustn't breathe once you're through. The air is poisonous. We'll only be ten paces from the next way, but inhale, and it will be your final resting place."

The sound of drumming increased. Perfect, I thought. Luckily, we had gas masks. Oh wait, we didn't. I glanced at the street, and the drumming stopped. It hadn't been in my head at all.

A robot stood on two legs at the bottom of the stairs, its bulk reaching at least twice my height. I took in robust legs, a horizontal wedge-shaped torso, arms extending from either side, rose-colored paint with checkered lines of white and yellow. My eyes returned to the arms. They finished not with hands but with dull barrels. Every science fiction movie I'd ever seen told me this couldn't be good.

Blackbird cursed. "Another world tainted. Martin, ignore the machine and help me open the way."

Sure, ignore the death machine and think horrible thoughts about myself. Yay. I closed my eyes.

A smooth, synthetic voice boomed, "Organic systems, exit this facility and face judgment."

I looked. The barrels shifted as the robot adjusted its aim.

"Hurry," Blackbird demanded. "Or a few thousand flechettes will rip your body to shreds."

I glared. "Thanks. That's a big help."

Squeezing her staff, I tried to float above the fear, the self-recrimination that promised an easy source of magic along with a free flaying of my soul. I just didn't want to be hurt anymore. Surely, that couldn't be the only method to release it? I dared to close my eyes again, all too aware of how little time we had, and considered my growing sense for distortions in reality. Could I use it to find my own magic?

I peered inside, not judging, but open to whatever I found. It was a moment of vulnerability, one that I wouldn't have dared before I'd met Blackbird. Logic said I should do what had worked before and leave this experimentation for another time, but I'd reached my limit. I wasn't going to give up, but I wasn't going to follow the same path. My sense of self wouldn't survive it.

And I was rewarded by the presence of my magic, swirling, bubbling, splashing like lava. Awe washed through me. How had I never noticed what lay within? Pushing aside the wonder was difficult, but the robot focused my mind. I imagined a shallow channel between myself and the staff, a finger dragged through sand. *Yes*. The magic poured into the channel, churning as if there were rocks, but still flowing toward the staff. I wouldn't have to rip my psyche open.

The runes on the staff flared. Those on my cutlass warmed in sympathy. Blackbird caught a rough patch near the top of the way, and directed rune-activated magic through the sphere, sending it out with a fine focus, burning through reality like a surgical laser.

It was done. I staggered, surprised at how weak I felt.

Blackbird grabbed me. "Boy, we weren't trying to cut through ten worlds at once. You must control your flow. Now, pass through."

A deafening chatter accompanied her command. Bits of wall exploded, one after another, forming a line that walked in my direction. The robot's makers had forgotten to program it for due process.

Blackbird barreled into me, and we both passed through the way. I hadn't taken a deep breath—or a shallow one for that matter.

I staggered as the ground jerked beneath me. A bitter stink scraped at my nostrils. Thick wisps of green hung in the air, shrouding the view. Beneath my feet, gray-blue metal trembled. It jerked again, sideways. At the edge of visibility, I saw why—the teeth of gears meshed with others.

Jerk.

We were on some kind of mechanism. I was about to take a breath to ask Blackbird about its purpose when I remembered her warning that I mustn't breathe, which meant the urge to do so swooped down and crushed my chest. To add to my sense of impending doom, the poisonous mist swirled as flechettes entered from the way. That wasn't fair.

Jerk.

Blackbird stood to one side of the way, gesturing with her staff, and it shrank. She crossed to me, glared for a second, then examined the gear on which we stood. Faint etchings marked its surface, but I couldn't focus enough to read. Blackbird paused at the edge of the gear.

Where was the way? Fast-spinning gears whined on a level further down, ready to crush anyone who fell. Why weren't we moving? I needed oxygen. Didn't Blackbird get that?

She shoved the staff toward me, but there was no way. I couldn't feel it, and I would have, I was sure of it. Panic rattled inside me, and Blackbird's silent demand only made it grow.

Jerk.

The magic wouldn't come. I'd need to take a breath first. I needed to take a fucking breath. Right now. Blackbird raised her hand. The slap didn't come. She put her hand on my cheek, the touch almost gentle, tender. Her eyes spoke of confidence. She believed in me.

Holding back my primal need, I felt for the magic. It was there. I couldn't do it carefully, but I threw magic into the staff. The runes flared. But there was no way. We were too late. God, how I needed to breathe. Dizziness rocked me more than any slap could have.

Jerk.

We'd moved across from another gear, and Blackbird dragged me across. The way revealed itself, the tension so obvious that I should never have missed it. I threw a hand over my mouth, unwilling to trust it. Too late. My vision flashed, then faded to black. I couldn't hold any longer. I had to breathe. It was inevitable. I gave in.

Blackbird hit me with her staff, knocking me forward, and I stumbled, breathing in sharp gasps, before dropping to my knees. The air was fresh, clean.

I swore. A lot.

"I told you to take a breath before we went through the way."

Hurt and angered by the injustice, I stood, my hands out for emphasis. "I wasn't ready."

"Always be ready, or death will find you. It never rests. It never gives up. There is no room for mistakes. I despair that you will ever take this seriously."

"*This?* After what I've done? And you constantly dance around what *this* is."

She shook her head and started down a dirt path. Green grass and wildflowers stretched away on either side. Ahead, a fenced orchard held trees heavy with red and white fruit. Though it was too far to see what kind, my stomach grumbled.

"Come along."

I kicked the grass. She was such a pain in the ass, demanding this and that, using me, demeaning me, and never explaining why —not the whole truth. I'd give her a piece of my mind.

When I caught up to do so, she sniffed and said, "If you apply yourself, there is hope, and in these last days, we must make it however we can."

Confused, I lost the chance to unload the frustration that threatened to boil over inside me.

"Listen close, boy. Some in your world talk of the language of creation. They have no idea of what they speak, and yet language is a form of symbols, and symbols are more than mere representations. If one were to integrate the ideas of mathematics, structural field dynamics, and symanomancy, then perhaps, aspects of all that is—"

Enough. I shook my head. "What the hell are you talking about? Simon Nancy? Dynamics? You sound like you're about to sell me herbal pills for only a hundred dollars a bottle, guaranteed to cure everything from bad breath to cancer."

The butt of her staff came down hard on my foot.

"Ow!" I shouted and hopped away.

"My mistake. I'm an old lady. I'll speak as to a child. The runes on the staff direct energy—"

"Magic?"

"If you will. The magic distorts the local reality, allowing for certain manipulations, and to cut it."

"Like the ways."

"When one world presses against another. Those like us can feed magic into the runes for specific results. It's limited but useful."

I thought of the water and fire she had called as well as the portals. That seemed a pretty big deal to me. What even was magic? Forgetting my sore toes, I wondered if we were like catalysts, making certain reactions possible.

"If we worked together, could we do more?"

"Yes. Under other circumstances. The wayfarers of old achieved much in part due to their great numbers. For the ordinary folk who inhabit the worlds we've traveled, rituals are needed to contact the magic and fuel the runes. The airships were an example of this, though they would think of it as manufacturing. Through ritual, the possibilities are expansive—if one knows which runes to use. Other methods exist with their own limitations, but that is moving far from our present needs."

Damn her. I was bitten by curiosity. "Is it easy to learn the runes?"

"No."

She turned off the path at the edge of the orchard and walked alongside. A fruit picker waved from atop a ladder pressed against a nearby tree. I waved back, nothing they were furry and with floppy ears like a puppy.

A quiet scream sent a tremor through my body. I watched the fruit picker closely, and the fruit.

The fruit watched back.

Eyeballs. The fruit was apple-sized eyeballs in a red protective skin. The fruit picker slid a hand around one, deftly pushed back the cover like opening an eyelid, and plucked it free with a twist. Another quiet scream accompanied this—a scream from the tree, even though it had no mouth. The fruit picker dropped the eyeball into a heavily laden bucket and climbed down.

I walked faster in case the fruit picker offered an eyeball. Fresh. Juicy.

May I never be that hungry.

"Slow down," Blackbird complained.

"You're the one always in a hurry."

I stopped. When Blackbird caught up, I stayed still.

She turned around. "Childish games do not become you."

Screw her scolding. I was exhausted and sore and fed up.

"I'm the one playing games? You're talking to me about runes, but you won't even tell me where we're going. You use me like a battery. And I'm pretty sure you'll be happy to toss me away when I'm out of charge."

"Martin," she said sharply. She looked more haggard, more tired, than at any time since we'd met. "You may have spent your life explaining, but that is not my way. It is true—I have been putting off the inevitable. Fear breeds mistakes. Walk with me until we are away from prying eyes.'"

I looked at the trees. Several eyes looked back. Was she being literal? I forced the distraction aside.

"Then you tell me everything."

"Then I tell you what you need to know."

CHAPTER 25

HARD LESSON

We walked on, me fuming and wondering how she was going to wriggle out of answering this time. It was better than imagining Gwen's take. If we could have teamed up to push Blackbird... I rubbed the back of my neck. Gwen wasn't here, and that was that. Just Blackbird. Just me. The corner of the orchard came and went, and we continued toward a small dam.

"I am transporting ambrosia."

Her statement surprised me. Was she actually going to spill the beans? Or the ambrosia? "You mentioned it before. It's from Greek mythology, right? The food of the gods."

"It is not the food of the gods; it is the essence of a god. In this case, the essence of a dead god."

I tripped and stumbled. "You're carrying around the juiced body of a dead god? Jesus, no wonder we're screwed everywhere we go."

"Not the body—the essence. And yes, it could be considered the cause of our troubles, but not in the way that you mean."

"How?"

"You have heard the name Tenekal from my lips. And I believe Nyashoth told you some? I expected so. She does like to interfere. Understand this: as difficult as it is for us to move between worlds, it is far harder for a god, far slower, and for most —impossible even if they wished. I tell you because Tenekal moved between many until he encountered his first real opposition."

"Wayfarers?"

"Ha! We wayfarers are not what we once were. That is by design and with reason. Those who roam can be like strangers to others of the Order. We meet at our hall and libraries by chance. Some settle and tend to the sites, conduct research, or waste their lives in pointless contemplation. We don't trust ourselves, and so we are weak."

That was a dubious claim. Blackbird had plenty of faith in herself. "Should you?" I demanded.

She glared at me. "What?"

"Should you trust yourself?"

"I don't trust anyone. Neither should you. I studied the signs, seeking a cause for the degraded worlds I walked. As time passed, I met others who had found the same or studied the growing ripples. But could we agree on a course of action? No. We should have heeded the dire nature of these warnings and acted as one. Instead, they either desired to waste time convening the council or spend endless days confirming this was more than a natural phenomenon. Fools. Off I went, in search of the eye of the storm. What I found was not a calmness, but a foulness that threatened us all. I stood in Tenekal's presence for but an instant, and yet I knew what he was and what havoc he would wreak. The instant I was away, I sent a rune bird with bearing a warning, but there was little hope it would reach the council."

Blackbird rubbed the back of her neck, a gesture I was prone to. She didn't like what she was going to say. "On the world of

Rayandani, there lived a devout people and a strong pantheon. I believed Tenekal would soon come upon them, creating our best chance to end the destruction. If the gods of this world united, they may be equal to a single god far from his own soil. I warned them. The gods were ready."

"They beat up Tenekal and sent him packing?" I asked, already sure of the actual answer.

"They lost. He had grown more powerful than I anticipated. And his reach was longer—his servants already walked the land, undermining the very foundations of society. More than a score of the scum fell to my fury. Not enough, not nearly enough. The gods went to war and lost. Kesaphus, Rayandani's god of wisdom, fled the battle after receiving a fatal wound. He manifested before me as I sought to leave."

She shook her head and looked everywhere but at me. "He revealed that he had entrusted his daughter to wayfarers who had arrived before I stepped foot on the world. Did Kelwyn or any of the council share that with me? No? Did he still hold a grudge? I had long let it go. Damn him and damn the council. Though in fairness, I had been out of touch for some time. Now, Kesaphus said to me, you must take of me and give to my daughter. He told me that the essence was a beginning, a seed of hope that may one day sprout into an answer—a way to defeat Tenekal. Then he gave me a bottle, held his shimmering hand over it, and let his golden blood drip until it was full. I suspect they fought the battle to buy his daughter time. They should have fought longer."

"And then," I said, needing more. I thought of the golden being that had called out for help.

"And then he faded away, and Tenekal was robbed of his meal. For now. I felt the fury from across the world. He does not take well to being thwarted. I remind myself of that every time I feel tired or weak, and it makes it all worthwhile."

Now there was a grudge. I let that thread go and picked up another.

"So, you're Ubering his god juice to—you do know where his daughter is, right?"

"Obviously. There is only one place she could be. And that is the cathedral of the Order of Wayfarers."

Well, didn't that sound grand. "And this goddess, can she defeat Tenekal? Kesaphus didn't sound confident."

"Confidence is the sign of a flabby mind. The bottle is proof against my senses, hiding the ambrosia, but Tenekal follows, a hound sniffing a wounded fox. If I'd assumed I could saunter instead of make haste, it would already be over. Put aside such childish desires, and focus on what matters. I've said before that our hope is slim, but it is still hope, and that hope lies in the ambrosia and the goddess."

Blackbird sounded even less sure. It sounded like the sort of plan a half-assed writer of a TV show would put together if he didn't know that a second season was going to be made. There had to be more.

"Couldn't you get the gods from different worlds to work together? If we can add our magic, a dozen gods, a hundred, a thousand, they'd kick Tenekal all over the universe."

"Gods are of their own world. Tenekal is an aberration for this reason. Any god that desires to rip themselves from their own world, their own believers, to traverse worlds would not be the kind to work with us."

The implications weren't good. "If this daughter, this goddess, is willing to go after Tenekal, isn't she as dangerous as he is?"

"I don't know."

Great. I rubbed my face, dreading the answer to my next question. "And what makes this goddess so special when all the rest keep dying?"

"I don't know."

We reached the dam. Several white shapes swam beneath the surface of the murky water, and it exuded a meaty stench. Blackbird settled on a large rock near the edge. Her shoulders were stiff, and the hand around her staff was pale.

"Easy answers are for fools and cowards. What has been is just the beginning. It will get harder from here. Hope may fray to a single thread, one so fine it cannot be seen. But it will only snap when it is abandoned altogether."

I picked another rock and sat, my eyes on the water in case one of the fish decided we looked tasty. Call me paranoid, but I was seeing a trend.

"And after we hand over the ambrosia to this goddess?"

"I will take you to your Earth if I can."

And to Gwen. I cricked my neck. Blackbird had said a lot, but I wondered how much she'd left out. I wanted it all. Or at least enough to reach my own conclusions. The blanks needed to be filled.

"What is the Order of the Wayfarers?"

She worked her mouth before answering. "We are those who can walk between worlds. We watch for those who threaten strife between them and put an end to it."

Her explanation should have been accompanied by the tacky animation of corporate PR.

"So, you're inter-dimensional cops? More like CIA, I bet. Take down a regime here, assassinate there. Wait. You can go between worlds, and that's all you do? You could disseminate knowledge, help cure diseases—"

"Or spread them. Think. You can't slow a river by rolling a boulder into it. You can dam it by rolling in many, but the water must go somewhere, and it may not flow where you wish. We are limited in number, especially now. We cannot chase every new stream and bend them to our will. More important than all that, we are fallible. Hubris stalks all with power. The less we do, the less we damage."

I snorted. Blackbird had been pretty happy to inflict damage so far. I started formulating another question, but she tapped my knee.

"Collect some wood. We'll stay awhile, and I am cold."

Surprised by her admission, I got up and gathered stray twigs, snapping the larger pieces down to size as needed. Staying sounded awfully good. When had I last managed a proper night's sleep? Days ago? Did that mean anything when days and nights could be of any length? Moving further afield, I looked for branches that would keep the fire going longer. And yeah, I checked for eyeballs. I inspected the ends of the branches for bones. There weren't any, thankfully.

With my arms full, I returned. Blackbird was crumpling in on herself. We should have stopped in that modern city for a med kit or a drugstore. But we always had to keep moving. So why stay now? She just sat there, staring into the water. How many worlds had she traversed to get this far?

Once I'd placed stones around a cone of wood, I set the fire alight by striking a powder Blackbird supplied with a rock. The ambushers had stolen all of our food, so we'd stay hungry. I looked back at the orchard with eyeball fruit. Not a damn chance. Not yet.

"Draw your sword," Blackbird said as I was about to relax. "Show me your form."

I raised my hands indignantly. "You're not the only one who could do with a break. I'm done."

"You are young, and time is short. Show me."

I glared. She was just like Nana. I deserved a moment to myself. A chance to rest physically and mentally. I'd earned it. And I'd proved myself fighting. She had a stick. What did she know?

"I don't need an aged crone telling me how to fight."

"I have forgotten more techniques with more blades than you have ever known. Show me that what I taught my child all those years ago has been passed down through the generations. Humor this *crone.*"

She wasn't going to give up. I sighed, scowled, and drew my cutlass, wondering if she'd noticed the runes before and if she'd comment on them now. She said nothing. I stretched, then worked through a series of guards, cuts, and parries.

"Your balance is forward. Any retreat will be slow and clumsy."

"You have a go," I shot back.

"Do not deflect. Do better."

I adjusted my stance, my lips pressed tightly together, and moved onto thrusts, determined to show that I was capable.

"Don't stay still at the end of the thrust like you're waiting for an artist to paint you. Step out of range. You have many bad habits. Consider where your opponent's weapon waits. Bring your blade to a stronger parry."

I didn't have an opponent. I was fine. A grunt of annoyance escaped my lips. Damn her for being right.

No fencing action should be considered as uncontested. Every offensive action needed a defensive component. My form was awful, and I'd been lucky to survive this far. I worked back and forth across the ground, shifting between attacks and parrying an imagined foe, my muscles burning as I kept at it. Eventually, I stepped back, my heel wobbling on a stone, and fell.

"You're dead," Blackbird said with a laugh.

"Bitch," I said as rubbed my back. My bruises had bruises.

"You think I'm a bitch? Let me tell you about my mentor, a real hard-assed bastard. Thought he knew everything. Acted as though he'd been born before the first star shone in the sky of the first world to form. He never let up, sunrise to sunset and beyond."

"Sounds familiar," I said, wiping my blade, then sheathing it.

"I'm coddling you by comparison. Year after year, never a day of rest, never a song, a laugh, a spice. No matter what chore I finished, he demanded more. It took me years to realize the truth. I was so desperate to learn that I failed to see he was teaching nothing. He'd been using me as free labor. I suspect he'd weakened my will, but for whatever reason, I eventually threw it off. All wayfarers have unique quirks. I guess mine is being stubborn."

Shocked by the idea of someone getting one over her, even temporarily, I asked, "So what did you do?"

"I went right up to him when he was having his bath so he couldn't escape, and I told him I knew what he was up to. He had the cheek to claim he was teaching patience. I told him, I'd pack up my patience and be gone in the morning if he didn't change his ways."

"And?"

"He did, grudgingly. The forms of the worlds. The flow of energy. He'd written many treatises and had copies of those written by others. I learned to read his words, and eventually, he schooled me in the basics of the runes."

"Like you haven't with me?"

"We don't have years. I was impatient, too. Once I had enough of a foundation, I stole into the library whenever I could and read voraciously. Out of sight, I practiced every day." She touched her leg, and I wondered whether she'd branded herself.

Blackbird put a hand on my forearm. "I understand what you want."

The fire popped, and I stared into the flames. "After my parents… left, my nana took me in. She was a real bitch. She started training me on the second day. And everything had to be just so. I couldn't breathe in that place. She was obsessive, nuts about these family traditions. After school, she'd force me to learn all these fairy tales and old place names and heraldry and this creed of hers. She'd make me recite it until I'd burned it into my brain."

"Honor thy ancestors. Always be ready. Keep the faith. Learn the way. Darkness will always find you."

"Each phrase could mean whatever she wanted depending on her mood, her temper."

Blackbird took a deep breath. "I can hear my words echoed in that, but they have become confused over the generations. I did not mean them to be an heirloom. That can't be changed. For what it's worth, I apologize."

I shrugged. "It doesn't matter. I haven't lived with her for years. You know, she didn't even believe in Christmas presents. She said it was paganism. So, I stole one from a store and hid it under my bed until Christmas day. I thought I was a good boy because I waited. I woke up early on the twenty-fifth, my eyes glinting, my hands shaking as I took the wrapped box out. The paper had this thick, expensive feel. I carefully loosened the ribbon and cut the tape. Inside was a cardboard box. I opened it. There was a piece of metal taped to the base—a weight. It was just a damn decoration. I had nothing."

My hands curled into fists. Why the hell had I shared that?

"Life can be that way." Blackbird leaned over and sorted through her backpack, pulling out a bottle. She took a healthy gulp and passed it to me. "There's no point waiting for gifts. You do the things you can and don't expect the universe to drop a reward into your lap."

I took a swig, and the liquid burned my throat as I tasted cinnamon and caramel. "So, you've never had a present, even a birthday one?"

She took the bottle back. "Oh, I've had one or two. The surprises are the best."

After another drink, she passed the bottle back.

"It's not always like this. When the chaos allows, live as best you can. There are pleasures to be had, diversions to pursue, company to enjoy. Such times make memories that you can hold tight, and there is no harm done, as long as you don't let them pull you away from your responsibilities. Hmm. I think we should get some sleep, or I'll show you bitchy."

I gazed at her with wonder. A wall had come down between us. I wouldn't describe us as friends, but we were companions, and I'd hold tight to this moment.

Throwing more wood on the fire, I imagined it screaming, and made myself as comfortable as I could. I looked at the bright sky, annoyed that I couldn't even see a star to imagine that Gwen might be orbiting it. But then, did that even make sense? Was Earth in another universe altogether?

Blackbird had been generous with answers for once, leading to yet more questions. I could live with that. I'd get her to her cathedral if I had to carry her on my back. And when she helped me return to Earth, I might even give her a hug of thanks.

And then I'd be under a familiar sky without a target painted on my back by a mad god. No more ways. I'd find Gwen and make sure she was okay, and we'd see where things went. Blackbird—we'd say our goodbyes, and that would be that.

I shifted, suddenly uncomfortable.

Stop thinking and get some damn sleep, I told myself, but it took its time to claim me. It might have been the sun or my various hurts or, as likely, the fish waiting in the dam.

I dreamed about them, too, bodies flicking this way and that as they writhed their way out of the water and to our sleeping forms where they sucked at our flesh and stole little bites of our magic.

At least, I really hoped it was a dream.

CHAPTER 26

WHAT CAME BEFORE

I woke first to a chill air. Night had slunk over the land, accompanied by the hiss of insects and a distant squawking animal. Blackbird shivered in her sleep, and I gently rearranged her cloak. If only I still had my blanket. To warm myself, I drew my cutlass and worked through a series of combinations with Blackbird's corrections in my mind.

As I paused, she grunted, and I decided practice was over. She hadn't gotten to her feet by the time I sheathed my cutlass, so I offered her a hand. She accepted it with no fuss, and I could see by the set of her jaw that the effort pained her.

With no food, we had little to do except spread dirt over the fire and move on. I threw a rock into the dam, causing the fish to dart away. Petty? Yeah, I'll own that.

Our pace was slow as we left a narrow track to walk across the gentle descent of untended grassland. Uneven ground combined with rocks and burrows to make our passage tricky. Blackbird was downright slow, leaving me too much time to dwell on how the last world could have gone differently.

"We are nearing the end of our journey," she said when we

worked our way around a patch of bushes with spiked canes like blackberry that ended with fuzzy tufts which shook on occasion.

Unexpected relief danced across my mind before I brought it to a halt. Experience told me to wait for the penny to drop.

"There are two worlds between us and the cathedral. The first is not unlike your own—at least when I last walked its roads. The second is harmless enough, a land of giant mushrooms and friendly folk well used to the passage of wayfarers. The Order's presence there remains strong, and though we shall bypass all who may recognize me, the path should be safer."

Two worlds. We could manage that. Blackbird's news was encouraging, but her tone possessed more resignation than excitement. I guessed she wasn't that keen on some of her co-workers.

She continued, "I am not my old mentor nor am I yours, but humor me, and let me teach you a little."

My eyes widened. Earlier, I might have dismissed what was coming as a plan to deflect and confuse, but she deserved the benefit of the doubt. "Okay, I'm listening."

Blackbird spoke of the many ways connecting worlds, and how their geometry couldn't be considered like a crate of bottles, each touching in a predictable fashion. Instead, they were more like brain cells—she questioned my knowledge of anatomy at this point—where each cell connected to many others through strands called dendrites. This complexity made it difficult to remember routes, and relying on physical objects such as maps was a good way to end up stuck somewhere unpleasant.

She paused her explanation at this point and stared into the distance. Eventually, she sniffed and continued. Everything a wayfarer needed, according to Blackbird, should be held inside the brain. For if that was lost, then nothing else could help. I said nothing about the staff she clung to.

"To anchor these places, a good wayfarer uses a memory aid

peculiar to the individual. One now passed, used an extensive spice rack they kept in their quarters, securing details with taste, texture, and scent. I use the streets of the town where I grew up running around barefoot. The texture of the ground, the knotted wood of the houses, the little flowers in pots in the middle of spring, the businesses, the little petty feuds—each is a way connected by the people I knew. To ensure my memories aren't contaminated by changes, I never returned."

"That's a memory palace," I said. Some of the external training I'd received as a teacher included dubious topics such as speed reading and memory enhancement.

"A palace? That's a foolish name, but call it what you will, for it matters not. Now, think of something in your life that is rich in memory and detail."

Wow, she didn't understand my life. I'd worked hard to forget as much as possible, especially the details. Add in the amount I'd moved, and I had a big fat nothing. I watched her carefully push aside a dried knot of grass with her foot before continuing and decided that she didn't need to know. Despite struggling with injury and exhaustion, she was making the effort to connect with me. It didn't hurt to be gracious.

"I can use a school. It had a few buildings with several levels." Highbury Middle School. I'd stayed there for the whole three years, longer than at any other. I remembered walking in, all the other kids pushing past. The school office on the left behind a glass window, holes cut for speech and a slot spot to push documents through. That should do.

"Do you remember all the details—the stains, the scratches, any broken furniture—"

"Yes." I tapped my head to indicate it was all in there. A complete lie.

"Good. Think of the entrance. Did it have a door? If so, what was it made of? The color, any sound when it moved, its thickness, its age, any marks or writing. Every time you need to map your journey, this will be the door you open, and opening it will tell your mind to dredge up the details you need."

"I've got it," I said, perhaps a little too fast as she gave me a searching glance.

"Then think of another object visible as soon as you enter. A chair, a shelf, a door, a hook for coats, a weapons rack, whatever comes first. This will represent the world where we stand. Consider the way we arrived. Pick a characteristic of this object that in some fashion can represent the way. Perhaps flaking paint or a poorly hammered nail."

"Done."

"Then let's put it to the test."

She rattled off a series of street names, then demanded that I repeat them. I didn't need a complex method to do that.

"Very good," she said. "Now for the second world."

My eyebrows rose. The directions she had given mattered. And now, those same streets dodged when I tried to recapture them. My attention returned to Blackbird, who had already started sharing details of towns, cities, roads, and distinctive buildings. Much of it made no sense, as she was referring to land-marks I'd never seen and found difficult to imagine.

"Repeat it all back."

I didn't cover myself in glory.

"Martin, that is not good enough. If you get lost once, then nothing else will make sense. Listen carefully, as your life may depend on it."

It wouldn't, but now I was in deep. She went through the directions again, and I did my best to pick out the important names and descriptions: mushrooms, city gates, gardens, and more. I said them back to her before they could slip away, and this time she nodded.

We made our way to the top of a shallow ridgeline. A white

rock formation in a shallow depression lay ahead where the land otherwise flattened out—another henge, I realized as we closed, this one made from crystal. Blackbird used the time to test me on the details she'd shared, demanding answers out of order, and then sighing when I got them wrong. I should have stopped her at the start, and not only for my benefit.

Her voice was strained, suggesting she needed to conserve her energy. When her pace slowed even further, I offered my arm, which she accepted, and the questions ended. Had her wound become infected? We had no elves this time, but she had said the next world was modern, which meant hospitals. I decided to carry her into the first one we saw even if she protested—getting treated would make the rest of the journey quicker.

Once we passed through the great standing stones, I felt the stiffness in the air denoting a way. Perhaps the wayfarers should have built henges to mark each one. That would make navigation easier. Or had the henge caused the way?

"Martin, go to the fifth stone on my left and dig."

The weakness in her voice stole any resentment at her command, and her ashen face sealed my willingness. I walked to the fifth upright stone and tested the soil. It moved easily, and I quickly dug deep. My nails scraped on a hard surface, and I worked to clear the top of a heavy clay pot covered in glazed runes. At first, I tried pulling it free, but it proved too heavy, so I used my cutlass to cut away the wax seal around the lid and opened it.

Fresh bread tickled my nose, along with a mouth-watering savory odor that I couldn't place. I moved my head to one side to allow light, and found a loaf of bread wrapped with a cloth, two smaller clay pots, two glass bottles of water, and a rectangular box. The clay pots were surprisingly warm to the touch when I removed them.

I wiped my hands and brought the haul to Blackbird, who lay resting against a stone.

"A hundred years or more ago, the goddess Chitzetrikri bid me store these. I think she knew."

"Knew what?" I asked.

"There's the rub with gods. You can never be sure."

Inside the pots was a thin yet hearty stew, still steaming. I soaked my share of the bread in it and ate my fill. A hundred years, and it was still fresh thanks to the runes. And it was good, filling me and invigorating me. I gave it my compliments in case Blackbird had made it. She ate slowly, so I opened the box. It was made of thin wooden strips with bumpy lines like bamboo. Inside were bars of soap, roughly cut as with the handmade sort at markets.

"Clean up as best as you can," Blackbird said when I sniffed a bar. "Remember, the first impression matters."

Given the torn and filthy state of my clothes, I doubted I'd be making a good one. But I pulled off my shirt and used the soap and some of the water to wash away blood, dirt, sweat, and whatever else clung to my skin.

When I poured water over my head to rinse, my vision blurred. I squinted, seeing fuzzy gold ahead but out of reach. A distorted voice called out to me, though not by name—the goddess Blackbird sought?

I shook my head, disoriented, and the henge filled my sight. So, the journey was almost at an end, as Blackbird had said. Why wasn't I reassured? Had that vision been real or merely a phantasm from my tired, at sea mind? It didn't matter, I thought as I dressed. Two more worlds and it would be done. I considered sharing the experience, but Blackbird had enough on her mind.

"You sense the way?" she asked.

"Yes," I said, joining her at the center. "So, which came first, the way or the henge?"

"The way. Before my time, the Order liked to mark them for ease of navigation."

Before her time. How long had the Order been in action? But I had another question. "They don't mark them anymore?"

"No. Too many things slipped through. The Order decided it was best to stop advertising their locations."

What slipped through? I didn't ask because I didn't want to know.

Blackbird settled her cloak. She moved a little easier than before, I thought. The food must have restored her as it had me. This time, I didn't wait for her to ask for my magic. Extending my senses, I found it ready inside me as if it had always been there. I reached out for the staff, happy to be the battery if it took us another step closer to the end. Magic flowed into the staff, and I worked carefully by thought to limit it.

"Good," Blackbird said. "Now pay attention as I cut the way."

I extended my attention along the staff and noted the subtlety as she directed the magic into particular runes in a rhythmic fashion that resonated in my blood. She guided it from the runes to the crystal sphere, the energy now more a weave of fabric than a fluid. And the sphere narrowed it to a blade thinner than an atom. She moved this, seeking the point where it would catch, and then brought it down, cleaving reality.

ORNATE LAMPPOSTS GLOWED a warm yellow in the pink of dusk. Cool, dry air lingered on broad sandstone buildings of three and four stories that stretched down six roads. These culminated in a grand circle where Blackbird and I stood. Neat pavers dissected a lawn of sapphire grass dotted with stylish artificial trees with broad rectangles taking the role of leaves. Bicycles waited in stands of wrought iron, surely some kind of tourist service. Four motorcycles stood next to small fuel pumps, their designs curved but without the aerodynamics of modern street racers or the brute force of a Harley. The seats supported by springs were closer to an old bicycle I'd seen in a history book.

I walked closer to one, curious about the lack of tailpipes. A cord ran from the first to one of the pumps. There was no smell of gas or oil. It was electric. I glanced at the trees—solar. Neat. The fourth motorcycle bore a sidecar, a real throwback for such modern tech. This had possibilities. I checked for a button to start, but the motorcycle had an old keyhole, and it was empty. A glint caught my attention. A key rested where pavers met grass, near a smear of gritty black.

What were the odds of it being the right one? No harm in trying. I slid it in and gave a turn. A series of display lights flickered into being, a full heads-up display with no glass. Nice. I thanked Gwen's Blind Lady.

"Hey," I called to Blackbird. "I've got us a ride. It can't be too hard to handle, and hopefully, the owner won't miss it before we're long gone."

"They won't," she said sternly and pointed toward the smear with the base of her staff. "What do you think that is?"

I crouched by the smear. It did kind of resemble the outline of a person.

Ah, shit. Of course.

This city should have been bustling. I'd been so enamored with how it looked that, like with the robot apocalypse we'd escaped, I hadn't considered what was missing. I tilted my head, listening for the buzz of a drone or the stomp of a coffee machine with a bad attitude. There was nothing, but nor were there the sounds of a living city. It should have been obvious, especially the second time. I hoped Blackbird didn't think I was a complete idiot.

"Tenekal?" I asked.

"It must be so. He expends vast energy to push his way between worlds. The ripples of his passage extend far ahead, pushing, bending, crushing reality."

"Unless he's closer than you think," I pointed out.

"Unless he is. In which case, he is coursing after the ambrosia like a hound with the second blood, his rage at being denied overpowering his sense. Or—"

"Or," I repeated when she stopped.

"Or he knows, and that is very bad indeed."

"Either way, it sounds like we should get moving."

I helped Blackbird into the sidecar, surprised that she didn't complain. Her staff went along its length, resting under her arm like a lance. When settled, she pulled two pairs of goggles from within the sidecar. I laughed at first, then slipped on a pair. Enjoy the small pleasures, she'd said before. I wanted a mustache to tweak the end of, but as she didn't pull one of them out the sidecar, I merely unplugged the charging cable and rolled us clear.

First, I tested the brakes, making sure they worked as expected, then sat down and gave the throttle a gentle twist. We shot forward, and I let out a shocked grunt while dodging around a solar tree.

"Do you know how to ride?" Blackbird complained.

"The throttle is sensitive, that's all."

I tried again, very carefully, and the motorcycle cruised forward, silent apart from the sound of the wheels chewing up grass. More black marks stained the pavers I steered onto. I'd learned to ride a dirt bike thanks to Nana, and drive a car. I think she would have made me take flying lessons if she could have afforded them. Needless to say, I was rusty, which didn't help with the differences of a motorcycle held upright by a sidecar. At least there was no clutch to worry about. There was a mechanism that allowed for a little leaning into turns, and it didn't pull left or right despite the sidecar. Five stars. Would recommend.

"So where do we go?" I asked.

Blackbird glared, and I remembered that I was supposed to have memorized the directions. "Oh, yeah."

The starting street was easy, so I took us around the circle, checking for signs. At first, there didn't appear to be any, then I spotted letters stacked vertically. On the second loop, I found The Low Pass and took us down the road.

Abandoned motorcycles and bicycles littered the way, requiring frequent zigzagging. I might have driven over one or two wheels in the process. Black smears added to the challenge. Avoiding them soon became impossible, and they frequently blended into each other. Worse, they often had little piles of black cubes that released a sharp, burning stink when crushed.

"What could do this?" I asked after one particular stretch of scorched silhouettes.

Blackbird, who kept scanning the way ahead, drummed her hands on the metal shell of the sidecar. "Best not to wonder. Focus on getting to the next way."

"And after that?" I asked, remembering the friendly world she promised. "Is anywhere unaffected?"

"Many. Their number is vast. If we're lucky, the worlds he has disturbed but not destroyed will settle down given enough time."

"And if not?"

"There will be many empty worlds to walk for a start."

We passed through several intersections. The traffic signals consisted of four lights in a circle, but all were dark. I rode us past, growing more confident in my steering and less so in our journey. What had killed the locals?

The road hit a final intersection. Neat gardens led to

guardrails along the concreted bank of a broad, fast-flowing river with a salty odor. The road continued to the left and right, but ahead, it dipped into a tunnel wide enough for the four lanes that disappeared into gloom.

I brought the motorcycle to a halt. "I don't like this. Is there another way across?"

Blackbird tapped the edge of the sidecar with her staff as if she were using a riding crop. "We don't have time for delays. I've spent too much already. Are you afraid of the dark?"

The world of absolute darkness with bones and hungry creatures came to mind. I definitely didn't like the dark. But there had been worse. I remembered being locked in a closet, the air stale and heavy, the sides of cheap veneer pressing in like a cave ready to collapse, muffled sounds that warped into a two-headed nightmare prowling unseen, ready to attack if I so much as dared to beg to be let out. How I had cried.

I placed my hand on my cutlass to steady myself. That was all in the past. I wasn't helpless. I wasn't a victim. I twisted the throttle and put my feet back on the rests, wishing the motorcycle could roar in defiance, but that was not to be.

It wasn't pitch black in the tunnel. Weak emergency lights flickered, candles in a storm that played merry hell with my vision and my efforts to steer around yet more abandoned vehicles. The thin sound of our passage echoed, announcing our presence. To what? To whom? This was childhood fears preying on me.

That though reminded me of a nightlight, which reminded me that I was an idiot. I searched for the headlight control, finding a little illuminated switch to toggle, and sent a beam of brilliant white ahead, dazzling my eyes.

The beam didn't reach as far as I hoped, but as my eyes adjusted, I noted more light further along the tunnel. Were we close to the end? Rather than one light, there were many bright spots, as if a dozen motorcycles waited for us to join them. This wall of brightness hid anything behind, yet the hairs on the back of my neck raised.

Letting the throttle go, I coasted the bike to a stop. "I don't like this. We should turn around."

A deep growl hit my ears, followed by more. An engine? A monster? A pack of them?

"Wait," Blackbird demanded.

I watched nervously as she retrieved a thick marker from a hidden pocket and started drawing runes on the bike and sidecar in gold paint. Next, she poured magic into them, her body shaking with the effort. It didn't take long, but I felt a definite tension and wished she'd let me power whatever she'd done.

Panting, she looked up and said, "Martin, turn around. Ride fast. Ride well."

Ride like my life depends on it?

CHAPTER 27

DEMON RIDER

I threw my weight and turned the handlebar, bringing the sidecar off its wheel as I gunned the accelerator, throwing us around to the music of screeching tires. The growls intensified, deep, gravely, ferocious. We dodged back and forth, scraping against the side of the tunnel, then catching the handle of a downed motorcycle. Sparks flew from the wheel of the sidecar on impact and the runes glowed, but when we were clear, I could see no more damage than a slight scratch to the paint-work. Rune shielding: nice.

My back itched. We were being chased. It wasn't just the noise—there was more, a feeling of wrongness. The light at the tunnel entrance beckoned us on, and when I crossed the threshold to open air, its weakness surprised me. Dusk leads to night, I told myself. Well done, Mr. Teacher. With no plan, I careened to the right at the intersection, keeping alongside the river, and dared a glance back.

"Holy shit!"

Demons. Huge, hulking brutes chased us on stocky motorcy-cles with wide tires. Cracks in their wine-red skin emitted a writhing pulse of dirty yellow. Slab-like hands appeared comically large against the handlebars, and their shoulders belonged on gorillas. The heads resembled a minotaur's that had taken a turn into ugly town: snouts, lethally pointed horns, beady eyes, and a long mouth filled with serrated teeth. And, I decided, the growling came from their mouths, not their motorcycles. Worst of all, a number held bizarre guns, big metal things with glass cylinders filled with a red syrup. Something told me it wasn't strawberry topping.

"Are these the locals?"

"No. Maybe. Not as they used to be."

I took us around a tandem bicycle leaning on its stand as if the owners had gone to buy ice creams. A flash of scarlet light hit it, and the bicycle disintegrated into cubes of flying incandescent metal. Hot spots burned into my back, then went numb. I shouted, dodged a raised garden bed, and thumped our wheels down several steps, the motorcycle shaking furiously.

Blasts of scarlet whizzed by. Damn it, I thought, demons and guns? Couldn't this world decide if it was fantasy or sci-fi? Did this place have its own celestial George Lucas? I just hoped he wasn't writing the script.

My leg hit the railing, stinging like hell, but I was grateful we hadn't ended up in the water.

"Left, Martin, up that ramp."

I followed her advice, throwing the motorcycle into a hard left that threatened to roll us. We zipped up the ramp, and at the end, soared over the sidewalk and back onto the road. Once the shock wore off, I grinned at Blackbird. This was insane. We were going to die. But I felt so alive. To my surprise, she chuckled.

The moment didn't last. A demon rider caught up on my right, shedding a stink of sulfur, charcoal, and soured meat. Was it too much just to get from one spot to another, to maybe have a second of fun? I was sick of this shit.

The demon leaned and grabbed for me. I was already in motion, drawing my cutlass and slicing in one action. Runes on the blade gleamed as it cut through the air, though I hadn't meant to feed it magic. I barely felt the impact when metal sliced through demonic flesh, severing the clawed hand.

As I worked the throttle—awkward with a sword in hand—the demon bellowed, lost control of its motorcycle and veered into a pole. A terrible crunching led to a boom—the battery pack exploding. A blue fireball tossed metal fragments and red goop, but we were clear before it all rained down.

Blackbird whacked me with her staff as she switched it to point backwards.

"Hold steady."

I kept my mouth shut and steered the motorcycle back to the center of the road. Blackbird unleashed several blasts of fire, blooms of heat washing against my side. More demonic bellows followed, along with the groans of metal and bangs of cooking batteries. She'd aimed well.

"Not bad," I said with a grin, "for an old lady."

A blast of scarlet zapped by my head, making me duck instinctively.

"Less smack talk, more riding, child. We have to find a route with fewer sightlines."

She was right. I made a sudden choice and turned sharply to the left, the momentum lifting the sidecar once again. Blackbird leaned out to shift the balance and slowly brought the sidecar back to the ground.

We entered a narrow road with wide sidewalks, a café precinct, I thought. The demon fire stopped as they lost us—for a few seconds at least. Streetlamps of black iron still functioned, the historical kind you'd expect to burn gas, but the light was bright and focused downward, creating circles of detail among a sea of shadows. Tables and chairs mingled with food carts and what could have been mangled pots and bent grills or the remains of a shattered vehicle.

I risked a glance, and sure enough, the demons had cornered and were back on our tail, though they'd lost ground. A plan formed. I only need to do a few turns and we'd get ahead, perhaps enough to double back into the tunnel. I shuddered at the thought of enclosed darkness. Didn't that sound fun?

Ahead, a strange machine moved to block the road. It had long spoked wheels, large enough for a tractor, and several demons sat at either end, their legs going round and round. It was pedal-powered.

What?

A wooden lump with metal edging filled the middle. The lump turned, revealing a long barrel, a cannon. We were racing toward a pedal-powered demon tank.

I said the only sensible thing.

"Fuck!"

We were sitting ducks in the middle of the road. I swerved, knocking over a chair, and weaved us down the sidewalk as a huge blast of red and white—some kind of plasma—ripped apart a cart we had passed seconds earlier. The shockwave hit like a whip against my back, and glass shattered all around. The motorcycle belched sparks with every impact, but the tires maintained pressure, and on we went.

"Good work, Martin. Keep to this side, then when we're close, cut across the street and go around. That turret's slow."

She had nerves of steel. We'd have to cross the barrel to do what she wanted. I watched the barrel as it tracked us. The heat of its first attempt had left it bright orange. How long before it could fire again? A smaller blast disintegrated the sign dangling from a nearby building. Oh, yeah, we had more than one problem. Demon riders were still on our asses.

I held our course as long as I dared, then wrenched the

handlebars and took us across the tank. Adrenaline swamped my body, sending my heart into a crazed beat and slowing time. I was more alive than I'd ever been, and perhaps, closer to death.

The barrel followed. Another blast of plasma erupted from the end and shot down the street only to engulf two demon riders. I clenched hard on the brakes and zipped around the side of the tank, demons growling as I passed. No translation, I noted. None needed, really.

The next crossroads was far ahead, and the turret may be slow, but it'd have plenty of time to get off a shot or two or three.

"Martin," Blackbird said, her voice cracking though her eyes glinted, "didn't you hear me? Turn around, right now."

Hesitation was out of the question. I hit the brakes and brought us around in a screeching one-eighty. Yeah, the barrel was already spinning, but I trusted Blackbird, and whatever she had planned, I was happy to sign on.

"Full speed ahead!"

"Aye, Captain," I said in my best pirate voice—blame the adrenaline—and twisted the accelerator hard. The rear wheel spun, gripped the road, and we launched forward.

"Almost there," Blackbird shifted her staff once again so the sphere faced ahead. "Steady."

We were almost about to crash into the tank. The barrel was lining up on us.

"Steady." Blackbird thumped my leg with her fist. "Care to lend me your strength?"

I reached for the staff. "All yours."

Rather than a gentle flow, my magic came as a ragged waterfall. I was too on edge to manage any better.

Ahead, the demons on the tank stared as if they too couldn't believe a motorcycle wanted to play a losing game of chicken with a tank. Blackbird adjusted her staff, bringing it in line with the tank's center of mass. A series of runes glowed as she sent magic through them. I sensed aggression in her efforts. She scooped more of my magic, taking rather than accepting, but how much of her own reserves had she already exhausted—too much?

A wave of dizziness sent me rocking, and it was all I could do to keep us on a straight path. A whipcrack echoed, loud enough for my ears to ring. Blackbird had pierced reality, not with a cut, but with the smallest of incisions, releasing the crushing gravity beyond. Debris clattered forward, and the air shook. The tank imploded, folding, crushing inward, metal screaming, demons crying out, smaller, smaller, gone. The way closed.

On the other side of the vanished tank, demon riders paused in evident confusion. It wouldn't last. I turned us around once more, my thoughts still fogged by the use of so much magic. I missed a ramp and went up over the curb, shaking us violently. A streetlamp loomed. I dodged, spotted a gap between two building, and took it.

Sparks crackled as we bounced between sandstone walls over and over. I fought to keep the front wheel facing forward. We shot out onto another street. There was no time to turn. Plate glass shattered, sparks flying like fireworks, and I had an impression of clothing on racks before I veered right and relaxed my grip on the accelerator.

The motorcycle came to a halt, and I brushed glass out of my hair and off my clothes with a shaking hand, amazed that I hadn't become a pincushion. Yet. I raised the goggles to my forehead and looked around.

We were in a shopping mall, similar enough to ones I'd walked, but different enough to feel like an anachronism. Elaborately carved columns ran along either side of the main walkway. Light fittings possessed the same antique ironwork elegance I'd seen elsewhere. Painted shop signs hung from horizontal poles. Chesterfield couches huddled around coffee carts. Further down the mall, which went on and on, wood and brass travelators led up and down.

Blackbird leaned forward, her head resting on the opening of the sidecar.

"Are you all right?"

She looked up. "Good enough to do what's needed. Don't stop on my account."

I gave her hand a squeeze. We were both at our limits, but I admired her tenacity. She set an example that I wanted to follow.

Growls brought me back to the situation at hand. A demon rider shot out of the alley, heading for the window that I had conveniently *opened*. Like me, it didn't have time to pull aside, instead grinding over broken glass, until it attempted a turn and lost all traction, smashing into the shop's wall. A second demon fared better, made the turn, and slammed on its brakes as it tried to come alongside us. Its momentum was far greater than ours had been, and as it screeched past, I shoved my cutlass into its front wheel.

The force wrenched the weapon from my hand even as it sheared through numerous spokes. The front wheel locked, and the demon somersaulted, hitting the ground heavily. I zipped forward and grabbed my cutlass, finding the blade unharmed by the experience. Which was handy because I then rode over to the demon as it struggled to rise and stabbed it in the back three times.

Its body started sagging to goop before it dropped to the ground. A blast of red hit the back of the sidecar, spewing sparks. That was our cue to move. I sped on, steering behind the line of columns to gain cover. Concrete, plaster, and wood exploded into hot little cubes as the demons took potshots. Merchandise inside the stores we passed received their fair share of devastation, too, and our passage was followed by smoke and flying debris.

Ahead, overturned boxes blocked the gap between columns

and stores, so I darted back onto the main strip. Blackbird used the chance to toss bolts of fire at the demon riders, frying three. I raised my cutlass and cheered, remembered I needed to look where we were going, and jinked to the left, ending up on a travelator with about a hairsbreadth of space on either side. If they'd been as narrow as on Earth, the result wouldn't have been pretty.

"You're kicking ass!" I said as we zoomed up.

"We are kicking ass, Martin. We are."

We were more than companions; we were partners—a team. My heart swelled. Was this what it was like to have a proper family? Blackbird might have been several generations removed, but that was close enough for me.

Clearing the top of the travelator, I slowed to get my bearings. A blast hit the rear of the motorcycle, tearing off the light in a shower of sparks and cubes. Another caught the sidecar, denting the paneling as it ricocheted off. Apparently, there was only so much the runes could do.

The mall kept going, so I accelerated, once again bringing us behind the columns. Demon riders leaped off the travelator one after another in dogged pursuit. The first angled closer until we rode side by side. I switched my cutlass to my left hand, and leaned over for a swing, barely dodging a column, and completely missing the demon.

It snorted at me and raised its gun, beady eyes glinting with an unholy hunger for victory. Blackbird prodded it with her staff. The demon lost control, wobbled, then crashed into the next column.

The blast from its exploding battery rocked us, and I had to pull back down the center of the mall to regain control. It was good timing—we were close to a travelator leading down. This was our chance to ditch the mall and get back on track.

I shouted with pure joy. We had this. We'd pick the demons off one by one, or we'd lose them. It didn't matter which. We'd get to the way, and then we'd sit around a fire and tell each other how it had gone down until we sounded like heroes and our stories were even more over the top than the already crazy truth.

Wilted flowers poked out of buckets on either side of the travelator. As we drew close, I spotted a cart halfway down the slope, flowers painted on the side. Black smudges marred the art and the travelator. A barricade? One I was about to crash into. I hit the brakes and tried to bring us around.

We were going too fast. The turn was too tight.

The motorcycle toppled, trapping my leg as we slid along, the tendons of my neck tight with agony.

Bang!

We crashed into the side of the travelator. I spun, bounced, and then my leg was clear. The cutlass clattered, lost. My head hit the floor, bringing nausea and flashes in my vision. I writhed, confused, bile pushing its way up.

No, I didn't have time for that. I needed… I shook my head to clear it and almost vomited. There wasn't time for weakness. I forced myself up and limped over to my cutlass, taking two goes to grasp it with unsteady fingers, then returned to the motorcycle, blinking over and over to reject the weakness that wanted to pull me to the cold floor.

Growls proclaimed the demons' arrival. I squinted. Eight or so formed a semicircle, blocking any remaining hope of escape. Thick, clawed fingers opened and closed, no doubt anticipating the kill. They were ready for some payback.

I held my cutlass out, attempting eye contact with the monsters while putting myself between them and Blackbird. There was only one way this could end for me. I wasn't sad or bitter. Hell, I'd been lucky to get this far. I'd met Blackbird and Gwen and traveled worlds. I'd been changed by desperation and horror, but also by beauty and friendship. Yes, I was going to die, but I wasn't giving up.

"Go," I shouted, not daring to look back. "Get to the way. I'll delay them as long as I can."

This was the right thing to do. If destiny was a thing, fate a path to be walked, then I did so willingly. To find family and make the ultimate sacrifice? It could be worse.

I scowled as the demons dismounted.

"Blackbird, did you hear me? You have to leave."

She had a mission. She had to be okay. Billions of lives were counting on her, trillions.

"Blackbird?"

CHAPTER 28

DENIED

The demons raised their guns, focusing my vision. Red sludge bubbled, and I decided they resembled a team of burly paintballers. The glowing cracks in their skin threatened my stomach. It was better to be disgusted than terrified. Would they shoot me or rip my guts out and watch me bleed to death? With those serrated teeth, it was just as likely they'd eat me alive.

"Blackbird?"

"Back away, Martin."

Relief flooded through me, and I dared a glance. Blackbird stood, her feet planted, her staff pointed aggressively forward, her gray, matted hair hanging over her face, unable to conceal the blood dribbling from her scalp. She looked like a force of nature. A wounded one. An angry one. Nature had nothing on her.

But she needs me. She doesn't have enough magic in her tank to take them on.

I checked the demons. Guns it would be, I decided, looking at the tension in their arms. We'd earned their fear if not their respect. My cutlass was useless. We were too far away, and it would only be a gesture. Blackbird should have slipped away when she had the chance.

"Martin, drop!"

I dropped, the command bypassing my consciousness. I trusted her. The cold floor stung the palm of my left hand and the knuckles of my right. A stink of ozone filled my nose. She'd cut another way, small once again, but larger than when she'd crushed the tank. My hair stood on end as the air pressure shifted. Lightning flashed, and a loud crack was overwhelmed by a tremendous boom. A hundred panes of glass shattered.

A slap of air pushed me along the floor, and my eyes filled with white cobwebs followed by black afterimages. I rubbed my face, trying to make sense of what I'd experienced. Blackbird— she'd cut through to a storm or something and fried the demons. Had she?

I walked over to them. They were all on the ground, but twitches of horned heads and fingers confirmed that all lived. That wouldn't do. Gripping my cutlass tightly, I went to each, stabbing again and again until they dissolved to red goop. For the last, I grabbed a horn and twisted its head until our eyes locked together. It groaned weakly, and I put my blade to its throat and slit it from one side to the other.

Over. It was over. We'd won. I wanted to dance, but I was too exhausted.

"We did it," I said, puffing and bent over, hands on my knees. "What a team, right? We've dodged ghosts, escaped lava, outwitted a giant cat, and now slaughtered demons. Tenekal can kiss my ass. We've got this in the bag. Goddess, here we come."

I turned to give Blackbird a hug—it seemed the right moment if ever there was one. My eyes locked on her staff. The wood lay in two pieces, the wood scorched, the ends smoking. The sphere glittered in a million scattered tears.

Blackbird sat against the jagged remains of the glass at the start of the travelator, surrounded by decayed flowers and bloody shards. My throat closed. My eyes burned.

No, no, no.

Over and over it went through my head—a mantra. I sprinted to her, sliding on the floor and holding her gently.

"Blackbird, are you okay? Tell me you're okay."

Her hair wobbled, and she slowly met my eyes. The lines on her face were deep, her skin pale, but her lips quirked, and her eyes were bright. She was happy. I swallowed. She'd live.

Move over, Terminator—you've got nothing on Blackbird.

"The thing about gods of wisdom," she whispered, "is that they know their shit. It took me a while to understand. Fate has been stalking me for so long that I thought I'd dodged it." Her hand went to her shoulder, the same one that had taken two shots already. A piece of metal from the motorcycle sidecar stuck out an inch. There was so much blood. Her clothes were wet with it.

I looked over her head. "Don't talk. Save your energy. There has to be a drugstore. I'll get you bandaged up more than a mummy. And if I can't find a car, I'll get a wheelbarrow—whatever it takes. We've only got one more world to cross, right? Your wayfarer friends will know how to patch you up. They must have the best medicine in existence."

She bent forward and coughed a bloody spittle. "Martin, you special boy, my journey is over, but yours has just begun."

I shook my head. "Don't say that. It's not true. I'll get you there. You'll be okay. I promise."

Her head pressed against my shoulder. "I've traveled long enough. Always knew I'd die like this. I chose my fate long ago, and I don't regret it. But I always believed I'd die alone. And, Martin, I never thought I'd die in the arms of someone I—I trusted."

My heart ached, as crushed as the tank. I held her tight. I

wouldn't let her go. Tears trickled down my cheeks. This moment was the sweetest of my life and the most awful.

She looked up again. "You will finish this for me? You'll take the ambrosia to the goddess?"

"I will. I'll swear it on whatever you want."

A piece of glass scraped as she picked it up. "Lift your shirt."

Refusing her anything in this state was out of the question. I bared my stomach.

"Hold still."

I tensed, and she cut into my flesh. A whimper escaped, but I kept still as she worked, cutting me over and over.

"The third. That must do."

She released the glass and gripped my arm with weak fingers. "To the goddess alone. Remember, do not worship her. Power can seem overwhelming, but you fight to stop Tenekal, not to become a slave nor to give up your reason."

"I'll remember," I managed to choke out. "I'll make you proud."

"You've already made me proud. There may be a few spare generations, but I couldn't ask for a better grandson, a better son. So much I haven't said. Kept too close. Too late for that. But be careful, Martin, bold but careful. Nothing has gone as it should. Why? I ask myself where are all—"

Blackbird's eyes closed. I put my head on hers and felt her body go limp. A woman who had lived for countless centuries, who had the ability to walk between worlds and call down fire and lightning, was gone, just like that.

I sobbed—for the innocence denied to me, for the fear that stalked my life, for the loneliness I had thought conquered. But mostly for lost love. She *was* the nana I'd always wanted—the mother. Our relationship had been messed up, but it was there, and it had been real. She never had to save me, but she did. I'd always had the choice to leave, and I'd stayed. I now knew why.

Losing her ripped up my heart, but the pain was worth having the chance to know her. Walking down that alley had been the best choice I'd ever made.

She'd called me special. She'd made me feel like I mattered—she, a giant in the universe. Tenekal might create ripples, but Blackbird, she created waves.

I RAIDED shops in the mall to build a pyre from furniture and clothes, liberally coating the result with spirits from a third-level bar. The smoke had a chemical overtone that suggested I keep a respectful distance. To set the blaze going, I tossed a lighted cigar, and that seemed an appropriate tribute, though I'd never seen her smoke.

"Goodbye, Blackbird, wayfarer, family, friend. There are gods, so I don't know if that means there are afterlives, too, but if there are, I know you're walking between them, doing what needs to be done, and kicking the ass of any god or devil that needs it. While you're doing that, I'd appreciate it if you kept an eye out for me."

The crackling of fire was my only response.

She would have told me I was being sentimental and wasting time, but I couldn't leave her body to rot. In fact, I stayed while the pyre turned to potentially toxic ash, thinking of how we'd met, the tense moments that became something more. When I found Gwen, I'd have to tell her there was more to Blackbird than a grouchy attitude and a domineering manner. If she didn't already know. Blackbird had driven us because she, too, was driven—by the most desperate of circumstances.

More demons could have ridden in to interrupt my mourning, but I knew they wouldn't, or I didn't care. Either way, my vigil remained undisturbed. To my surprise, daylight spread through the mall. The night couldn't have been longer than a couple of hours. That, I decided, was a small mercy.

I slung Blackbird's backpack over my shoulder and adjusted the leather straps to fit my larger shoulders. The staff was a lost cause, but I crouched to pick up a small shard from the sphere. A childish notion, but I thought if I took it to the cathedral of her Order, it would be like a small part of her had completed the journey. I cleaned my blade and sheathed it.

Time to go.

The motorcycle lay where it had fallen, the sidecar having snapped off when we crashed. Originally, I'd planned to find another in better condition, but I hauled it up, inspected it for obvious signs of imminent detonation, and tested the throttle. It bucked forward, so I mounted and searched for a clear travelator.

On the ground level, a door provided a better exit than my entrance. I passed the broken window at a sedate pace. There were no signs of demons by the time I reached the river, and if I ignored the abandoned vehicles and streets, I could almost imagine it being a quiet Sunday morning, a Christmas Day or New Year's. I wanted so much for that to be true, for the senseless deaths to be reversed. For Blackbird to walk around a corner, waving, ready to go on to the next world.

At the tunnel entrance, I stopped and checked my cutlass. In a city this large, there must be other routes. A nice bridge, for example, not at all dark. But that wasn't the way to start this leg of the journey. Screw the demons. I had somewhere to be. Pursing my lips, I rode down into the darkness.

When I turned the headlight on, the motorcycle pinged a warning: fifteen percent charge. Plenty. I weaved my way forward, bicycles and motorcycles creating shifting shadows, but I wasn't afraid. I *wanted* there to be demons. I wanted to end them, to dice their bodies like tomatoes.

"Come on! I'm here, you ugly bastards. Give it your best shot."

My taunts were unanswered, and I soon reached a spot filled with empty bottles, cardboard boxes, and an assortment of cans and other household crap—a demon nest. Empty now. Well, they wouldn't be coming back. Blackbird and I, we had cleaned them out. It was a big city, I warned myself. There might be more.

When I left the tunnel behind, my mind turned to more immediate problems. Where next? While I didn't remember all of Blackbird's directions, I had the gist, and only needed to backtrack or scout a few times. The motorcycle didn't quite make it to the last street, failing to respond when the battery hit seven percent. I patted it and continued on foot.

The buildings I encountered changed to shorter, more ornate designs—fussy slate-clad homes interspersed among professional offices in sandstone. Surgeons, lawyers, accountants, and demonologists according to the signs I passed. The last one gave me pause, but it looked as respectable as the rest.

One more turn, and I stopped on a short street with half a dozen wooden garage doors that finished at a dead end thanks to an old tree, the low wall around it suggesting a monument. The tree had bent over so far that its crown touched the dirt, forming a natural arch. Even if I hadn't felt the way's tug, its position would have been impossible to miss. I had made it.

Which brought up the problem I'd been pushing aside. Blackbird hadn't seen her shattered staff. She hadn't known that it was beyond use, that I might be stuck here unable to take the ambrosia any further.

"No," I said. "This is going to work. I have what I need. I won't give up."

My words echoed in the empty street as I stepped beneath

the tree and drew my cutlass. The blade shone except where dark runes promised the key to my problem. Blackbird had given me a summary of her encounter with Kesaphus. Did wisdom equate to prophecy? By her words, he didn't know everything. Nyashoth had etched the runes. The ex-queen was old and thoughtful. That must instill its own reserve of wisdom. Blackbird had talked about fate. Had she known I'd need the runes one day, or had she been preparing a contingency?

Martin Drake, the chosen one…

Hell, no. The arrogance needed to believe that would collapse under its own gravity. Yet, if I was the backup plan, the situation was dire. Doubt flooded into me. Yes, I had the ambrosia, and I was willing deliver it, but I had no idea what I was doing. I didn't even know which bottle held the stuff. And now, a god would be on my tail. A god so damn powerful that its mere approach twisted and corrupted entire worlds.

It wasn't new, not really. Just a matter of scale. I'd had my own demons trying to bring me down all my life. And there'd been troubled kids in my classes who faced the same. They weren't deities, but they were real enough. What would I have said to the kids? Be true to yourself. Remember, tomorrow is another day. It won't always be like this. Platitudes. But some of them had been so brave, even as they acted out, even as they were the monsters that others feared. If they dared to keep going, how could I not?

My best chance lay in preparing my mind. I slowed my breathing, making it deliberate, consistent, and deep. Then, pushing aside a feeling of vulnerability, I closed my eyes and turned my senses inward. My mind had always possessed a hard core—I would have died long ago without it—but determination now coated it like steel, reinforced by actions I'd never believed myself capable of. I was a killer. I was ruthless. And I was more.

Shifting my attention deeper, I found my magic. It was lethargic, the pool smaller than before. Blackbird's disappearing tank trick had cost us both. Judging by her example, it was likely to recover if I was willing to wait. I wasn't. It would have to be enough.

I guided the magic down my arm and into the cutlass. The runes all glowed as one, a brilliant green visible even with closed eyes. I focused on them. Some runes had microscopic channels linking them like strokes connecting letters into words, but I was sure they didn't all form the same sentence. This blade had more than one function, which made my task even more difficult.

When I taught, I provided a model for kids to copy in the beginning. Pulling away the supporting scaffolding came later. Did I have a model? I thought back to the runes on Blackbird's staff, to the ones I'd felt her activate. Yes. They matched a set on the cutlass. I guided the magic toward these. It flowed, sloppy enough that other runes fizzed, but the brightest were those I needed. There was an order to how she'd done it as well, a rhythm.

Exhaustion tested my focus, turning my arms heavy. How had Blackbird managed this and so much more? I pushed the magic through the runes and let it retreat to build the rhythm. My hands shook. Whether or not I had the blade ready, if I didn't try now, I'd be tapped and lose the chance.

I licked my lips and opened my eyes. The cutlass glowed, dripping magic like a car with an oil leak. I raised the tip, swinging it left and right, searching for the edge of the way. The blade went right through, catching nothing. I tried again and again, more desperate each time. No matter how many times I swung, I couldn't feel it at all.

I was fucked.

Was I wrong about the runes? There were so many combinations. What if they served a different function and this would never work?

Calm the hell down, Martin. You're acting like a child. What would Blackbird tell you—after calm the hell down? She'd say you were rushing. Take your time. Relax.

Whether that was her advice or mine, I took it. I raised the tip, keeping my hands loose, seeking the smallest friction. A little to the left. No. That's okay. A little to the right. Not yet. Up. Down.

There. Something. A quiver ran through my body, but I kept the cutlass still. Was it real? I steadied the magic with my will and pressed gently. The air resisted. Reality puckered. I held my breath and thrust the blade forward. It took more force than I expected, and I had to put my whole shoulder into the action to get a third of the blade through. Sparks erupted, and through them, I couldn't see the tip.

I'd done it! Almost.

I cut down, using my weight, feeling the way open. The edges were jagged and close together. It wouldn't last long. I didn't care. I was going to fulfill my promise.

"Don't you worry," I told Blackbird, wherever she was. "I've got everything under control. I'm going to finish this."

One last world. I could do that. I had to.

I crossed the way.

CHAPTER 29

WORDS OF ASH

Darkness waited beneath my raised foot, and my body rocked as I teetered on the edge of an abyss. Blue-tinged mist billowed off the moist soil of a path stretching to my left and right, throwing itself lemming-like into the void. A mad vertigo threatened to do the same to me. I could go either way with nothing but the gentlest breeze.

Panic threatened to seize control. The hole pulled at my body like a magnet. Damn vertigo—unless this was twisted physics or a malevolent force.

Not helping, Martin.

Had the way closed? If I didn't fall forward, the only other option was back—the ground on the sides looked ready to fall away without help. But what was behind, the way or another hole? If I turned to check, I'd go over the edge for sure.

I arched my back and willed my center of balance to shift. It did, slowly at first, then gravity gripped me tight. I accepted my fate, whatever it would be.

Dirt puffed as my body sank into soft soil rich with a scent of decaying wood—not exactly unpleasant, but cloying. I wasn't falling. On balance, things were good. I bent my neck to check the size of my way. Closed entirely, which came as no surprise given how badly I'd made it.

I rose and brushed myself off. This was not the start I wanted, but it could have been worse. And that was a solid benchmark these days.

The pathway on which I stood connected to others, and between them, waiting for the unwary, were enormous holes. Together, these formed a winding latticework similar to honeycomb made by drunk bees, more hole than surface. And just how deep were the holes? I kicked a lump of dirt over and watched it fall into darkness. Even after waiting for a count of thirty, no sound of impact echoed up. Yikes. More endless voids than holes.

This was not what Blackbird had described. My memory wasn't perfect, but I knew that for sure. And as far as I knew, a way couldn't take you somewhere else. I hoped. I really hoped. Which meant the destruction had spread here, too. I was glad that she hadn't seen it. Witnessing so many worlds she knew rendered into chaos and horror must have been awful.

Above, a huge broken moon, perhaps even a planet, filled a good quarter of the twilight sky. An almighty divot had been carved out, the debris coalescing in a rough line. Had a glancing collision ripped the gaping wound, or had the moon exploded? What if it had been dug out by the hand of an evil god? There was an image I didn't need. I lowered my gaze.

Mushrooms dotted the paths, some small with flat caps, others taller than me with luminescent gills and a decidedly phallic shape. I wanted to make a joke about not being intimidated, but I had begun a slow turn and the town Blackbird had mentioned in her instructions was either shrouded by the mist or had fallen into the ground.

Was I even sure which direction I'd entered this world? Nothing would stop me from wandering off in the wrong direction. Getting around without GPS sucked. I studied the wrecked moon and wondered if artificial satellites could survive the hail of debris from that. A pinprick blue star poked out from beneath the intact side. Blackbird had mentioned it. I wiped my face, relieved. I might not have GPS, but I had a compass of sorts.

Walking the paths required concentration and caution. Sections were liable to slide away or compress under my weight, and I had to cut back and forth to keep heading in the right direction. It was lonely, dirty, exhausting work, and a nagging fear whispered that I followed the wrong star.

Eventually, the mist diminished, and the holes grew smaller and the paths wider until only land greeted me, silver under the light of the night sky. I took a small break, but I was restless and without food—which I could have easily picked up from the demon world if I'd thought about it.

When I continued, small homes stood here and there in the distance, their roofs low and wide with turf covers. Next to these were fields of mottled white and green plants, their leaves curled, sickly, blighted.

Diverting a little to the left, I crossed to a road heading in what I believed was the right direction. The hard-packed dirt improved my pace, but I soon paused by an abandoned two-wheeled cart to rest. Opening the way had really sapped my strength. The wait gave me time to observe my surroundings. Not a single person worked the fields, and no animals—birds or sheep or whatever—took advantage of helpless crops.

What moved me on were the occasional long, thin strands of white that drifted by as if the mist had dried up rather than evaporated. They stuck to the cart like cotton candy and hurt like hell when I had to pull one off my arm. Thankfully, my bikini line was covered.

On went the road, seemingly extending as I advanced along its surface. And with each step, my throat dried a little more and my stomach shriveled. Given what I remembered of Blackbird's description, at least half a day's travel lay between me and the final way. A thousand things could go wrong between here and there, and that was before I considered my own needs, like water and food. Logically, I could have left the road to search any of the houses in the fields, but I didn't know what I'd find and inertia kept me moving on. Instead, I chose to the one place Blackbird had warned me against—a wayfarer outpost.

"We'll walk right on by the library," she had said. "Remember, no contact with wayfarers until we reach the cathedral."

I figured it had to be the safest place around, especially given they didn't know me from a bar of soap. I wouldn't tell them a thing, that I had come from Earth, that I had ambrosia, that I had traveled with Blackbird. But they knew what had happened here, and if I played my cards right and dredged up the tiny measure of charm I reserved for job interviews, they might be willing to tell me. For once, I wanted to know what I was getting into.

The library proved easy to find.

A waist-high wall sprouted at the side of the road with flowering bushes of many kinds lining the inside. The different textures and shapes didn't go together in my mind, and none of them resembled the flora I'd seen so far. Pillars rose at regular intervals along the wall, each topped by carvings of animal heads, some familiar, some unsettlingly alien. Chiseled runes ran down the sides, and I sensed a latent power within them.

Further inside and beyond a variety of trees, I spotted the peaked roof of a building. A small, neat wooden gate opened with the barest of touches, and I was inside, walking down a cobblestone path worn smooth by countless feet.

A blur in front of my eyes. I stopped and jerked back. A fine line rested at eye-height, taut against the bridge of my nose. It was one of the sticky white strands I'd encountered earlier, and it stretched across the path between two plants. Blinking, I pulled back until the strand ripped away a layer of skin and twanged like a guitar string. A few choice words followed.

My nose hurt, but something stuck to my eyeballs? I shuddered and gritted my teeth against the thought. No way would I let that happen. I drew my cutlass, ducked beneath the strand, and advanced, the extended blade protecting my face.

My eyeballs remained unstuck. Yay, excessive caution.

The path opened onto a structure with a municipal design—chunky, imposing chocolate-brown stone with tall, narrow windows set deeply, and a pair of ebony doors reinforced with decorative iron. One was ajar.

Large chips of stone lay beneath divots in the walls, and I thought I saw the remnants of runes. Someone had taken to them with a sledgehammer, but it could have occurred years ago for all I knew. Perhaps the process of shutting down the outposts was ongoing. That didn't bode well for my thirst, or the situation in general.

Cutlass in hand, I pushed through the doors—which creaked as if made for a horror movie prop—and entered, wishing I had both Blackbird and Gwen at my back.

Gloom wrapped a wide corridor, sullenly nesting in the corners. Polished wood paneling climbed the walls to waist height, followed by smooth white plaster almost entirely covered by portraits. I'd assumed they would be dull oil paintings. But those catching the limited light from outdoors displayed a discordant variety of styles. Several lanterns hung on ropes dangling from the ceiling, but I couldn't see a switch to turn on the blocky shapes.

My pupils expanded as far as they were capable while I listened. I wondered if I should have knocked, but there was no sound beyond my breathing. If someone lay in wait, there was no point in giving them warning. Floorboards groaned as I walked deeper inside. I glared at them. So much for sneaking around.

The painting of an iridescent dragon person caught my attention, which meant I didn't see a lump on the floor before I tripped and slammed my hands and knees on the ground, my cutlass hissing as it slid along the floor. I swore, then cursed the noise that I was making. Master thief I wasn't. Why hadn't I brought a flashlight? I needed to do better.

The lump proved to be a hard rectangular object, with a loop of metal on top. My fingertips traced patterns down the sides. Runes? Only one way to find out. I fed a sliver of magic into the object, and light flared—a lantern. My eyes watered as I waited for them to adjust.

Above, an empty hook hung from a rope. I stood and dusted myself off, noting a pulley mechanism and spots high on the walls for tying off. Lowering the hook would allow the lanterns to be attached, and to turn them on and off. Which would require someone with the ability to use them. I'd found the wayfarer's library for sure.

I reached for the lantern, but a face froze me—no eyes, a grinning jaw with missing flesh and tiny mushrooms sprouting from an ear. Fear jolted me into action, and I darted back to the front doors.

The face remained still. My gaze followed its form to shoulders, a body, pressed against the wall. Very dead. I took a deep breath and told myself it was perfectly reasonable to have acted how I did and that collecting my cutlass was a sensible precaution, not because of the body, but in case I and the body weren't alone.

It didn't move. I knew because I watched it long enough for my eyes to dry out. Dark patches and gaping holes marred flowing robes of tan linen, proving the death wasn't from natural causes.

Look at me—I'm Hercule fucking Poirot.

What else could I deduce? The body hadn't been removed, so it was unlikely I would meet anyone alive. It also meant that someone or something had been happy to slaughter the poor bastard. Why, I had no idea. How long ago? Same. Surely more than a few days to allow the mushrooms to grow.

"Can you tell me anything else?"

The corpse gave no response. I didn't complain—there was nobody to play the part of bad cop. Doors waited along the corridor, and with lantern in hand, I selected the first and went through. Comfortable leather seats with small side tables had been pushed against the far wall. Bookcases covered the one to my right, but they were empty. I ran a finger along a shelf, finding little dust.

Crossing the corridor, I checked the next room. A long table dominated this, with several shorter benches filling either side. Fine porcelain plates with intricate patterns dotted the table at one end, each paired with long, narrow, two-pronged forks that could also have been a variation on chopsticks. Six places set in all, and none of it looked used. If the place had been looted, these would have been worth taking. Unless only the necessities mattered.

I moved onto the third room, this one being much larger than the others. Holding the lantern high, I inspected the troubling sight before me. Empty bookcases lined the walls, leaving only space for the door and a few narrow windows. Three bodies lay near one, close enough in line to hint at an execution. Two were robed, a man and a woman, both with gray-tinged skin and corn-yellow hair. The third was shorter, almost child-sized and thinly built, details easy to observe as they wore only a skirt and Roman sandals. A patchwork of coal black and luminous yellow covered their skin. The ears were no more than holes, and the fingers were long and delicate.

All of them showed signs of attack. Swords, knives, or guns—I didn't look close enough to be sure. There was little reason to check, though I felt sorry for them. No one deserved a violent death. Well, few people did.

In the center of the room, a substantial pile of charred wood and ashes promised an answer, even if I wasn't asking its question. I put down the lantern and ran a hand through the ashes. A corner of a page of thick paper caught in my fingers. I held it close to the lantern, trying to read the remnants of words on the blackened edge, but the whole thing crumbled to nothing. Gently taking another piece, this one curved, gave me what I thought was part of a title.

GUCHANGS WAY MAP OF

"A good old book burning," I said to no one. "Perhaps the wayfarers got on the wrong side of the local priests." Or, I continued silently, the nearby farmers wanted someone to blame for whatever befell them. And the wayfarers couldn't hold them back. I rubbed my stubble, which was rapidly becoming a beard. Blackbird may have been more militant than the average wayfarer.

The next room contained what I needed. Sinks, wooden benches, drawers, a large squat ceramic object with panels and handles, an oven. I'd found the kitchen. Boxes, barrels, and jugs lined the walls, each with rune markings, and each intact. I investigated several, finding raw fish, fresh bread, butter, jam, green speckled eggs, dried fruit, and more. Some jugs held water, others a pale sweet wine.

I couldn't believe locals would have left this food untouched, even if they'd been superstitious. Some enterprising bastard would have snuck back in. Better to have a full belly than a moral high ground.

The occupants and the books had been the only targets, and the attackers hadn't bothered to give their victims a decent burial. I was standing in a mausoleum, but it didn't stop me preparing a meal and scoffing the lot down far too quickly. There were sure to be bedrooms further inside, but sleeping with the dead nearby didn't appeal. And who was to say the murderers weren't nearby waiting for new victims?

But in truth, neither of those reasons mattered. I was close to completing Blackbird's mission. All I had to do was push on. Once I reached the cathedral, I could sleep for days. And I'd sleep better knowing I'd fulfilled my promise.

I collected a few supplies, water, several fluffy rolls of bread, and a small bag of dried fruit, stowing them in the backpack along with the lantern, and left the library behind. Night stubbornly refused to give in to day, and the sky kept its visage of a titanic impact.

Nebulous worries followed on my heels as I continued along the road. The food was good, but it wasn't answers. If only there'd been convenient writing scrawled in blood on the floor. Watch out for pint-sized leopards, or the farmers are psycho. I sighed, resettled my backpack, and focused on the way ahead, or did as best as I could.

Gwen, I hope you're having better luck. I do think you make your own. Can I borrow a little?

CHAPTER 30

WALLS AREN'T ENOUGH

The route went gently uphill. A pointed triangle poked upward where road met sky. As I continued, it became taller and taller. When the road crested, the peak turned into the tallest building of a white city glistening beside a lake with a castle at its center. Behind these were the silhouettes of elongated hills.

On the plains between, the soil was heavily tilled, the pattern of crops broken by occasional orchards, huts, and sod-covered houses. The white fibers I'd encountered had clumped together in many spots, giving me the impression of a gossamer fabric laid atop the land. I wished Blackbird walked by my side, caustically reassuring me that this was normal for the world. Still, the end was within sight, and that gave me a boost.

I pressed on, missing my companions but finding an unfamiliar peace in walking alone. There was little point in thinking ahead, so my mind relaxed, and I enjoyed the little details: grooves from the passage of wagons, an old sandal at the road's edge. When passing a grove of trees, I noted white fibers turned them into cotton candy on a stick, and massive white seed pods dangled from the branches. These trees tugged at my memory, but I couldn't shake loose the reason.

Strands floating in the air grew annoying. Several times, I anchored one to nearby crops and pulled away to clean myself. When a pile of rocks presented itself at the side of the road, I sat and rested. Both the castle and the city filled the way ahead, but it was a seed pod from a singular nearby tree that caught my interest. I grumbled and walked over to it. A darker mass was inside. I leaned closer, wondering what kind of fruit it would bear. My cutlass made surprisingly quick work of the strands—they were dry and brittle.

A shriveled, upside-down head greeted me, the mouth in a rictus. I stumbled back, my heart pounding, my cutlass searching for an enemy I couldn't see. A memory crept out of the recesses of my mind.: a video shared on social media, trees during a flood, with millions if not billions of spiders seeking refuge and spinning countless webs. Shivers chilled me as details merged into a new understanding.

The city wasn't white—webs covered it. An entire city. I swallowed and retreated to the road. Had I known this earlier? Had I buried the obvious to keep my courage intact? My gaze went to the castle, where the way should be, according to Blackbird. The more I looked, the more cocoons resolved. At least, I wasn't going to have to negotiate entry based on Blackbird's instructions. Which was handy because I couldn't remember them. Yeah, handy. Squeeze past a few webs and be home free. The castle defenders had obviously done so well. Ah, shit. This was going to be bad, very, very bad.

"You don't have far to go," I told myself. "Just into the courtyard. That'll be nice and open. A few paces, do the magic thing, and you're through. Would Blackbird hesitate? You bet your ass she wouldn't. Would Gwen? She'd call it a fun challenge and tease you. So, Martin, what's it going to be, running away or getting the job done?"

I trudged toward the castle, taking a fork in the road. The other led to the closed city gates. Beyond the city walls, great ropes of web hung between the rooftops. Equally chilling was the utter silence. I thought of spiders and their far-too-many legs. What use were walls against them?

The road to the castle transitioned to a cambered surface studded with flat stones and bordered by well-maintained drainage ditches. My toe caught on a cracked clay cup, shattering it and sending pieces airborne. Closer to the castle, a variety of debris covered the road and filled the ditches. The population must have fled. Had any escaped? Or had they run to the city, hoping for protection within its walls?

A breeze played over my skin, cooling my clammy forehead. I sniffed at a mustiness in the air that suggested the entire world was decaying. Would it shrivel to nothing, or remain a lifeless husk?

Movement above drove me into a hasty crouch near the lake. A yellow speck, bright against the dead moon. I peered intently, wondering if it was a meteorite burning up, but it began a slow circle over the city.

Life. I gave it a tight smile and a wave. I'd have to finish the journey by myself, but it was good to know I wasn't alone in the world. A second red dot flew in from the hills and joined the first. I thought I could make out large wings and a thin tail, but the light was too poor for certainty. The pair landed on the top of a distant building, shrill cries barely reaching my ears.

Ahead, a stone causeway led from the shore to the castle. I gave the birds one last glance, then jogged to the crossing. At the far end, the castle waited, rough unworked stone coming out of the water, topped by neat mortared offset squares no bigger than my head. As the walls climbed, a row of arrow slits spread. Square towers reinforced the corners, and a solid gatehouse waited opposite the causeway. The angles of the corners were wider than I expected and must have formed a hexagon if seen from above.

Web covered it all, from turrets to the open entrance of the gatehouse. Passing through would suck. I was considering ways to clear the webs, such as with a flamethrower I didn't have, when the ground trembled, nothing violent, but the vibrations moved my whole body. The start of an earthquake? I spun round and round, searching for danger. Could the water of the lake overflow its shores? Would the ground open wide and chew me up?

The vibrations came with noise, a beat, a thousand drums. There was activity in the city. Rust-colored creatures crawled out of windows. Only one was remotely clear due to the distance—a long body, perhaps segmented. I dived for the nearest drainage ditch, figuring if I could see it, the reverse might be true.

Hairs on the back of my neck stood erect. How many were there? How big were they? What if they were smart? I wiggled beneath the broken half of a barrel and waited. The vibration increased, rattling my nerves as well as my bones.

I dared a glance. The city wasn't the only infested location. Creatures slipped over the castle wall. They were massive, their form shooting jolts of terror into my amygdala. Two huge dripping fangs, fourteen legs, and four glistening eyes—a diabolical chimera of a spider and a centipede, but as long as a bus and half as high.

Spiderpedes.

The abominations scuttled toward me along the causeway. I wanted to close my eyes, but I dared not and settled for wriggling as deep into the ditch's muck as possible while peeking through a hole in the barrel. With every pulse, I fought the urge to run for my life, knowing it would lead to certain death. Bristled legs thundered past. And then I saw corpulent spinnerets swaying before the fangs of the next spiderpede.

They kept coming, and I whimpered, my teeth clenched, every ounce of bravado pouring from my body. A rusty, hairy leg slammed down onto my barrel, bending damp wood and pressing down on my chest hard enough to stop me breathing. Which stopped me from crying out.

An eternity later, the leg lifted.

I don't know how many spiderpedes there were or how long it took for all to pass, but at some point, the thuds grew distant, and I scraped together enough courage to look. The last were up over the city walls, joining their brethren who massed on the taller buildings, upper bodies outstretched. The two birds I'd seen earlier soared upward, dodging the writhing spiderpedes, and gaining altitude quickly. Good on them.

"I hope you starve," I whispered to the spiderpedes. They were going to live in my nightmares for a long, long time.

Legs quivering, I made for the causeway. Vulnerable wasn't a strong enough word to describe how I felt on the open ground. You're lucky, I told myself. The birds had cleared my path. Which didn't help with the tunnel-direct-to-hell look of the gatehouse. My pace, fueled by a simmering dread, increased until I jogged without meaning to.

A voice caressed my brain, ignoring my ears. "Hurry."

Checking over my shoulder to see who it was, I found no answer, but I did collect a fresh problem. A spiderpede had climbed back over the city wall and was heading toward the causeway. It must have given up on a feathered meal. I watched the complex undulating pattern of its legs as it closed the distance. A second spiderpede joined it.

"Oh, shit!"

I sprinted, my boots slapping the stone. If I could get to the gatehouse, I could close the doors. Except they could climb. All I had was speed, and they were faster than I could ever hope to be.

A tickle in my brain brought a glint of good news. The way was ahead. If I could get close, I'd find it. A big if. And if I could find it, I could escape. The first spiderpede reached the far end of the causeway, its legs pounding the ground like hammers, its long fangs twitching with delight at the sight of my juicy body.

My arms pumped, and a reckless urge to throw away anything of weight trapped my thoughts until I realized the act would cost precious, unaffordable seconds. The gatehouse appeared farther than I expected, then I was suddenly at its murky entrance. The low height required me to bend a little, explaining my confused perspective.

Darkness enveloped me as I entered, but the fine pressure of a web strand on my cutlass stopped me dead. I couldn't walk blindly into the gatehouse and its hidden trap of webs. Even with the plan to cut through, my body refused to budge, a prisoner of instinct.

Tick, tick. Seconds crumbled to nothing.

The lantern! I dredged it out of my backpack, sent magic into its runes, and, with the aid of the light, picked a side of the gatehouse tunnel with marginally less web. My cutlass sliced strands steadily, but the ground rumbled beneath my feet. The walls and ceiling pressed in, and I imagined myself walking through a spider burrow, a dark form waiting patiently for me at the end.

When the gatehouse gave way to the evening sky, I stumbled out into a courtyard, my eyes wide, my limbs leaden. Webs covered everything from small lean-to buildings to the battlements. Cocoons dangled from every high protrusion.

The way called to me, its tension welcome. It wasn't far from the heavy doors of the keep. I ran over uneven ground, dodging shields, spears with curved blades, rags, and lumpy sacks. The echoes of a terrible slaughter beat at my sanity. How many had poured into this space to defend the civilians, only to be grabbed and spun, encased, to feel the bite as venom flowed into their bodies, their insides turned to soup? How much had it hurt?

Distracted by this macabre image, I stumbled and kicked a wooden bowl. It skittered a short distance before webs caught it. I licked my dry lips and looked back. The first spiderpede had chosen the wall over the gatehouse, and was breaching the top.

I backed up, then stopped. I'd reached the way. All I had to do was cut through. Which I'd managed. Once. Barely.

Webs connected to the nearby keep trembled. Smaller spiderpedes shifted within, about the size of cats. That was in no way a relief. They were everywhere, swarming out of the deepest shadows, chittering, a carpet of legs and fangs and death. That wasn't fair. They shouldn't make sounds. There shouldn't have been so many.

I stared, trying to feel the pool of magic within, while struggling to ignore the oncoming tide without. So many legs. Sweat dripped down my forehead. My cutlass shook in my hand. The adult spiderpede leaped off the wall, its legs flexing like shock absorbers.

"Come on, Martin—" I was about to tear into myself, make myself bleed with the worst moments of my life, but it didn't have to be that way. "Martin, you can do it. For Blackbird. For the promise you made. For everyone."

Dirty strands beneath my feet flexed as the mass of spiderpede young climbed over each other in their haste to claim me for themselves.

For Blackbird. For Gwen. For everyone. For Blackbird. For Gwen. For everyone.

The magic awoke, and I guided it down into the cutlass, urging it to the needed runes in a ragged rhythm.

Please. Please.

The runes erupted in bright green.

I grinned triumphantly.

"That's right, bug central. This night, you go hungry." I sliced the air, catching the way by luck rather than skill, and tore it open. With sparks waterfalling from my efforts, I added, "Next time I drop by, I'll be coming with a tanker of insecticide and a flamethrower or twenty."

I threw myself into the way, a weight slamming into my back.

Another world.

I rolled, screaming, my mind unable to process the location. A spiderpede scuttled from beneath me, its legs having scratched deeply in my flesh to the side of Blackbird's backpack, my shirt providing no protection. I crawled away, my face twisted in horror.

A second spiderpede scurried through just as the way closed. It leaped at me—a disturbing motion with flexing legs—and I slashed wildly. A weight pulled at my leg. I looked down. The first spiderpede was climbing my leg.

So close.

So far.

So dead.

CHAPTER 31
VENOM

My breathing ceased. There was no sound, only a sense of emptiness, of loss that followed the cessation of a drum roll. My body was as frozen as my gaze. The spiderpede grasped me with all fourteen leges. Its four eyes were black globes of alien menace. Two fangs dripped clear fluid. The rust-colored body was arched mid-undulation.

Out of the corner of my eye, I spotted the second spider, still airborne, two severed legs spinning. My cutlass was off to the side, coated with yellow goop. This spiderpede's fangs were raised, ready to sink into my flesh. I'd failed to keep my weapon between me and my opponent. Not that it mattered. Surely one bite was enough when they were as big as cats.

Time rushed forward. I crouched, wrenching my cutlass back to cover myself—too slow, far too slow to help. My left hand rose by instinct and caught a leg, the sensation like grabbing a bottle brush. Fangs of the airborne spiderpede missed my nose by a hair's breadth. Lips curled in disgust, I tossed the creature as far as I could.

The first spiderpede was up past my bent knee, sinking its

fangs into my thigh. The wound burned. Pain and revulsion hunted my sanity. I'd been violated in a way that beatings by hand, shoe, or blunted weapon had never managed.

Screaming, I swung my cutlass at a shallow angle, slashing its body and removing half its length. Yellow goop sprayed. The fangs remained lodged in my leg as its remaining body twitched, upper legs still gripping firmly.

"Get the fuck off me!" I slid my blade under it and flicked with all my might. More agony, but the spiderpede launched into the air.

"How do you like that? Let's see who cuts the best, yeah?"

I remembered the second one. Two missing legs weren't going to put it down. Sure enough, when I spun to face it, pain digging needles into the muscles of my wounded thigh, the little bastard was darting forward. I angled to cutlass to skewer it, but the clever little thing stopped and reared, its body compressing for a jump.

Screw that. I thrust forward, driving the blade through its abdomen. The spiderpede went for my hand. I let go and retreated. The creature felt the weapon with its legs as if attempting to remove it. Yellow dripped steadily from its wound, however, and the monstrosity flopped to one side, its legs writing.

Overcome by a wave of nausea, I, too, collapsed. My head fell in knee-deep grass, brightened by wildflowers: reds, delicate blues, vibrant whites. Very pretty. My skin was clammy. My pulse raced. And my hands wouldn't go where I wanted.

Venom. My insides were going to dissolve into goop, and I'd feel it all, at least until my heart stopped.

I tried screaming for help, but my mouth remained still. That wasn't good. I remembered an Australian documentary about snake bites. I needed to immobilize my leg. But I was already immobilized.

The sky was a rich blue. The flowers were sweet. It really

would have been beautiful if I hadn't been dying. My body went limp. My eyes flickered. They closed. The world went dark.

BLACKBIRD LEANED OVER ME, hands on her knees. There was nothing else, just her against a dark that had never known light.

"Are you done?"

My brow furrowed. Done? Was I dead, did she mean? Surely, she'd be the one to know. She had more experience, after all.

"I—I'm not sure." My head rested on a soft surface. I should stand, I thought, but I didn't want to. "Am I… dead?"

Blackbird sighed. "You're a good boy, but you're mighty thick sometimes. The answer is obvious."

I tried to sit up, but my body didn't respond. "Easy to pretend you know when you won't share the answer."

Blackbird sniffed and stood, her staff appearing in her hand when she opened her grip. She stared at me for a moment, then walked away, accompanied by a rustle of feathers.

Panic tingled along my skin, its roots deep in my flesh. "You're not leaving me here, are you?"

"We're never done."

"What?" That didn't make sense. But Blackbird was gone.

Gwen put a hand on my forehead, which rested in her lap. "She can be a real pain in the ass."

"I wouldn't change her," I said. "I wouldn't change you either."

She ran a finger along my cheek. "We all change, Martin. Do you know what I've had to do to survive? Who I was? Who I will be?"

I closed my eyes, ashamed of abandoning her. "I swear I'll come for you."

My head shifted. I could raise it, barely. She was gone. I let my head thump down against a hard surface.

The darkness was no longer absolute. Pinpricks of light blossomed. Sparks leaped between, trailing faint lines in curved geometric patterns. Worlds—that was what they represented. More appeared, fizzing.

I expected a path of them to wink out, one after the other, a metaphorical cliché of Tenekal's progress. Instead, multiple lines coalesced into a vaguely human shape. Long hair, a small nose, perhaps wide cheeks and a surprisingly large head. A thin, shapeless shift covered her body. She leaned against an unseen object, her knees held tight to her body.

The goddess. I knew this was her, but I couldn't be right. Surely, she should be clad in armor, wielding some kind of mystical sword or spear? Hell, I'd have accepted a baseball bat or a holy rocket launcher.

I wobbled to my feet and staggered toward her, but no matter how many crude steps I took, she remained out of reach.

Her head shifted. She was looking around. Was that a tear on her cheek? Her head tilted. She was aware of me. I waved my arms, but she didn't glance my way.

"You need me," I said. "You need the ambrosia. I'm close. And I'm trying, but I—"

"Help me."

The despair, stronger than any acid, ate away at my soul. "Please."

"I'm almost there," I shouted. "I'll get you the ambrosia, I promise."

"Can anyone hear me?"

Sobs followed, almost child-like.

The pleading burrowed deep into my unwanted past. I knew

that tone. I'd been there. How could a goddess be so upset? Anything she wanted—a click of her fingers and zap, there it was, right? She couldn't be that desperate for a cold glass of ancestral frappe. And why couldn't she hear me if I could hear her?

Something was *wrong*.

The questions swirled, becoming murkier as they blended. I'd been so focused on Blackbird's quest to bring the ambrosia to the cathedral that I hadn't worried about what happened next.

I'd fucked up, though I couldn't say how.

"Hang on! You're not alone."

I stopped shouting. She hadn't responded at all to my words. I was wasting time in this… this nothing. That didn't mean I was done. I had an answer for Blackbird.

"I'm not done, do you hear?"

My voice echoed, and yet there was nothing for it to bounce off. Worlds flashed, then blinked out of existence. A rough line of darkness headed toward the goddess. There was the metaphor. Unless it was real.

"Heal me," I called to the goddess. "I can't help you from here."

Her head cocked.

I raised both my arms and shouted, "Here. I'm here. Heal me, and I'll help you."

She faded.

"No! Don't go."

My body was heavy. I dropped to my knees, then to the smooth nothingness of the ground.

Was I done?

I COUGHED, a hoarse rattle. A thousand scalpels were cutting into my skin. Water hadn't passed my lips for a century or more. Someone nearby muttered steadily, the words slurred and wholly unintelligible. My joints ached, but I pushed on my hands and opened my eyes.

Grass and flowers surrounded me as before, stalks scratching my face and hands. A bird perched precariously on the broken stem of a reed, its black feathers glistening. To my right, a stream bubbled and gurgled as it headed downhill. Overwhelming thirst demanded hydration at any cost, so I dragged myself along, my legs the tail of a snake.

The water was clear, revealing a bed of amber pebbles. I dipped my head low and drank—I would have done so if it had been green and slimy. My raw throat soaked up the cool moisture, and I wanted to throw myself in, to clean myself, though of what, I could not say. Too weak to manage anything more, I lay at the side of the stream, and darkness took me again.

A gentle breeze tousled my hair a short time later. I groaned. My mouth tasted of ash, and my body was sticky and damp. After rubbing my eyes clear of sleep, I took in my position.

The stream remained. That was the voice I'd heard before. Water danced playfully, and a small, dumpy creature flew off when I ran my fingers along the surface. A warm yellow sun slowly rose above the distant horizon, and insects chirped to each other. If this was an afterlife, it could have been worse. I could stay for some time and be quite happy.

My toes jerked and my leg muscles cramped. I clenched my jaw and stretched my legs, bringing my toes up. My legs worked. That was great. The pain, less so. The spasms receded, then came back stronger, only to fade to a determined ache.

As an experiment, I sat up. When my body remained in one piece, I peered over the grass. The scent of salt wafted by, reminding me of the one time I'd seen a beach, but there was no sign of water. A distant forest of pale blues and greens stretched behind me. In every other direction, the ground undulated gently, each view picturesque enough for a tourism influencer to snap. *Taking a walk. Living the Dream.*

Was it too good to be real?

A black bird ceased circling above to land on a nearby reed. Its head moved to follow me as I struggled to my feet. At first, I thought its feathers were real, but leaning closer revealed a metallic glint, a hardness to the edges, and faint rune lines. The legs were gold, beautifully crafted, but with visible articulations. The left had a slight scratch.

"Blackbird?"

Was this an afterlife? Was she my spirit guide?

The bird moved its head from side to side, watching me with one eye, then the other. I looked for a sign of intelligence, body language mimicking the woman I had known. It was just a bird, albeit an artificial one.

"No, you're not her, are you? But you are Blackbird's, right?"

I tried to imagine her taking care of a pet. That seemed unlikely, but a mechanical bird might suit.

Edging closer, I held out my hand. "Hello, aren't you adorable?"

Yeah, I had never owned a pet, and that was the best I could muster. To my surprise, it leaped on, sharp claws tightening around my pointer finger, sending a tingling sensation up my skin and all the way around to my back. It cocked its head, one beady little eye staring at me as if I'd forgotten to do something.

"Sorry, little one. If you were waiting for Blackbird, I have some bad news. She's not coming back for you. She can't. We were on this mission, and she died. I'm going to finish it for her. You see—"

The bird gave a four-note mellow series of chirps and launched off my hand, circling me once, then darting upstream.

"Okay, not much of an attention span. Have a good life or whatever. You're welcome."

In the direction it had flown, sat a small hut of intricately carved wooden slats painted a luminous white with gold highlights. Set around this were lustrous red marble park benches. Its incongruous placement compelled me to survey the area once more, and now that I knew what I was looking for, I spied more huts on the surrounding hills. Was this a hiking trail for wealthy retirees? Some paradise of unearthly delights?

The idea was unbelievable. Instead, I grew certain that I lived. I felt too awful for death, and a hell wouldn't be so subtle. Which meant—

I've reached the final world. I'm almost done.

Energy coursed through my body, and I forgot about the bird and amateur metaphysics. I'd made it. The wayfarers were here. I tested my balance with a step, ready to finish. Pain lanced from the wound in my thigh. Blood and dirt had dried, forming a glue that held to the material of my pants, while hiding the extent of the damage. I'd survived the venom, but the wound needed cleaning.

Where was my cutlass? I remembered stabbing the spiderpede, then… then nothing. Shit. The grass looked identical in every direction. My passage hadn't crushed it. I walked the area slowly, searching fruitlessly until I remembered the attack occurred at the way. Extending my senses, I found the spot and the carcass. The spiderpede's body and legs had folded around the blade like a giant murderous lobster. I kicked it to be sure it was dead and held it firmly under boot to draw my cutlass free.

"You," I told the blade, "will need a good clean and a thorough oiling."

It didn't respond, which was good for my shaken mental health. I set off for the hut, boots swishing through the grass.

Blackbird hadn't given instructions for this world, and it seemed as good as any other direction.

One side of the hut was open to the air, and within there were shelves and a small table. Robes of light woven fabric lay folded on the shelves. I'd seen them before or something similar on the dead wayfarers back at the library. I looked down at my torn shirt and pants. Anyone seeing me would think I'd been attacked by a swarm of giant moths. I'd be much more presentable if I changed.

My mouth twisted. No, I decided. I wasn't a robe kind of guy.

A wide, shallow wooden bowl rested at the center of the table, and a copper jug filled with water stood next to it. On the bowl's other side, a small glass box contained pink flakes.

I opened the lid and sniffed. Soap.

"Martin," I said, stripping. "You have hit pay dirt."

The chill water invigorated my flesh. I took my time rubbing, rinsing, and picking at my leg until I could see the damage. Two pencil-sized holes surrounded by red puckered skin. Less than I feared. Despite the obvious need for antibiotics, I'd been lucky. The juvenile spiderpedes had weak venom—not enough to kill but enough for an unpleasant trip. Blackbird had been there. I couldn't remember all the details, but her earlier words about cleanliness came to mind.

"I'm already on it," I told her.

I enjoyed the sloshing of water as I poured from the jug and took a generous handful of soap to wash my hands and face. It was glorious. A sniff test of my armpits set me back to work, and when I was as clean as practicality allowed, a robe served as a towel. The same robe also served to wipe my blade, which I then oiled. The wayfarers couldn't complain, given what I was bringing. And yet, there was no basket for dirty robes, so I folded it up and hid it under another.

My efforts had soaked my shirt, but the sun was warm, so I

slipped on the backpack and tossed the shirt over a shoulder, confident it would dry. It was good to smell not-terrible, and a bit of sun on my skin connected me to a life I'd almost lost.

Ready to go, I circled the hut. Where next?

The answer came easily. A slight depression in the ground formed a path that I followed a short way, and from my new vantage, the destination was obvious.

A large, yet unassuming building waited on the next, lower, hill. Its white, two-story square design had a large garden in the middle. It came across more monastery than cathedral, but it couldn't be anything else. Windows on the first floor were narrow and set high. On the second, they were larger and decorated with open shutters. The roof was all red tiles, and every wall a satin white. Fields of neatly planted crops surrounded the site, and small figures moved among them.

Beyond all this, a blue-gray sea spread to the horizon with cresting waves a jaunty white.

Yes, this was it. I knew it. My chest hurt with anticipation. Finally. After all I'd been through, after the sacrifices made by my companions, I was here. I tried to run down the path, but my leg sent shocks like high voltage with every footfall. So, I settled for an impatient walk, and ignored the fresh blood.

All I had to do was hand over the ambrosia and get one of those way bridge stones. If they needed to make one, I could wait. Once I popped back to Earth, I'd find Gwen and make sure she was okay. Earth would be an adjustment for her, but even with all its problems, it beat being fried by lava or attacked by monsters elsewhere. Maybe I'd show her around.

That would be that. Life back to normal. I wouldn't need to hop to another world again. I'd hang up my cutlass and find another job. It would be different this time. There was nothing I couldn't handle. It was hard to picture what I'd do, but I'd been through a lot. It'd take time to sort it all out.

I reached the base of the hill and hiked up the next. The discomfort of my injuries and the exhaustion were nothing. I'd never doubt myself again. My parents had judged me, but they didn't know me. They'd never understand who I had become. Perhaps every abused kid harbored a fantasy where their parents would see how wrong they were and come begging for forgiveness. I no longer wanted that, and the realization made me laugh like a maniac, tears streaming down my cheeks. I didn't want it because they didn't matter.

I'd moved on.

And I'd gone far. Worlds. I'd walked them, and now I was saving them. I wasn't a superhero, just the guy in the right place at the right time. And I didn't even need a reward—or praise. I'd done this for the right reason: for others. Eventually. It had been a journey in more ways than one. Sometimes we had to embrace the good we could do in the here and now and not hold back for some convenient future.

All I wanted in return was a shortcut home.

And maybe a shower.

CHAPTER 32

THE THIRD

Tightly packed cobbles took over dirt and grass when my route met the first crops. The expectation of being stopped and challenged brought an uneasiness, as if I'd slipped behind the counter of a café to make myself a coffee. Instead, short-robed workers waved briefly before returning to their toil. With wayfarers coming and going regularly, had I been mistaken for one of their own? Given the chaos in world after world, I'd expected caution.

The wayfarers didn't fear Tenekal. That made sense, though unease persisted in my core. Not only did they wield powerful magic, but they had the goddess to protect them. All they needed was the ambrosia. The cathedral and its world might be a sheltered harbor in a storm. I'd never actually seen a harbor outside of movies. The style of the place had more of a monastic vibe with Age of Sail tech rather than grungy-dock-filled-with-container-ships.

Or maybe it was more akin to a train terminal? On my way up, I'd felt the familiar tension of ways. When I let my senses extend, even more prickled at the edge of my awareness. The selection of destinations was vast. The Order could have built the cathedral here to take advantage of a natural nexus, or repeated use might have scarred the local reality so much the ways were hard to miss.

Either way, they confirmed I'd made it. I forced myself to relax and take in the little details of my surroundings.

Plants with fuzzy green leaves drooped, their branches thick with lavender berries. Slick red vines climbed wooden poles driven into the soil. Between clumps of long thorns, lobed fruit hung, some split, revealing dark, glossy pods. A tart cherry scent wafted to me, and my stomach grumbled.

The cathedral revealed its age as I drew close. The walls weren't perfectly even, and variations in patches suggested repairs hidden beneath the whitewash, some recent given the brighter shades of white. I liked that. The building's condition represented a solidity my life lacked. Year after year, likely century after century, it remained true to its purpose, scarred but functional.

When the path took me alongside, I paused and leaned against the wall. My new sense for magic prickled. There was power here, hardly a surprise, but I'd never encountered so much, and I wasn't sure I wanted to again. It churned in a way I couldn't understand—almost a rejection. Maybe it knew I wasn't a true wayfarer.

Even if the building didn't accept me, I needed to show my respect to its occupants, so I slipped my shirt back on—there wasn't much left of it—and ran my hands through my hair. Even with my cutlass sheathed, I must have looked like a random marauder coming for a cup of coffee and a friendly slaughter. Best to keep my hand clear of my cutlass, I decided before continuing.

Ahead, two steps led to a small paved area and a wide door made of a weathered material veined like a leaf. Several carved faces stared out of this, each surrounded by runes and flowering vines. The impression it gave was more mysterious-forest-people than hippies-in-love-with-nature.

A woman in a scarlet linen robe scoured the paving with a stiff brush, occasionally dipping it in a wooden bucket filled to overflowing with suds. She was young, maybe still a teenager, I decided as I closed. Two stubby horns protruded from the front of her scalp, and what I had at first considered as high-heeled shoes proved to be hoofs.

A satyr.

She sang to herself, a song of a lost love who went to war.

"Excuse me."

She dropped the brush and stood quickly, her gaze taking in every detail of my state before resting on my sword.

"Good day to you, sir." That came with a deep bow.

"My name is Martin Drake." I considered how much to share. If the goddess was hidden from Tenekal, I didn't want to out her. "Can you take me to the person in charge?"

She shook her head, concern in her wide eyes. "The Guardian ordered that we must not enter."

That was worrying. "Who is we?"

She gestured to the fields. "Those who serve the order."

"The Order of the Wayfarers?"

"Yes, sir."

The Guardian hadn't ordered me, and no door was going to stop me, either. That said, I needed information. "Martin, just Martin. What's your name?"

"Melia, sir."

"Nice to meet you, Melia. When did the Guardian give you this order?"

"Yesterday, sir. After the…"

"The what?"

She looked anywhere but at me. "There was a loud noise. Carmine and others tried to get in to see if we were needed, but the door wouldn't open. Later, the Guardian told us to keep outside as it wasn't safe."

Dread scurried down my spine, and my hand went to my sword. That wasn't good at all. Damn. Couldn't things be simple for once in my life? I let out a breath, wondering how much I should be panicking—in a very heroic way, of course. No wonder the goddess had been upset.

"That was a day ago, and no one has gone in or out?"

"Since the Guardian? Not that I have laid eyes upon. Some of us have family working inside, but we must be patient."

If the Guardian had been to come out to give that order, then they likely had the situation under control. Maybe Tenekal's agents had attacked, and now the wayfarers were holed up inside, guarding the goddess, ready to fight off a second attempt. But why was she still upset? One thing that I could be sure of was that the ambrosia was in danger outside, and much needed inside.

"Thank you for your help, Melia. Hopefully, this will all be sorted very soon. Once I've done what I need to, I'll see if I can get information on your people."

"You're going inside?" she asked with trepidation as I moved to the doors. "Are you a wayfarer?"

"That is an interesting question. Not really, I guess. I'm more of a freelancer."

Apparently, my answer wasn't reassuring. She backed away, and once off the paving, turned and fled.

"Have a nice day," I said to her back.

I didn't waste any time pushing on the door, but avoided the carved faces because that would just be creepy. The damn thing didn't budge, and I wondered if it was locked or barred from the inside. I rapped on the surface as hard as my knuckles would bear.

"Hello, anyone home? I have… something for the goddess. Blackbird sent me. I need to get in, right now."

After a minute with no response, I tried again, hammering with the end of my cutlass and shouting as loud as I could. Not so much as a rattle greeted my efforts.

I was sore, exhausted, and really done with the quest thing. Could I bash the door down? It wouldn't be much of a defense if I could. I pressed my head against it, letting frustration flow over me.

Magic writhed in the wood. The wayfarers didn't need a lock, not a physical one. I licked my dry lips and sheathed my sword to press both hands against the wood. The magic flowed out of the carved heads and into the runes. Could I disrupt them like picking a lock? I directed my own magic flow down my hands and into the door.

The skin of my back burned, then twin lines of fire ran down my arms and into the wood. There was a loud clap, and I found myself airborne, the backpack sailing away as I passed over the pavers and crashed into a vine.

Above, the sky that was a shade too blue for Earth had birthed pink clouds. Idyllic was the only appropriate word, and yet, that was hard to square with getting tossed around like a piece of trash. Gathering my wits, I rose, tearing the back of my shirt on thorns, and brushed myself off. The fabric was nothing but rags. Great. I took it off and threw it down, figuring I looked slightly less stupid wandering around bare-chested. Only slightly. Who needed dignity?

"I'm going in," I told the door as I retrieved the backpack. "And if you want to be more than splinters, you'd better let me."

I marched back over and pressed on the wood, on guard for a second attack. But the magic was gone, and the doors pushed open.

"That's better," I told them, wondering how I'd managed

that. Perhaps it was only meant to block non-wayfarers, and I almost but didn't quite fit the magic keyhole.

I'd never really fit in, so that tracked. That hadn't stopped me before, and it wasn't going to stop me now.

"Let's take a look."

HONEY-COLORED timber struts covered in runes held up the vaulted ceiling of a corridor. A scarlet-robed man lay on a board held high by ropes, a chisel in one hand and a wooden mallet in the other. Curls and chips of wood lay on the clay-tiled floor, which was noticeably sunken along the middle of the corridor. On each side, a simple wooden door punctuated white walls with no indication of where they led. The one on the left had a large chip missing.

"Hello up there? I need to see the Guardian."

The man didn't respond. He also didn't move.

"Hey, can you hear me?"

Nothing. I drew my cutlass—screw getting misidentified as a threat. If the guy was dead or injured, they should have taken him down. And my entrance should have brought someone running. I glanced at the nearby doors, but hurried down the corridor, keeping my footsteps as light as my condition allowed. A building this size must have a hundred rooms or more, and I wouldn't resort to searching door-to-door unless I had to.

Bright light streamed in from the far end, promising nothing but peace and quiet. I passed through into a cloister, a covered walkway with repeated arches facing onto a garden. This was repeated on all sides of the formal garden, which itself was massive. I spotted short decorative hedges, complex flowerbeds, vines, trees, bushes, and varieties I had no hope of classifying. The incredible array of colors was restrained by careful placement—smooth transitions of hue giving way to bursts of intensity from complementary colors.

Peaceful. Apart from all the bodies, and the stench of rotting offal. I swallowed hard. Damn it. What the hell had happened here?

More scarlet-robed workers lay broken, or torn up, spread out as if a giant hand had dropped seeds. But they weren't the only ones. Near thirty bodies of a variety of species joined the workers, clumped as if they'd chosen to die together. Scorch marks, great divots in soil, broken stonework, and more destruction told me none of this had been voluntary and no Kool-Aid had been involved.

Some of the dead wore robes similar to those I'd seen in the hut. Wayfarers, not servants.

Other dead wore less-ascetic outfits, no two styles the same. A long leather jacket, a miniskirt, a plastic pair of overalls committing a crime against fashion—clearly these were wayfarers from different worlds. Around them: sticks, staves, crystals, a sprayed deck of cards with runes, a chunky marble revolver, an axe, several spears, and a few swords. There had been a battle, though I couldn't tell who was on what side, or if the attackers had removed their dead, leaving no evidence.

Stalked by fear and doubt, I went among them, unsure where to go next even as a sense of urgency filled me to bursting. Was I too late? Was the goddess dead?

"Come on, where are you hiding? Give me a sign, anything."

"You," a voice croaked.

I spun, weapon ready, my eyes scanning the cloisters.

A figure shifted among tall flowers that looked like a crossbreed of roses and sunflowers. I approached cautiously, noting a pleated kilt in yellow and brown, black sandals, a sleeveless sky-blue jacket of thick wool. That and a two-handed sword as long as I was tall. I dared a glance at their owner, a woman with tangled blue hair. She looked nothing like Blackbird, but I wondered how similar they had been. She'd lost an ear, but it was the large hole in her stomach that was going to finish her off. How she'd held on so far, I had no idea. Wayfarers didn't like to give in.

"I'm Martin. Who are you?"

"I don't know you," she gasped.

"Yeah, I'm not from around here." I wanted to offer help, but getting close was a risk I wasn't willing to take, even given her grievous wounds. "I'm a friend of Blackbird"

"I know." Each word came with a pause. "I saw her sigil on your back."

We laugh at dogs for chasing their own tails. Did I try to look at my back for a second? Yeah.

"Sigil?"

She coughed, a juicy effort that sent spasms through her body. "Why are you here, friend of Blackbird?"

"To see the goddess. And I need to do it right now."

"Why?" She closed her eyes.

Trust was in short supply. I glared at her, wishing I could see her thoughts. "I'm here to complete Blackbird's mission. That's all I'll say."

"It is… enough." The last word was so quiet, I wondered if my mind had filled in the silence.

Ready to shake her if I had to, I demanded, "Tell me where the goddess is. I need to find her."

Her trembling hand rose. "Bird saw."

"What?" I scowled. What was a bird-saw?

"Summon." The woman gasped, went rigid, then relaxed, lifeless.

"Oh, wait," I said. "You mean a bird saw where the goddess

went? And now I'm talking to a corpse. And now I have to summon the bird. Seriously? I'm all out of seed, lady."

I rubbed my forehead. So close. So damn far. I kicked a plant, snapping it in two.

"Hey, bird, wherever you are, can you show me where the goddess is? If it helps, I officially summon you."

Not a bird in sight. I stalked around the dead filling the garden, reconsidering a search of the building. No, I'd been right in the first place—it would take too long. Tenekal had been chasing Blackbird the whole time, and he wouldn't give up on the ambrosia just because she was dead. The goddess needed the ambrosia now.

Then it hit me. Not the bird, but what the woman had said. Somehow, Blackbird had stuck a sigil on my back without me knowing. I wasn't sure what the difference between a rune and a sigil was, but it all sounded like magic symbols to me. And magic symbols had a purpose.

Calming enough to feel the pool of my magic, I directed it to my back rather than down my arms like usual. A prickly warmth suffused my skin. "In Blackbird's name, I summon you. Direct me to the goddess. Come on bird. I need this. How about a break?"

The sky was empty of everything except pink clouds.

A bush shook. I drew my cutlass and retreated. The black bird sang its four notes at me in a mocking tone and hopped into sight. At least, that's how I interpreted it.

"Good to see you again. I have a favor to ask: can you show me where the goddess is?"

It stretched its wings, but didn't take off.

"Come on." I advanced on the bird, dropped to one knee, and whispered, "I brought the ambrosia. I need to give it to the goddess. Will you help?"

The bird scratched at the ground as if considering whether I was worthy. It chirped once, then launched into the air. I sprinted after it, hopeful but fearful as I lost sight of the bird when it swerved through an open doorway.

My steps were clumsy on the soft soil, and my leg burned with pain, but I followed with every ounce of energy I had. Back in the building, more bodies, broken furniture, and scars of battle filled my path, but I only had eyes for the bird. It pulled at me like a magnet. Three more times, I lost sight as it veered around turns or sped through archways, but finally it hovered like a humming bee before an imposing door of gleaming wood and wrought iron with runes inscribed above its lintel. A faint noise escaped.

"This is it? Good job. Thanks. I'll take it from here."

The bird flew out of the way, watching me the whole time as if I were about to change my mind and wander off. I sucked in a deep breath and pressed my ear to the door. Definitely some kind of intoning, quite possibly chanting—the sort of shared voice that could have been beautiful, but instead filled my ears with a disturbing, punctuated passion for nothing good. The bad guys, whoever they were, had beaten me here. I knew it for sure. After everything, I'd done, I was too late.

Or was I? The goddess was there. I could feel her—not like a way—more a wave of sadness that washed against me, over and over. All I had to do was get the ambrosia to her. There was still a chance.

I upended the backpack and sorted through the contents with careless speed. Which container held the ambrosia? I opened several, sure that none of them were right, then realized my mistake. A tingle of anticipation went through me, and I felt for the hidden compartment in the bottom where I'd discovered Blackbird's medical bundle back on the airship. It hadn't been the only contents.

I worked the mechanism and pulled out a pouch holding a

flask with a wax seal. The flask was made of clay with an uneven glaze of navy blue with dull golden runes tracing thin lines around its flat body. The translucent seal covered a metal clip that held the top in place. It hardly screamed blood of a dead god. I'd seen fancier designs at dollar stores. But then, perhaps that was the point: a layer of security through obfuscation. I used a blade from the medical supplies to cut the wax free. I probably should have left it alone, but if I was wrong, this was all for nothing. There wouldn't be time to come back and try again.

With the wax cut off, I pressed my thumb against the metal clip, slowly raising it until the lid loosened.

Pure magic erupted from the thin gap, and I staggered back, almost dropping the flask as the intensity of the power blinded my new sense. It beat at me, seductive, overwhelming. I forced my hand back to the clip, my fingers burning as if stuck in lava. I fumbled the mechanism, then tried again. As the lid closed tight, the assault stopped, and I blinked over and over to clear my mind as much as my eyes.

"That's some serious juice."

A thought came unbidden. What would happen if I drank it? Would I have the powers of a god? I could charge in, destroy Tenekal's goons and get the goddess out of there. What could stop me? Could I raise Blackbird from the dead or teleport Gwen right to me? What would that make me? What sort of person would I be? What kind of god?

I stared at the flask. I could walk between worlds thanks to Blackbird, but there was a difference between that and controlling them. Perhaps I'd have wanted to be a god when I entered that alley back on Earth, fixing all my problems with a mere thought. But I knew all too well how people behaved when they had power over others. It was easier to force than to guide. I never wanted to be that person, taking while saying they were giving.

What had Ms. Hart said? *I need teachers who will put in everything they have.*

Well, I was going to do that. Everything. I'd repay Blackbird's trust. I'd earn Gwen's forgiveness for sending her off alone, and I'd stand up to the bullies of this world and more. And I'd do it as myself.

"Martin, you've got this. You're going to save a goddess, and she's going to save everyone. Don't fuck it up."

I slipped the flask back into the pouch and tied it to my belt, then pushed the doors open and walked through, ready for anything.

Or so I believed.

CHAPTER 33

AN ALTAR OF CONCEIT

Two rows of hexagonal columns framed a hall immense enough to embarrass any Earth cathedral. A ceiling of twisted quartz branches sprouted from these—beginning a good four stories up. There were no windows in the crudely dressed gray stone walls. Blue marble tiles covered the long floor. Runes of bruised purple glowed on each except for an aisle down the center that led to a distant set of three steps at the base of a dais. In front of these curved steps lay numerous long dark lumps.

All of this was entirely impossible. None of it could fit within the confines of the outer structure's dimensions.

"It's bigger on the inside," I whispered while striding forward, my attention settling on figures moving atop the dais, their details shrouded by the serpent tendrils of an oily haze.

The same chanting I'd heard before I entered helpfully concealed my footsteps. My nose shriveled at an unpleasant smell that intensified the closer I came. I dared a sniff. The stench of bloody raw meat and a long-uncleaned toilet. There was more as well, a pungent, cloying floral overlay that reminded me of shops selling overpriced crystals and tarot cards.

Shadows behind the columns shifted back and forth as the runes on the floor pulsed in irregular bursts. I scrutinized both sides as I progressed, expecting cultists to leap out, tossing magic or swinging blades with maniacal glee. Or, knowing my luck, a giant gerbil with flaming farts, spiked tentacles, and razor fangs.

The air itself possessed a nauseating thickness that clung to my skin, and yet it didn't exist, at least not physically. It was magic—unlike any of Blackbird's workings—a nest of corruption, an invitation to hurt, a capitulation of hope. Through it, another note, faint, clean, fragile.

The goddess. I knew exactly what was going on, and it was bad, very bad.

I shifted to a jog. Why not run? Because I wasn't going to sprint headlong and assume my pigheadedness would get me through. I didn't have Blackbird's experience, nor Gwen's flair for surfing chaos. I needed to play it smart. But barging into the ritual sacrifice of a goddess conducted by shady wizards with a little sword and a lot of ignorance was all I could think of. I used my mind's eye to glare at myself.

Run it was.

Details resolved as I reached the steps. The lumps were bodies. Thirteen in all, adults, children, and a few beings with fur or feathers. All were dressed in wayfarer robes, the fabric marred with cuts and blossoms of wet blood. Death was becoming familiar. I'd been the cause often enough of late. Yet this slaughter brought me to a halt, my jaw tight, as I took it all in. The floor runes needed a power source, and these poor bastards were the batteries. How little was a life worth?

"Blackbird," I whispered, kneeling momentarily to wipe my hand in the pooling blood. "They're lucky you're not here to tear them a new one for this."

Five figures occupied the dais. Two wore burnished plate armor, the chests etched with dragon heads. Fluted lines in the steel added decoration and strength, articulations aided movement, and yet they lacked helmets as if they were ready for a photoshoot rather than trouble. One was a man with a jaw you could have used as a jackhammer, the other, a woman with high cheeks and a broad, crooked nose. Scratches and dents in the armor suggested the victims hadn't gone down without a fight. Single-handed arming swords hung from the warriors' thin belts, the kind of weapon everyone thought of when they imagined knights.

Dragon knights—if I was sure of anything, it was that these assholes were as far from chivalrous as you could get. I expected them to charge, but they remained where they were, eyes on a central figure, their lips moving. Still, I wiped the blood on my hand from my heart to my stomach, cleaning it so I could grip my weapon, and maybe to make a statement.

Two in standard wayfarer robes painted with red runes lurked at the back of the hall, arms outstretched, chanting praise to Tenekal in a mix of steady rhythm punctuated by jolting pauses that echoed with unholy power. I was disappointed they didn't have candles.

The figure beside an altar in the middle of the dais was different. His hair was thin and white, including a long, narrow beard that spread beneath a broad smile. Over his plain robes, he wore a threadbare stole with gold-embroidered runes, the effect one of a priest gone wild. He could have been christening a giggling baby.

In one hand he held a staff, the top carved into six tentacles in such a fashion that they appeared to writhe whenever at the edge of my vision. In the other, he wielded a long, thin dagger with short quillons, a misericorde, the sort of weapon used to stab between gaps in armor. On the opposite side of the altar, a bath had been sunken into the floor, its water a dirty red that rippled without being disturbed. Near this, a square table covered by a rune-embroidered tablecloth. Numerous small bowls holding a colorful array of powders crowded one end, while the other side held pure white sheets of paper, a glass of water, and a paintbrush.

I climbed the three steps, stony-faced, and absorbed the horror of the altar.

A girl, perhaps ten years of age, lay in a pool of blood on the altar's black marble top, her long, dark hair spilling over the sides like a frozen oily waterfall. Her face held the chubbiness of youth but none of the innocence. Tears dripped from her closed eyes, igniting a fury that boiled my flesh. Her puffy cheeks were discolored with bruises. She wore a sleeveless, short dress of blue velvet with gold filigree. Cords bound her arms and legs to holes bored into the stone, but there seemed little point in securing the child. The skin of her limbs had been sliced up, runes carved in soft flesh, an obscenity beyond comprehension. And from these came a weak golden glow that I recognized.

Her body twitched on occasion, and her chest rose and fell—alive but unconscious. The goddess. The goddess was a child, and they'd abused her, tortured her.

"Enough!" I shouted, my voice thundering with rage, my body shaking. Heat suffused my every cell. Damn them. Damn them all to hell.

The head priest, or whatever he was, lowered the misericorde slowly and faced me while the rest chanted and mumbled. The old man's eyes gleamed, the skin at the sides crinkling with joy, as if he had been waiting for me to arrive.

"Who do we have here?"

"Martin Drake, descendent of Blackbird. Who the fuck are you?"

He chuckled. "Why, I am Kelwyn, Guardian of the Order of Wayfarers."

Oh, shit. Oh, hell.

That was bad, very bad.

"Ah, Martin, well met, well met, indeed." The so-called guardian tilted his head and grinned as if sharing a joke. "And where is she?"

"Dead," I admitted. "But I swore to carry on her quest, and here I am."

"Blackbird chose most wisely. I knew we could rely on her. Though she may not stand here, her shadow stretches far, sheltering us from that which comes. Yes, I see the resemblance. Boldness, courage. Just like my former student: a resilience beyond most mountains and a determination as hard as diamond. Well met. Now, Martin, it is time for you to complete Blackbird's task. Hand the ambrosia to me, and it shall be done in her name."

I blinked, trying to steady my racing thoughts. He knew about the ambrosia. Maybe Tenekal had told him, or the father god had known he'd die when they took the goddess away. But Kelwyn had spoken utter nonsense. He talked as if Blackbird had been in on his scheme the whole time. I knew Blackbird. That couldn't be right.

"Whatever you're selling, I'm not buying. Drop your weapon."

Kelwyn placed the misericorde carefully on the altar and took a single step closer to me, the empty hand extended.

"Oh, young boy, you are mistaken. The dark god Tenekal is near, and our hopes for survival dwindle faster than an apprentice's first way. Fear breeds mistakes. Do not let fear take away our only hope."

Gesturing at the altar with my cutlass, I said, "*This* is a mistake, one I'm going to correct." I swept my free hand back to indicate the dead, though the carnage he had inflicted outside was far greater. "How the hell can murdering your own people and torturing a child stop Tenekal?"

"That *child* is—"

"A goddess, I know. It changes nothing. She's an innocent."

"It changes everything. Did Blackbird not teach you the hardest lesson of all? Survival requires sacrifices. Some must fall so that others live. Heed this if nothing else: Tenekal cannot be stopped. A mortal cannot defeat a god."

His claim beat at me with its fervor, with his certainty. But if this girl was a goddess, then he must be wrong, or he couldn't kill her. The child whimpered, and I made for the altar. Screw his bullshit.

The two armored wayfarers put their hands on their swords. I was not getting through this without a fight, but the odds weren't in my favor. I needed to keep him talking and watch for an opportunity. How long did the girl have for me to play diplomat?

I'd give it one chance. "Tenekal can kiss my ass. Blackbird said he could be defeated, and I believe her. This girl can do that. She just needs the ambrosia."

Kelwyn ran a hand down his beard and looked at me with sad eyes. "Listen to yourself, boy. That is the naivety of youth speaking. This child has no hope, no chance, no power. Tenekal will never allow another god to threaten him, and this one never could. You see worlds, but he sees the full omniverse. You see a battle, but he sees the war, and it must end soon. Tenekal makes a statement that he cannot be stopped and thus puts an end to the destruction. This message is not for you or me, but for all other gods to know what will come. His might is without end. In his generosity, there is room for us lesser beings. All mortals must know to worship without question and without reservation, and thus we gain our freedom. His servants are many, and we must join them. That is our only path to deliverance—your only path."

The muscles of my shoulders tensed. The fucker. He'd created an elaborate argument to conceal his real reason: he wanted to save his own hide. None of us wanted to die, but to put himself above every other being in existence. Damn, that was some conceit. None of us matter that much.

I advanced, and his dragon knights drew their swords. I didn't care—I'd had enough. There was no special plan to invent. Just me, my sword, and my stubbornness. I extended my arm, the shaking cutlass tip toward the evil son of a bitch.

"You aren't trying to hide from him. You're kissing his ass. Worse, you're bringing him here so you can serve up the kid. And what, the ambrosia's a sauce? How many worlds have been trashed as your boss homed in on her? No, Blackbird wouldn't have gone along with this. I know it in my bones."

The walls of the cathedral shook, and the wind howled right through the stone. Kelwyn ignored it and laughed in my face.

"How few days did you spend in her company? Blackbird, the Endless Walker, the Breaker of Stars, is far more ruthless than I could ever be. For this reason, I cannot blame you. She certainly had me fooled. But she wanted both goddess and Ambrosia for herself. She wanted the protection for herself. She used you poorly."

His eyes were deep pools of sympathy. Here, they seemed to say, is a man that could be the grandfather you never knew. Blackbird was gone, but I could find family once again.

"Young Martin, I would not do so. I would like to know you in the many years ahead. I sense what she saw in you—promise. Whereas she saw the promise of an unwitting tool, I see the potential of a future wayfarer of consequence, maybe even the next guardian. After all this is done, if you wish, you may stay at my side, and I will teach you all that Blackbird withheld.

However, I can no longer delay. What must be done requires precision and cannot be rushed. Hand me the ambrosia, and let's move on from this grisly task."

I lowered my sword, my thoughts as hazy as the air around us. Blackbird had been ruthless. I'd seen that aspect of her many times. But this? She wouldn't have. And yet I'd seen her kill many without a second thought. Perhaps not for herself—but for the greater good, she would have had no limits. What had been her true intentions? Had I been fooled by her gruff care? Could Kelwyn have duped her? Had she meant for me to finish this abomination of a ritual? These thoughts tangled with each other like skipping ropes in a P.E. closet. The ridiculous image stopped my mental spin.

What had Kelwyn said earlier?

In you, I see much of my former student.

He had been the mentor that Blackbird tricked? The answer came to me. I knew what I had to do.

I looked into Kelwyn's entreating eyes. "I don't like it."

"None of us wants to get our hands dirty. Do not fear your part. Your task is at an end. The true burden lies upon my soul alone."

What's next, he's going to tell me that I'm just following orders?

A wave of invisible pressure wrapped my mind, firm yet soft, choking like plastic.

"That's right. Hand the ambrosia to me."

The only sensible choice was to do as he said. What a relief to put aside the weight of decisions. He really was a nice old man.

"You are generous. Thank you for doing this. Please forgive my transgressions. Let me be your servant, though I am not worthy."

I believed every single word. BELIEVED.

A searing pain dug into my blood-smeared stomach. I

grunted, my mind clear, then forced my face to a neutral expression. The rune Blackbird had carved just before her death, this was what it was for. Blackbird was a crafty one. I didn't think she'd known for sure what the bastard was up to, but she must have had her suspicions. Kelwyn didn't know what she had done.

Blackbird had earned my trust. Kelwyn had tried to force it. And now I was going to return it to her. The circle of life or something.

I placed my free hand on the pouch holding the flask of ambrosia as if I were about to hand it over. Going for the pouch also masked the testing of my balance. I launched an explosive thrust at the old man's heart.

He dodged with incredible speed, deflecting my blade with his staff. Damn. He'd been waiting for this. Apparently, I wasn't going to win any Oscars. Before I could pull back to a safe guard, Kelwyn swung his staff in a two-handed swipe and smashed the end into my head, knocking me down the stairs. I rolled over and over, scraping my fingers and slamming my knees.

"Oh, you are Blackbird's, that much is clear. We were right to exclude her from our plans from the very beginning. But the bitch still collected the ambrosia and fled before we could run her down, exactly as Tenekal foretold. Distrustful whore. She thought she was so clever. She thought she had us. Well, she brought the ambrosia right to my feet in the end. In her arrogance, she wanted to prolong the suffering—all for a future that will never be. She failed, and now, so have you."

He turned his back on me and raised his staff. Runes of fire appeared along its length, dancing, crackling. I felt him thrust power at the rear wall. Sparks fizzed along the mortar. The stones groaned, they rattled, then flew back, launched by an invisible blast.

A chill wind tugged at my hair as I forced myself up. The new opening revealed an ocean view—enormous white-crested waves crashing under the light of six red moons glaring through thin breaks in a ceiling of ominous clouds. Was this the sea I'd seen before or a way through to another world?

A web of lightning cascaded across the sky, as red as the moons, followed by a barrage of thunder that pounded my eardrums. I climbed the steps. With that visual display of might came a fog of malevolence, a miasma that settled in, a rancid hunger, a cloying brutality. Tenekal. The god that Kelwyn wished to appeal to was a thug, nothing more, nothing less.

"Our master comes!" Kelwyn returned to the altar and said to his dragon knights, "Ograin, Vordami, kill this fool and bring me the ambrosia."

There it was. The games were over. He knew I had the ambrosia and that I wouldn't be playing a good little boy. Why he'd been so cautious, I didn't know. But now it didn't matter. The guards advanced, eyes hard and jaws set. There was a family resemblance, I thought, brother and sister if not fraternal twins. Their swords were longer than my cutlass. They had armor. There were two of them, and that was if I didn't count Kelwyn and his chanting minions.

I was screwed.

Behind the knights, Kelwyn set his staff to hover horizontally above the altar while he hunched over the table, paintbrush in hand. He was the key to the situation. Could I get to him, upend the table, and put an end to the ritual without another drop of blood spilled?

A prickle of magic brought my attention back to the knights. They had moved apart, blocking any path to their boss. That wasn't their only trick. Their faces distorted, growing snouts, ivory scales, wicked horns, and long teeth. Their hands shifted, too, taking on the same scales while gaining short, pointed claws. I'd called them dragon knights, but I hadn't meant actual dragons.

I took an involuntary step back and glanced at the altar. I was the girl's only chance. How long before she bled out?

I was out of my depth. And I was alone, just like Blackbird had said I'd be.

We all walk alone.

And just like her, I was going to die.

CHAPTER 34

SPAWN OF A LESSER WORLD

Having been entirely clueless about magic and what it could achieve meant I'd never considered the possibility of using it to turn oneself into a monster. Then again, knowing didn't really help. All I could do was cut ways, and for a region filled with them, this hall was remarkably barren.

Tails flopped to the ground behind the dragon knights, the tips spiked like a stegosaurus. Perhaps, I thought with rising fear, I should have classified them as dinosaur people. Wouldn't their bones really confuse paleontologists? Actually, I decided, I should leave labels until after confirming whether or not they could roast me with fiery breath.

Keep it together, Martin.

"I claim this one," hissed the male dragon knight through his dagger-like teeth.

The female dragon knight snarled at her brother. "No, Ograin. He is mine. You slaughtered the apprentices."

Was their manner affected by the magic, or did the magic paint the ugliness of their insides on their skin? The answer might be useful, but I couldn't see how. Instead, I rolled my shoulders and memorized the layout of the dais, hoping to avoid another fall down the stairs.

Ograin opened his mouth inhumanly wide and growled at his sister, who must have been Vordami. "There was no sport in that. You claimed the dire boar's death blow in the forest."

"You ate the head librarian. Didn't even tell me of the hunt."

My nana had once said that the quickest way to end a fight was to be the first to strike. That had worked well when charging the wagon. Would it now? My balance was even, the cutlas tip a little low, but I could work with it. The range was long but manageable.

The secret to a surprise strike is the lack of tells—no shifting or bobbing, no buildup of tension in the shoulders, no withdrawing of the blade to wind up the body. Kelwyn had been ready, but were these two as insightful?

I drove the blade forward, launching my body using my back foot and a twist of my hips. Whether through desperation or the return of my youthful competence, the timing came together with deadly precision.

Air whistled as I crossed the dais, my cutlass flying toward Ograin's chest—his armored chest. At the last moment, I lifted the tip. The point hit steel, slid between fluting on its path up, and caught on the rolled top of his breastplate. I threw my weight to the side to avoid crashing into him and landed with a jolt, keeping hold of my blade thanks to a miracle.

The dragon knight spun, sword cutting in a horizontal path. I rotated on the ball of my front foot, bringing my cutlass up, catching his blow, and riposting with a downstroke. When he pushed my blade away from his snout, I continued the blow, and was rewarded by slicing off a pointed dragon ear.

His shock gave me a half-second edge, and I retreated, blade out as he attempted a vicious backhand slash. The bastard should have gone with a helmet, I thought. Which reminded me that I had no armor at all. He hacked at me again and again, driving me to the stairs. The blows were strong, but not inhumanly so, giving me a small sense of relief—right until Vordami stepped beside her brother, picked an opening, and tested me with a thrust.

I barely parried and executed an awkward sidestep, hoping to use Ograin as a shield. Yeah, I was right back to being completely screwed.

I carefully went down a stair, then another, and another. Good. I hadn't tripped. My next step landed on something soft that rolled under my weight. I landed on my ass painfully and rolled back up with desperate haste. The brother laughed at my antics, and the sister claimed the opportunity, leaping over both stairs and the dead with an overhead swing. I twisted my cutlass to catch the attack, edge to edge, angled my tip and tried to slide it down her blade. She pulled her sword back, and using the mechanical advantage, parried with ease. Panting, I retreated again. There was no way to fight both at once.

My back hit a pillar. I'd retreated to one side of the cathedral while stopping either dragon knight from getting behind me. They had a silent partner of stone. There was only so far I could go. I dodged behind the pillar, and an instant later, steel clanged on stone that could have been my neck. Chips of stone flew. Maybe the pillar was more a neutral party.

"Can't we talk about this?" I said, trying to buy time. "You're wayfarers. Didn't you train to save worlds?"

A spiked tail lashed around the column. I darted back to the next before the knights could slip around the first and pincer me. This wasn't going well. I was alive, but I'd been lucky. I put a hand on the pouch holding the ambrosia. I was so close to the goddess. With my attackers off to one side, could I run past? But they'd be on me in seconds, and I'd be caught between them and Kelwyn.

"We," Vordami said, "were trained to keep the worlds apart. That is no longer possible." Her voice grew louder, as did her footsteps. "Any fool must see that."

They seemed so sure, but Blackbird had thought otherwise. "The goddess—"

"The goddess was a mistake. The weakling council should never have thrown its lot in with her. Like vermin on a sinking ship, they paid the price for clinging to what had been, and we turned it to our advantage. We survived. We will survive."

Blackbird had once said she was a member of the wayfarer council. Were the bodies by the dais the rest of them?

Clomping footsteps stopped on the other side of the column. Was it closer to my right where the shadows dwelled safe from the rune-light? My skin prickled. Why was Vordami being so obvious? Why was she so happy to share?

Ograin exploded from the right of the column, his sword whistling as it chopped toward my neck. The talking had been a ruse. I ducked as the blade chopped stone once again, and the dragon knight followed up with a kick to my stomach and a left-handed haymaker.

Blood vessels ruptured. Pain blossomed on my cheek and nose. Broken, I thought foggily as the force of the blow sent me sprawling to the floor, barely able to keep hold of my cutlass.

Ograin closed. "Mine!" He swung. I was royally screwed.

A flap of wings, a high-pitched cry, and a black shadow flew at him, sending the strike off target and buying me precious seconds to live.

"Get out of it!" the dragon knight shouted, batting the mechanical blackbird away.

The brave little creature called out, then darted at him again. But this time, the knight was ready and flicked his sword, catching its body dead-center. The bird exploded into a cloud of artificial feathers and a thousand little glowing cubes of rune-etched glass that fell on me like rain before dissolving to nothing. Gone. Just like Blackbird.

I screamed in fury, but that only wasted time. Ograin snapped his teeth and struck down at me.

I parried desperately and tried to return the favor of his earlier kick, but the bastard easily avoided my boot with no effort, and followed up with a tail swing that drove a spike an inch into my thigh before I could wriggle out of the way.

Agony. Blood.

There's no coming back from this. They're going to take the ambrosia from my dead body, slaughter that kid, and feed her to their asshole of a god.

To my surprise, it wasn't as terrifying as I would have thought. In recent days, I'd lived more than I ever had before. But that was me. There I lay, as vulnerable as when I was a kid, fear on a leash, feral, but under control. It was no victory, though. I was on the cusp of failing the girl and Blackbird in equal measure.

All those times I waited, trying to appear small, unworthy of attention. The punches, the wooden spoons, the belt, being dragged out in front of the house to add humiliation to the beatings. They stirred deep within, strengthening my resolve rather than sapping it. The students I'd seen while teaching—long sleeves on ill-fitting clothes to hide the hurt. Haunted faces that told me all I needed to know. The system that took my reports and ate them.

I'd wanted to make a difference. I'd wanted to stop the bullies and save others the way I'd never been saved. These assholes might be wearing masks of dragon flesh, but I saw through them. They didn't frighten me, not enough to give up. They were bullies who only cared for themselves. I'd survived worse. Screw them and the dark god they were sucking up to.

I reached for the pouch, dodging a thrust at the same time. My shaking hand worked the opening as I parried a chop.

"Stay still, vermin," Ograin hissed.

"Let me have my turn," Vordami demanded.

"No. Stay away."

The flask was light in my hand. If I hadn't seen the ambrosia myself, I would have believed it empty. Such a small thing to be fighting over. But it was the ambrosia and not me the dragon knights were after. I thrust the flask up like a shield as Ograin readied another attack.

"The ambrosia," I called out.

The Ograin halted mid-swing. Seizing the moment, I flicked my blade without hesitation, finding the asshole's hand and slicing two clawed fingers off. His sword dropped, and I rolled up, thrusting beneath the armored plates protecting his hips. Thin padded fabric resisted, then the cutlass found skin and slid deep, splitting flesh.

A torrent of blood poured down as he stepped back. I staggered to my feet, ready, but he collapsed, arms twitching while his body returned to its original form. It shouldn't have been possible to defeat someone far more experienced. How had I done it? Deception, yes. But he'd been arrogant. The bastard must have relied on intimidation for far too long.

"Ograin!" Vordami screamed and kneeled by her fallen brother.

She was the smarter of the pair—I was sure of it, which meant hanging around wasn't going to end well. I made a stumbling dash for the dais, every step with my wounded leg forcing me to swallow cries of pain.

Kelwyn was up there, letting go of a sheet of paper with a mustard-colored rune that flared magic as it dropped toward the bath. Its descent laughed off wind resistance, suggesting a weight beyond its physical dimensions. It hit the water, spewing an oily magical energy, and was drawn beneath as if by a hand.

As I approached, the guardian retrieved the dagger, raising it aloft, crimson dripping from its thin blade. The chanting reached a crescendo, and all of my existence narrowed down to this murderous traitor.

I leaped up the stairs, my teeth grinding to manage the pain. Kelwyn stabbed down at the girl, and I threw myself at him. The dagger spun away. We tumbled to the floor, and I cut wildly, but the old man held my wrist with both hands, stopping the blow.

"Curse you," Kelwyn growled, spittle flying from his lips and splashing on my face. "I will have to reset the ritual. Understand, boy—you haven't stopped me. This is merely a delay."

We struggled for a breath or two, but with neither of us able to gain control, we separated. I took the chance to check on the girl. So much blood. I hacked through two of her restraints, surprised that the guardian hadn't come back right at me. I saw him look to my side. Not again.

I wrenched my cutlass around, just in time to parry the dragon knight's sword. My wrist shook with the impact.

"Hurry, Vordami," Kelwyn barked. "I need the ambrosia!"

I executed a flurry of blows to drive her away from the altar.

"You will die here, and none shall mourn you," Vordami snarled and seized the initiative, cutting this way and that, forcing me to parry wildly to save myself.

Each time I left larger openings, despite my frantic efforts. She was a better fencer than me, and she was uninjured. The altar brushed against my hip. She executed a back-handed swing. I shoved my cutlass to the right, catching the blade, but she leaned forward and bit my left arm.

I looked down in horror as shock dulled the pain. She'd actually bitten me. That wasn't fair. Her fangs found bone as I instinctively pulled away, and the flask slipped from my grasp to fall on the altar by the girl's head.

Kelwyn hurried over to the table, sparing me a look of open-eyed glee as he dipped his brush into several powders at a frantic pace.

Vordami released my arm, her fangs bloody. She licked them sensuously with a long, forked tongue—toying with me. I couldn't outfence her. I couldn't outrun her. And though I might have been a hair stronger, I couldn't outwrestle the dragon knight either, not when she could take bites at will. Blood soaked against my hip, the girl's, not mine.

Think, damn it, Martin, think. Stop wallowing in what you can't do, and work out what you can.

I had my sword. I could cut open ways, but there weren't any inside the cathedral. Would that have stopped Blackbird? No, she would have used her staff to call forth fire or water or that crushing force. How?

Oh, shit.

The answer was obvious. I was an idiot. Blackbird had been cutting where there weren't ways, where it wasn't hospitable for life or where there was nothing at all. That was why the location affected what she could do.

Vordami lunged at me, and I beat her blade away, snapping back to gain a precious breath. I felt inside me for the pool of magic. It was there, fizzing and popping, hungry to be used. And when I guided it into my cutlass, it flowed effortlessly.

"Kill him!" Kelwyn demanded, his voice rough as he stood, paper in hand, over the ritual bath.

The runes along my blade glowed, and the dragon knight hesitated. Perfect. I needed the time for my act of madness. The cut would need to be paper thin, or it would last long enough to trap myself and the girl. If only I could be sure what lay on the other side, if there was anything at all.

I swung my sword toward Vordami, willing a cut through her body. The runes flared, and she dodged.

"You are pathetic."

There was no sign of a tear. Had I fed magic to the right runes? What about the rhythm? Had there been any resistance? I tried again, and she danced to the side, drawing a shallow slice along my forearm. Wincing, I searched my memory. There'd been something—a pressure, a frequency. I let this sensation slosh back and forth in my mind. I'd failed twice, but the thing about failure, the thing I'd tried to pass on to my students, the truth that only now settled in my soul, was that failure was a good thing. Failure meant trying. And trying again was the only way to get better, to succeed.

I steadied my mind. Vordami had called me pathetic, but I'd heard it before—water off a duck's back. I flowed magic through the runes, like an amateur playing with a piano's keys to hoping to produce a pretty sound. When I found a pattern that matched what I'd felt in the air, I slashed outward, picking a single point in front of her. I didn't need to rip a whole fresh way. Small and simple was enough.

The cutlass tip caught, and beyond its reach, a shower of sparks exploded from a minuscule hemorrhage in reality. A tremendous bang followed, and air flew toward this pinprick, screaming. The dragon knight, only a foot away, was dragged inward. She twisted furiously, and the steel of her breastplate buckled inward as the sparks vanished.

The vacuum caught me as well. I used the momentum and attacked. The dragon knight was bent over but managed to parry my first strike. My second hit her shoulder, sliding uselessly off the steel pauldron. She deflected my next two, far too mobile despite her damaged armor.

Weary beyond description, I wondered if there was any value in ripping through once again, this time going larger and taking us all out. Nobody would win, and we'd all die. The innocent girl would to, goddess or not.

I gritted my teeth. Hell, no. I'd do whatever it took to stop these traitors, but I wouldn't do that. An idea came, something childish, and I didn't have time to reconsider.

"So," I said as she blocked yet another attack. "Were you brother and sister, or were you both looking for someone as ugly as each other to fuck?"

Her face contorted in rage, and she threw herself at me. Her blade was longer than my cutlass. In fact, I thought, noting the grip, it verged on a bastard sword. How appropriate. Her advantage lay in keeping distance between us, allowing her to control my blade before I ever truly threatened to slip through.

The answer? Get inside her tip. Make her advantage a disadvantage. And avoid those bladder-weakening teeth.

I slapped her blade aside, surprising her, and stepped in. As close as we were, I still had the space to bring my cutlass high while her sword swung back. With satisfaction, I buried my blade deep in her eye socket. She slammed her blade into mine, but the damage had already been done. The force drove us apart, and we staggered back. After three steps, she collapsed, her form reverting as it jerked.

Two down.

Kelwyn had recovered his dagger and was circling around the altar. My eyes dropped to the flask. That's what he was after.

"Does it have your name on it?" I said, grabbing the flask. "No, then it's not yours."

I followed up with a couple of half-hearted swings to drive him back and give me a chance to steady my breath and calm my aching muscles. Beneath the fury of Kelwyn's expression, I thought I saw a touch of fear. The old bastard hadn't expected me to defeat his goons. Who knew that we would have something in common?

Doubt in my abilities was the only thing we shared. I used the chance to sever the girl's remaining restraints.

"I'm taking her out of here," I said, my voice flat. It was a statement, not a request. "You can die trying to stop me, but I'm going to do it."

"Arrogant spawn of a lesser world. You are too late. This child is dead. You will die. Tenekal, the hungry, will consume her and the essence of her father. Two more gods to fuel his might. Nothing can stop him."

Dead? I looked at the girl. Her chest wasn't moving. I reached out with my senses. Could I feel her? There was something, perhaps only a fading echo. I squeezed my eyes shut in horror.

"Yes," said Kelwyn. "You understand. Your pain is a prayer to him, a call to honor me, his most faithful servant."

I lay my cutlass down on the altar. There was a different between dead and dying. I didn't know which was true, but it didn't matter. I had only one chance, only one choice.

I opened the flask.

The brilliance of a sun beat at my vision. The entire hall was thrown into stark relief, bleached of color. My chest expanded and contracted with the waxing and waning of a bass buzz.

"What are you doing?" Kelwyn demanded, his teeth bared.

I leaned over the girl, opened her mouth, and poured the fluid between her lips.

"No! It is not for her." Kelwyn threw his dagger.

It hit the flask, ripping it out of my weak grip and sending it spinning away.

Ambrosia sprayed, hissing when it splashed on the floor, only to evaporate faster than my job prospects. I leaped for the flask, but my movement was clumsy, and it rolled away, spilling more. I crawled to it on hands and knees, but it was all gone by the time I held it.

Tossing it away, I stalked toward Kelwyn. The girl was still on the table, a drip of ambrosia at the side of her mouth, defying the evaporation of its brethren. It hadn't been enough. I was too late. She was dead, and I'd failed Blackbird.

Kelwyn appeared as shocked as I. The asshole hadn't thought through the consequences. He'd lost the ambrosia for his master, and Tenekal wasn't likely to be the forgiving sort.

Neither was I.

Runes glowed on Kelwyn's fingertips, and he held his hand out. His staff leaped from above the altar, right into his grip. It was on.

I sprinted to the altar and grabbed my cutlass, my gaze falling to the girl as I did so.

I'm sorry, I told her silently. *Know that you weren't alone. I couldn't save you, but I was with you.*

Her lips trembled, and she took the shallowest of breaths.

She lived.

Grinning like a lunatic, I walked around the altar toward Kelwyn.

He brandished his staff. "Worthless gutter trash. You've ruined everything. I'm going to erase you from existence."

"You can't," I said, realizing that Blackbird lived on through me, and that I could live on through the girl—if I could get her to safety. "He—or she—who lives for others is immortal."

You non-binary folks, too.

Kelwyn raised his staff, runes along its surface spitting purple drips of energy, and slammed it down on the marble floor. The air in front me ripped open, and I lurched to one side as head-sized chunks of rock shot through. They crushed floor tiles, sending shards into my skin. I stumbled away as more rocks poured through, seeming to chase after me. A veritable landslide crashed into a wall, shattering the stones. The wall shifted, and old, dry magic leaked through, invisible, but scratching at my awareness.

I took refuge behind a column, but the rocks smashed into it, ripping off pieces, until it teetered and collapsed. This couldn't go on. Kelwyn had to be stopped, and stopped now. I ran toward the dais in an awkward, limping gait, the earthen assault continuing. A small rock bounced off the floor in front, ricocheting toward me. I brought my cutlass up to protect my head, but the force knocked the weapon from my grip. Dodging another and nurturing an idea, I raced to the rear of the cathedral, running by the chanting wayfarers, moist air buffeting as I passed the seaward opening that Kelwyn had wrought. On I went, around the gesticulating guardian and back into the cathedral proper.

The rock blasts halted, the cacophony replaced by random thuds as the last few tumbled and crashed. I slowed, then halted, holding my heaving chest as silence came to the hall. Even the chanting had stopped. The two wayfarers had been pulverized as I'd hoped. The thrum of their dark magic dissipated, along with the rune light on the cathedral floor.

I grinned savagely. Kelwyn had wiped out his own ritual.

A second column collapsed, stones crashing onto the floor. Dust filled the air, tasting as dry as the magic in the cathedral's bones. I brushed myself off and spied the dagger. It would do. I picked it up with my left hand, blade against the back of my forearm to conceal it, and navigated slowly around the debris.

Kelwyn's rock storm had created another opening in the hall. Beyond this rent in the wall lay a meadow bathed in the moonlight of a different world.

"I'm still here," I said, climbing the dais with leaden legs.

"You have no sword or staff," Kelwyn gloated, "no friends, no allies, no hope. I have you beaten."

Beaten? He was screwed. It was only a matter of whether he'd take me down with him. Or, given how weak my leg was getting, whether I'd collapse on my own accord. Still, I wanted him to feel powerful.

"You're right. I don't know why I believed Blackbird. I thought I had you there for a moment, but who am I kidding? You have centuries of experience. I didn't stand a chance. Why didn't I just go to the bar and have a drink?"

I stood before Kelwyn, my legs shaking, then dropped hard on one knee. The thing about bullies, I knew, was that they loved to feel stronger. They craved others to proclaim their superiority.

Kelwyn sniffed. "You expect mercy?"

"Blackbird taught me not to. One of your pets put a hole in my leg. Give me a minute. I'll get back up."

Kelwyn swiped the staff at my hand, knocking the dagger into the air. It landed between us with a clatter. "She didn't teach you enough. I am no fool."

Now, I was screwed. My shoulders drooped as the extent of my injuries pushed through the waning adrenaline. Centuries of experience really did give him the upper hand. Kelwyn raised his staff and thrust into my stomach, driving the pointed butt deep into my flesh.

Fire and electricity exploded along my nerves as he ripped it free. Gravity punched me down. I dropped onto my hands, darkness sweeping my vision. My limbs were numb. There wasn't enough oxygen. All I could feel was warm blood flowing from my body. I was going to die.

Why had I hoped for so long? Why had I thought I could keep my promises? The pool of blood on the tiles held no answers.

A delicate cough dared me to look up. Kelwyn craned his neck to see as well. The girl lifted a hand. The runes cut into the flesh of her arm were gone, healed. I chuckled, then groaned as pain wracked my body.

"It can't be," Kelwyn said, lowering his staff, his bushy eyebrows high on his forehead and his mouth opening in horror. "What have you done?"

He should have been worrying about what I was going to do. I grabbed the dagger and threw myself at him, stabbing over and over, each effort drawing fresh blood from my own body, hastening my own death. It was worth it. Kelwyn collapsed to his knees, and we watched each other, eye to eye, both humbled.

"I thought Blackbird taught me to be ruthless. But I think what she was really teaching me was to never give up trying to make a difference. Your ritual failed. The goddess is alive and free. What a shame. I guess you're the one who lost in the end."

Kelwyn wobbled back and forth. He leaned closer. "Is that what you think? Look outside, fool."

I looked over his shoulder. I froze.

Oh, shit.

CHAPTER 35
IT WILL HURT

Beyond the first opening Kelwyn had ripped lay the edge of the cathedral's lands, where great waves beat against a crumbling coast. Lightning arced across clouds, pulsing with an organic rhythm. A roiling fog of shattered reality burned away as a form strode through the sea. Oozing slime of fetid magic dripped from its bulk, forming wet strands that would snap and fall away.

Its thick, scaled thighs of murky blue cut through the sea with ease. Judging by the white crests that exploded against its bulk, the entire being had to be near skyscraper tall. Four great arms extended from its body, spines erupting haphazardly along their lengths. Curved claws of gleaming black sliced the waves, leaving trails of froth. Deformed mouths opened and closed on its muscled torso, at least a dozen of them—fanged, toothed, beaked, round, wide, bloated, thin—each unique, each macabre.

Its shoulders were heavyset like a weightlifter's and fringed with rows of hard, lumpy serrations. A head sat neckless, low and forward. Its ridged brow stretched between two chipped horns that swept forward, each ending in wicked points. The gaze of six bloated yellow eyes, each scabbed and leaking pus, swept across the horizon, vertical pupils narrowed. Beneath, a mouth of sword-like teeth opened with the lower jaw dropping impossibly far.

Tenekal, the hunger for power made real, had manifested.

An invisible force slapped the sea, expanding outward at a rapid pace. Pressure built against my skin, popping my ears. A boom punched me, a vile roar of rage combining physical force with an agonizing grating on my soul. A command to supplicate myself. An order to debase all I valued to honor the Great One.

I wavered. There was no winning. This being, this god, was untouchable, unstoppable. It had defeated other gods and eaten them. It had smashed between worlds and killed untold billions. I was nothing compared to it. Not an opponent, not an obstacle, not even a gnat flying around its head. I should give up and accept my fate. I wasn't worthy of more. Tenekal would win, for it was ever thus.

My cutlass glinted among the rubble, and the moment was broken.

"No." I closed my eyes and tightened my jaw. "I don't know how, but you can be stopped. Blackbird said so, and I'll see to it."

Kelwyn cackled. "You worthless little snot. He will shred your soul. Bow to him and beg forgiveness."

"Sounds tempting," I said, pushing the traitorous guardian away and forcing myself up through sheer will. It hurt so much. Tears formed in my eyes, and I wasn't ashamed of them. "Unfortunately, I'm a little busy."

I staggered over to my cutlass, picked it up, and made for the altar. The girl struggled to rise but had even less control over her body than I had over mine. A drop of ambrosia still glistened at the corner of her mouth, reminding me of how much had been wasted. It all would be if I didn't get her out of there.

Sheathing my cutlass, I said gently, "Stop moving. I'm going to pick you up and carry you. I'll get you somewhere safe, I promise."

I looked at my collection of wounds. Promises were cheap.

Her eyes opened. They were brown, flecked with green and gold. She managed a trembling smile. "You came for me."

"I did, but we need to go. Will you let me carry you?"

"Yes."

I slipped an arm beneath her knees, the other under her back, and lifted. Agony forced a whimper from my lips, and my torn innards clawed at my strength, at my resolve.

"You can't go," Kelwyn said, lying in a pool of our collective blood. "I killed you. Accept it."

I held the girl against my chest and staggered toward the second hole he'd created, the one leading to a meadow.

"I have. I have accepted it."

Each clumsy step weaving through the shattered stone took everything I had. I'd made it through world after world, each corrupted or crushed by the so-called Great One. Every time, I'd kept going. This was just another one, except it had been people who had defiled it long before Tenekal had shown up. To do what Kelwyn and his minions had done, that had to be true. Maybe they were afraid, or maybe they'd embraced their new god wholeheartedly. It didn't matter—they'd chosen to leave the world, every world, worse than when they'd entered them.

A cool breeze tousled the ends of my hair as I stepped through the stone wall. A wrenching sensation followed, and I staggered to one side, almost toppling.

"Don't worry," I said. "I've got you."

I turned around. There was no wall, just the opening. Kelwyn or one of the earlier wayfarers had somehow built the cathedral proper between or in several worlds. Wayfarer magic was far more versatile than I'd known. But there was other magic at play. Tenekal's power writhed at the opening, little more than a dark shimmer, hungry and callous. The god was closing, and he either couldn't contain his nature or didn't care to.

One thing was sure—I couldn't fight a god on my best day. I knew the only viable chance for the child I held so tight.

Closing my eyes, I sought through the dark god's taint that spread all around. Yes, there were several ways. This place, like the lands of the order, had been traveled extensively. The energy of other worlds dripped through, each with its own tang brushing at my senses. I picked, not the one with a bright sweetness or the one with an earthy promise. Instead, I chose one less likely—an edge of metal and shattered hope—and carried the girl there.

"How are you feeling?"

She put a hand on my shoulder. "I—I think I'll be able to stand soon, good sir."

"Sir?" I remembered a joke I'd heard. "I'm no sir. I work for a living. Call me Martin."

"Thank you, good Martin. I am named Amaleia."

"Nice to meet you, Amaleia. Do you know what's going on?"

Her little brow furrowed. "I lived in a small temple, and then the wayfarers took me. They said they were going to protect me, but they hurt me and made me drink something awful… and I was caught in a dream. It was horrible."

She shifted to look around, and I had to let her slip slowly to the ground. I groaned, my arms shaking, my cheeks cold as ice and sweaty. She sounded far too much like a little kid rather than a goddess. And that was going to make the next step harder.

Blackbird's words haunted me.

Always walk alone.

"I need you to be brave," I told her. "I'm going to open a way for you to escape—a door between worlds. You need to go through and keep moving. I don't know what it means to be a goddess, but you're going to have to use whatever power you have to get away. And when you're older," I closed my eyes, biting down on the *if* that wanted to come out. "You'll have to find a way to stop Tenekal. It won't be easy, and I'm sure you'll be scared. But no matter what, don't lose faith in yourself."

Her wide eyes stared up at me as I drew my cutlass. I found my magic quickly, but the pool of energy was low. Too much of me had bled out. Yet what remained would have to do. I took a slow breath and grounded myself in the moment, in the reality, not the taint. The scent of nature, the cool air, the little imperfections of soil beneath my boots, the gentle pressing of a lighter gravity. Steadied, I used the reserves of my magic with care, funneling them into the blade's runes, building the rhythm, and quickly feeling for the tension I'd sensed earlier.

There. I sliced, and the way parted, sparking, more beautiful than ever before. A new world awaited. But not for me.

"Go through." I turned back toward the cathedral opening. "Crawl if you have to. There isn't much time."

"Aren't you coming with me?" Her voice trembled, a sense of betrayal cutting as sharp as any sword.

I winced and took several unsteady steps away. "I can't. This is the end of the journey for me. I'm bleeding out. You need to go through. The way will close soon enough, but that one," I pointed my cutlass toward the cathedral hole, "that's going to need a little help. I'll slow Tenekal down and give you a fighting chance."

Each step was a battle, but I continued toward the cathedral. A low steady rumble came through the hole, and the broken stones lining its edge shook. I felt hunger, hunger for power, for worship, for a future with no opposition. It sickened me all the while it tempted me. I could take my rightful place as the nothing I was, show obeisance, and offer up all that made me *me*. I barely resisted, but heeded the message well. Tenekal was almost here.

"You can't leave me," Amaleia cried.

I squeezed my eyes shut, not daring to look back, and pressed my left hand against my stomach. The searing pain steadied me, helping me push away Tenekal's demands, along with my urge to return to Amaleia, to scoop her up, and offer comfort. It would be a lie. I had to abandon her.

"Go. It's not your fault, but people have died to get you to safety. You can't let them down. You can't let me down."

"Please! I don't want to be alone."

I kept walking, tears streaming down my cheeks, until I reached the opening. There, I raised my bloodied left hand, trying to sense the state of the damaged reality. Strips of existence dangled, the edge all in loose threads. It wasn't closing. There was no shrinkage, no healing to encourage. I'd made a dramatic gesture, but how in the hell was I going to back it up? This was no ordinary way.

Through the hole, I saw the cathedral shake, and slabs of ceiling crash down, shattering the altar. A torrent of vile power flowed out, and I staggered. Was I too late? Fuck that. I wracked my brain for a solution, but a bone-shaking roar stole the last strength in my legs, and I dropped to my knees.

The cathedral went dark. Tenekal was blocking the light from the moon. How close was the god standing? Were its hands reaching in to tear the cathedral open, its claws raised to slice the hole to this world wider and push through in some grotesque parody of birth?

Slice.

How would a doctor treat a wound that wouldn't heal? Cut away the dead flesh—I'd read that or seen it on a medical show. I lifted my cutlass, my arm shaking. It would be easier if I were closer, but I'd never stand again. I felt inside for magic. There was so little I had to search, to scoop, to squeeze and still there wasn't enough.

Kelwyn had taught me one thing—the power of blood, of life and death. Maybe I wasn't a god or goddess, but I still had a few drips of the red stuff to bolster my remaining magic. My death would fuel Amaleia's escape. I pressed my left hand against the wound in my stomach, then wiped the blood onto my blade. This was my ritual, and the universe had better damn well accept it as good enough. It would work. It needed to.

"This—" I said, charging the runes on my cutlass, "this is for everyone who ever needed someone. I can't save every kid. I couldn't save myself, but I can save one child, and damn it, that's enough."

The runes fizzled, glowing weaker than even my first time. I raised the tip of the blade toward the top of the hole. Projecting my will beyond the cutlass by pure instinct, I searched for a weak spot, anything that would let me start. I found it, a little to the left, barely enough to catch. It would do. I gritted my teeth and cut slowly, tracing a line around the wound between worlds. Sparks erupted, and energy splattered. I forced the blade along.

An almighty crash stopped me halfway. The air changed, a pressure. A great claw scraped past, shifting slabs of stone even as more poured down. Razor-sharp chips ricocheted, several lodging in my face and hands, fresh stings reminding me that I still lived and that I had a task to complete.

Roaring my defiance, I made a second cut, continuing my incision around the hole, draining myself until I felt hollow. Nothing held back. The second cut met the first, and the shreds of damaged reality fluttered away.

I froze, waiting, hoping.

The sparks erupted anew. I blinked, clearing my vision. The hole was closing. It was still there, but it was closing.

I laughed and let the cutlass fall from my hand. I had nothing left. I fell and rolled a short distance downhill, stopping with my face to the hole. A hexagonal chunk of column slipped partway through, then was guillotined as the way shrank further.

Anger flared. At first, I thought it was my own. How dare any flee? How dare they steal? How dare they refuse what I was owed, what I was promised? It was Tenekal, his thoughts bleeding into mine. He had figured out that I'd screwed him over. Damn, it felt good.

A black claw tip pushed into the hole, far too big for more to enter, its surface gnarled and scratched, and not getting sheared off by the shrinking way. To be touched by it was death, I knew that to the core of my being. The claw pushed against the freshly cut edges of the way, stretching it like a rubber band.

The nearby grass wilted, and the ground cracked. My hope remained. I'd failed to stop him, but perhaps I'd slowed him down enough that he wouldn't see where Amaleia fled. I went onto my back, spent, not caring for the sky above, or the sickened land beneath.

"Martin!" The girl was over me, looking down, the corner of her mouth still glowing with ambrosia. It was such a kid thing to do.

My face twisted, and I tried to lift a hand to push her away. "You can't be here. You have to be a big kid. You have to survive. Go."

"I'm too scared. Please, please, don't leave me alone."

My eyes blurred. "I'm sorry. I'm done. I'm dead. My body will work it out soon enough. But you have a chance. We're counting on you. Leave me here. It's okay."

"It's not. I won't. I won't leave you. You saved me. You were with me when I was all alone. I know it was you."

I turned my head. The claw pushed further into this world, shedding menace like dandruff. The poor goddess. She was innocent. She didn't understand that the world couldn't be changed by thought alone, that all you could do was keep going, keep trying, keep watching for a break, and seizing it when it showed up.

Blackbird had given me a break in that alley, one I hadn't

realized I'd needed. And now, I was doing the same to Amaleia, but she was too inexperienced to see it for what it was. I had to make the choice for her.

I reached for my cutlass, groaning and whimpering with the agony that accompanied every movement. As I was about to close my fingers on the grip, she picked it up.

"You are very hurt. I'll hold it for you." She tugged at me even as I looked at her with horror. "Let me help you up."

Help me up? She was clueless or so damn stubborn it made no difference which.

Goddamn it.

If I stayed here, she was going to die. It wasn't fair. I'd done enough. But I hadn't. I flopped over onto my stomach and screamed over and over. Amaleia pulled at my shoulder. Somehow, I wedged a hand underneath myself and pushed. A rat burrowed into my stomach, or at least that was how it felt. I managed a second hand and wobbled to my knees. Amaleia took my arm, and I ended up on my feet, my sweat-slick skin too tight.

She looked into my eyes. "Lean on me. It's not far."

Little girl or goddess, she had no idea what she was asking of me. Not far? Might as well say Earth wasn't far. But I had to get her to the way. I leaned as much as I dared on her little shoulder and took a step, then another. Only pure determination gave me the energy, the fortitude to continue.

We passed a closed way.

"Give me the cutlass."

Her cute brow creased, but she passed the weapon without a word. I felt for the tension, blade quivering, and tried to catch it. On the third attempt, I succeeded, the runes on the blade weaker than a false dawn. I hacked at it again and again, ripping it open, and then walked away.

"Why did you do that?" she asked.

"I don't know how Tenekal senses us, but if he can't tell which way you've gone through, it might buy some time."

I directed her toward another way and did the same, feeding the runes with my desperation, like a driver with the fuel light on red. At last, we reached the original way I'd cut. I'd opened it surprisingly well, but it was shrinking. Good. I collapsed at its base.

"Martin," Amaleia shook me. "Please get up. It's only a little farther."

Tenekal's entire hand was through the cathedral hole, the four claws large enough to mince a T-Rex. As I watched, it pushed through further, a giant wrist, a colossal serpent slithering over the meadow, claws gouging the soil. It would reach us soon.

"I wish I could go with you," I whispered. "Be brave. And remember, you don't have to be alone. Make friends, ones that will be there for you, and you be there for them."

Gwen's face came to me, and I smiled. She'd be okay. She was a survivor. Maybe I should tell Amaleia about her. Gwen would keep her safe. But my mouth wouldn't work. My body was shutting down.

Amaleia hit me. "You can't die. I won't let you. I'm a goddess. You have to do what I say."

I tried a smile. She didn't mean it. And that was a good thing. No one with real power should believe that.

I closed my eyes.

"Please, Martin. You were there in the darkness. Knowing that you were coming was my only comfort, even though I didn't know who you were. I never had a father—not one I could see or speak to. It wasn't allowed. If I had one, a proper one, I'd want him to be like you."

She hit me again, and my eyes opened in reaction to the pain. "So don't die. I won't let you."

Amaleia wiped her eyes, then her cheeks, and looked at her hand. Her eyes shone.

"I think it might help."

I couldn't say a word. The edge of my vision clouded. All I could see was her staring down at me.

"I'm going to try. I think it will hurt."

She raised her finger, revealing the tiniest remains of ambrosia. It had stayed at the corner of her mouth the whole time, only coming off when she wiped her face. How had it lasted? Perhaps being on her skin had stopped it from evaporating. It didn't matter. It was hardly going to give her enough of a boost to take on Tenekal. She was wasting time.

Why was she ripping at my shirt? I wanted to push her away to get some peace, but my arms were numb. In fact, my whole body was. Relief swept across me. It was over. I heard a bird song and felt welcomed.

"Hold still," Amaleia told me in her little, serious voice.

I'm not going anywhere, kid.

She plunged her finger into my stomach—right into the open wound. My body arched, a million volts surging through me.

Then nothing.

Finally.

Peace.

CHAPTER 36

THE WAY AHEAD

A steady beep itched, too complacent to be an alarm. It should go away. I had endured—the violence, the loneliness, the fear of my youth. I kept on going, struggling to be more than a broken kid, to be someone who could help. Reality had told me otherwise. I'd been ripped away from the life I'd made and thrown into chaos and danger. I'd found family and had it cut away with the jagged knife of fate. I endured. I stood up to dragons, a wizard, and a damn god to help a single child. Enough. It had been enough. Couldn't I stay asleep a little longer? Was that too much to ask?

Other noises jostled for my attention, but that steady beep drilled into my skull. Why hadn't anyone turned it off? I raised a searching hand, but couldn't see the tone's source.

Open your eyes, stupid.

I did so, and a blinding intensity burrowed into my pupils, biting, clawing. Wait. That was odd. I shouldn't be able to feel anymore. I shouldn't be able to see or move. That was the deal when you died. How could I hear?

Shading my eyes allowed blurred objects to take form. A

machine stood on a trolley, graphs zigzagging up and down. Numbers on the side changed, too. I knew this. It was a medical thing. I grasped at tendrils of memory. Vital signs. It was measuring the heart rate and oxygen concentration and probably a few other things. My vitals. The sort of equipment in hospitals.

Martin Drake, you are in a hospital.

I took a sudden breath as my heart jolted, and the machine beeped a complaint. How did I get here? My eyes were adjusting to the light, so I lowered my hand.

Fluorescent yellow bandages covered my arms, the gaps between making me look like a first grader's attempt at a mummy costume. A tube was taped to my right arm, the other end leading to a brass box hanging from a pole with a braided wire connected to the beeping machine. This too was brass, with the numbers formed from spinning disks, and the lines being scratched on rolls of paper.

That didn't make sense. I tried to sit up. Pain coursed through my abdomen as if an angle grinder was bouncing its merry way along. I lay back down. Running a hand over the blanket confirmed there was a bulky wound dressing beneath, and of course, the very painful wound.

It didn't make sense. I'd been in a meadow, dying as Tenekal pushed into the world from a hole torn in the side of a cathedral.

And that makes sense?

Where had the weirdness started? With the wolves. With the alley. Had a delivery truck hit me? Maybe there had been stray wolves, and I had been attacked, and I had hit my head and fallen unconscious, and had a bizarre dream. Yes. A very, very realistic one. That felt reasonable.

Forcing my gaze to travel beyond the strange equipment, I considered the rest of the room. There was another bed near mine occupied by a man in his fifties, his scalp covered in yellow bandages. He was asleep on his back, and yet he almost stood at attention. The set of his chin, the prominent cheekbones, and the weathered skin suggested a hard man. A shelf on the wall to his far side held a military hat of some kind, a khaki green with unfamiliar symbols of rank, and a short, forward-pointing brim. Next to it were folded clothes of the same khaki, blotched with dark grays and tans. A camouflage pattern, but nothing I'd seen before.

There were other unfamiliar details as well. Large ceramic tiles on the floor extended to wood-paneled walls that reached a ceiling of beaten brass. At each upper corner of the room, grotesque figures, no larger than a fist. They possessed wings, bulbous noses, and pointy ears, and their faces held watchful expressions. Were they guarding us, or keeping us prisoner? I watched until I decided they wouldn't move. Decoration. Hopefully.

A scent of artificial mint came with each breath, perhaps from a cleaning detergent or antiseptic. Even more than what I saw, this completed my discomfort—it hammered home my situation. This was not Earth. I hadn't dreamed it all. I wasn't Dorothy waking up.

That was strangely comforting—not the Dorothy bit. Was I in an afterlife? I wondered. Had one of the gods taken me? One thing was obvious: this place sure as hell wasn't the handiwork of Tenekal. That would have a lot more fire and tentacles. No, I concluded, the most reasonable take was that this was real. Real —for what that was worth.

Which meant Amaleia was. Which meant she was in danger.

"Amaleia?" My throat was dry, my voice croaky.

No answer.

Where was she? The machine blipped in concern. It was damn right to be. She could be anywhere, on any world, without protection.

I tried to rise once more, but the pain in my stomach forced me down, and the machine complained with urgent tones. I slapped at it, but it was out of reach. Grunting, I pulled the tube and wires connected to my arm. The tape was strong. Hair ripped as I yanked it all free. A needle slipped out of my arm in a sprinkle of blood, and I pressed down on a piece of tape to seal the spot as best I could.

The machine bleeped urgently at me, as if scolding. I used the wire to pull the machine close. When it was within reach, I hit the various buttons, switches, and knobs, each one clicking loudly, until it finally stopped. Only at this point did I remember that I could have looked for the label reading *off*.

Next came movement, and this was going to hurt like a son of a bitch. I'd partially rolled onto my side to work the machine. Keeping that position, I threw off the thin blanket. I was wearing a dark red gown, the overlapping front fastened with eight buckles down its center. My legs, visible below the knees, were covered with several rectangles of yellow dressing held down by tape. Removing them would give me a free waxing.

"Amaleia?"

Damn it. Where was she? I had to know she was safe. I wiggled over the edge of the bed, accepting the bursts of sharp pain.

"On the count of three," I told myself. "One, two—"

I flicked my feet out, as if I could trick myself by not waiting to three, and when gravity pulled them down, I used the momentum to swing up into a sitting position.

"Aaargh," I gasped, my eyes moistening.

I held still, swearing a mantra, until I felt in control of my abused body. That had hurt. But I wasn't done. How many times had I seen this in movies and thought the character was an idiot? Fleeing the hospital without even checking with the doctor was asking for trouble. But they'd usually been right to do so.

I slipped off the bed, my feet thankfully holding my weight on the cold tiles.

"That wasn't so bad," I told myself. My inner voice was too polite to point out the lie.

An enormous boom shook the floor, the entire room, and objects clanked and dropped off shelving. A cup dropped, porcelain shattering and releasing beige drips of someone's forgotten drink. I grabbed the monitoring machine for balance, hugging it as I'd once hugged Gwen.

What the hell was that? I wanted to check outside, but unlike a normal hospital room, there were no windows, and the single wooden door was shut. My heart beat faster. What if Amaleia had been near whatever that was? I had to hurry—but hurry smart.

I looked down at my gown. If I wore these, I could get asked a lot of awkward questions. My gaze switched to the soldier's uniform. If he was some kind of colonel or general, stealing his outfit could be a bad, bad idea. But my own clothes were nowhere to be seen. Which, given my habit of turning material to rags, wasn't surprising. No, I'd go as I was. Getting dressed in my condition would take too long, anyway.

After walking with tiny steps to the door, I opened it and peered outside. The sound of misery assailed me. Hanging lights in brass fittings rocked gently. I was partway along a corridor. Beds lined the far side, each filled with wounded, many still in uniform. Scarlet blotches stained sheets and blankets. At the far end, a sole woman attended a wailing patient.

Three distant explosions, one after the other, sent the lights swinging in sympathy. Was the hospital being bombed? What kind of scum did that? I scowled, admitting that it was hardly unknown on Earth. We could be real bastards.

"Amaleia?"

I entered the windowless corridor and turned right. An arm

touched mine, some poor guy with a face cut up by shrapnel, I guessed. Where were all the doctors and nurses? I pulled free, hating myself for not offering comfort. There was the sound of faraway gunfire, perhaps anti-aircraft. I couldn't be sure, as I'd never been in a war zone. Not this type of war, at least.

My sense of urgency grew. Where was she? I moved as fast as I could toward a distant corner, holding a hand against my stomach and wincing with each fresh jab of pain. Yet, it hurt less than I had any right to expect. My eyes went to each wounded soldier, in case they turned out to be a little goddess, abandoned by the man that should have protected her. Anything could have happened while I was out. What if she'd been captured and interrogated as a spy?

"Amaleia!"

She stepped around the corner. Her dark hair was neatly brushed, and she wore a clean blue dress with puffy sleeves, a stiff bodice, and a full skirt—an old-fashioned look. She held a miniature duffel bag, which she dropped as soon as she laid eyes on me.

"Martin? You're alive!" She hurried to me and inflicted a big, painful hug. "I knew you would be."

I swallowed a cry of pain and put a hand on her shoulder, feeling the same relief she was expressing. "That might change if you keep squeezing."

She let go, her eyes wide and glistening. "Sorry, good Martin. I did not mean to hurt you."

"That's okay. It's good to see you, too, kid. Though I thought I told you go through the way. I didn't say to drag me through after you."

"You were being very silly, and I didn't want to be alone."

I sighed. "We'll talk about that later. Are you hurt?"

"No, I am well."

At least on the outside. I couldn't fathom what she'd gone through.

"Where are we?"

She tugged me toward the corner where her bag waited.

"I don't know. I rolled you through the magic door, and there was mud and people with loud sticks. I was very scared. When a man found me, he was very shouty and made me cry. I *compelled* him to carry you—I didn't want to. It makes me feel sad and angry—and he took us to a spot with a carriage that moved by itself. And then I *compelled* the owner of that to deliver us from there. And then—"

"Okay, kid," I said, running a hand down her hair as if calming a cat. "I think I'm getting the picture. We landed in the middle of a war, one that's still close. And you got me some help. I appreciate it. I truly do. But right now, the details will have to wait. We need to get out of here, find a way, and put more distance between us and Tenekal."

My hand went to my waist automatically. "My cutlass. Shit."

"That's rude," Amaleia said. She picked up her bag and held it high. "It's in here. And I've found some food."

That was a relief. She was clever and resourceful. We stood a chance, but I was barefoot and certain to stick out if we left the hospital.

"I don't suppose you found my clothes?"

"Not yours. Follow me."

Around the corner waited a set of stairs on the left and a door on the right. Ahead, a sheet had been spread across the corridor and nailed to the walls. A sign read:

DANGER: STRUCTURAL DAMAGE. DO NOT ENTER.

She pointed to the door. "There are clothes in there. And a dead man, too."

I pushed the door open and checked inside. Copper basins and bars of soap rested on tables pressed against one wall. A row of lockers stretched along another. Each door was open, and clothes were strewn across the floor. Looted for items of value? That seemed likely.

The body was easy to spot. A man lay by one of the tables, a pool of blood around his head, and a pistol in his hand. He wore a uniform. A soldier who'd seen too much? A deserter who realized there was nowhere to run to? What a world for me to have picked.

"Can you watch the door?" I asked, hating to let her out of my sight for even a moment.

Amaleia agreed, and I searched for clothing that fit, scrunching my face to control the pain as leaned down to pick each item up. I found a pair of smooth-soled boots that fit well enough, though they were too soft to be sturdy, and underwear that was thankfully clean. To these I added tight pants that itched, a buttoned and collared shirt in a dazzling emerald green, a waistcoat that I first rejected before deciding I needed to fit in, and a matching jacket, all three pieces of the outerwear in a charcoal wool. The cut fit oddly, making my shoulders appear larger, and I felt like a two-bit villain in a B-grade historical series, the kind that would be canceled after the first season—or the pilot. At least the image distracted me from the teeth-clenching pain of dressing.

When done, I looked at the gun in the dead man's hand, but I couldn't find the resolve to bend over one more time to pick it up. I'd found a limit, and I was already stretching it.

"All right," I said as I rejoined Amaleia. "I don't know much about this whole god and goddess business, but I've learned a thing or two about running. I'd rather not do it blindly. Do you know what you should be doing?"

Her eyes were large as she stared at me, her little brow creased with earnestness. "My tutors said that I needed to be kept away from all that would come lest I be diverted from my true path. I am not due to take my station until I reach ascension."

I raised an eyebrow. "Ascension?"

She nodded. "Yes, when my aspect is revealed."

"Aspect?" Was my translation faulty?

She crossed her arms and pressed her lips together as if annoyed by my obtuseness.

"I mean it, Amaleia. I don't have a clue."

She rolled her eyes, and I saw a kid that could have grown into a wonderfully annoying teenager in other circumstances.

"When I ascend, I will learn what my responsibility is as a goddess, who I really am. My father's was wisdom."

"I see. So, you know barely more than me about what you're meant to do, and I know barely more than nothing about all the worlds out there in which you can do it. Wow, don't we make a pair?"

Another explosion, this one closer, sent dust falling from the ceiling. We hugged each other until it was clear the building wasn't going to collapse. Yet.

"I guess," I said, leading her to the stairs, "that we'll have to make it up as we go."

We took the stairs down, me leaning on the handrail. The slow progress gave me a chance to worry. We couldn't blunder around forever. She was going to need a teacher, one that knew about whatever she was. Until then, I'd have to do.

Two flights down, I was panting, grateful for the nice, flat floor that took us to a wide corridor. There were more filled beds, and plenty of wounded and dead lying on the ground. There was no smell of cleaning chemicals here, only the stench of meat and misery. An open door at one end led out to glorious sunlight. A sandbagged circle sat at the border of light and dark, an abandoned machine gun drooping as if it, too, were a casualty.

We walked to the entrance and stopped. Trucks filled the

road outside, some burned to rusted skeletons, others still painted with camouflage, doors open. All were abandoned. Barbed wire coils blocked off side streets between terraced brick houses. Craters had turned the road into Swiss cheese. Above, four-winged aircraft banked, spiraled, looped, and threw themselves into barrel rolls as they shot at each other with angry bursts of machine gun chatter.

I gestured for Amaleia's bag, took out my sheathed sword, and checked the blade. She hadn't cleaned it. That was okay—it wasn't her responsibility. She'd saved it, and that was enough. I buckled the belt and slid the sword back in. Yeah, it would be out of place, but if lugging around a staff had worked for Blackbird, then the cutlass would do for me.

Tenekal couldn't just teleport between worlds, or he would be on us already. But that didn't mean we were free of immediate danger. I needed to be ready. I was no longer a traveler or a courier—I was a bodyguard.

A distant blast sent a cloud of smoke into the air, its boom arriving several seconds later. I looked down at Amaleia, and she took my hand. She'd been brave and resourceful. We could work with that. But we needed answers. Hell, we needed enough information to know what questions to ask and which bastard to extract the answers from.

But step one: keep ahead of Tenekal. I gave her hand a squeeze. "Shall we go for a walk?"

We navigated around the twisted wreckage of a small vehicle and started down the road, slowed by my injuries. I opened my senses as we went, searching for any disturbance that could suggest a way.

"You'll stay with me?" Amaleia asked, her voice tight like she'd had to build up the courage to ask.

"You bet," I told her as we passed an abandoned checkpoint with a snapped boom gate. It looked how I felt, and yet here I was, putting one foot in front of the other. "You and me, Amaleia, kicking ass and taking names."

She gave me a look. I'd used a bad word. Well, I guessed there were a lot of things she was going to learn on her way to defeating an evil god. You weren't doing a quest right if you didn't.

I'd certainly had to deal with some interesting sorts. And I'd come out the better for it. An idea nudged me. If there were going to be two of us, why not three?

"You and me, as I said, but there is someone I'd like you to meet." I smiled, the pain of my body irrelevant. "I think you'd like her."

MARTIN DRAKE WILL RETURN IN:

WAYFARER'S BLADE

About the Author

Robert writes gripping science fiction, urban fantasy, and epic fantasy for adults and children. When he's not writing, he's swinging swords for fun and bruises. He has previously written works for adults and children under the name R Max Tillsley.

You can find him at:

https://www.tillsley.com

and:

ACKNOWLEDGMENTS

While recovering from wrist surgery, I watched a movie with a broken structure, and in considering why it didn't work, I developed a concept for a portal fantasy filled with disasters. I thank the movie makers, though it would be unfair to name their effort. All art has value.

Monika Tillsley helped me tighten the fine details of this novel and took a flamethrower to my usual mess of punctuation and remnants of edit cycles. My thanks are as endless as my affections.

Beta reader Michael Walley challenged me to ensure the story structure was solid, and as a result, had to read three different versions of one section. Thank you, and I look forward to reading your own published works.

I am lucky to have two author groups that have my back. Those of the Dead Robots' Society keep me focused through weekly check-ins and shared support. As well, my Australian author colleagues are ever generous with feedback on the publishing and business side of being an indie author.

Finally, I'd like to thank the fans who keep me going through the time needed to write and publish. You make it all worthwhile.